Journey Through a Land

of Minor Annoyances

or

How I Came To Embrace Being

an Insignificant Speck of Dust

on a Meaningless Trip through

an Apathetic Cosmos

Al Kline

Livingston Press

The University of West Alabama

ISBN 13: trade paper 978-1-60489-264-2
ISBN 13: hardcover 978-1-60489-265-9
ISBN 13: e-book 978-1-60489-266-6

Library of Congress Control Number 2020940002
Printed on acid-free paper
Printed in the United States of America by
Publishers Graphics

Hardcover binding by: HF Group
Typesetting and page layout: Joe Taylor
Proofreading: Tricia Taylor, Joe Taylor

Cover Design:Regan Chase, Maine Photo Works

6 5 4 3 2 1

Journey Through a Land

of Minor Annoyances

Chapter 1

This is my life and by the time you read this, I'll be a distant shadow in the past, the present, and the future. A footnote in someone's fading memory.

This is my journal, and what you're about to read is the Truth, pure and eternal and delicious. At least my Truth. Everybody has their own version of the Truth and this is mine.

Max interrupts, "Not a very good beginning. Start over."

Damn. I knew he'd criticize. I tap the delete key and start again:

I'm a newly born snowflake, formed in the frozen womb of the night sky, fluttering down onto an unforgiving lake of ice, taking flight again as the winter wind eddies, sending me aloft toward the cold, apathetic stars.

Max rolls his eyes. "Are you writing Hallmark cards for the permanently stoned?" he barks. Goddamn, he's a grinder.

Take three. I type again:

My mind is different now and I'm not sure who or what I was am now or will be and although I may appear to be here I am not all there.

"Chaz, don't be afraid to use a comma. Rest."

"Max, I don't have time to rest."

He chuckles. "'What can I tell you, kid? You're right. When you're right, you're right, and you're right.'" He shoots me an inquisitive look, "You know where that line's from, don't you?"

"Ah... *Dog Day Afternoon?*"

"*Chinatown.*"

"Oh, yeah. The Nicholson character."

"Jake Gittes. Did you see it?"

"Well, ah..."

"Put it in your bucket," he laments.

My fingers return to the laptop:

My Life has morphed into Lewis Carroll, Hugo Ball, and Luis Buñuel as it cascades into places and experiences that are esoteric, euphoric, abstract and liberating. My existence is Dadaist, free from conventional norms, now on an uncharted journey of self-exploration.

This is my Reality, even though I question whether Max is real or anything I'm about to write is real. Both Max and I may be a product of my own imagination or psychosis or drugs. The following pages contain the grains of salt to help you understand. Take as many as you need.

Max exhales and with a patronizing smile says, "I'm so glad I could be here to help you live out your avoidance of reality. Your drug-induced fantasy."

"Just shut up. You're real. I know you are," I snap.

"Illusion."

"Don't mess with me."

"Chaz, you're an illusion too."

"God, you're an annoying little mutt. Leave me alone and let me write this." Max snickers like a machine gun on helium HEE-HEE-HEE-HEE as I inhale a deep toke from my Northern Lights and continue:

I am clear about one thing: In spite of the danger, there's no sense in worrying about Death: Been there and done that. It's where I am now. I do not fear having a near-death experience. My concern is that the last twenty years was only a near-life experience.

Max feigns a yawn and closes his eyes. "Wake me when you're done taking this metaphysical crap."

I ignore him. I'll begin this story soon before it ends. In August of 1999. I type: It's 168 degrees and the shimmering highway lies ahead, a glistening black serpent coiled on the horizon of this Utah desert, or Arizona wasteland, or perhaps planet Mercury, maybe even "Planet Claire," but it's hot enough to make a dead man sweat. With the pavement a scalding ribbon of molasses my tires leave a puddle, my sandals are liquid and I'm feel like a Dali pocket watch as Hell pours into my 1959 Cadillac convertible, as all around tumbleweeds burst into flames, spontaneous combustion taking place both within me and without, a fire that's hotter than anything I ever set, burning worse than the Death Valley conditions where Von Stroheim directed *Greed*, and this Inferno world is melting, melting, with buzzards circling overhead piercing the arid air with their Margaret Hamilton cackle laughs, looking down at this poor bastard trying to find himself but in imminent danger of losing himself.

The vultures are drowned out by Brenda Lee's "Rockin' Around the Christmas Tree" blasting from the rear right speaker that vibrates like a tuning fork. The left speaker died years ago when it was peed on by Max, my Pitbull, my trusted traveling companion and a damn-fine unique canine with astonishing abilities and a brilliant mind. He prefers to be called a Staffordshire Bull Terrier but whatever his breed, he is a true Mensa dog. The only dog I ever met who quotes Kierkegaard and can expound at length about the hidden messages in Kubrick films. Max would read the *Paris Review* and smoke expensive Cuban cigars if he could, but his lack of opposable thumbs prevents him from doing so. Besides, I don't want him to damage his lungs. There's nothing more pathetic than a dog toting around a portable oxygen tank while rasping like Pat Welsh.

The air conditioner died long ago, but playing holiday tunes as I plod through Hell makes me feel cooler, like *trompe l'oeil*, but this is more like *tromper l'oreille*. Max, with a heavy pant, barks, "Remove the fucking fedora and you'll feel even cooler." But I need to wear my black fedora because I never know when I may be thrust into a film noir and I want to be ready. Paul Muni always kept a Tommy gun under his bed after filming *Scarface*. Ann Sheridan was never without the necklace she wore in *Nora Prentiss*. Bengt Ekerot kept the chess set he used to play Antonius Block. It's why I keep an old pack of Chesterfields in the glove compartment and practice blowing smoke rings from the corner of my mouth while talking about dangerous dames with nice gams who fire off a few rounds from a gat. I want to be prepared for any opportunity that may present itself on my doorstep.

Max is so erudite he pronounces the 'G' in 'fucking' instead of dropping it and substituting an apostrophe. That canine has class they just don't bottle anymore. He makes Asta come across like a mangy street mongrel.

I found Max at a shelter, or as the saying goes, perhaps he found me. We connected with an instant, metaphysical bond that transcended the ages, communicating as though we had known each other for centuries. Max may be four or five years old or maybe ageless, but he's accompanying me on this journey, just as he's accompanied me on countless journeys before. Max kids me, saying he was so desperate to get out of the shelter he would have gone home with a starving Vietnamese family. At least I think he's kidding. Owning Max has been both a blessing and a curse, all rolled into one big hairy package.

I take a final swig from the piss warm Coors nestled in the crotch of my underwear. I stripped off my pants and stuffed them into a trash barrel at a highway rest area many miles and inhibitions ago somewhere outside of Ogden. My decision to go pant-less was not impulsive. I thought about it since Idaho and finally decided to do things in life without regrets. I never want to limit myself because of fearing someone else's disapproval. Max tells me that's the way to write: Write from your heart, but edit from your brain. Write like you don't care who reads it. "Create with no inhibitions," Max says. It's become easier for me since every-one I may have worried about reading and judging my writings are now dead and gone.

It's so freeing to not wear pants and I vow to never wear them again. How would Mormons react if they knew a man was driving through their state wearing only his underwear? I know Mormons have their own special underwear, magical shorts that ensure happiness on their own planet in the cosmos, but I'm wearing Hanes boxer-briefs and the exhilarating feeling cools my jewels. There can't be a law against driving around in your underwear. I never see road signs showing a stick figure remov-ing their underwear with the international slash mark through it. I hope I'm not breaking the law because I don't want to be sent back to Ju-vee Hall. I drown out Brenda:

> "Let's be jolly, deck the halls
> with boughs of holly."

In the rear view mirror Max shakes his head, "You sound like you're getting a root canal without anesthetic."

"You wouldn't know good singing if it bit your hairy little ass."

"You sing as well as you write," Max mumbles. The words sting. He may have a point. Inside one of the totes in the trunk are my thirteen screenplays, in written form but also stored on my laptop and burned onto CD's. All homeless, all unwanted, and all with no destination. Like me. Paraphrasing Capote's remark about Kerouac, maybe I don't write. Maybe I only type.

Brenda wails:

"Everyone's dancing merrily in the
new old fashioned wwwaaaayyyyyyy."

Max throws back his head to howl, drowning out both me and Brenda, which may be a good thing. The shadows from the blood-red mesas hang like death heads in the torrid atmosphere as the Caddy darts through the desert air like a honeybee slicing through August sunshine. We're moving about 50 miles per hour in some deserted part of the universe, past sage brush, beer bottles, pieces of a shredded tire from a semi, and other people's unwanted memories. I open Final Draft on my laptop and catch Max in the rear view mirror cutting me with a stare. Just as he barks, "Keep your eyes on the road!" I'm rattled by the ear-splitting blast of a big rig horn as I swerve the Caddy back to my own lane with the semi thundering by, missing the car by inches. The laptop flies onto the floor and Max bounces around the back seat like he's on a trampoline. I'm shaking and I feel like Dennis Weaver hunted by an 18-wheeler.

"Okay! Okay! Everything's under control," I tell Max, my voice quivering like a katydid on speed. I take a deep breath and retrieve the laptop.

With cautious furtive glances from the road to the screen and back again, I type the scene as if I were handing it to John Ford to shoot.

EXT. DESERT — DAY

LONG SHOT *Pan left to right. A lone car on a dusty road is dwarfed by towering sandstone buttes.*

MEDIUM SHOT *Through windshield. A man and a dog look distraught and sweaty as they anticipate death.*

Max looks over my shoulder to read it. A blast from another big rig's horn and I hiss "Fuck!" as I swerve the Caddy back into my lane with tires screeching. Max screams, "Oh, that's just brilliant. Multi-tasking while driving. Just hasten your death and just get it over with. Spare yourself any insight as to why you're on this journey."

I gulp hard, "I can't let the writing muscle atrophy. When I got the itch, I have to scratch it. Gotta write something, even if it's a last will and testament." I throw Pam Grier into neutral, turn off the engine, and coast to a halt in a dirt clearing off the road, kicking up a cloud of dust. I leave the ignition on to continue playing the holiday tunes.

I grab a Blue Dream from inside the brim of my fedora, light it up and take a long drag. It's as welcome as another tomorrow. Blue Dreams are usually good for priming the creative pump even though I suspect the well has been running dry.

"Max, I wanna tell you something. Even though you probably don't care."

"You're right. I don't care."

"My face is gonna melt like *The House of Wax*. Ever see it?"

"The 1953 version was the best," he says. "In 3D. Directed by Andre de Toth."

"Wasn't that Charles Bronson's first movie?"

"No. He had a bit part in a 1951 movie you probably never saw. *The Mob*."

"Damn! You're an encyclopedia of film." Max retained his cinematic knowledge from his previous life when he was a Hollywood director. He claims to be Samuel Fuller reincarnated as a dog and who am I to doubt that? Reality has proven to be too painful the last two months so with much exuberance and weed I've embraced fantasy which is much easier to grasp in one hand. I don't know what Mr. Fuller did during his life to warrant the Big Wheel of Karma returning him to Earth as a dog. Especially my dog. I never thought to ask but I think I know the answer. It's probably because Fuller made *Shark*, a film so bad he asked the director's guild to remove his name from the directing credits. Perhaps being yoked to me is his cosmic punishment for making that film. Guess everyone has at least one door locked tight to keep any embarrassing incidents from flying out and being exposed to the light of day.

I ask, "You wanna talk about *Shark*?" just to poke him with a stick.

Max lifts his leg and hisses, "Listen pinhead, you mention that movie again and I'll obliterate your right speaker."

He's a hoot when the fur stands up on his back and he flashes his canines to appear so intimidating. Trying so hard to resemble that genetically engineered dog in *Man's Best Friend*.

Next up is Burl Ives and I singyell:

> "...oh by golly have holly jolly
> Christmas this year..."

"He'll always be Big Daddy Pollitt," Max says, staring at me for several beats like Alex Trebek eying some dumbass contestant who goes the entire show without ever buzzing in. I know this is a test and Max waits for an answer.

"Ah... *East of Eden*?" I blurt out.

Max makes a buzzer sound BBBBZZZZZ and sighs, "*Cat on a Hot Tin Roof*."

"I'll put it on my list," I say and Max snorts. I return to my attempt at singing, which Max says sounds like Ethel Merman on crack:

> "Oh, ho the mistletoe hung where you can see.
> Somebody waits for you, kiss her once for me."

Max joins in:

"Have a holly, jolly Christmas and in case
you didn't hear, Oh by golly have a holly
jolly Christmas this yeeeeeeeaaarrrrrrrrrrrrrr."

I step out of the Caddy, look both ways down the road, and inhale. My windpipe and lungs are singed like a newbie circus performer attempting to eat fire for the very first time. No one approaches from either end of the serpent. I could be the last man on Earth. I envision being on a David Lean set and seeing T. E. Lawrence riding his steed over a dune. Without the car's muffler growl, the desert is still. The quiet of a cemetery after a snowstorm in January. The only noise is the sun sizzling in the liquid sky.

I pop the trunk to grab Max's bowl and a bottle of water from the cooler. The ice cubes melted miles ago, but I pour the water bottle into the bowl and place it on the back seat. Max takes a few laps and winces. "My own piss would be cooler," he spits.

The trunk contains empty Subway wrappers, Jack Daniel's bottles, beer cans, books about writing screenplays, dirty socks and underwear, a sleeping bag, my cello case, and novels. When I was about ten I remember seeing a list of the top 100 greatest works of literature and I was determined to read them all. By the time I was 15, I had.

Also in the trunk is dog hair. Lots and lots of dog hair. It's where Max usually sleeps. I tell him, "They told me at the shelter you don't shed."

"And they told me you weren't an asshole," he replies.

I survey the mess, and with a flamboyant wave of my arm while holding an imaginary cigarette, I take a puff with mock-disgust. "What a dump!" I Bette Davis-ized.

In the food tote several soggy burritos and potato chips float in warm water. The rejection tote is filled with form letters from studios and agents saying my submission was "Not right for us at this time." Max asks why I even keep the rejection letters, "Why dwell on the negative?"

"To keep me humble."

"Then use the negativity as an incentive. Adopt an 'I'll show those bastards' stance."

In the clothes tote are tees, jeans, socks, and underwear, and a garment bag contains a black tuxedo and a purple ruffled shirt in case I'm invited to the Oscars. Or a funeral. There's also a plastic bag for dirty clothes, although I admit my clothes are no longer washed with the same frequency as when I lived at home. You can always get an extra couple of days use from your underwear if you turn it inside out. Tucked into the glove compartment, the side pockets of the doors, and the trunk, are paperbacks. Well-worn pages by Vonnegut, Camus, Kafka and others.

Also in the trunk is a secret cutout camouflaged by carpet. It's behind the rear seat, with another cutout hidden under the front seat on the passenger side. One is for my Bliss Box, filled with meds and some other pills that are not so medsy, as well as baggies of cannabis, like Northern Lights, Blue Dream, and Cookies and Cream, and rolling papers, glass pipes, and tinctures. I stayed in touch with a couple of guys from Ju-Vee Hall who supply me with whatever rockets of escape I need to blast away from these earthly confines. The other cutout hides a box sealed tight with cash. Lots of cash. A very generous inheritance from my grandparents.

Also occupying the Caddy's trunk is my cello case and an emergency gasoline container, with enough room left over to house a family of five.

The food tote is a mess, thanks to my alter ego who represents all of my errors, mistakes, and imperfections and attempts to make me perform acts that are either embarrassing or just plain hazardous to my health. If I ever do anything out of character or just wrong, like the time when I was seven and decided to piss on a hornet's nest, I blame my little Thai friend, 'Dum Phuk', who's a permanent patient in the mental institution of my imagination. I think everyone has a Dum Phuk voice they can either listen to or tune out. Giving in to your own personal Dum Phuk can sometimes be a learning experience, but could also shorten your life span.

I crawl up and stand on Pam Grier's hood and turn a slow 360 while staring at the distant horizon. I don't know what I'm looking for but whatever it is I hope it provides some answers. I raise my arms and yell, "I'm king of the world!" and Max says, "Get down from there Jack before you have a titanic injury." I get the reference. What a clever dog!

I mumble, "We're in dire straits." Max picks up the musical reference. "Sultans of Swing," he responds.

Sweat gushes from my face.

"We're done," I whimper.

"Over-done," Max counters.

"We're past done."

"You're not very well-done."

"Max, I'm going to fly away." I raise my arms higher and close my eyes. My fedora falls to the ground as the blistering heat waves of the desert lift me off the hood an inch at a time. I imagine consuming a gallon of Fizzy Lifting Drink as I elevate off the metal surface and in moments I'm hovering fifteen, maybe twenty feet above the car like I'm in *The Matrix*.

"Hey Max, is this fuckin' cool or what?"

"The flying is imagined but your fall will be very real. Now come back to Earth, Neo," he deadpans and with that I collapse with a metallic THUNK onto the hood and with a pathetic whimper slide onto the ground in slo-mo with a painful "OW" like Wile E. Coyote slamming into a painted fake door on the side of a boulder.

"I'm okay. Don't call 9-1-1," I wince as I struggle to stand up and then stumble to the fedora and place it back onto my head. I amble back to the trunk and grab an empty Heineken bottle and with a few running steps throw it hard against a sandstone rock some twenty feet away where it explodes into a thousand pieces.

"There you have it ladies and gentlemen," I yell. "THAT is the meaning of life!"

Max is amused. "Chaz, my boy, you may be right."

Chapter 2

> The real voyage of discovery consists not in
> seeking new landscapes, but in having new eyes.
> — Marcel Proust
> All the roads we have to walk are winding
> and all the lights that lead us there are blinding.
> — "Wonderwall" —Oasis

Back at the Caddy trunk I find an old Dunkin' Donuts cup containing an abandoned joint just begging to be smoked. "I don't think we're gonna make it." I croak. "Gotta leave a note for any-body who finds our remains. My last will and testament."

Max has heard this song and dance before. He snorts, "You make Annie Wilkes sound sane."

"Okay, so maybe just a testament. No need for a will when there's nothing to leave or nobody to leave it to."

He tests me. "When you got nothing you got nothing to lose."

"Dylan," I yell.

Max stretches and sighs. "Chaz, everyone has something to leave. Even if it's an organ donation."

"Max, when I die you can have my spleen."

"How about your brain? It hasn't been used much."

I scratch him behind the ears and wail, "The end is near, my faithful companion. Things must be put in writing. Apologize for stealing. Apologize for setting fires. Acknowledge certain people. Tell 'em how much they meant to me. Maybe even tell a few that I'm sorry for being such an asshole."

"There were more than a few," Max smiles, displaying his shiny whites like Jack Torrance about to put a hatchet through a door.

"You're right again. You're always right. Except when you're wrong. And that's most of the time."

Max sighs, "Chaz, you're more melodramatic than a Pabst film."

"A movie about the beer?"

"No. George Pabst. Directed *Pandora's Box* with Louise Brooks." With a smile drenched in smugness.

"I'll put it on my bucket list."

The fire in the Blue Dream goes out, but I don't need a match to re-light it. If I hold the joint skyward like I was offering the sun a toke there would be a spontaneous combustion of weed. I grab the laptop from the front seat and sit against the rear tire in the car shadow, the joint between my lips and the fedora tilted down to my brow. Max jumps from the back seat and strolls to a nearby saguaro to lift his leg. The cactus, its arms heavenward, appears to cry out to the Great Spirit, "Why is this little pissant pissing on me?" Then Max marks a nearby rock. And another spray nails the front tire. I'm thinking that if he could run alongside a tumblin' tumbleweed and piss on it he would. Max seems to have an inexhaustible supply of pee. After urinating the desert he returns to my side and collapses with a deep exhale.

I close my eyes and reflect on my life as consciousness evaporates in the heat. I'm 20 years old, but I admit my emotions sometimes place me at the age of 10. My intellect is that of a man of 60. With every passing day though, my body feels like I'm 90. I can convince myself that I'm ageless if I never celebrate another birthday. That's why I refuse to have another birthday cake. I don't need a reminder of my own mortality.

I open my eyes, look at the laptop screen, and type: To Whom It May Concern. I, Chaz Chase, being of sound mind...

"Hah!" Max interrupts.

I ignore him. "Maybe I should leave Pam Grier to the NAACP."

"Explain the name so the poor sap who finds this note will know what the hell you're talking about."

I exhale a cloud of delirium at the screen and type: I call my 1959 Cadillac convertible 'Pam Grier' because she's black, beautiful, and her top is easily removed. Remember *Foxy Brown*?

Max howls, his tail wagging.

My Pam Grier used to be beautiful. She was a molten slick attitude of leather and chrome, spit metal so shiny you could shave your face in the reflection. A raw seductive, sensuous gem that turned heads and quickened pulses. But now my Caddy has seen better days; a dusty, decrepit Norma Desmond who no longer receives wolf whistles. But if Pam Grier could read, I'd write her fan mail so she believes she is still adored.

Pam Grier's A-C is busted, only one speaker works, the windshield is cracked, the back seat torn up, duct tape holds the glove compartment shut, and the word DICKWEED was keyed onto the front hood by an ex (Was it Lexi? Or Ashley? Maybe Amber?) a few months after I inherited it. When the car was new she was the *Foxy Brown* Pam Grier. Sensuality on wheels. Kick ass lustiness. Today she's more like *Jackie Brown* Pam Grier. Still smoldering sexuality and quite interesting but now a faded beauty. "Max, I've always loved Pam Grier and black-ploitation movies," I RichardRoundtree-ized.

He nods.

"*Coffy* was as sweet as honey at the bottom of a jar."

"Nothing better than *Shaft*," Max says.

I sing, "That Shaft is a bad mother..."

Max interrupts, "Now shut your mouth!" and we laugh.

I take a deep drag of the joystick and think about what I want to include in my will.

Max interrupts my thoughts, "We're not far from Monument Valley. If we leave now we'll be there by sunset." He believes that visiting locations around the country made famous in movies may inspire me to write screenplays.

Being a former member of Hollywood's prestigious director corps, Max has a soft spot for Monument Valley. It's where John Ford, a director he admires, filmed *Stagecoach*, *She Wore a Yellow Ribbon* and several others. The backdrop is also used in *Forrest Gump*, Milepost 13 on Highway 163, where Forrest jogs while leading a group of devotees.

But right now Monument Valley seems like a destination and destinations mean endings and endings have the finality of a cemetery. It shows on a road map from point A to point B. This is where you're born and here is where you die and all the stuff in the middle is life. I want my life to be a circle that never ends. My whole short life has been a roller coaster. I want to be on a merry-go-round.

I continue typing: I hereby leave Pam Grier to the NAACP.

Max says, "What are you, a fucking Quaker? Nobody uses 'hereby' in this day and age." When Max snarls, he reminds me of Edward G. Robinson in *Kid Galahad* with a fat cigar dangling from his mouth.

I type again: Sorry NAACP that I don't have time to clean my ride, because I'm about to step into the Great Unknown where time is fleeting and madness takes its toll.

"From *Rocky Horror*," Max barks. "Must you always think in terms of lyrics?"

"I can't help it. I can't turn off my inner juke box." It's the byproduct of having worked as a disc jockey at several oldies radio stations after graduating from high school, and always being surrounded by music. When I was young, my parents always had oldies CD's or a classic hits radio station playing on the stereo. Mostly stuff from the 70's and 80's. Many of the files in my brain have been deleted over time, things I used to know, like my ex-wife's middle name, or the address of the last radio station I worked at, or my parent's birthdays, but files about songs and the artists who sang them are all still alive and well and ready and eager to pop into my consciousness at any given moment.

I grew up in a musical family. Dad played the violin and mom the flute, and I wanted to play electric guitar and be the next Eddie Vedder but since my parents were footing the bill for music lessons they suggested cello, and it worked out well because I got hooked on Yo-Yo Ma. Lessons and a strict practice schedule helped me stay away from the bad crowd I was starting to hang with. Although I didn't need others to get in trouble, I was able to do that quite well on my own, thank you.

When I was younger I stole stuff. Stuff I didn't even want or need. I'd go into a Target and leave with a Hamilton-Beach waffle maker duct taped to the inside of my pant leg. Home Depot was an easy take down. I'd walk out with a wrench set, a Mikita cordless drill, or a Moen bathroom faucet. I didn't need any of that crap but the very act of stealing was a rush. My shrink said it was the rare situation I could control.

And then there were the fires.

Nothing serious, I didn't burn down any houses, but I lit up a neighbor's tool shed and an old, dried out Christmas tree set by the curb for the trash guys to pick up. Also my fourth grade teacher's Chevy Vega. Mr. Hannigan was my personal pain in the ass who loved giving me detention. I think he would have worked without pay if the superintendent guaranteed him that he could give me detention every day for the rest of my life. His Vega was always breaking down, so I figured I was doing him a favor by lighting it up. It's a Chevy Vega... it's supposed to burn! Hannigan took the insurance money and bought a new Honda Accord. He never even thanked me. Of course he never knew it was me, but I'm sure he had his suspicions.

My psychologist, from the age of 8 through high school, called my crimes a desperate cry for attention. He said I had an "impulse control disorder" but all I know is the actions made my adrenaline kick into high gear. A definite endorphin rush. I remember when I was six years old and visited Alexandra, a girl who lived a few houses away. She was 7 and I was madly in love and wanted to greatly impress her, so when she left her bedroom to go to the bathroom, I set fire to her doll house with matches I stole from my parent's kitchen. Alexandra ran back into the room screaming, even though the doll house only had a corner that was ablaze. I reached in to 'save' her dolls and then smothered the fire with a wet towel I had conveniently kept nearby. She thought I was such a hero, but her parents must have been wise to the charade because I was never invited into their house again.

Yeah, for a while I was a card-carrying pyromaniac. Until I lost the card in a fire.

I stare at the burnt red mesas and beg for guidance from Yeii, the Divine Navajo Spirit. The sun closes my eyes and a thousand years are reversed in a blinding white hot tempest. I've vanished, along with Max, my car, the road, and all the cigarette butts and Bud lite cans that mar the land and the jet trails that scar the sky. Innocence and purity reign, before the White Death rode in on horseback to steal the land. Soon the sandstone columns will be owned by corporations. The beauty of Mother Nature usurped by Big Business. This mesa is brought to you by McDonald's. The Yellowstone geyser Old Faithful is now sponsored by Ford. The granite face of El Capitan in Yosemite is painted over with a two thousand foot tall Coca Cola logo. And on a small ice floe in the Bering Strait, a yellow Shell icon is spray painted onto the fur of a lone polar bear. Our Mother is slowly dying, and I'm sure that will be sponsored too.

Announcer: "The end of the world tomorrow is brought to you by Viagra, urging you to go out with a bang."

And Yeii cries.

A long tongue licks my face and Max snaps me back to the

current Hell of the moment. "I'm hungry. Feed me," sounding like Levi Stubbs as Audrey II.

"Yes, your royal highness. That's why I'm here. To serve your every need."

"If I had opposable thumbs I'd do it myself," then Max contorts around, lifts his left hind leg, and licks his dick. I prop the laptop against the rear tire, wondering how my thoughts drifted to my nefarious past while avoiding work on my last will and testament.

I walk to the trunk to open a dog food can and ponder this human-dog relationship. Max is brilliant. Lassie was able to alert humans if Timmy was stuck at the bottom of a well, but Max can pontificate for hours about the use of montage in Eisenstein films or about the symbolism of extreme weather in many Kurosawa movies. And for my money, that's much more important than saving Timmy.

Most dog owners burst with pride if their pets know 'sit', 'stay', and 'play dead', but Max is a renaissance dog, well versed in music and art and cinema. Damn, if Timmy was stuck at the bottom of the well, Max could solve the crisis by explaining how deep the well is, its circumference, and its area, because he knows $V = \pi r2h$. Still, as much as I want to anthropomorphize Max, he is a dog. Most of the time, anyway. I'm sure that on a movie set John Ford never yelled, "Cut! Okay everybody, take five. I gotta go lick my dick."

Max wolfs down his food. Another dog trait. His DNA demands it. "At least it's real food instead of some of the shit you find on the side of the road," I tell him.

Max replies, "Chaz, I'm still a dog, even though my spirit and essence and intellect is Sam Fuller. You're just going to have to accept my reality. I accept your reality that you're some stoned out of your mind, babbling lunatic."

"Thank you."

"I still have 39 pairs of chromosomes and I'm still a canis lupis familliaris and my definition of food is anything I can fit into my mouth and chew."

"Sometimes you don't even need to chew."

Max lets out a dismissive sigh. "Maybe Monument Valley will inspire you. You should seed the clouds with ideas and the words will rain down."

I know the answer is out there, so I throw back my head, stretch out my arms high to the Spirit and sing "Let it rain, let it rain, let your love rain down on me."

"Clapton," says Max, and of course he's right again.

Faster than you can say 'Maria Ouspenskaya', we're back on the highway, the tires droning like a distant swarm of anger. We don't speak. I'm thinking about my situation and my frustrating inability to change it.

Max is asleep and dreaming in the back seat. He's in pursuit of something, his paws claw the air and with quick gasps and tiny yelps, his nose twitches. The only thing I ever pursued in a dream was Diana Templeton, the bustiest girl in grammar school. I always tried to sit to her left in class so I could steal glances down her blouse. Without a doubt she was my first wet dream.

The CD plays "Sleigh Ride" by Leroy Anderson, but my brain plays 'We're on the road to nowhere, come on inside, taking that ride to nowhere, we'll take that ride'. Max says my jukebox tunes always reflect my subconscious thoughts, fears, and desires.

For some unknown reason I flashback to when I was three years old and lying on the front lawn of my parent's house. I gazed straight into the sun, trying to stare down the burning fire.

It was a wretched attempt to destroy my vision, not unlike that disturbing scene from *Un Chien Andalou*. My father was on the road at some dentist convention, but my mother must have seen what I was doing and rushed from the house, grabbed me and screamed, "Don't ever do that. You'll go blind and I'll have to take care of you." The self-mortification thing was dumb and I don't know why my retina was not destroyed, but the only permanent pain I felt was my mother's rebuke. Years later my psychologist said in my subconscious I wanted to blind myself to the arguments and tension created by my parents. It may also explain the fascination with fire. Maybe on some level I wanted to burn.

And then there were the thefts. The first thing I stole was a package of baseball cards from a 7-11, but then I felt bad and returned them the next day, minus the bubble gum. Okay, I'll be honest. Also minus the Cal Ripken Jr. card. But I sealed the package up like it was brand new and slipped it back into the original box and 7-11 was never the wiser. The thefts were never anything too serious. At least I never removed the tag from a new mattress under penalty of law. I try to never question anything. If you question something, you end up with more questions than answers and get sucked into this vortex of the unknown. Everyone has their own raggedyass Truth, but somewhere is the Real Truth in caps and underlined and in a wavy aurora Borealis fluorescent neon sign a thousand miles high that shouts down from the heavens with the thunder voice of James Earl Jones. That doesn't mean I won't raise a challenge and get all pissed off if something doesn't go my way, but I am trying to achieve that higher state of consciousness, which is Total Acceptance. Since my diagnosis it hasn't been easy. I've felt alienated my entire life and I tell this to Max.

"Chaz, part of your maturing process will take you from feeling alienated to feeling accepted."

"Wouldn't it be easier if I just accepted my alienation? Or alienated my acceptance?"

Max says acceptance adds years to your being. He's right. My Mom's father accepted nothing and he paid the ultimate price.

Grandpa Don was always at odds with his world and later in

life became a recluse. He disagreed with everything and every-one, especially his wife Helen. They would argue over anything. They once fought over which time zone was better. Their battles probably could have been used in *Fists of Fury*, except Bruce Lee would have found them to be a little too over the top. Grandma could be stern and intimidating but she always stood her ground. My Mom said Grandma was lactose intolerant. I think she was just plain intolerant. When I was growing up we rarely saw them since they had a farm in Iowa and couldn't get away because they had to take care of the livestock. They would send cards on my birthday and Christmas and the envelopes always contained $20 bills.

Don's coil was wound tighter than the rubber inside a golf ball and that final massive heart attack was the Universe telling him, "It's the contented leaf that just drifts downstream and never fights the current." That pesky Ego can sure shorten your life. It's all about Acceptance.

Take Max, for example. I have yet to find anyone who can hear Max talk. I may be the only one, and I accept that. I don't bring it up to anyone. I may be insane but I'm sane enough to realize I shouldn't act insane in front of others. There's a time and place to display crazy.

If no one can hear my dog talk, well... it's their loss. I do know Max and I are on the same wavelength. I read somewhere years ago, maybe in a Ripley's 'Believe It or Not' column or an Ant Man comic, that if the atoms that create audio waves are in tune with each other, it's possible to have communication be-tween species.

I remember my science teacher Mr. Billings explaining that anything is possible if you harness the power of atoms and neutrons and protons. This was just before he placed a chemical solution too close to a Bunsen burner and lost his eyebrows. The students got used to his browless feature until one day he showed up in class with faux eyebrows, resembling two woolly caterpillars. They looked like Martin Scorsese's brows. I'll admit it was difficult to sit through Mr. Billings class and watch him wear his new brows, because he sweat a lot and it appeared those strips of hair were always in motion as they slid to various spots on his forehead. Like rearranging the eyebrows on a Mr. Potato Head.

Yes, we've entered the Golden Age of Possibilities with the 21st century on the horizon and anything and everything will be achieved. The colonization of distant planets. Transporting matter through air. Even having a conversation with your dog.

Just last night Max was bemoaning the current state of cinema. He says there's too much emphasis on Computer Generated Imagery and not enough on the story. "The script is king," he declares. I respond, "What about your script for *The Naked Kiss*? It was less king and more joker." He didn't laugh at my joke but curled back his upper lip to display his canines, like Bogart in *The Big Sleep*, and snarled, "If a script doesn't give you a hard-on in the first couple of scenes, throw it in the goddamned garbage!"

I continued my assessment, "It started off okay with the prostitute beating the shit out of the guy with her high heels. You can take pride in knowing you influenced Tarantino. Then there was the shot of the movie marquee showing *Shock Corridor* which was just a shameless self-promotion and there were too many jump cuts. I didn't buy her sudden transformation from a hard-as-nails hooker to a nurturing therapist for crippled kids."

Max lowers his voice to a throaty growl. "It was all raw emotion. The kinetic energy of the script flowed through the actors. The public didn't get it. It was over their heads. You know how I feel about the public. Three percent of the population are assholes. The other ninety-seven percent are dipshits."

Max can be so caustic and cynical and disagreeable. Why can't we have more of a Mr. Peabody and Sherman relationship?

I know it was only two dimensional but at least it was cordial. They never fought about a choice of destination for the Wayback Machine. They never disagreed about anything.

Speaking of cartoons, I knew a guy in high school who confessed that some of his earliest masturbatory fantasies involved Betty Rubble of *The Flintstones*. He also would stare at *Josie and the Pussycats* for hours with the volume turned off. I was never that fond of animation, although I once mentally undressed Jessica Rabbit.

I do enjoy talking movies with Max. I aspire to have that much knowledge. I've read a lot of books about film noir and the French New Wave and Italian Post War cinema, but just hearing Max spout his point of view is a real learning experience. I've spent many days at the cinema or at home watching DVDs and each two hour escape is such a rush. Any time you can avoid reality it's a good thing.

It feels like Max and I have been driving for months. When you drive mile after mile, Tuesdays become Saturdays and Mondays are Thursdays, and you're under the hypnotic spell of the rhythm of the passing mile markers. But I love being on the road, and now more than ever being in motion is very important. It's when I stop I fear my heart will stop and my world will cease to be. I wouldn't be comfortable settling down in one place. I have R.S.S.: Restless Spirit Syndrome. It seems that my roots have always been grounded in the wind.

Chapter 3

"The gladdest moment in human life, me thinks,
is a departure into unknown lands."
— Richard Burton

"Everyone keeps asking, what's it all about?
I used to be so certain and I can't figure out."
— "Barely Breathing" —Duncan Sheik

We pass an old rusted sign used as target practice. The sign reads: Just ahead - Eat and Get Gas. Max observes, "Cliché. Avoid them. Just a verbal crutch. It would be much more interesting and unexpected if the sign read: Just ahead The New York Philharmonic Orchestra."

Trying to top his suggestion, I offer: "Just ahead: the Secret to Immortality," and Max nods.

In another mile I see the gas station and store, with a very rusty Texaco Flying A Pegasus sign that has also taken its share of buckshot. I don't understand why anyone would waste their time shooting at a sign. I pull into the dirt parking lot, dust churning into the air as I roll up to a pump.

Sprawled on a beat up purple sofa on the store porch is a guy of about sixty. He's tall, wiry, and tattooed, ripped jeans, grease streaked Harley-Davidson white tee shirt, and with his long, gray ponytail, sort of looks like Ginger Baker. The man's arms are chiseled tan rock formations tattooed with a fiery dragon and a black skull. He looks like someone who never turned down an invitation to a barroom brawl and probably won his fair share. His skin is the texture of a worn saddle. With obvious discomfort he rises to his feet and winces-shuffles to the Caddy. Maybe he's been in one too many bar fights. His herky-jerky movement makes him appear as though he was created by Willis O'Brien. I step out of Pam Grier, expecting to receive a puzzled look, but he seems unfazed by my minimalist attire of shorts and fedora. I have a feeling he's seen it all and done it all.

Max jumps out from the back seat and strolls around marking rocks and cacti. I yell, "Don't piss on a Gila monster," which would probably be a popular bumper sticker in these parts. I move to unscrew the gas cap, but the man grabs it first and then reaches for the pump nozzle. It's clear he doesn't want me to fill 'er up by myself. He grunts, "Hey, how's it goin'?" with a raspy voice that sounds like two sheets of sandpaper mating. His steely-blue eyes pierce into you, as if he can read what's written on your soul.

On his shirt is a hand-stitched tag reading 'Leroy' and on his belt is a sidearm reading Glock. He tells me he used to wait in the store for people to come in after filling their tanks but there were too many who decided to gas and dash. Leroy says showing the pistol promotes honesty.

Leroy mumbles "Nice boat," as I stare at the blurred numbers on the gas pump spinning like a calliope on crack.

Tendollarstwentydollarsthirtydollarsfortydollars.

If I only had solar panels on the hood I could ditch the gas tank and break from the gravitational bonds of Earth. I'm sweating like a sow giving birth to a litter but there's not a drop of perspiration on Leroy's face or his tee. "You sell beer?" I ask.

He gestures to the shack. "Ginger'll fix you up."

Max has finally stopped peeing and is now by my side. I gaze up at the sky at several buzzards in the distance looking like check marks made by a black Magic Marker onto a sheet of cobalt blue paper. I leave the ignition on so Leroy can be entertained by Christmas tunes. As I walk toward the store, my steps on the gravel sounds like Frosted Flakes being chewed. Before entering the store, I hear Ella Fitzgerald croon, "Baby It's Cold Outside" and Leroy joins in, sounding remarkably like Bing Crosby.

There's not much of a selection of brews in the cooler but they're cold and wet and that's all that matters. I don't think Ginger notices me because she's riveted to a soap opera on a portable TV on the counter top and talking to the actors, "Come on Karen, tell Luke the baby's not his," but after a few moments she realizes I'm in the store. She murmurs a stage whisper "Howdy" as I grab a six pack of Coors, a bag of Doritos, and a bottle of water. Maybe the stage whisper was meant not to interrupt the actors on TV. It worked, because the actors didn't miss a beat.

Ginger is about 55 years old, her complexion the color and texture of a well-worn toilet seat at a Greyhound station in Trenton. She straddles a stool, although I can't see much of the stool because her flesh envelops the seat and cascades down like a lard waterfall. Doctors on TV talk shows would diagnose her as being 'morbidly obese'. Ginger must weigh at least 300 pounds soaking wet, and dear Lord, I never want to see her soaking wet.

"Fourteen dollars and twenty-five cents, hon." She speaks on tiptoes, not much above a whisper so as to not disrupt the universe. As she makes change at the cash register, I sneak a peek at her large, pendulous breasts. She's not wearing a bra under her white t-shirt and her raspberry nipples resemble a pair of distant red silos on the snowy, rolling hills of Iowa. Ginger looks up and catches me staring but her smile tells me she hasn't been stared at for a long time and she's flattered, although I feel my face redden. My alter ego inner voice Dum Phuk pleads, "Go ahead. Tell her the doctor gave you only six months to live and you'd like to grope a woman one more time before you croak."

"Supposed to hit a hundred and eight in the shade today," she murmurs.

"Guess I'll avoid the shade," I tell her, cracking open a cool Coors.

"Where ya goin'?"

"Oh... same place I came from. Nowhere."

Again Dum Phuk shouts in my subconscious, "Do it! Grab her boobs!" and I feel my blood pressure quicken.

"Your dog wanna treat?" she asks.

"God damn it, no!" I blurt out to Dum Phuk, but Ginger thinks it's directed to her and says, "Geez, sorry. I was only asking."

"Sorry," I try to recover. "I was thinking about something else. Yeah, he'd love a biscuit."

She grabs a biscuit from under the counter and places it in my hand. One last glance at her face and I realize she looks like a much older, heavier version of Tura Satana, the femme fatale in *Faster Pussycat! Kill! Kill!*. Max watches the scene unfold and says, "Want to do it again? Give it the Russ Meyer touch?"

I trot out to the car and grab the laptop, open up Final Draft and type:

INT. CONVENIENCE STORE – DAY

Chaz *enters, checks out 25-year old Ginger sitting behind the counter. She's a beautiful blonde, with a slim figure and large breasts under her low-cut tee. The jiggle of her boobs could be picked up by a seismograph in San Francisco. Her breasts are proud, yet defiant. He grabs a six pack from the cooler and approaches Ginger.*

GINGER

Supposed to hit a hundred and eight in the
shade today.

Her hand rests on mine as her tongue circles her ruby-red lips. She stares at me like I'm a pistachio ice cream cone about to be licked.

CHAZ

I like it hot.

My index finger goes to her cheek, but she moves my finger to her inviting mouth and sucks on it.

                    CHAZ *(looking out the window)*
                    What about him?

                    GINGER
                    Hugx pewqun mdlsanfdlndee doplf.

                    CHAZ
                    Huh?

She removes Chaz' finger from her mouth.

                    GINGER
                    He's not the only one who knows how to pump.

                    CUT TO:

Leroy pumping gas, looking bored.

                    CUT TO:

Chaz and Ginger make love inside the cooler, steaming up the windows. The cooler door opens to reveal Ginger   straddling Chaz and wildly waving his fedora in the air like Slim Pickens riding the H-Bomb.

                    GINGER *(squeals)*
                    Yippee ki-yay!

Gallon milk jugs break open and milk splashes onto their bodies.

                    GINGER
                    Milk! It does a body good!

Leroy suddenly bursts into the store, his pistol drawn.

                    LEROY
                    What the fuck...

Shots are fired, hitting cans of beer in the cooler.

                    LEROY
                    I'll kill you, you little pencil dick!

Chaz grabs his shorts and fedora and dashes out the door with Leroy in pursuit.

                    EXT. CONVENIENCE STORE – DAY

Chaz jumps into his car and revs the engine, as bullets

fly everywhere. Chaz high-tails it from the parking lot, the car's
tires churning up gravel and dust. A bullet hits the gas pump and
ignites a huge explosion.

I finish typing. Max gives the script a quick once-over and sighs, "It's not giving me a hard-on, but what the hell. Let's shoot it" and in a flash we're surrounded by silent, faceless, shadows that make up the movie crew. Everyone from the assistant director to 1st Camera to sound guy to script girl, all appearing as gray, human-shaped vapors.

Max yells 'Action' and I enter the store for the very first time as we follow the script.

Following the gas pump explosion Max yells, "Cut! Nicely done" and the shadowy movie crew disappears into a pure white fog. "See how you can make a routine scene interesting?" Max says, and suddenly in real-time I'm back at the counter facing 55-year old Ginger and she's placing a dog biscuit in my hand.

"Thanks," I tell her and pour the water into a dog bowl. By the time I reach the gas pump the Coors can is empty.

Fiftydollarssixtydollarsseventydollarseighteencents.

Leroy and I already talked about the weather, but I feel like I should offer more small talk. "Where's this road go?"

"Wherever you want it to," he grins. "About thirty miles from here is a motel."

"I don't need that. I sleep in this Cadillac Motel. I didn't expect to see this out here in the middle of nowhere."

"Yeah, it surprises a lot of folks," he says, removing the nozzle from Pam Grier. "I don't even think I'm on most maps. Right here may be the only place on Earth that doesn't exist. Like the dark side of the moon."

A quick, knowing glance at Max and he says, "Pink Floyd."

"How long have you been out here?" I ask.

"'Bout twenty-two years. Ginger and I were trying to figure things out. Make sense of it all. We were driving around aimlessly and came upon this. The old man who owned it was dying of emphysema and he sold it to us for eighty-five hundred bucks. Gas station, store, and a cabin beyond the ridge over there. I think when Ginger and I finally sobered up, we said, 'What the fuck have we done?'" We laugh.

"But now I can't picture us being anywhere else," he continues. "At night we'll sit outside and look up at all those stars and say, 'Man, this feels comfortable. This is the way it's supposed to be.'" Leroy talks like a man who was rescued after being shipwrecked on a tropical island and is anxious to have a conversation with a fellow human being.

"She's my rock. My soul. My anchor. We've been together for almost thirty years."

"Congratulations. I consider a relationship successful if it lasts thirty minutes," I WoodyAllen-ize.

Maybe Leroy's parents didn't emphasize proper dental hygiene when he was a boy, or maybe he dumped his bike and got a mouth full of asphalt, but I'm curious about his jack o' lantern smile. Perhaps it's because my father was a dentist and he wanted me to be one as well.

When I was five or six, Dad would use dental x-rays as flash cards for me to identify each tooth by its number. He'd flip x-rays in rapid succession and I'd yell "Second molar, two!" then he'd hold up the next x-ray and I'd shout, "Lateral incisor, twenty-six!" and then another "Second bicuspid, thirteen!"

Dum Phuk urges me, "Go ahead, ask him."

In real life I wouldn't attempt it, but everything is possible in movies. I think it could be a cute scene and Max shrugs, as much as a dog can shrug since they don't have shoulders. Max says, "Okay, let's play it out. I'll channel Preston Sturges."

"No, the scene I have in mind plays more like Peter Farrelly," referencing *Dumb and Dumber*. I re-open my laptop and write up the scene with Ginger standing next to Leroy at the gas pump.

Max yells, "Okay, let's shoot it," and from nowhere the shadowy-gray crew suddenly re-materializes and a movie set takes shape. Max shouts, "Roll sound. Roll camera. Slate it! Action!"

EXT. GAS STATION — DAY

Leroy and Ginger stand next to a gas pump, filling up the Caddy.

CHAZ

Leroy, I don't mean to pry but... how many teeth have you got?

LEROY

What?

CHAZ

Ever count your teeth?

LEROY

Naw, I got better things to do than that.

CHAZ

Mind if I count 'em for you?

LEROY

What for?

CHAZ

Because knowledge is power and if you know how many teeth you've lost, you'll do whatever it takes to preserve the remaining teeth. I know this because my father was a dentist."

Leroy leans in, bends down and opens his mouth wide. Chaz recoils from the mixed odors of Skoal's, whiskey and barbecue sauce.

Al Kline

CHAZ

Got your back molars, 17, 31 and 32. But
you're missing most of your 20's, and up top 3, 4, and
7, and 11 are gone. And no 14, 15, or 16.

LEROY

Not good, huh?

CHAZ

You're supposed to have 32. You have 17.
Poor dental hygiene can lead to cardiovascular issues,
diabetes, and even dementia.

Chaz grabs a box from the back seat of the Caddy.

LEROY

Seventeen? I had no idea.

CHAZ

And make an appointment to see a professional
dentist. Not someone like Dr. Szell.

*Max rolls his eyes, getting the movie reference. Chaz
jumps into the Caddy and tears off into the sunset. Leroy and
Ginger watch the car disappear on the horizon. Leroy opens
the box.*

LEROY

I don't know who that guy was, but he may
have saved my life.

GINGER

Did he leave behind a silver bullet?

LEROY

Nope. Something even more valuable.
(Holds up a Water Pik) And I never even thanked him.
Leroy and Ginger embrace.

FADE OUT.

Max yells "Cut!" I wait for his assessment. Max says,

"You're right. Nothing like Preston Sturges" and shakes his head in displeasure. He then walks to a nearby canvas chair, lifts his leg and attempts to pee on the laptop but misses. Laughter from the invisible crew is heard off stage. I smile at Max and say, "Geez, everybody's a critic." Max barks, "Okay, back to reality" and in a lightning bolt the film crew evaporates in swirling pure white vapors and in real-time Leroy and I are back at the gas pump.

"Doesn't seem like this road gets much traffic," I tell him.

Naw. A few truckers takin' shortcuts. Biker gangs. Photographers checkin' out the desert. Had one guy yesterday studying cactus for his doctorate. And then there's the occasional person who just wants to disappear and not be found. You fit into any of those categories?"

"I don't fit into anything."

"Square peg in a round hole, huh?"

I nod.

"Good lookin' dog ya got."

"Max. A good traveling companion. My alter-ego." I offer Leroy a Coors, "I don't like to drink alone."

"You in a hurry?" he asks. I shake my head no.

"I didn't catch your name." I tell him and he continues, "Chaz, I got something better than that weasel piss," which sounds strange since he sells that weasel piss. Leroy motions me to follow.

We walk to the store where he sinks down on the dusty and torn sofa in the shadow under the eaves. I plop down next to him. "A friend of mine is Navajo. William is a big poo-bah holy man on the rez," Leroy says. He takes a business card from his pocket and hands it to me. "If you ever head down that way, look 'im up. He's good people."

Leroy sticks his hand under the sofa and pulls out an antique milk bottle half-filled with a thick, brownish liquid. "This is special tea that William brewed just for me. Peyote. Ever hear of it? It's supposed to only be used in religious ceremonies," he continues, "But I figure this is kinda like a religious ceremony. Whenever I drink it, I always see the Divine Spirit. And lots of other shit too." We laugh. He continues, "Last week I had a few sips and within an hour I was a raccoon playing accordion in the Lawrence Welk Orchestra," and there's more laughter. "It's even good for my arthritis."

Leroy unscrews the bottle with excitement and tentative anticipation as if he were releasing a very powerful genii upon the world. My mind races and I wonder: Is this gonna have the same taste and effect as Pan Galactic Gargle Blaster?

Leroy takes a sip and winces. He wipes his mouth with the back of his hand then swallows. "You're gonna feel like pukin', but don't. Hold it in. Let it do its job. Respect it."

I take a swig and start to gag, but force myself not to. It was the most disgusting taste imaginable. I felt like my innards was being eaten by cockroaches and I had to fight an overwhelming urge to vomit. Leroy kept urging me, "Keep it in. Keep it in." I nod and groan and fight to keep it down. Leroy says, "Didn't your mother tell you the best medicine tastes the worse?" Leroy and I talked some more but later I didn't recall our conversation. In fact I don't remember anything about the last eight hours on this plane of existence, but I do recall thinking, yeah, this is Ginger Baker giving me "Strange Brew."

After swallowing the concoction I don't think anything happened for an hour or so. Maybe longer. But then I physically shed my skin and grew a colorful plumage of feathers that were fluorescent 4th of July sparklers, and then eased into an omnipotence where I became larger than life, a large bird of changing vibrant colors engulfing the world, soaring above the desert and taking in the rocks, cacti, snakes, and mesas, accompanied by a wailing Hendrix riff and knowing that I was in Oneness with Everything and time no longer existed and I was the moment and my universe was perfect and pure and holy. I also felt like I was trapped inside the Sun, trying to peel it open to escape.

After the magic carpet ride stopped, the day died behind rock formations and turned the valley into a tranquil crimson sea as several bold stars stepped forward to introduce a new night. I remember lying on the couch and Ginger whispering into my ear, "I fed Max. He's okay."

I murmured, "You're right. That was better than Coors."

It could have been minutes or maybe eons that passed before I finally managed to rise from the couch and stagger into their home, all the while shaking cobwebs from my mind.

The cabin had rows of solar panels on the roof and nearby was a utility shed with solar panels. The cabin looked small like a boxcar from the outside but seemed much larger inside. There were two golden exotic fish swimming in a large aquarium on a table, and many books lined the bookshelves. I'm curious about what people read, and I believe you can understand them better after checking out their library. Many of Leroy and Ginger's books were about nature, and some about Native American mysticism and world religions. There were also a few poetry books by Mary Oliver.

My peyote experience, or 'metaphysical exploration' as Leroy calls it, worked up an appetite. Ginger made the best burritos I ever tasted and Leroy served up tequila. I contributed my bag of Doritos and we laughed and talked as if we had known each other for years.

On a shelf is an older, framed Kodachrome photo of a smiling Leroy and Ginger standing next to another woman I didn't recognize. Leroy is holding a Gibson guitar and Ginger has a fiddle resting on her shoulder. I asked them about the picture. Leroy grinned and Ginger blushed.

"Oh that. From 1970. Taken at the Missouri State Fair. That's Tammy Wynette. We were her opening act."

"So you guys are famous musicians."

Leroy laughs, "More like infamous." I ask them to play and after some coaxing, they agree. They remove their instruments from cases and Ginger says, "Now bear with us, we're a little rusty." Dum Phuk says, "Get your cello. Join in," but no, this is Leroy and Ginger's moment.

Leroy strums random chords and tunes the guitar. "We called our act 'The Love Birds' and played a lot of clubs and weddings in Tennessee, Kentucky, Ohio."

Ginger bows the strings, "We had a hit ... well, a small hit, that a few radio stations played."

Leroy adds, "We made it into Billboard's Top 100 Country Chart. It was called, "Two Peas in a Pod." Ever hear of it?"

"Maybe once I hear it I'll recall it," I reply with much diplomacy.

"Ready hon?" Ginger nods and Leroy counts one, two, three, four and they launch into their tune and I could tell by their expressions they are transported back thirty years. At my insistence they play three more tunes, all with clever lyrics, good hooks, and tight harmonies. As Ginger put her fiddle back in the case she says, "Okay, I think we've bored you enough. You'll never come back," and Leroy and I laugh.

The conversation turns to hopes and aspirations and they ask about my road trip. I tell them, "I'm seeking the Truth."

Leroy asks, "Wisdom and Truth?"

"No, just the Truth. I gave up on Wisdom years ago."

"That was very wise of you," Max snorts.

Leroy says, "Truth is an elusive woman. Did you ever know a woman who was beautiful, smart, the whole heavenly package, but unattainable? You would have done anything for her. Anything. Walk around the world on broken glass, but she wouldn't give you the time of day? You were invisible. Well that, my friend, is Truth." I immediately thought about Sara, who I pursued briefly in high school but she never acknowledged my existence. I felt invisible, like Claude Rains as Dr. Jack Griffin.

Leroy pours more tequila, then sighs when a car horn is heard. He straps on his pistol then ambles to the door and says, "Another desperate nomad with a camel runnin' on fumes has found our oasis."

I compliment Ginger again for the burritos. She smiles, but her eyes hold a deep sadness. Or maybe I misread her and she's melancholy after playing music that brought her back to happier times. I ask if they have any kids. She closes her eyes and sighs.

"We do. She's in heaven. Waiting for us."

She moves to a sideboard and reaches for a photo of a young girl with long golden hair and a smile like warm apple pie.

She hands me the photo. "Our Anna. Eighth grade graduation," she says with a pain that will never go away. "We were living in Memphis at the time. Had a nice place right on the Mississippi, and..." Her voice trails off. I put my hand on her arm, "That's okay. You don't have to tell me." But she continues. "A few weeks after this photo... well... they found her body in the river. Our baby..." she sobs. "Raped and killed by a deacon in our church. A deacon. Why would God allow something like that to happen? A kind and merciful God? A God I used to worship? Why? Why?" It's a question she's asked a million times.

Ginger lowers her head, sadness enveloping her like a cold, dark fog. The door opens and Leroy says, "Some guy from Nebraska on his way to the Grand Can..." but his voice trails off as he looks at Ginger and says, "Oh, hon," then walks behind her chair and wraps his arms around her shoulders.

"I'm okay," she whispers, "I'm okay." Ginger had become as vulnerable and powerless as a tiny leaf tumbling over a waterfall.

"I'm sorry. Just got a little overcome. I'm real sorry." Women tend to say "I'm sorry" much more than men, although I think men have more reasons to say it than women.

It was almost 2 am before I said, "I should go. The highway is calling." They insist I stay the night and get a fresh start in the morning, but their one bedroom cabin is too small for another person, so Ginger hands me a blanket and pillow and the sofa turns out to be quite comfortable in the night air. Even better than a night in the Cadillac Motel. They say their goodnights and Max stretches out next to the sofa, puts his head between his paws and lets out a deep sigh. As I look up at the stars, I hear Ginger's voice asking, "Why? Why?"

The universe unfolds before me, watching, appearing close enough to touch, the timeless Milky Way pinwheel coming around once again. The voice of Bogart as Rick in *Casablanca* enters my thoughts, "...it doesn't take much to see that the problems of three little people don't amount to a hill of beans in this crazy world" and I wonder, "Why would an Energy that creates beauty also destroy beauty?"

Max looks up, "Do you remember the Grant Williams character in *The Incredible Shrinking Man*? Just before he disappeared, he said, 'To God there is no zero. I still exist.'" I nod, but even as I'm overcome with deep sadness, I stare at the apathetic night sky and curse the Energy.

"I don't know if God is dead, but I think He's gone deaf," I moan. "Probably blew out his eardrums being too close to the Big Bang. That's why He doesn't respond to our prayers. He can't hear them."

Max edges close to me and whispers, "You do know we're not going anywhere, right? We're always here. Everybody and everything." I reach down and stroke his fur. He's a dog. What the hell does he know?

At that moment my *Charlie's Angels* ring tone sounds. I receive a text and it reads: NOT NOW.

I stare at the cell phone screen for eons and murmur, "That's weird." I re-read the message, but it wasn't sent by anyone. How could I receive a text without a sender? I look at Max and shake my head in bewilderment. Maybe it's just the residual effects of Leroy's brew. Like Scrooge believed the apparition he saw was the result of "an undigested bit of beef, a blot of mustard, a crumb of cheese."

When I check the screen again the message is gone.

Chapter 4

"We do not take a trip, a trip takes us."
— John Steinbeck

"I used to think that I could not go on
And life was nothing but an awful song."
— "I Believe I Can Fly" — R. Kelly

Ahead lies the highway, clutching my dreams like un-opened presents. I tell Max, "Tomorrow at this time we'll be clos-er to home," and he counters with "Wherever you are is home." I stick my finger in my mouth and gag. Goddamn, sometimes he sounds like Rod McKuen. I don't need Max spewing nauseating adages. I can get quite nauseous on my own, thank you.

The cruise control is locked in and the hot desert engulfs us in its womb. Our next stop is Monument Valley. To kill time before time kills us, Max and I play a road game, a variation on the old Burma Shave signs of the early and mid 20th century. Max tells me hundreds of these signs used to dot the highways of America. Like, 'Every shaver/Now you snore/Six more minutes/ Than before/By using/ Burma Shave' or 'Your shaving brush/ Has had its day/So why not/Shave the modern way/With Burma Shave.'

Max says, "Slow down or we'll meet our maker. The rough road ahead is a real tit shaker. Burma Shave."

I counter with, "The seat is cramped and the road is long. I have to get out and stretch my schlong. Burma Shave." Both the mile markers and my life speed past like a warm dream.

On my laptop I open a poem in Word that I wrote a few days ago. I ask Max for his feedback and critique. It's titled "Chal-lenge":

When the time comes
I hope I don't struggle and gasp
and try and make
the last breath not be the last.
Just let me sleep
and not battle fate with machines
take what you want
but I get to keep all my dreams.
When the light fades,
and the shadows win out
I can only ask,
"What the hell was that all about?"

I wait for his reaction. He said, "Well... yes, it's good, but somewhat derivative."

"Derivative?"

"It screams Dorothy Parker. Has everything but her signature."

I figure if you're going to steal, steal from the best.

Max says, "Oscar Levant once said, "Imitation is the sincerest form of plagiarism."

"I'll make a copy of that."

I always bounce my writings off Max to get his reaction. I tell him a recent idea for a short screenplay: The scene shows a family opening Christmas presents. Like a *Saturday Evening Post* cover by Norman Rockwell. Everybody gathers around the 94 year old grandmother as she opens her gift. Somebody has given her one of those hideous holiday sweaters that you buy as a gag gift. Everyone's laughing, except Granny. She stares at the gift giver, and then reaches for a shotgun above the fireplace mantel. As we fade to black, we hear the shotgun being pumped.

"Like it?" I ask with much anxiety.

"Yeah, terrific," Max says, soaked in sarcasm. "I'll call the

Academy and have them engrave your Oscar."

I know it's crap, but taking a crap is better than not taking a crap. If I keep writing stuff maybe something good will materialize. I figure if you shuck enough oysters you're bound to find a pearl.

Miles pass by as Bruce Springsteen sings:

> "You better watch out! You better not cry
> You better not pout, I'm telling you why.'"

Max howls while thumping his hind leg like a hairy metronome:
> "Santa Claus is coming to town
> Santa Claus is coming to town."

For some reason my mind drifts to thoughts of my dad's parents.

I remember my grandparents always having horehound candies in a purple cut-glass bowl on a lamp table in the living room and their house smelled of African violets. A jigsaw puzzle scene in bright Kodachrome of the Matterhorn or a buffalo herd in Yellowstone was a work in progress on a card table. The big wooden stereo cabinet from about 1960 played records by Montovani or 101 Strings. Just once I wanted to throw a Nirvana or Pearl Jam album on the turntable and crank it up from ten to Spinal Tap eleven for my grandparent's reaction. But I never did. I loved Grace and Maxie and didn't want them to be uncomfortable. Although if I had played *Smells Like Teen Spirit*, Grandma would have said, 'Delightful! I wonder if Bert Kaempfert has a version of that.'

Grandpa Maxie, who I named my dog after, was gregarious and friendly, perfect traits for a successful traveling salesman. He worked at Gizmonic Institute and was usually away from home for weeks at a time. Maxie showered my Dad with presents when he was growing up, often surprising him at school and interrupting one of George's classes so he could pile gifts onto the teacher's desk to show everyone how much he loved his son, but once the "Oh's and Ah's" of his classmates faded, Maxie quickly returned to the road again.

Maxie left me his '59 Cadillac convertible with only 7,227 miles on it. It was a present he gave himself upon retiring, but it sat in their garage under a tarp for years because he lost his license on a drunk driving charge. He would either walk to the American Veterans Club and stagger home or take a bus and stagger home. He promised that once I got my license the Caddy would be mine. When I inherited the car I named it Pam Grier and gave it a few modifications, like a new stereo with a CD player, two big speakers in the back, and wide, retro whitewalls. I also custom made a few hiding places for various goodies and diversions.

Grandpa Maxie also left me his collection of erotic Pez dispensers. There were about fifty male and female nude plastic figurines that shot candies from various orifices. I sold the collection on eBay for $625.

Maxie used to take me aside and tell me dirty jokes he'd heard on the road. He told me the worse part of getting old: "When you ejaculate, dust shoots out of your pecker." I laughed at that for days. He also advised, "When you tell a girl the size of your penis, always give it in centimeters because it sounds a lot longer." With his many romantic interludes on the road, he considered getting a vasectomy. "I'd be just like a Christmas tree. With balls for decoration only."

Grandma Grace was warm and sweet, just not to Maxie. I suspect she was aware her traveling salesman husband was not living the life of a choir boy, and if he suddenly transformed overnight into Gregor Samsa, Grace would have found that to be an improvement. My Dad says his mom was very pious and moralistic. She once wrote a scathing letter to the *National Geographic* because an issue showed a photo of a bare-breasted Kenyan woman working in a field. Grace also once called a local TV station to complain after they ran a story about an infestation of rodents and the announcer said the word 'titmouse'. I sensed she viewed sex as only a messy and evil requirement to procreate and if you enjoyed the disgusting act it was downright blasphemous.

Grace taught Bible class in a private Catholic school and decided after a few years of dealing with snotty nosed brats that she didn't want any children of her own. But accidents happen. In rapid succession, she and Maxie went from a daughter to a son to separate bedrooms with her bedroom door dead-bolted at night. I imagine she wore a chastity belt just in case Maxie tried to break down her bedroom door. Maxie probably didn't mind her celibacy because according to family whisperings, he never longed for female company in his travels. My dad says Maxie never gave him the birds and bees talk because he was seldom home, and his mom never broached the subject. When talking about her husband, Grandma's frequent admonishment was to refer to him as a "half-ass."

Grandpa used to have a crude habit of putting his hand down the front of his pants to adjust his genitals. It bothered him that his equipment flopped either to the left or to the right of his pants crotch with great frequency. Maxie didn't care if it was at the dinner table or in the produce aisle of the local A & P, if his package needed adjusting, he adjusted. He referred to it as "Rearranging the furniture." He'd stop whatever he was doing and proclaim, "Excuse me, gotta rearrange the furniture" and Grandma would grumble "Such a half-ass." Years later I wanted to believe that if Grandma had offered to help rearrange his furniture, they probably would have had a happier marriage and fewer road trips for Maxie. It's the romantic in me.

Grace died three years before Maxie, and Grandpa insisted on giving her eulogy, even though the family felt he was in no condition because he had been drinking Rum and Coke all morning long. I was twelve years old and don't remember much about the funeral, except Grandpa Maxie staggering to the front of the gathering, leaning on Grandma's open casket and slurring, "Friends come and go, but dead people last forever." My dad shook his head and hissed, "Oh, Christ," but Maxie continued with, "I'll keep this short and sweet. Just like Grace," Then he mumbled on for about ten minutes comparing the ups and downs of her life to the Pittsburgh Pirates road to the World Series in 1960.

I remember looking at her in the casket with two aunts by my side. One mumbled, "Well, she's on her way" like Grace had just been jettisoned into space like Ildebrando Zacchini, the human cannonball.

I whispered, "I wonder where she is?" and the other aunt said, "Oh, she's everywhere," and I replied, "Or nowhere" and the aunt glared and admonished me with "Now that's not nice. You apologize to your grandmother now."

"Sorry Grandma Grace, wherever you are."

Later when we left the cemetery, my Dad said, "When you die you'll see her in heaven." I blurted out, "Do I have to?" and he laughed and hugged me. I'm sure heaven is crowded with so many more interesting people to meet than Grandma.

I always wanted to believe in a Heaven where everybody and everything you ever cared for was waiting for you, but it's a stretch of the imagination that I can't even comprehend, even if I'm smoking a stick and drinking Southern Comfort. I can't grasp the concept and it kind of freaks me out to think that folks who are now dead, like Grandma Grace, are with you all the time and watching you because they are everywhere. It gets me out of the mood to jerk off knowing I'm being watched by my grandmother.

Maybe dead people know when you're horny and they just leave you alone for twenty minutes. I wonder if there's sex in Heaven. I'll bet there's great sex in Hell. At least I'd like to think so. It's the romantic in me.

Maxie met his own demise a few years after Grace. After leaving the Vet's Club late one night, he decided to rest on a curb before staggering home. He didn't realize the curb was in fact railroad tracks, and for once the Boston & Maine freighter was on time and its wheels neatly severed Maxie's ass from the rest of his body. Grandma's admonishment proved to be prescient. I don't know where Grandpa is now, but wherever he is, he's probably rearranging the furniture.

Max interrupts my thoughts with, "I'm hungry." I tell him, "Okay, the next restaurant."

Ten minutes later we pull into the parking lot of 'Ollie's Omelet's and Oil Change.' Many semi's and pick up's dot the lot. Volvos and Subarus need not apply. I assume the joint has a 'No shirt, no shoes, no service' sign on the entrance, so I decide to wear a shirt. How about formal? I put on my purple ruffled shirt that goes with my tux and sing "Purple Rain" to Max:

"Purple rain, purple rain
I only wanted to see you
Bathing in the purple rain."

He barks, "Stop it. You're ruining my appetite." The sign on the door doesn't mention pants being required. Besides, my underwear is clean. I place a Service Dog vest around Max, tuck the laptop under my arm, and stride toward the cafe.

The place is packed with what appears to be the former cast of *Hee Haw*. In the background a jukebox plays Patsy Cline. Near the cash register are scores of photos tacked to a bulletin board, displaying proud and beaming hunters holding the heads of their fallen deer conquests. The place is mobbed and the only vacant seat is a red vinyl stool at the counter. I scan a menu. Things could be worse. It could be me on the menu, I HannibalLecter-ize.

On either side of me are two customers, the one on the left bearing a close resemblance to Junior Samples. But it could be a female. There's lots of belly fat overlapping belt buckles and pants held up by over-stretched suspenders screaming in pain. Even though the suspenders are doing the best they can, they seem to be losing the battle of the bulge as there's still a display of a hairy butt crack. I quickly look away but the image is burned into my memory forever. It could have been my imagination but it seemed to be much more raucous when I first entered the cafe. It sure quieted down a lot, and I notice my attire is being checked out.

Max giggles, "I feel like we're on the set of *Deliverance*. Cue the banjo music."

I tell him, "I hope they don't make me squeal like Ned Beatty. The 'oinking' part I don't mind. But getting on all fours and squealing is where I draw the line."

"You'd go from an oink to a boink."

Dum Phuk suggests I stand on a chair and yell, "Anybody here want to join me for the gay rights parade?" but I think better of it and try to disappear as I slide onto the lone bar stool. A waitress approaches carrying a pot of coffee. She has the facial expression of someone with an infected tooth. She quickly puts a cup in front of me and pours. I look at her name tag and it reads 'Bunny'. I'm surprised it's not 'Flo.' She looks at Max and says, "Sorry, but we don't allow dogs in here, hon. You can get your food to go."

I point at Max's vest. "He's a service dog. You know... service dogs for folks with disabilities."

Her eyes narrow and she gives me the once-over like a carnival barker trying to guess my weight. She leans in close and whispers, "I don't mean to pry but... what's your disability?"

I put on my most pathetic expression and whisper, "I suffer

from C-M."

"Oh, well I'm sorry, hon. What... what's C-M?"

"Chronic masturbation."

She recoils like she just found a snake in her bowl of spaghetti. "You ain't gonna do that in here, my friend. No offense, sir, if I don't shake your hand." She makes an expression like she's going to vomit, then quickly runs off.

The guy to my left glances at me and with a mouthful of sausage mumbles "Good mornin'." The guy to my right, signing his tab and appearing to be in a hurry, asks, "Where are you headed?"

"Oh, just drivin' and lookin' around," I say, purposely dropping my 'G's.' "Takin' in the good ol' U-S-of-A." I figure it won't hurt to do a little flag waving.

"Yeah, before China owns it," he huffs.

I thought it best to not bring up the China-Wal-Mart marriage, so I answer, "Ain't that the truth" and I take a sip of coffee. Always best to listen, agree, and sympathize. "So, where you headed?"

"Salt Lake City."

I thought I'd really sound like a local and ask, "Whatcha haulin' these days? Pork rinds out of Yuma?"

He stares at me for a moment with a quizzical expression and then smiles, "Just hauling my butt. I'm a singer with the Mormon Tabernacle Choir and I'm running late for a performance tonight." Maybe the shock registers on my face, because he leans in close and says, "You can always get the best breakfast at places like this. Trucks stops are not just for truckers." He tosses a twenty on the counter and leaves. Max reprimands me, "What have I told you about stereotyping?"

With great reluctance the waitress returns, like Commander Shears being told he has to return to Burma. She takes a deep breath. "Okay, Mr. C-M, what can I get you?"

"Mexican omelet and a blueberry muffin." She scribbles the

order on a pad and leaves.

Max says "Thanks" knowing he gets the muffin. He's addicted to blueberry muffins.

The guy on my left, the ringer for Junior Samples, says, "Gonna be another hot one."

"Yep. At least it's a dry heat." Max rolls his eyes. Dum Phuk says, "Tell him you'll play 'Help Me Make it Through the Night'on the juke box, but only if he slow dances with you." I stifle a giggle.

Junior says, "This place is the best. I haul all over the southwest, but this place kicks ass."

"What do ya haul?" I ask, taking a swig of coffee.

"Pork rinds out of Yuma."

I gag and the coffee jettisons out of my nose and onto his bib overalls. I burst out laughing but try to sell it as if something is caught in my throat. "Excuse me. Sorry!" I croak feebly while gasping, my face reddening.

He slaps me on the back and says, "You okay, buddy?" and I'm thinking please-don't-pin-me-to-the-floor-and-perform-mouth-to-mouth-resuscitation.

Junior continues, "Where else can you get grub like this and drop your rig off next door for an oil change? I tell ya, it's a gift from heaven. Hehehehe."

"Well..." I say, still trying to catch my breath, "The lord works in mysterious ways."

"He sure does. He sure does."

Dum Phuk says, "Tell him the only lord you believe in is Jack Lord." I close my eyes and shake my head to eradicate my annoying inner voice.

Junior asks, "So mister, what do you do?"

"I'm a writer."

Max paws my leg and says, "Don't lie to the man." I attempt to kick him under the counter but miss and stub my foot against the chrome base of the stool next to me.

"What do you write?"

"Screenplays. Short stories. Poems."

"The only poem I know starts out, 'There was a young lady from Nantucket...'" and he laughs. "Wrote that on the blackboard in the second grade, and Miss Kendricks paddled my bee-hind real good. I couldn't sit for a week. Hehehehehehe."

I'm feeling bolder. "I don't mean to impose, but I'm always looking for feedback. Would you mind reading one of my poems and tell me what you think?"

Max says, "Oh Christ, this is going to turn into a bar fight like the one in *Dodge City*. If you need me I'll be over there cowering behind an overturned table."

"Thanks. Glad I have a dog for protection."

Junior ponders my request then says, "Sure why not?" like someone had asked if they could dump a load of manure on his front lawn. I open a page on my laptop. It's titled "Prayer."

Junior removes a pair of reading glasses from his shirt pocket and inches closer to the screen. He reads out loud:

> I don't have what it takes
> to digest carbon monoxide
> or put weights on my feet
> and stumble into the tide.
> I guess I've no backbone
> to pass a noose 'round my throat
>
> or take handfuls of pills
> and leave a final goodbye note.
> So God please help me out
> make the decision heaven-sent,
> couldn't you just arrange
> some quick, painless accident?

He folds up his glasses, and smiles but doesn't say anything. There's a long, uncomfortable silence as he nods his head for what seems like ten minutes. Like he was a Junior Samples bobble-head doll. Finally I prod, "So... what do ya think? Be honest."

He takes a deep breath and shrugs, "Well, it's purty good. I like it. Hehehehe."

I beam and say, "Thanks."

He places his hand on my shoulder, "But... it is kinda derivative of Dorothy Parker, don't cha think? Especially her earlier pieces in *The New Yorker*."

Max is in hysterics as he rolls on the floor and pees. I feel my face redden and turn to Max, "You told him to say that, didn't you, you little shit?" His laughter is a high-pitched machine-gun cackle like Snoopy battling the Red Baron. HEH-HEH-HEH-HEH as a yellow puddle forms on the linoleum.

"So much for man's best friend being loyal," I say like a woeful and pathetic Charlie Brown.

Junior asks the waitress for his check then turns to me and says, "No, really, I liked it. Good luck, mister. Hehehehe."

The waitress shoots me daggers. "Sir, would you clean up after your dog, please?" She smirks and adds, "Your service dog?" Emphasizing 'service' like the *SNL* church lady emphasizing the word 'Satan.'

"Want to re-write reality?" Max asks. I think about it and say, "Yeah. Get me out of this scene and into another."

"I'm thinking Busby Berkeley meets Mel Brooks. Type it up."

I open my laptop to Final Draft and write the slug lines and descriptions:

INT. CAFE – DAY
The diner's tee shirts, jeans, and bib overalls morph into

mermaid costumes, as the scene transitions to:

EXT. POOL – DAY

A large, round swimming pool is filled with the diners cavorting in an ocean of blue. The waitress, morphed into King Neptune, wears a long, brown beard and crown and sits upon a huge throne while holding a trident. The shadowy movie crew materializes to set up a camera above the pool and add klieg lights and microphone stands around the set. The mermaids take their places in the pool.

Max mumbles, "Your script is still not giving me a hard-on."

I whine, "Come on, Max..."

He rolls his eyes and yells, "Okay, quiet on the set! Roll sound, roll camera, and slate it." One of the shadows operates the clapper, and Max says, "Action!" A tune by Paul Whitman and his Orchestra plays in the background.

An overhead shot shows the synchronized swimming of the mermaids forming a pinwheel that churns up the water and spins in foamy blue patterns. The billowy truckers-turned-mermaids blow water into the air in sync, like trained orcas.

"Beautiful," I whisper to Max.

"Breathtaking," he responds. He yells, "Cut!" and the shadowy movie crew disappears as soon as you can say 'Esther Williams,' and the scene reverts back to reality. I remember Max's pee on the floor, so I grab a handful of napkins and kneel down to clean up. I'm suddenly aware of being up close and personal with a pair of shiny black pumps, and my gaze moves up a great pair of legs, belonging to a girl now where the Mormon Tabernacle Choir singer sat. I follow her legs from her feet all the way up to heaven. Her legs appear to have no end. I imagine them wrapping around me. Twice. Max mumbles, "Nice gams," trying to sound like Robert Mitchum. On the floor next to the stool is an oversized canvas handbag and a pink suitcase plastered with the names of hair bands from the 1980's, like Bon Jovi, Motley Crue, and Van Halen.

I didn't notice her enter the cafe. She must have breezed in like a soft cloud on a warm July day.

I get to my feet and check her out. Stylish brown hair with blue streaks under a wide-brim yellow beach sun hat. A couple of tats and oversized sunglasses with a paisley blue summer dress. She also has a few piercings. On a windy day she probably whistles.

She's a bit overdressed for Ollie's Omelet's and Oil Change and I notice a few of the truckers staring. She's wearing tiny headphones and gyrating-dancing to music from a CD player tucked inside her purse. She could be 22, or even 32, with smooth, porcelain skin seldom kissed by the sun.

"Good morning" I offer, taking a seat next to her. She removes one headphone from an ear and tilts down her sunglasses. Her eyes are wide and vulnerable, like in a Keane painting.

Deep blue pools of experience, the wisdom of a thousand years, telling me this had better be good because there won't be a second chance.

"Good morning!" I repeat.

With a voice as quiet as a butterfly fart, she says, "Buy me breakfast and I'll pretend to like you."

I can live with pretend until the real thing comes along, so I grin, "It's a deal." The waitress approaches, and with a look of disapproval, pours the girl a coffee, obviously wishing it were hemlock, and then flits away like a bat seeking moonlight.

The girl smiles and says, "Cool!" She's a total blam-blam as I think of the Bowie tune with the lyrics "Oh, don't lean on me man, 'cause you can't afford the ticket" but at least I want to try. I notice her perfect teeth, although there is a slight gap between her left maxillary lateral incisor and left maxillary cuspid, but that's perfect too.

The waitress returns. "You ready to order, miss?" emphasizing the S's like a cobra.

"Can I get an order of veggies?"

The waitress can't hear the girl's soft voice over Garth Brooks on the jukebox. "Sorry, hon. Gotta speak up."

The girl repeats it louder and the waitress snaps, "We don't sell veggies by themselves."

"But your menu says you've got veggie omelets."

"Yes, ma'am. Best in the valley. And that includes toast and home fries."

"But I'm vegan and I don't want the omelet. Can't you just charge me for the omelet but only give me the veggies?"

I'm amused by the exchange and tell Max, "It's like Nicholson trying to order toast."

"*Five Easy Pieces*," Max says with a self-satisfied grin.

The waitress' eyes narrow. "What I can do for ya hon, is bring you the veggie omelet and a separate plate and you can remove the veggies yourself."

The girl's voice gets louder. "You can't remove the veggies for me? What is there, some kinda state law? Remove veggies, go to jail." Some of the diners have stopped their eating and conversations.

The waitress digs in, not about to concede. "Miss, our omelets are the best in the west."

"I'm sure they are. But I don't want an omelet. I only want veggies."

"Hon, I was havin' a good day today, so don't you be a fly in my ice cream."

"I don't want ice cream, I want veggies! Geez, don't get your sphincter all twisted into a knot."

"Leave my sphincter out of this. Missy, I've been here 23 years and I've never had anyone order just veggies and nothing but veggies."

"First time for everything..."

"Now don't get sassy..."

"...and that probably includes you getting laid."

"That's enough! Get outta of here! Out! Out!" the waitress screams. Complete silence until the cook, clutching a blender, bursts through the kitchen door and scans the now silent dining room. "What's goin' on?" he roars, holding the blender above his shoulder.

The girl smirks at the cook and says, "What are you gonna do with that? Puree somebody?"

I decide to intervene before the melee begins. I take a fifty from the brim of my fedora and hand it to the waitress, telling her, "Here. Keep it. Can we just get the veggie omelet to go? I'm very sorry but my friend here is on medication for life-threatening depression. She's extremely distraught over the loss of her parents in a terrible accident during the Macy's Thanksgiving Parade." The waitress and cook glance at each other and appear to cool down a bit. I'm encouraged and want to embellish the story.

Max senses it and says, "Chaz, quit while you're ahead." I ignore him.

I lean in close to the waitress. "Her mom and dad were on 5th Avenue in New York City, enjoying the parade, when suddenly a gust of wind picked up and they were crushed by Mr. Potato Head." The girl coughs like she's choking and turns away to laugh but quickly buries her head in her hands with loud sobs. The waitress' expression softens as her hand goes to her mouth and she appears to fight back a tear. "Oh, hon, I am so sorry" she whispers. The cook returns to the kitchen.

I put my arm around the girl's shoulders, and through teary eyes look at the waitress and mutter, "And to this day, she can't even look at a French fry without crying." The girl's shoulders are in spasms now with her head almost between her legs in a laughing-crying fit.

Max closes his eyes and murmurs "Oh God..."

We get the food then dash outside faster than a wife having an affair jumps out of bed when she hears her husband come home early from work. We dart through pick-ups and semis and a few SUV's and find a picnic table under a small stand of juniper and pinyon pine trees. Max wanders off to mark his territory. The girl is still smiling as she opens the to-go container and with a plastic fork separates the veggies from the omelet.

"That was good. I almost peed my pants," she says. "What's your name?"

"Chaz. Chaz Chase. You?"

She takes a cigarette from her purse and places it between her lips. She then murmurs something that sounds like Kitty.

"Nice to meet you Kitty."

"No. Clitty."

I stare at her for what must have seemed like a month. Did she say what I thought she said? I ask, "Clitty?"

She shrugs. "My parents were hippies with a fucked up sense of humor. When I was born, they combined their first names, Clint and Doris, and came up with Clitoris. Some joke, huh? My friends call me Clitty. Kids in school used to give me shit, but I'm used to it now." She takes an imaginary drag from the unlit cigarette.

"The name or the shit?"

She smiles and says, "Both."

"Oh well," I say, "Things could always be worse."

Clitty continues, "Yeah. As Mother Teresa used to say, 'It's better than a kick to the nuts.'"

I'm not sure Mother Teresa ever said that, but if Clitty says she did then I accept it. I reach into the brim of my fedora for a book of matches and offer them.

"You'll probably inhale more smoke from the cigarette if you light it first."

"I don't smoke. Used to. I figure if I just go through the motions and make believe, I can trick my brain. I know. It's lunacle madness."

"Want a real smoke?" I ask. Clitty smiles and I take two Blue Frost joints from inside my fedora lining, fire them both up between my lips, then hand one to her, like Paul Henreid sharing a smoke with Bette Davis.

Clitty takes a long drag and whispers "Thanks. I meant to say that I don't inhale nicotine anymore. This is a healthy smoke."

"Where are you going?"

She whispers "Hollywood" like Marilyn Monroe having an orgasm, as she blows smoke rings that form the letters H-O-L-L-Y-W-O-O-D in billowy clouds above her head for several moments and then disappears like an innocent starlet's dream.

"An actress. Cool. Maybe I've seen you in movies."

"Doubt it. Mostly summer stock. *Chorus Line... Guys and Dolls*. Some off-off-Broadway crap. Last year in the second national touring company of *Beauty and the Beast*. I played Babette. I also did a horror movie. An indie. I was a scream queen. I played Bimbo Number Three. No shit, that's actually how it read in the script. I still remember my line."

"What was it?"

"'You may take my head, but you'll never take my soul.' And then the psycho cuts off my head with a machete and my head lies on the ground screaming. AAAGGGHHHHH!!!" Her piercing scream is heard for miles around, setting off car alarms.

Max says, "Like Fay Wray being grabbed by Kong." A couple of truckers walking to their rigs stop and stare.

I yell to them, "Everything's okay here. Nothing to worry about. She's just giving birth." Clitty laughs.

"Good scream," I say. Max agrees, "Like Jamie Lee Curtis in *Halloween*," and if he could applaud, he would.

"So where are you going?" she asks.

"Oh... just wandering around trying to find myself. But I'm proving to be very illusive."

She inhales a final hit of joy and gets up from the picnic table. She extends her right hand. "Okay, Taz..."

"It's Chaz."

"Oh, I was thinking Tasmania Devil."

"No, Chaz."

"Gotta go. Nice meeting you," she says, shaking my hand. "Hope you find yourself."

"Hope to see you in the movies." She grabs her suitcase and handbag and trots toward a driver about to step up into his rig.

I yell, "Don't you have a car?" but she doesn't hear me as she jiggles-wiggles toward the parking lot with a stride that looks like she's vying for a gold medal in cock teasing.

Max says, "Now she is a chunk of change that doesn't make any cents."

"What movie is that from?"

"None that I know of, but it sounds like something from a film noir."

I watch Clitty gesture to a driver, then he grabs her suitcase and crams it into a compartment in the cab as she runs around to the passenger side and leaps up onto the seat. The rig starts up, the engine revs, and it moves out of the parking lot, gaining momentum as it grabs the asphalt.

Max asks, "Did you see my film *Pickup on South Street*? That girl has the same smoldering sexuality and toughness as Candy, my femme fatale played by Jean Peters."

"Didn't see it, but it's on my bucket list."

"That figures. Well, Candy is thrown around an apartment, hit over the head with a beer bottle, and shot. But she survives. Why? Because she has an indomitable spirit that no man can crush." Max sighs, and with his best Bogart impersonation says, "They don't make dames like that anymore."

I stare at the receding semi as it becomes a shimmering silver bullet traveling in slo-mo past saguaros on the distant highway. Max asks, "Why didn't you offer her a ride? You should have run after her."

I shrug.

"Come on, Chaz. It's never too late to get your heart broken."

I sigh.

"We could have dropped her off in L-A and then continue on south of the border. We really should go to Mexico," he Dean Moriarty-ized.

"No. Whenever I think about Mexico, I imagine banditos stealing my shoes and then beheading me," I Alphonso Bedoya-ized.

I feel that a relationship at this time would freeze me like a step backward, and besides, it wouldn't be fair to her. I exhale a deep contented cloud of Blue Frost and soon the shiny dot vanishes on the heat-wavy horizon. And just like that, she was, as Chuck Berry sang, "Gone like a cool breeze."

Chapter 5

"It's not how far you've traveled,
it's what you've brought back."
— Tiziano Terzani

"There is a deeper world than this
That you don't understand."
— "Love is the Seventh Wave" — Sting

The sun rises again in the east only because old habits die hard. Max and I ride in silence on Highway 163 on the Navajo rez with the desert air caressing the convertible like a mother with a newborn. A deep inhale of a Blue Dream stick while passing the sandstone buttes makes me feel like I'm in a scene in a John Ford movie. I expect to look toward a distant hill and hear Ford yell "Action!" into a megaphone and see a thousand Navajo warriors ride toward a wagon train led by John Wayne. I'll bet John Wayne never smoked weed in his life. Or maybe he did. He sure had a funny way of walking. I sort of walk like the Duke when I'm stoned.

I'll be staying with William, a Navajo who knows Leroy and supplies him with magical bottles of insight. The card Leroy gave me should be my door opener.

My mind always plays mental leapfrog and for no particular reason I think of my Dad and the funny story he told me about his mother, highlighting how uptight she was about all things sexual. A lot of that sexual uptightness got passed down to my dad.

My dad played football during his freshman year in high school but after a few games he quit. "Lucky to still have my nuts," he told me. Lucky for me too, because if I wasn't here this would be a hell of a lot shorter journal. His father Maxie was away from home during the Fall peddling who-knows-what, and Dad was too embarrassed to ask his mom to buy him a jock to wear during athletic contests and she was too embarrassed to ask her son if he wore a cup when playing sports, so he played his entire freshman season with his jewels just swinging free. He said, "In my young, developing mind, I thought if I don't acknowledge my testicles and my mother doesn't acknowledge my testicles, then my testicles don't exist." It's like what Descartes talked about existence being property. His mom must have thought her two kids had Ken and Barbie doll genitalia.

It was very fortunate that during games and practices he never took a hit to his sack, but after leaving the team he decided to forgo any high school sports and get involved in acting. Of course with acting your ego can take a bruising, but at least you get to keep your nuts.

George's dad was never around and his mom was too uptight to ever give him the 'birds and bees' talk so he was pretty much clueless until he finally lost his virginity as a sophomore in college. My dad once told me that when he was about eleven, his mom took him to a nearby farm to observe the ewes coming into heat and being mounted by the rams. His mom would say,

"We're similar to sheep." Dad said for the longest time he thought a woman's vagina was surrounded by wool.

George always had a few extra pounds around the midriff, but as he got deeper into the bottle the weight increased. He had long hair on the sides and back and for years mastered the illusion of the comb over, but eventually genetics won out and he was left completely bald. He had an older sister, but insists his parents never wanted children and had sex only twice resulting in two mistakes. I vividly remember my Aunt Lucy and was drawn to her because she was the polar opposite of Dad. She was gregarious and flew about like a wild, exotic bird on acid. Lucy always wore bright, colorful clothing, called herself a bohemian, could recite passages of *Howl*, claimed she had sex backstage at Woodstock with the drummer for Ten Years After, and was always with a different boyfriend.

She worked as a nurse and frequently said, "Nothing shocks me. I've heard it all and seen it all." I had a feeling she also may have done it all.

Aunt Lucy eventually married, the ceremony performed on the beach with the couple's wedding song "Sympathy for the Devil," but the marriage lasted about five weeks and was annulled. She used to take me aside and tell me dirty jokes, just like her dad, my Grandpa Maxie. I'd laugh at her jokes, although at the age of six I seldom knew what she was talking about but I wanted to appear jaded. Just a few years ago she drowned in a boating accident in upstate New York. It rained the day of her 'Celebration of Life' but a huge tent was needed for the hundreds of friends who paid their last respects. I cried for weeks after she died. I totally related to Aunt Lucy, much more than my own father, who could be moody, melancholy, withdrawn, with bursts of an intimidating temper.

My love of music came from both parents, but it was my dad who encouraged me to play the cello. After lots of practice I got good at it and was a natural. The Roy Hobbs of the cello. Whenever I played Barber's "Adagio for Strings," Dad would sob. I eventually stopped playing it for him because it hurt me too much to see him cry. Yes, I held animosity for my father but it didn't bleed into cruelty.

The *Charlie's Angels* ring tone jars me out of the daydream. It's a text reading: NOT NOW. The same message I got before and somehow still untraceable. How could this be happening? Maybe Max is right. Perhaps I'm smoking too much weed.

Max interrupts with, "Barrel rolls and a loop-dee-loop, you'd better pull over cuz I gotta poop. Burma Shave."

I ease Pam Grier off the shoulder of the highway and onto a dirt road, turn off the engine and open the door. Max jumps out and makes a beeline for a patch of sagebrush. Cars with tourists pass by on Highway 163, occasionally pulling over to the shoulder to take photos or videos of the majestic burnt red monoliths rising up from the desert floor. A tourist bus pulls over next to the Caddy and about ten thousand Japanese tourists depart, all clicking their cameras at once. The noise sounds like billions of cicadas awakening from a 17-year nap as it echoes around the mesas. I get out to stretch and for some reason my thoughts turn to my mom.

Sara divorced George just before I graduated from high school. They had already separated when I started my senior year. He lived in the house where I grew up, and she bought a townhouse about thirty miles away. She was tired of his anger and depression. From the time I was in the eighth grade, they were working very hard on their divorce, with more determination than they ever worked on their marriage. They tried individual therapy, couples counseling, the Gottman Method, Couples Boot Camp, a month at a nudist colony, Primal Scream Therapy, Narrative Therapy, and a weekend of shooting each other with paint balls but nothing could stop the inevitable derailing of the train, so it came as no surprise to anyone when they finally filled out the papers at city hall, gave each other a brief and uncomfortable hug, then walked away in opposite directions. In reality they had been walking away in opposite directions for years, but this final act was just the official stamp of putting distance between themselves. It was a relationship that from day one had an expiration date stamped all over it. But there was one thing Mom and Dad never tried which seemed to bring them closer: Divorce. Once they lived apart they became friendlier and more civil and refrained from pushing those well-worn buttons.

Although Dad was a dentist, he dreamed of writing the Great

American Novel, and while attending college and med school he worked part time jobs as a radio copywriter and newspaper sportswriter and wrote his own creative stuff in his spare time. Mom was the breadwinner for many years until my father got his own practice. Sara was an award winning real estate broker who owned her own company and supported my Dad through those lean years when he didn't have a job and struggled to get through med school. In the last several years I would ask from time to time how the novel was taking shape. He'd joke, "Still waiting to be seduced by the Muse of Writing." He admired all of the great writers who were also great drinkers, like Ernest Hemingway, F. Scott Fitzgerald, Robert Benchley, and Dylan Thomas. My father thought it was Thomas who said, "Write drunk. Edit sober." Dad followed part of Dylan's advice.

Dad talked about "Alcohol opening up the spigot of creativity." George mastered the drinking part, but the writing part seemed to elude him. At least that's what Mom and I thought. He never showed us anything he wrote so we couldn't judge it. The drinking eventually cost him his marriage and his dentist practice. He was not a 'happy' drunk, and although he never struck my mother, she did suffer emotional bruising as he could get nasty and sarcastic. He and I sparred a few times too. My parents life resembled an Albee play. I guess everything looks distorted when you view the world through the bottom of a bottle.

Unlike many other kids my age, I placed my father under a pedestal.

Sara was a career woman who loved the real estate business and was dedicated to her clients. While pregnant with me, she showed a house to a young couple, then went back to her office to write up an offer before her water broke and was rushed to the hospital. Years later after their divorce, she met a man from Spain who was buying investment property in California. They dated, she sold her real estate firm, and they were married less than a year later and were very happy. I heard the contentment in her voice whenever we spoke on the phone. But while driving to their villa in Madrid, his sports car veered to miss a dog in the road and they were both killed. Dad and I were devastated, and I believe it led to a more rapid deterioration of his health.

His life had stalled out over an ocean of frustration but right after my Mom's death, it took a nosedive. I believe he still loved her even years after the divorce. At least I like to think so. It's the romantic in me.

I believe every family is dysfunctional, some more than others. I don't think I was planned and I wasn't born until my folks were 40 years old. I'm sure they thought their lives were going along pretty well until I showed up and ruined their plans. I often wonder how my parent's lives would have turned out if they didn't have me and how much happier they would have been if they never had to deal with my outbursts, pyromania, thievery, and need to disappear. I can only imagine how much better things would have been if I had never existed. I feel that the soundtrack to my bitter, short life has always played out in minor keys.

Max barks, "Snap out of it, George Bailey."

I lean against the car, taking in the overwhelming stillness of the landscape as if I were alone on a distant world and perhaps I am. But somehow I don't feel alone. I hear the faint whisper of a distant voice, not much louder than my own thoughts, a single musical note echoing off ancient mesas and times. A female voice.

"Max, you hear that?"

He rolls his eyes and with great pride says, "Of course. We hear decibel frequencies humans can't. Our hearing is four times greater than yours."

"Well, congratulations. You are so advanced. Then why do dogs eat their own shit?" Max strolls over to Pam Grier, all the while glaring at me. He curls his upper lip then unleashes a pee of defiance on my front tire, changing it from a whitewall to a yellow wall.

I'm curious about the sound, whether it's real or imagined. If there is no sound, maybe it's the desert heat fueling my imagination with an auditory oasis. Or maybe residual effects of Leroy's tea. Either way I'm drawn to the Siren's beckoning call, but unlike Odysseus, I decide to ignore the danger and pursue the sound.

As I follow Max to a short hill of sagebrush and cacti, the sound intensifies and is more like a hum, a middle C on the musical scale. Not the five tones played in the movie shot at Devil's Tower, but just as intriguing. Some fifty feet away, connected to an inclining ridge, is a lone mesa, probably less than twenty feet tall and some thirty feet in circumference. Max and I approach and begin our ascent of the ridge as the sound seems to grow in volume and appears to be emanating from atop the mesa. We ease closer, and then stop.

Seated in a lotus position, arms reaching high to the sky, is a nude woman chanting "Ommmmmmmm" and holding it until a new breath creates a new "Ommmmmmmmm." I recognize her blue-streaked hair, oversize sunglasses, the blue paisley dress folded neatly on the ground, and the suitcase and bag by her side.

Clitty catches our gaze and nods to acknowledge our presence, but continues her "Ommmmmmmm" and in her trance-like state makes no attempt to hide her nakedness. I'm sure the Navajo Great Spirit approves. I certainly do. I want to make love to her right there in the desert like that movie scene with Mark and Daria directed by Antononi. I'm spellbound as Clitty continues her meditation for another ten minutes, then rises to put on her dress. Dum Phuk encourages me, "That was great! Give her a hand!" and I'm about to applaud, but Max interrupts with his paw on my leg. He hisses, "This isn't a titty bar, dumbass."

All I can blurt out is, "I'm so glad to see you," and I really am, as I hold the image of her naked breasts, pubic hair, and ass in my mind forever.

"Just staying centered. Getting my metaphysical connection. Being in oneness with the universe. Practicing Mindfulness. And all the rest of that New Age whacka-whacka."

"Where's your trucker friend?"

"He wanted to give me more than just a ride," Clitty says, adjusting her sun hat. "A couple of miles into the trip he started playing with himself."

"So he just dropped you here in the middle of the desert?" I ask, as she slips on her black pumps.

"He didn't have a choice." She pulls a handgun from her bag. "I told him 'You lay a finger on me, and your tiny dick is gonna get even tinier.'"

Max smiles, "Ah, now there's my femme fatale. Like Phyllis in *Double Indemnity*."

Clitty strokes the barrel of the gun and purrs, "My little friend, a Springfield XD." She waves it around a little too close to my head and briefly takes me out of my comfort zone. Like a Bond martini, I'm shaken but not stirred.

"I guess if you're traveling alone," I say, "It's good to have a little protection."

"My Daddy taught me how to shoot when I was six. He used to tell me that Al Capone once said, 'A smile can get you far, but a smile and a gun can get you further.' I never forgot that."

"You any good with that?"

"Won a few marksmanship contests. Some folks in town called me the New Age Annie Oakley. Wanna see?"

"Go for it."

Clitty looks around for a suitable target. "See that cattle crossing sign over there?" She points to a yellow sign with the silhouette of a cow. It must be a hundred feet away.

"That's quite a distance."

"Pretty much anybody could hit that sign from here, but I'm gonna shoot the cow right in the ass. Ready?"

She draws a bead and squeezes the trigger and then the POP and the sign flips back and recoils with a PINGGGGG. I walk to the sign and sure enough, a bullet hole right underneath the cow's tail. I applaud.

"Ever have to use it?" I ask.

"Just showing it usually gets my point of view across."

"My daddy taught me how to identify teeth when I was six. He was a dentist."

As soon as I said it I wish I hadn't. It sounded so Eugene Felsnic. Like I was the King of the Nerds. Out of the corner of my eye I see Max laugh, "My boy, you really know how to impress the dames."

"Cool," Clitty sayd, but I can tell she is underwhelmed.

"I never had a gun," I murmur, digging myself deeper into a dweeb hole.

"Guess they're not for everyone. Some folks would like to take away my gun. They say I shouldn't own one. Well, as Mother Teresa once said, 'If they don't like it, fuck 'em and feed 'em beans.'"

I smile, and wonder how I never knew Mother Teresa used such colorful language. Clitty grabs her suitcase and makes her way down the mesa. I offer to carry the bag but she refuses. "Need a ride?" I ask.

"Sure, Taz. You going to Hollywood?"

"It's Chaz. My name is Chaz. I'm kinda, sorta goin' in that direction. As long as you're not in a big hurry."

"I don't have time to waste while you drive around the country trying to find yourself."

"It's no problem. I don't have much time either. Gonna stay tonight on the rez, but should be back on the road tomorrow."

"That's cool," she says. "As long as I can put miles between me and my shithole hometown of Loserville, Arizona."

"Small town?"

"Everybody wastes their whole lives there. Go to school, get married, pop out young'uns, and die. It's what's expected."

"Must have been peer pressure for you to stay there."

"Hey, I never bow to peer pressure. I have no peers." She shrugs with a broad smile.

And I totally believe her.

Max and I follow Clitty as we descend the mesa and then walk the red sand carpet to Pam Grier. Max says to me, "Careful. Better get rid of her in the second act."

"What are you talking about?"

"Chekhov said if you introduce a rifle in the first act, you'd better use it by the third."

"Listen my little furry friend, this is not a play."

"It's all a play," he snarls. "You just shouldn't die before you're supposed to."

"Yeah, I'm sure that would ruin the natural order of things. The Big Cosmic Plan."

We arrive at Pam Grier where I pop the trunk and try to find room for Clitty's suitcase. I re-arrange a few totes, beer bottles, dog bowls, a cello case, and books and think it would be easier to figure out a Rubik's Cube while drowning in quicksand, but after some rearranging I manage to squeeze in her suitcase. Clitty sees the cello case and says, "That's a really big guitar." I tell her it's a cello.

I grab the beer cooler, put it on the floor of the passenger seat, take a bottle and hand it to Clitty. Max jumps in the passenger seat, I slide in behind the steering wheel, and Clitty leaps into the middle of the back seat, her arms spread wide across the seatbacks, her legs propped up on the top of the front seat. She takes off her hat, stares up at the sky, and with a large grin yells, "Come on, cowboy. Let's ride!" and chugs the brew. I fire up Pam

Grier, rev the engine, and kick out stones and gravel before the car grabs the highway and lunges forward with a saucy squeal. In a blink we're moving at 60 – 70 – 80 miles per hour, "Like a pneumatic railcar under New York City," I Alfred Beach-ized to Max. In moments we were a streak of black lightning slicing through the desert air in 9/8 time like a Brubeck rondo.

Clitty isn't crazy about hearing Christmas tunes in August, so she reaches over the seat to eject my holiday tunes CD from the receiver and slides in her own CD and soon "You Shook Me All Night Long" blares from the right speaker and Clitty and I bounce our heads to the beat like Myers and Carvey.

I realize more and more I'm staring at Clitty in the rear view mirror. A few more beers are downed. After about twenty minutes of head bobbing tunes she shouts, "So what do you do?"

I lower the volume of the music. "You mean like work?"

"Yeah," she says, putting on blood-red lip gloss.

"Used to be a radio DJ, but I got fired from my last job."

"What happened?"

"You really wanna know?"

"I really wanna know."

"It was at night. Nobody around and I had a groupie visiting the studio. Well, one thing lead to another and we had sex in the studio."

"What's the big deal?" she interrupts. "Nobody was around."

"Yeah, but I didn't realize that the song had stopped playing and there was dead air, and either me or the girl accidentally switched on the microphone so all of our moans and groans were being broadcast to fifty thousand people."

Clitty laughs. "Cool!"

"It would have been, except the boss was listening and drove to the station and promptly threw me out."

"Fuckalicious!"

"Funny thing though, my ratings that night were the highest of any time in the station's history." I take a joint from inside my fedora and fire it up.

Clitty laughs, "Yeah, I had the same kinda shit happen to me."

"Yeah?"

"I was working at McDonald's and hooking up with this guy who used to dress as McDonald's characters, you know, to entertain at kid's parties, that kinda crap. Well, one night we decide to have sex in the back room and I'm on my knees in front of him while he's wearing a costume when suddenly the back door flies open and there's about a hundred kids out back waiting for a party and they see me going down on Mayor McCheese."

"Those kids will undergo years of therapy."

She shrugs, "Another reason to avoid Mickey D's."

"I also once got canned because my boss thought I was having sex with an inanimate object," I said.

"You say that like it's a bad thing. Some of the best sex I've ever had has been with inanimate objects. What happened?"

"He invited me to this fancy luncheon to wine and dine some clients. A couple of brothers who were born-again Christians with a lot of money to spend on radio advertising. Anyway, I had to use the men's room, so I was in there washing my hands and I spilled water on the front of my khaki pants. Nobody was around and I had to dry my pants so I thought I'd prop my legs up on the sink and hold on to the hand dryer and put the hot air against my wet crotch while moving my pelvis back and forth and..."

"Fuckalicious!"

"Yeah, one of the religious guys came in and made an expression like he had just swallowed his own bile and said, 'Eewwww...' then turned around and left. When I returned to the dining room my boss called me a pervert and fired me."

"He was a dipshit."

"Yeah, but before I left I grabbed the bottle of wine and took dinner rolls from the basket and stuffed them into my sports coat. A small gesture of revenge."

"That's cool, Taz!"

"Chaz."

"So what else do you do?"

"I also write screenplays. I specialize in a certain genre."

"What kind?"

"The kind no one wants to read." She nods her head, smiles, and says, "Cool."

I'm starting to think I could tell her, "I swallowed a rat and it's eating away at my stomach" and she'd respond with, "Cool." I asked if she has a job.

"Up until two days ago I did," she says. "Then I up and quit."

"What did you do?"

"Sold used cars at my uncle's lot. Did that for three weeks. Uncle Larry used to say, 'If they got a pulse, they can be financed.' I was pretty good at talking poor folks into taking out a high interest loan on a bucket of shit. Most of those cars had been underwater from a recent hurricane and they had the life expectancy of a fruit fly. But that's what I did. Until I finally told him I was done. Didn't want to fuck with people anymore. It's bad karma. I know I'm going to Hell."

"That's where I'm going. All my friends will be there."

"Well, if you get to Hell first, would you leave a light on for me?"

I laugh. "Well, hopefully you'll pick up an acting gig when you get to L-A."

Clitty closes her eyes with a hopeful smile, like an ingénue auditioning for Busby Berkeley.

The conversation is free and easy, more like old friends then two people who had just met earlier in the day. We had both been married once before and we talked about our exes.

Clitty says, "I was 19 and had been seeing this guy for about a month. He was okay. Just kinda stupid. On the 'dumb-ometer' scale of one to ten, he pinned the needle at eleven. I used to tell him shit like, 'You must have filled your tank when you stopped at the stupid station' and he would just laugh like he had no idea what I was talking about."

"What was his appeal?"

"Sex was great. He could rock my world for hours. He was young, dumb, and full of cum. He wanted to get married, but I wasn't sure, until my parents forbid me to marry him, and that sealed the deal. We ran off to Vegas that night."

"How long were you married?"

"Well, counting all day Friday... part of Saturday... oh... about 39 hours. For the first 38 hours all we did was have sex, and then the last hour we talked and the more we talked we realized the less we had in common and in fact really didn't like each other, so we left the motel room and got an annulment."

"And it was over just like that?"

"Yup, just like that. We shook hands, wished each other a long and happy life, then he turned and walked away and I turned and walked down the Strip and within ten minutes got propositioned by a pair of Elvis impersonators who wanted a *ménage à trois*."

"So... did you?"

"Of course, but they weren't very good. They tried to get me horny by singing "In the Ghetto" but they each lasted about five minutes. Then Elvis left the building!"

"The story of my ex can't top that."

Clitty takes a deep drag, "I'm done with sex. I've had it with men. All of my relationships have the impermanence of clouds. If I don't make it in Hollywood, I may join a cloistered bunch of nuns." She giggles and says, "Now wouldn't that be fuckalicious!" She takes another drag and says, "It's not a 'bunch' of nuns. What's it called?"

"What is what called?"

"A bunch of nuns when they huddle together."

"A huddle of nuns?"

"No. There's a murder of crows, a flock of sheep..."

"Is a group of toads called a 'wartage of toads'?"

"Who the fuck knows. I'm talking nuns. Is it a gaggle of nuns?"

"Sisterhood of nuns? A Eucharist of nuns?"

"Runs of nuns?" she says, giving up. "Okay, your turn. Tell me all about Mrs. Taz."

"Chaz. Well, Amber and I were married for seven months. Less time than the expiration date on a bag of Cheetos. She was a nurse at a local hospital."

There's a long pause as I think about our relationship.

"That's it?" Clitty asks. "That's all you remember?"

"She had chicory blue eyes. Vibrant blue. Even more so when she cried and the blue burst forth like the twilight in a Maxfield Parrish painting. I never wanted her to be sad, but I gotta admit I was turned on when she cried."

"Very Freudian. Anything else?"

"She loved shoes. We had a separate closet for her hundreds of shoes. She could never drive by a Payless. I thought I was married to a centipede."

"What else?"

"She was a talker. She had frequent monologues but we had infrequent dialogs. I read somewhere that the average college educated person knows 28,379 words. My ex knew that many and probably a few thousand more and she was determined to use each and every one of those words in every conversation."

"What happened to the relationship?"

"Yeah. Good question. What did happen to the relationship..."

"Don't you know?"

"I'm still in the processing stage."

Clitty asks, "How long have you been divorced?"

"Little over a year."

"And you're still processing? You must have some indication as to what went wrong."

There was a long pause to consider the answer and finally I murmured, "She put the toilet paper so the sheets came off under the roll rather than over the roll."

"Now there's a good reason to get divorced."

"She wanted to have kids and I didn't. At least not right away. It just came unraveled. Lots of disagreements. The relationship was a gun with no safety lock and a trigger too easily pulled."

"How melodramatic!"

Max says, "Sounds like a line from *Double Indemnity*."

I heave a deep sigh. "I think we fell out of love. Well... at least I fell out of love."

"How come?"

I shrug. "Like I said, I'm still processing. It's kinda like when Max and I are out for a walk and he comes across a pile of crap. Well, he sniffs it to process it — what kind of dog pooped this? How big was the dog? What did it eat? How long ago was it here?"

"Interesting that you compare your relationship to a pile of dog shit."

"I should have seen the red flags when I noticed that none of my friends were invited to the wedding. Looking back, I wish I hadn't been invited."

Clitty laughed. What I said was not really true, but I said it to get a laugh and I always thought you should never let truth stand in the way of humor.

I mumble, "Whatever happened, I take full responsibility. It's all my fault. Everything. Everything that's ever happened since the beginning of time is my fault."

Clitty rolls her eyes and says, "Mellow out. You should practice meditation."

"It's more effective to practice medication. With all of my meds I mellow out very well, thank you."

No one says anything for about a minute, then I ask, "Hungry? I got stuff in the cooler."

She says okay and I ease Pam Grier off the highway and into a clearing under a shadow cast by a nearby mesa. Clitty gets out and walks behind a boulder to pee. I grab a joint from the glove compartment and fire it up and look toward a gathering storm in the valley. Then I pop open the trunk and grab a can of dog food and a cup of dry dog food and mix them in Max's bowl. I place it on the ground along with his water bowl. I open the cooler and the ice has almost melted, but I find a plastic container of egg salad, smell it, and judge that it hasn't quite reached the level of botulism. I learned long ago to never eat antique food. I smear a forkful of egg salad onto a couple of slices of multi-grain bread and put the sandwiches on two plates and then open up a bag of potato chips. The beer is still cold.

Clitty returns and says, "Can I ask you a question?"

"You just did."

"Okay, wiseass, another question: How come you don't wear pants?"

"Too restricting. I don't like to be confined."

"Is that the way it was with your marriage?"

"Maybe..."

"Well, you got nice legs so you can pull it off."

I smile.

"You know I never met a cellist before. Would you play for me?"

"In high school I played 'Kashmir' and all the stoners thought that was cool."

I hand her a plate with a sandwich and chips and a can of beer. I walk back to Pam Grier, open the trunk and remove the cello from the case. A nearby rock makes a convenient seat.

Several drops of rain ping against Pam Grier's hood and trunk. I tune the cello for about a minute then look at Clitty and ask, "Okay, you wanna hear another tune?" She laughs and says, "Yeah, that was really good." I'm about to place the joint under the strings at the top of the fingerboard, like Keith Richards does before playing "Jumpin' Jack Flash" but think better of it. I don't need char marks on my instrument. Keith can afford another guitar. I can't afford another cello. Besides, it was a Christmas present from my folks so it has sentimental value. I hand the joint to Clitty.

I close my eyes and take a deep breath. I'm transported back six years, a junior in high school, on stage about to play Bach's "Six Suites for Cello" to a packed auditorium. I glance at the audience and see my parents beaming with pride and love, even though an hour before they had another knock-down battle, like Keaton and Pacino in the second *Godfather*, but they came together for me, for my moment in the sun. I open my eyes, smile at Clitty, and then play "The Swan" by Saint-Saens.

The rain is soft and steady as it pelts the metal of the car in a rhythm that plays off the nearby mesas, which have now become violins and oboes and flutes joining the soul of my cello as the staff and notes are written on the clouds while the primeval music cascades around the valley with the occasional distant thunder like a timpani building in a life force that gladdens the heart of Yeii, the Great Spirit of the Navajo. During the performance I left my body and was transported outside the galaxy to became stardust in the cosmos, but when I open my eyes at the conclusion of the piece Clitty is applauding and my fedora is soaked.

I rag off my cello and place it back into the case as the rain eases up. Clitty is dripping wet and I have difficulty keeping my eyes off her because dripping wet is a good look on her. Max had the good sense to squeeze under Pam Grier to stay dry. He says, "Do you see the way she looks at you? Like Ingrid Bergman gazing at Leslie Howard in *Intermezzo*."

"I'll put it on my bucket list" I tell Max and he rolls his eyes.

"That was cello-licious!" she says as I pack the cello back into the trunk. I ask, "Do you play an instrument?"

"No. Just sing."

"What do you sing?"

"Mostly show tunes. In the eighth grade I was Julie Jordan in *Carousel*."

"Cool."

"In college I played Maureen in *Rent*, Always loved performing. I even took dance lessons."

I nod and feel that I want to know all about her and tell her all about me but what would be the point. Had I met her a year ago or even six months ago things would be different. Max senses my frustration and sadness and says, "Like Rick said to Ilsa, 'Where I'm going you can't come.'" I close my eyes and think of the possibilities of another day, if there is another day.

Dum Phuk interrupts, "See if she wants to rear-steer." Maybe I should have given this longer deliberation than a nanosecond knowing that nothing good can ever come from a Dum Phuk suggestion, but I blurt out, "Do you want to rear-steer?"

Clitty asks, "What?"

"Rear-steer. Using only your ass to drive."

"Why?" she says, looking at me like I had suggested she swallow a scorpion.

"Ah... just something to do."

"It's a guy thing, right?"

"A guy thing?"

"Like pissing in the snow to write your name."

"No. Rear-steer can be done by either sex. Everybody's got an ass."

She's very amused and somewhat curious. "No wonder the life expectancy of men is less than women. Okay, go ahead. Show me."

I tell Max to jump in the back seat and ask Clitty to sit in the passenger seat. I tell her, "I need you to control the floor pedals with your left leg. I steer with my ass while looking into a mirror."

"It's amazing you've done this and lived to tell."

"I've called the Guinness Book folks about entering this as a category but they never return my calls. The fastest rear-steer I've ever done is 47 miles per hour."

Clitty is up for the challenge. "47? I can do better. My ass is built for speed."

I strip off my underwear, toss it in the back seat, then grab a hand mirror from the glove compartment. I then turn and kneel with my back to the steering wheel and ease my naked butt against the wheel. Clitty snaps a photo and says, "You're next of kin will want to see what caused your demise."

"You gotta sit next to me to control the brake and gas and put it in drive. And you gotta keep an eye on the speedometer."

"Does this get you many dates? Maybe it's a turn on for some women."

"I'm gonna start a world-wide fad. Maybe we should shoot a video of this," I reply. "Turn the ignition."

Clitty turns on the engine and with her left foot revs Pam Grier. Max says, "When you got nothing you got nothing to lose" and I get the Dylan reference.

"Okay," I tell Clitty, "Put it in drive."

With her left leg Clitty holds down the brake pedal and eases the column shifter into 'D'. Pam Grier inches forward. I glance into the mirror and move my left butt cheek to the left and the wheels turn left and onto the highway. Clitty has a big grin as she controls the brake and gas pedals. She gives Pam Grier a little more gas and we pick up speed on the highway as I stare at the road in the mirror and make slight adjustments with my butt.

"I'm impressed!" Clitty shouts.

"Give it a little more gas."

Pam Grier is now up to 25 miles per hour. Soon accelerating to 30, 35, 40 as Clitty's eyes dart from the road to the speedometer and back again. On a straightaway 50 would be attainable, but this road serpentines like a desert sidewinder to the left and then to the right and then to the left again. I tell Clitty, "Okay, ease off the gas. What did I get up to?"

"43. I can beat that."

As Pam Grier stops on the shoulder of the highway, I joke, "My ass hasn't had a workout like that since I did time in a Turkish prison."

I get out of Pam Grier and slip on my underwear. Clitty kneels in place behind the wheel then removes her panties and hikes up her dress and gently leans her ass against the steering wheel. I hand her the mirror and sit next to her with my left leg touching both the gas and brake pedals. I take in more than just a glance of her naked rear before she says, "I'm ready" and I fight an urge to say "Yeah, me too."

I gently ease my foot onto the gas pedal as Clitty shifts her buttocks to the left and Pam Grier creeps forward like a cat stalking a mouse.

"Give it some gas," Clitty boldly says, and I do. The car pushes past 25 miles per hour. Then 29, 30, 31. "Damn, this is harder than I thought," she says.

I continue pushing down on the pedal as a sharp turn looms ahead. 35, 36, 37. The curve is coming closer and faster now as we exceed 41, 42, 43 with Clitty moving her right butt cheek to the right, and then a slight movement to the left. "Okay!" she yells so I push down the accelerator and we're now flying at 48, 49, 50 and she screams "No! No, let off! The brake!" and pulls her ass away from the steering wheel. I grab the wheel and hit the brake as Pam Grier leaves the highway and spins off the shoulder. Clitty screams, gets somersaulted into the back seat, and the car comes to a sudden rest onto a clump of sagebrush against a boulder.

Clitty is mildly shaken and hisses "Shit!"

I ask, "You okay?" and she nods. Her panties have fallen onto the floor and I hand them to her. Then I get out of the car to assess the damage. "Could have been worse," I say, looking at the dent. "Takes a lot more than a boulder to kill Pam Grier." Freud said there were no accidents but Sigmund never played rear-steer.

Clitty puts on her panties. "I'm sorry. When I said 'Okay' I meant, 'Okay, that's enough.'"

"No problem. By the way, you had it up to 51 miles an hour. The new record." She forces a smile as I high-five her.

"As soon as I land a job I'll pay for the damage," she says.

"Don't worry about it. The blemish gives her character. Like Marilyn's mole."

"Manson?"

"No, Monroe."

"Taz, you're funny."

"Chaz. Let's toast the new record."

I get behind the wheel and Clitty jumps into the front seat and eases next to me. I turn on the ignition and gently back the car onto the shoulder and then it turn off. "The new record in rear-steer calls for a celebration," I tell her, reaching under the seat for a half-consumed bottle of Jack. I take a gulp and pass it to her. We sit in silence for several minutes, alone with our own thoughts, but our smiling eyes are dancing together.

Clitty makes me happy, and I so wish the feeling will last. But all my life I've been able to temper my joy with negativity. I don't know why but I can't remain happy for long. Either anger or depression always enters my mind to extinguish any fire of elation.

My thoughts are interrupted by Clitty rubbing the back of my neck and whispering in my ear, "Chaz, do you want to make love?"

Chapter 6

"It is better to travel well than to arrive."
— Buddha

"Welcome to your life, there's no turning back."
— "Everybody Wants to Rule the World"—Tears for Fears

I thought I was still dreaming, and Clitty must have thought I was too because she repeated the question, this time close so our lips almost met. "Chaz, do you want to make love?"

At least she finally knew my name. Part of me, the part below the belt, screamed YES YES YES and wanted to rip off her clothes and take her right then and there in the front seat. I wanted to make love to her in positions you wouldn't even find in the *Karma Sutra*. I wanted our sweaty bodies to merge as one and explode in passion as we re-enacted the Big Bang. I wanted to... I wanted to... I wanted to... I felt the situation was an enigma stuffed inside a paradox, but with airholes so it could breathe.

I wanted to tell her, "I don't have time to make new memories." She sensed my rejection and murmured once again with more urgency, "So... do you? Do you want to make love?" But the sadness of her voice was now like the lonely whisper of a distant train at night. I had become the oncoming darkness of the day causing the petals of her sweet and precious flower to close. She wore the rejection like Rose in *The Mirror Has Two Faces*.

I looked for help from Max in the backseat and once again heard Rick's words to Isla: "Where I'm going you can't come." Max knew what I wanted and we made eye contact to seal the deal. In the blink of an eye my canine avatar sent Clitty to another land in another time in another universe in another dimension, and as quickly as you could say 'Billy Pilgrim,' she disappeared like smoke from a dying fire.

My answer to Clitty would have to wait.

The card given to me by Leroy was my introduction to William, my gracious host. That night we sat outside under the stars and full moon on the rez in southern Utah, the silhouettes of distant mesas in Monument Valley appearing as headstones in a cemetery. We talked, drank beer, and smoked weed. His perfect teeth are whiter than the moonlight, and contrast greatly to his dark rust colored skin. His lazy Husky-mix female dog named Yanaha lies sleeping in a basin she dug in the ground under the cottonwood tree. William tells me Yanaha means 'brave.' William lives in a modest ranch house in the shadow of a butte. A '72 Chevy Malibu, its yellow paint bleached to a cream, its hood up, sits tireless with the axles resting on cement blocks. Looming in the distance are black silhouettes of the buttes standing guard in Monument Valley, each with its own Navajo name, including Elephant Butte, the five Sisters, and The Mittens.

Every so often a car unfamiliar to William makes its way up the dirt road next to his house and with the speed of an arrow he tucks the beer bottle inside his jacket until the car passes. It's illegal for a Navajo to drink on the rez and a violation will bring you before the tribal elders.

William owns a hogan, a red mud and stick house not far from his own home and that's where I stayed. All the soil on the rez is a burnt red. William says it's because of all the blood shed by the Navajo people. Sometime after midnight, I had a dream. I was in a silent movie and my lover was Greta Garbo. We made love under a million stars at an oasis in the Sahara Desert. Then in a flash she's on a crowded train looking out a window at me running alongside. The train builds speed and Greta is yelling for me to run faster to jump onboard, but I can't run any faster as my feet melt onto the tracks and the train vanishes into the night sky as I fall to my knees and cry. I think about Clitty and wonder if the significance of the dream is related to my decision to leave her.

That morning I want to tell Max my dream but think better of it. The last time I told him about one of my dreams, he reacted with sarcasm and derision and I felt humiliated. That was the dream where I'm alone in the woods at night under a full moon and suddenly thousands of crows appear in the sky, swoop down, and carry me to the top of a distant mountain. I think dreams have tremendous significance, but Max would advise me to knock off the Coors and marijuana before going to bed.

The morning rays stream into the dwelling, because the entrance to every hogan faces east to greet the sun. I awake with a headache, which I attributed to leaning too hard last night on the fun button, and not anything more sinister. I hear William singing and playing Seger's "Night Moves" on his guitar. I leave the hogan and amble my way to the picnic table under the cottonwood where William is seated.

"Sleep well?" he asks. "I've got breakfast burritos if you want one." He hands me a cup of coffee. He strums a few more chords of "Night Moves" then smiles.

"I thought I'd have two guests in the hogan last night. What happened to your woman?"

"Oh, we decided to part ways. At least for now." I'm wondering, 'How did you know I was with somebody?' and just like that, William says, "Chaz, the rez is thousands of acres but Navajo people know everything that goes on. Who comes, who goes. We see it in the sun's rays, we hear it on the wind."

"Nothing gets by you."

"Nothing gets by us," he says laughing. We talk for a while about the Navajo Nation.

"How many Indians are there?" I Custer-ized. "About three hundred thousand," William replied.

He returns to his song, and I see how the deep red furrows of his brow match the surrounding dirt and terrain as his coal black eyes search the distant landscape. After the song we talk some more while finishing breakfast. He tells me with pride that his grandfather was a Code Talker during World War II. "They were all heroes, you know," he murmurs. We sit in silence for several minutes, each guarding our own thoughts.

I know my sadness is fueled by thoughts of Clitty. Maybe I should have made love to her. Maybe I need her more than I thought.

After feeding Max and filling the water jug, I thank William for his hospitality, we shake hands and hug. As I ease into the front seat of Pam Grier, I call out, "See you again," but his eyes tell me he knows that won't happen and I sense it too.

"Good luck with your journey, my friend," he says. I fire up the car and take the slow drive on the red dirt road away from his house. I glance in the rear view mirror to see William waving. Now the dirt road ends and we're on pavement so I blow the horn and look back at his house to wave, but he's gone.

Max and I cross over the Arizona line, heading south to the town of Page. Noticing that the gas gauge is leaning on E, I pull in to a Maverik gas station/convenience store and hand a young Indian man my credit card and ask him to fill it up. Since Page is on the rez, Navajo tribal music blares from outdoor speakers.

Max is checking out a young female puppy tied in the back of a nearby pickup truck. The pup makes high-pitched whining sounds to tease him. "Pretty hot, huh?" I ask him and Max sighs, "If I only had my nuts back..." Max sure likes the young ones. I would have named him Humbert Humbert but it didn't fit on a dog tag.

I enter the convenience store to buy a blueberry muffin for Max and use the rest room. While sitting on the toilet, I notice different Navajo music piped into the rest room from that being played at the gas pumps. Did the Navajos compose separate music to be played only for taking a dump? Sitting on a toilet in a public restroom can be chancy. If the seat is cold, it freezes your butt cheeks. But maybe that's better than sitting on a warm seat, indicating someone else's ass was just there. Once in northern Minnesota I pulled off the highway to a rest stop and entered the men's room which was not heated. I sat on the metal seat and was quickly gripped by fear: What if this is like the scene with *Flick*? Instead of a tongue stuck to a pole, I get my ass stuck to this seat. It didn't happen, but it did take a few minutes for my cheeks to thaw out.

In a few hours we're traveling the old wagon route along Highway 89 past the Vermilion Cliffs. The distant wall blushes in the late morning sun, appearing like a large open wound. We pass a hospital and I flash back to Amber, who worked in the E-R of our local hospital in Santa Cruz.

My mind can go in some fucked up directions. Maybe it's the weed, but I'm reminded of a conversation Amber and I once had about the unusual things guys put up their butts and then end up in the Emergency Room with some "Splainin' to do," I Desi Arnezized. Amber said one night a guy in a lot of pain was brought in via ambulance. The doctor on call removed a spoon from inside the guy's rectum. The doctor and nurse didn't ask how the spoon got there, but the guy volunteered a story. He must have felt that a lie was less incriminating and embarrassing than silence. The man said he was eating a hot fudge sundae when he accidentally fell and the spoon slipped. The doctor and nurse didn't question the guy. How the two medics could remain stone-cold sober and not laugh in his face always amazed me.

Another time a man came to the E-R with a carrot up his rectum. Amber was assisting the doctor that night and said the patient smelled of alcohol. The man was given a mild sedative and the doctor removed the carrot. I asked Amber, "How did he remove the carrot?"

She said, "Well, he held a hungry rabbit up to the guy's ass..." and we both fell on the floor laughing.

She told me that guys... mostly guys, but every so often there'll be a girl... will stick the weirdest stuff up orifices. A flashlight, a banana, part of a garden hose. Wouldn't it be easier just to carry this stuff in a backpack rather than your butt?

Even though the marriage didn't last long, I still think of Amber. I don't love her anymore but there's a bond that I feel will never disappear. Maybe it's not supposed to. I thought the pieces of the puzzle would fit together, but they didn't. There were too many pieces missing. After the divorce she told me I was a nice person and if I wanted, she'd give good references to any of my future dates.

As hard as I try, I'm like that preserved prehistoric fly in a history museum: There's just no escaping from Amber. The longest relationship I had was four years, which is the one I'm having now with Pam Grier, my car. That proves so many of my exes wrong when they said I was afraid of commitment.

Max senses I'm thinking about Amber and he says, "Dating is like going to the shelter to adopt a dog. You find one that connects with you, makes you smile, makes you believe you have a future together, so you take it home. But after a few weeks the dog shows bad traits. Pisses on your couch. Chews on your sneakers. Growls when you get near its food. Then you realize you picked the wrong dog."

"Thank you, Dr. Phil."

"Someday you'll figure it out. Or not."

"I'm sure her hours at the hospital didn't help. We only saw each other a few hours every day. I worked mornings and she worked overnights. That's why we moved to separate bedrooms, so we wouldn't disturb each other. Then after a while we just got used to not sleeping together."

Max says, "You guys could have found time to make love."

"I think we got used to not being intimate. Maybe I felt reject-ed. The male ego can be pretty fragile."

"Maybe she felt rejected, too."

I turn away and mumble, "Yeah... whatever..." as my head-ache pounds with even more intensity like a percussionist on up-pers playing a timpani.

"If you worked harder you could have made it work. She wanted to go to couple's counseling and you didn't, so..."

I interrupt, "I went twice! Okay? But it was a lost cause by then. The relationship was already flat lining on the screen." The conversation was getting as hot and uncomfortable as an attic in July.

"Did you fight? Have arguments?"

"I don't remember. Maybe I blocked 'em out."

"What did you say when she asked you to go to counseling?"

"I... I don't recall exactly..."

Max stares at me for several moments and says, "Selective amnesia."

"Damn, you drive me crazy."

"That's a short drive."

"Fuck you, dog face!"

"See?" Max says. "Getting all pissy about it tells me you're harboring guilt over not trying harder to save the marriage."

"God damn it. I had to get a fucking talking dog."

"Want to explore some of your other relationships?"

"No! But thanks for asking. Just shut up, you ball-less won-der."

"You're the one without a pair. If you had a set you would have left Denise when you found out she was banging the forklift guy at the factory. A real femme fatale. Like that dame Elsa in *The Lady From Shanghai*."

"Didn't see that one."

"That's the problem with you, Chaz. If you watched film noir, you'd have life figured out. No surprises. No double-crosses. Everything in glorious black and white."

"No. You're wrong. Life is only shades of gray." Damn, Max can be an irritating little snot and if he didn't talk and stimulate my mind I'd probably return him to the shelter.

I hiss "Fuck" and pull the car off onto a shoulder and jam on the brakes, dust and dirt erupting everywhere. I jump out and slam the door. I rip a Vortex from the lining inside my fedora, light it up, and walk quickly into an open field of boulders and sagebrush.

Max and I are tethered together like those characters played by Tony Curtis and Sidney Poitier but now I wish that chain was broken. I lean against a rock and take a deep drag of my remedy. I look up at cloud formations and see several buzzards circling off in the distance. After a few minutes I calm down and think about why I get angry every time I talk about my divorce. There must be some unresolved issues with Amber that I haven't dealt with. It's difficult to admit but maybe Max is right after all. He has a maturity and wisdom that transcends the ages and is evident in all phases of his life, from talking about the influence of Sergei Eisenstein to sniffing another dog's butt.

I shuffle back to the car and murmur "Sorry" and Max replies "No apologies needed."

I scratch Max at the base of his tail and say, "Really. I think you found an exposed nerve." I apologized again because I just want to go out with a clean slate and not leave behind any bad karma. Only a few months ago it would have been difficult to tell anyone "I'm sorry," so I must be making progress.

He says, "Don't give it a second thought," but lately I take pride in being wrong. It's something to wear like a badge.

Max locks eyes with me for a few moments then says, "You wanna meet up with her."

"Who?"

"Amber."

"Let me think about it."

Max says, "If you think about it, you won't do it. Over-analyzing an impulse can kill it."

I shrug, then get back into Pam Grier, turn the key, and ease the car from the dirt to the pavement. The thought of meeting Amber again fills me with apprehension, but I know there's unfinished business to resolve. When it comes to destinations, sometimes it's best to be on your way but never arrive.

I open a search engine on my laptop to find the nearest Wal-Mart, since Max is just about out of dog food and I need to stock up the cooler with food and beer. Besides, we can always crash for the night in the parking lot. There's one about 33 miles away in Kanab, Utah.

My ring tone sounds and the text NOT NOW flashes across the screen of my cell phone. I murmur, "What the hell is that all about? Who is sending these texts?" Max closes his eyes and rests his head between his paws.

A dark storm shoots across the plains and we appear to be in its cross-hairs. The ominous clouds rumble around the sky to "A Night on Bald Mountain." My mind flashes like lightning back to a dark time in my life. The months I spent in Ju-Vee Hall.

I gave my parents lots of grief being a young wiseass kid, like setting fires and petty theft, but things came to a head when my friend Mark stole a car and came by my house to pick me up. He told me he had bought the car, even though I figured he stole it. The cops stopped us for speeding and Mark told them I had nothing to do with the theft. My parents though were really fed up, especially when I later tried to joke about it by saying, "At least I didn't try to rebroadcast a baseball game without the expressed written consent of Major League Baseball." That's when it hit the fan and Mom and Dad pleaded with the judge to send me away to youth detention to get scared straight and the judge complied. Even though I had skipped a grade in grammar school, I lost some time because I was sentenced to two months at Warm Springs Youth Camp outside Sacramento, which sounds more like a getaway for 4-H club members to hone their skills making ceramic ashtrays. It was a hell of a lesson but my parent's goal was accomplished. I was scared straight.

I met Mark in my freshman year in California when his family moved from Dover, New Hampshire. It took me awhile to understand him, with his New England accent. He called himself "Mahk frum Dovah" and was a lot of fun. Always looking to get into trouble and get rich quick. He tried to lose his accent to fit in to his new surroundings until several of the cheerleaders thought the way he spoke was very sexy, then he laid it on thick like maple syrup. Mark and I had a great time together, but if I continued hanging with him we would have been doing time together. In prison, not Ju-Vee Hall. Mark also introduced me to amphetamines, and I never had a chance to thank him.

Mark was always doing crazy shit. I remember one time he told me that when he was a kid he wanted to visit his older brother who was doing prison time in Illinois. He checked on the price of an airline ticket and it was too expensive, so he talked a friend into putting him in a cardboard box and taking him to a local Fed Ex office to be shipped because Mark weighed 53 pounds and it would be a lot cheaper than an airline ticket.

The clerk at the office asked, "What's in the box?" and apparently the kid wasn't bright enough to have anticipated that question, so he blurted out, "Mark."

The clerk asked, "What?"

"My friend Mark. He wants to go to Illinois."

The clerk paused for an eternity while staring at the kid and finally deadpanned, "We don't ship human beings."

To his credit, the kid replied, "But he's got air holes. See?"

The FedEx guy shouted, "No!"

"And a bag of Oreos, too," the kid added, ripping open the

top.

When Mark told me that story, I almost peed my pants laughing.

Mark once bought an old car for three hundred bucks and thought it would go faster if he installed a spoiler on the back. It didn't. If that was true, I would have put a spoiler on my cello to help me get through allegro passages.

My parents had numerous meetings with my high school counselor and psychologist. The shrink was pure Jungian, always urging me to open my inner box of secrets, to expose my shadow archetype to the world. The counselor took lots of notes:

Mr. and Mrs. Chase, your son Chaz is a troubled genius BLAHBLAHBLAH with a drug-induced psychosis BLAHBLAH-BLAH a program of cognitive-behavioral therapy BLAHBLAH-BLAH and serotonin reuptake inhibitors BLAHBLAHBLAH Sorry doc, I prescribe my own drugs and they seem to be working very well, thank you.

I once took an I-Q test in the fifth grade and scored 168. I took the same test as a freshman and hit 174. I skipped the seventh grade, going from the sixth directly to the eighth. I knew I wasn't stupid but I was sure acting it by setting fires and stealing, although I couldn't seem to control it. I once overheard Dad ask my mom, "How can our brilliant son act so stupid?" I wanted to tell him that it wasn't an act.

In high school I felt alienated from everything, except my music. I had perfect scores in all of my classes, but the only thing I felt qualified to major in was Angst.

I pull off Highway 89, jump out and fold the convertible top back into place. Once I'm back in Pam Grier, a few drops of rain ping the front hood and dot the windshield. I tell Max, "It's gonna be a bad one" and right on cue we hear the rumble of the sub-woofer of distant thunder that shakes the hot desert air like the Cloudburst movement in *Grand Canyon Suite*.

Max says, "Did you know that a few movies and TV shows were shot in Kanab?"

"Really?"

"*The Outlaw Josey Wales. The Lone Ranger. Gunsmoke.* Clint Eastwood did a helluva job in *Josey Wales,*" Max says. "There was one line I remember. The lady says to Josey, 'Kansas was all golden and smelled like sunshine.' And Josey replies, 'I always heard there were three kinds of suns in Kansas, sunshine, sunflowers, and sons-of-bitches.'" Max howls and says, "Good line, huh?" I nod.

Max starts to ask, "Did you see Josey..." but his voice fades as I shake my head. "I know," he mumbles, "On your bucket list."

We don't talk as the miles pass by, the only sounds are the pelting of raindrops, an occasional crash of thunder, tires dancing on wet blacktop and the SHOOBSHOOBSHOOB of the windshield wipers. Lyrics to a song run through my mind, 'I finally see the dawn arrivin', I see beyond the road I'm drivin', far away and left behind.'

We pull into a Wal-Mart. After shopping, we'll drive to the most distant section of the parking lot to crash for the night. Wally World is a beacon for travelers who don't want to spend money on Motel 6 or Holiday Inn Express and don't mind no-frills boondocking. If you're not in an RV with all the creature comforts, you can bring your toothbrush and towel into the Wal-Mart rest room and freshen up and address the 3 S's — shit, shower, and shave — before heading back to the road. And you don't have to worry about your appearance with your hair mussed up and your eyes half-open as you shuffle through the store to the rest room. It's Wal-Mart. Nobody looks their best. I tell Max, "I'd like to see the company dish out a little truth in advertising and include under their sign 'Wal-Mart — Big Savings, Big Aisles, Big Carts, Big Asses.'"

Max volunteers, "How about 'Wal-Mart, Your Home for Cheap Shit?'"

"'Wal-Mart, making Chinese factory owners happy every day.'"

I grab a carriage to get dog food and a blueberry muffin for Max. Then I pick up a loaf of bread, a bottle of wine, a wedge of Gouda cheese, a package of Reese's Peanut Butter Cups, and I'm ready to party. I think how easy it would be to pocket this stuff and just walk out of the store. Ah, the good old days. Dum Phuk urges me to, but that part of my life is in the past. On the way to the checkout my carriage is rammed by another carriage pushed by a young boy who can barely see above the handlebar, but he's running out of control through the aisles like he's Steve McQueen racing a '68 Mustang up and down the hills of San Francisco. This happens almost every time I'm in Wal-Mart, and it usually ends with one of the parents whacking the kid on the back of the head and yelling, "Watch where you're going, idiot!"

At the check-out, a very cordial, very rotund woman with the name tag 'Tina' asks, "Did you find everything okay?"

"Everything except the meaning of life." She gives me a blank stare for several beats and then forces a chuckle.

"Well... Bibles are on aisle three, if that's what you mean." A polite smile. Ever notice that most folks named 'Tina' or 'Junior' are overweight?

She asks, "Paper or plastic?"

"Plastic. It has to hold a liver and spleen without leaking. At least until I get past the border guards," I respond, just to get her reaction.

She stares at me and blinks several times then forces a smile, "Ohhhh-kayyyyyyy" before placing my items into a plastic bag. I'm sure later on she'll tell her husband, "Honey, you'll never believe what happened at the store..." I feel pride in knowing I gave them something to talk about. Helped their communication skills. Maybe they shared a laugh. I'd like to think my wise-assery even saved their marriage. It's the romantic in me.

Back outside the rain has stopped and white cotton balls are stuck to the azure blue sky. I drive around the back of the store where the overnight lot contains several pickups, RV's, third wheels, vans, and a few cars. I pull into a space, leaving a space between me and a 30 foot Fleetwood with a sign on the back reading 'Happy Trails.' As I get out of Pam Grier, I hear the muted sound of guitar chords being strummed inside the RV and then it stops and at the window a curtain parts and a young boy looks out, eyes me for a moment, then disappears and the chords return. I expect to hear an ominous voice shout, "Pay no attention to the boy behind the curtain!" I can just about hear the guitar, and the boy's singing is even more faint.

As I stand before the open trunk scooping dry dog food into Max's bowl, the RV door opens and the tune becomes clear, as the boy wails:

> "I'm worse at what I do best
> and for this gift I feel blessed.
> Our little group has always been
> and always will until the end..."

I know the song. I could have sung along with him.

Standing in the open door is an attractive woman, early 50's, wearing jeans and a white blouse, no make-up, but her gray hair is perfectly styled. Her broad smile reveals perfect teeth. She says, "Kyle, you coming?" and the guitaring stops and the boy, about 12, all hair, acne, and attitude, follows the woman across the parking lot toward the store as if he were being lead to a guillotine. As she passes Pam Grier she smiles and gives me a quick wave.

I start on the bread, cheese, and wine and some fifteen minutes later my neighbors return to their RV. The woman stops at Pam Grier as the boy bolts back into the motor home, slamming the door behind him. How embarrassing it is for the world to see you with your parents.

She smiles and says, "Is that dinner?"

"Yeah," I grin, "All of the essential food groups. Wine is good for longevity, so I'm drinking as much as I can."

"I'm Cindy," she smiles, shaking my hand.

"Chaz."

"I've made more than enough fettuccine if you'd like to join us."

"Well..."

"Fellow travelers should look out for one another, yes?"

"Okay. I'll bring the wine and bread and we can..."

I'm interrupted by a loud stereo inside the RV screeching Metallica.

"Kyle!" Cindy yells. "Kyle! Headphones!"

But the music continues, and Cindy storms into the RV. Moments later the sound diminishes by many decibels and Cindy reappears.

"Sorry. He's at that age."

"We've all been at that age." I smile, sounding much older than I am. I'm only just a few years away from 'that age.'

"So... see you in a few minutes?"

I nod.

Cindy leaves and I wonder if she ever dreams what her life would have been like if she had never gotten pregnant. It's obvious she had Kyle when she was about 40. Maybe she had a professional career and decided to postpone having children until later in life. Was it a choice she now regrets? The situation makes me think of my own parents.

There is also something interesting about her manner of speech. Even her declarative sentences sound interrogative, like she's pleading. As if she has more questions than answers.

I put the cork back into the bottle, repackage the loaf of bread, and re-wrap the cheese. A homemade dinner sounds good.

Max says, "If I don't pee real soon I'm going to explode in a shower of urine" and I tell him, "That's an interesting visual." I take him out to a grassy area. Walking Max is not so much a walk, but an endless series of urine stops. I tell him, "I know wolves, your ancestors, peed everywhere 20,000 years ago, but it's time for a new paradigm. Time to be at the forefront of evolution and just piss all at once in one spot. Think you can do it? Are you ready to be the leader of your species?"

Max curls his lips, displaying his long, white canines. "Did you ever see my movie *White Dog*? Probably not. Didn't get distribution in the States."

I roll my eyes. "Oh, geez, here we go. Another one of life's lessons from Samuel Fuller."

"The movie is about racism. The dog is trained to kill black people, but the last thing the white dog does is kill a white guy. Tears him apart. You've been warned."

"Fine. Pee wherever you want."

"I will. Do we have an understanding? Let's shake on it" he says, extending his right front paw.

I curl my upper lip, displaying my teeth. Max feigns fear, "Ooooh, I'm so afraid!" then laughs. I shake his paw and lead him back to Pam Grier, where he takes a final urine shot onto the back tire.

"Thanks a lot," I wail. "Evolution will just have to march forward without you."

Max follows as I grab the bread and wine and approach the RV and rap on the door. Cindy opens it and waves me in. Max jumps in and curls up in a corner. Cindy is on a cell phone and gestures me toward a chair as she ducks into a back room. Her muffled conversation sounds like a gathering storm. After about a minute she loudly asserts, "Stop it! I said no more! Enough!" to the person on the other end of the line. The conversation ends without a goodbye. She re-enters the front room and tries to hide her anger and frustration.

"Hope you have an appetite, Chaz. I made plenty." I hand her the wine and bread. "Kyle, honey. We're ready to eat."

The RV smells like an Olive Garden. She uncorks the wine and pours the Cabernet Sauvignon into two plastic glasses. "You on vacation?" she asks.

"Well, not really. It's more like a trip of self-discovery."

"I think we all need one of those."

"You?"

"Oh... it's an extended vacation. Maybe throw in a little self-discovery too." She motions me to sit as Kyle enters in a cloud of reluctance. "Kyle, honey," she says, "This is Chaz." It's obvious he doesn't want to make eye contact. I extend my hand and after a brief hesitation Kyle offers his handshake. It's very brisk and weak and I feel like I'm trying to grab an eel.

"Nice to meet you," I say. Kyle wants to be anywhere but here. Cindy's smile has a touch of sadness and her eyes reveal she's 'living a life of quiet desperation.' Almost on the verge of giving up. A feeling of, 'What have I done?' Kyle is probably 12 or 13, just entering the asshole years. The time when parents secretly wish a very late, late, late term abortion could be performed without fear of criminal prosecution.

The conversation tip-toes across the surface, never going too deeply, although as we close in on the bottom of the wine bottle Cindy reveals she was divorced less than a year ago because her husband had an affair. She got custody of Kyle. His affair was predictable, "I was the other woman who he left his first wife for, so his behavior followed a pattern." Kyle, shooting her daggers, explodes, "Mom!" Cindy says, "I'm not speaking ill of your father. Just stating facts."

Cindy says she and her husband owned a start-up software company then sold it, and following the divorce she home schooled Kyle. She thought perhaps they could bond on a cross-country trip, although the boy's attitude reveals he'd rather be spending time with his dad or with his friends. She says her ex-husband does not agree with their road trip or home schooling, and I think back to her tense phone call earlier. I see a lot of my younger self in Kyle.

Cindy opens a cabinet and brings out a photo album, showing me many snaps of her and Kyle, standing at the south rim of the Grand Canyon, at Zion National Park, by a waterfall in Colorado, but in all the photos, Kyle is not smiling. Perhaps that's something she could one day fix in Photoshop or fix in counseling and learn to accept.

She asks me if I'm married, have kids, what I do for a living and the talk bores Kyle to death and he blurts out, "Mom, can I eat in the other room?" She lets out a deep exhale and waves him away just to avoid another battle. We sit in silence for several moments as I wonder if she wishes her life had played out some other way. Perhaps wishing things were different is a human condition. If so, it's an exercise full of futility and frustration.

Max knows what I'm thinking and he offers, "We all make choices. Sometimes things happen to us beyond our control, but other times we have to take responsibility." Such a wise dog.

I often wonder where certain people will be in five, ten, or twenty years from now and how my being with them at a particular moment may or may not influence them in the future. I believe everyone we meet influences us, either minutely or profoundly. I think about Kyle in five years. Will he be proud to be with his mom, talk with fondness about their road trip together, get serious with a girlfriend, become a track star, visit college campuses with his mother, maybe even Photoshop a smile onto his photos, or will hate and self-loathing build up inside until one day he enters his high school with an AK-47 to shoot up a crowded cafeteria?

Cindy brings me back to the here and now with "So... where will you be tomorrow?"

"Wherever my car decides to go. I have no say in the matter."
She smiles, and I suspect she's envious.

"How old are you, Chaz?"

"If a birthday is an awakening, then every day is a birthday."

"Oh, come on! Enough of the New Age babble!" She giggles. "How old are you?"

"I'm scheduled to be 21 in July."

"Scheduled?" she laughs. "That's a rather odd way to put it."

But I meant it that way. I can't assume anything.

"I would have guessed you to be older."

"I obviously have been ridden too hard in this horse race."

More laughter.

In the background Kyle strums his guitar and that gives me an idea. I tell Cindy, "I'm going to get something. Be right back."

A minute later I return with my cello. "Think he'd like to jam?" and Cindy breaks into a huge smile. I walk toward the bedroom and rap on the door. From inside an angry yell, "WHAT?" but I open the door and he's surprised and a bit embarrassed that it's me. Kyle is sitting up in bed practicing chords.

I tell him, "I'm a musician too. Wanna jam?" and the question, along with my sudden presence in his sanctuary catches him off-guard, but he stammers, "Ah... yeah... I guess..."

I take my cello out of the case and tune it. "I heard you playing Nirvana earlier. That's my music. Old school. Go ahead and I'll keep up with you."

As Kyle sings "Smells Like Teen Spirit," his face comes alive, he smiles, as I accompany him on cello. I love making music. It's like getting on the highway. It frees my soul from the bonds of the Earth and takes me to places I can only dream of.

Cindy enters with a glass of wine, sits on a nearby chair and taps her foot to the beat. We finish the tune and Kyle breaks into a grin while looking at me as if to say, "This guy's not such an asshole after all." We high-five and I ask him, "What else you got?"

and he strums a few chords and asks, "You ever heard of Alice in Chains?"

"Come on man. *Dirt* was one of my favorite albums."

Kyle says "Cool" and strums the guitar like he's trying to ignite it and sings:

> "I live tomorrow, you I'll not follow,
> As you wallow in a sea of sorrow."

Kyle is all smiles as he blurts out, "Shit man, that was great!" and Cindy admonishes him with, "Kyle. Language?"

I tell Kyle, "Okay, think you're up for classical?" and he says, "Bring it" and I launch into Handel's "Arrival of the Queen of Sheba" with vivace tempo but Kyle has trouble keeping up. I shout out the chord changes and after a few stops and starts he manages to stay with me and we end the song with much laughter. I tell him "One more," and play Dvořák's "Cello Concerto" with guitar accompaniment. At the end Cindy applauds and Kyle keeps repeating, "That is so rad" and I urge him to buy a few Yo-Yo Ma CD's to broaden his musical horizon.

As I leave, I thank Cindy for the food and company and Kyle for the jam. He says, "Thanks, Chaz" and we bump fists.

Rain falls again as Max follows me out of the RV and back into Pam Grier. It was a good night, but I keep thinking about Cindy's question: Where will I be tomorrow?

As I lay down on the back seat and close my eyes I think of Clitty.

Clitty. Yes, Clitty.

It is now raining question marks with no answers in sight. Despite being in a Wal-Mart parking lot, it is my temporary home, because home is anyplace you close your eyes and dream.

And eventually I did.

Chapter 7

> "One's destination is never a place,
> but a new way of seeing things."
> — Henry Miller

> "Nothing is forever, There's got to be something better."
> — "One Headlight" — The Wallflowers

A new day is about to be born, accompanied by "Ode to Joy," as the morning sun spills iridescent blotches of reds, oranges, and yellows across the skyscape like a canvas ignited by Peter Max. We're now traveling a secondary road in the Central Valley of California. Just a nameless two lane job with no beginning and no ending but many stories it keeps secret.

I used to spend more time on the interstates but now with much deliberation I avoid the I-5's or I-80's or I-10's of the world because the I's are bland and unmemorable and repetitious. Like a Ben Affleck performance. The secondary roads of William Least Heat-Moon are full of personality and interest and quirk and provide fodder for future conversations with friends. Like watching any movie with Steve Buscemi.

We may be near Fresno or Chico, I just don't know or even care, as the sun sneaks up behind the Sierra Madre Mountains with a lascivious playfulness, ogling the lushness of the San Joaquin Valley, with the golden light awakening Earth to new hopes and possibilities. The geographical location is not important, but what you take away from the experience is.

Wherever we travel, the locals always refer to their part of the planet as 'God's country.' But when you think about it, isn't every place? I can't think of a single location on Earth where you might say, "Yeah, God made this, but He had an off day. He is capable of so much better. What was He thinking when He made that lame-ass hill over there? Those gnarly trees? That uninspiring mountain that doesn't even have a peak. Sometimes He can be such an underachiever." I can't think of any place so void of interest and beauty that God would deny having made it.

Outside Fresno we pass an ominous black billboard with white Gothic letters: 'If You Were to Die Today, Where Would You Spend Eternity?' Hopefully not in Fresno, although a week would seem like an eternity. A few miles further along is another billboard: 'After you die you will meet God.' I'd like to climb up there with a can of paint and write 'And you'll be disappointed. You'd expect Him to be much taller and not stutter. Such a nebbish!'

I open a can of Coors and begin practicing a pitch of one of my screenplays. I'll be attending a writer's conference and get to pitch my script *Satan Bytes* to several agents and producers. Selling a script is my last great hope. I try to act excited as I practice my sales job to Max. He listens with attention, except for the few times he bends down to lick his dick.

"A 20-year old slacker named Nougat discovers that the love of his life made a deal with the Devil, so he hacks into Satan's mainframe to retrieve her Soul."

Max sighs. I wait a few moments, waiting for his response. "Sucks, doesn't it?"

"No. Good logline. I think it has real potential," he says. "You have to watch the special effects and CGI stuff and your movie would have lots of it. That means more money for the studio to shell out. If you're Stephen Spielberg or Terry Gilliam, that's one thing, but as a newbie, remember the acronym K.I.S.S. — Keep it simple, stupid."

I know he's right. "Shit, maybe I shouldn't even go to this conference."

"No! Go! It'll be a good experience. Help toughen your hide. I like what you've done with the characters. You have a flair for dialogue. But don't be afraid of creating more conflict. Aggravate the reader. Ever hear the line, 'If you can't annoy somebody with what you write, there's little point in writing?'"

He's right. I have to write like I don't care who reads it. Spill it all out with no concern about creating anxiety and unease. Self-censoring is the enemy of genuine creativity.

Max continues his writing seminar, "Don't get flowery in your prose. Write bare-bones. Knock off any superfluous words. This is most important: Don't use adverbs and never start a sentence with a conjunction."

"Exactly. But I hardly ever do," I reply.

My stomach is in turmoil, already feeling queasy about a pitch that's less than 24 hours away. "What if half-way through the pitch I vomit on the agents?

"They'll demand ten percent of it," Max replies.

Maybe I should pitch another screenplay. "What do you think of *Rocky, My Fairy Godmother*? Does that script give you a hard-on?" It's a question I never thought I'd ask a dog.

He smiles and says "No, but it has a quirky story. Unique characters. If only an agent could get it into De Niro's hands, they'd green light it in a New York minute."

"Yeah, if only... if only... IF ONLY!"

I visualize the pitch fest and wonder if I'd be more enthused about being water-boarded. I'm an agnostic, but lo and behold, just as I feel the need for divine intervention, we drive by Jesus on a bicycle.

He's a short black man riding an old rusted bike on balloon tires with a large wooden cross sticking up from behind the seat. A red bandanna, a black shirt, and a pair of tightie-whities flap in the breeze from the arms of the cross. Because of his stature, as well as his beard and red floppy hat, he resembles a lawn gnome in an English garden. I bring Pam Grier to a sudden halt, throw the Caddy into reverse and back up next to the Holy Man on a Schwinn.

I hold out a can and ask, "Hey buddy, wanna beer?" I now get a good look at his Rondo Hatton face. He has the look of someone who should have been wearing a helmet but didn't and had a horrible accident. His eyes are chalky-white and crusted over and resemble used ping-pong balls and his skin is rough with black lines, like the rumble strip on a highway. He may have three gray-yellow teeth in the front. Maybe four or five if I examined his mouth closely, but I don't want to get closely. His long Medusa-like gray dreads have a life of their own. It's obvious the man is blind, but he reaches for the can and in a gruff New Orleans accent says, "God bless ya, son." I pull off the road and pop open another Coors as Max murmurs, "This should be good."

I get out of the car and sit on the front hood. Max sniffs the guy's shoes. "Nice dog ya got," he says, his voice sounding like two emery boards wrestling.

"The good Lord takes all dogs into heaven," he says bending down to pet Max. "Ain't no dogs in Hell. Nononono. All animals are pure. All without sin. Cerberus guards the gates of Hades to keep the dead from leaving but he also keeps other dogs from entering the Underworld. Not many folks know that. Unscyldgung!" The guy scratches Max behind the ears and my dog's right hind leg spasms while pawing the dirt with a THUMPTHUMPTHUMP.

This man of God is less than five feet tall, but what he lacks in stature he makes up for in intensity. Even though he can't see, he appears to be staring at me, and with the x-ray of his glare, I feel like an ant under a magnifying glass on a hot summer day. He moves very close, looks up at me and says, "I know your modgemynd. Gears are turnin'. How'd the ugly ol' neofugol lose his orbs? Well, a jealous husband came home at the wrong possible time and shot me with a .16 gauge right in the face. The pellets went through my brain and out the back of my head and are still sailing through the universe like Voyager 2. Hahahahaha. I never did thank the man. Because without that epiphany, I never would have changed my evil ways and stop being a forsyngod and fing the Lord."

"Amazing," is all I can murmur, as I wonder what language he's speaking. He's sprinkling in some words I'm not familiar with. Max senses my confusion and says, "He was an Anglo-Saxon in the 9th century. Old habits die hard."

"So you're a man of God..." I say.

"All of them!" he interrupts with arm flailing, his eyes growing wider, his voice increasing in volume and excitement as he rattles off the names, "Adonai, Jehovah, Elohim, Shen, Nkosi, Allah, Brahma, Jupiter, Zeus, and Wakan Tanka, the Sacred Spirit of Lakotan peoples!"

His outburst seems to have covered most of the beliefs, the 'isms' of Man, except for Bokononism and Dudeism.

"But I see you carry the cross of Jesus. Are you a Christian?"

He laughs. "It's easier to hang my laundry from a cross than a Star of David. I don't follow any organized religion. I only follow those that are disorganized. I consider myself poly-theamorous. I shack up with all faiths. Love 'em all! And they love me! The best part of making love to all the religions is you never roll over on a wet spot. HaHaHaHaHa!"

After a pause I ask, "So... how are you able to bike the highway? Don't you ever veer into traffic?"

"The hand of the Lord guides me, son. You don't need eyes to see. The Almighty steers me in the right direction." All I can muster is a faint "Oh" and take a swig of beer.

"You appear to be a wegferend too." I shrug and look to Max for help. The man realizes I don't comprehend and says, "A 'traveler' as you might say in this millennium. Someone on a quest." He offers his outstretched hand, "Brother Benny is the name."

"Chaz. My dog Max. Nice to meet you," I say shaking his thin, cold, bony hand. I felt like he was dead but I didn't know how to break it to him. Like the lady in *Carnival of Souls*. He smiles at Max.

"I can tell that you and your furry little companion have transcended time and space," he says. "You're not alone. Every so often I meet a few of you celestial wegferends... ah, travelers.

As long as you spread the word of the Lord, you'll have a smooth journey. Hahahaha," and he takes a long swig of beer.

"We're not space aliens," I Klaatu-ized.

"Nononono!" Brother Benny says, climbing up onto the hood of Pam Grier. "That's where you're wrong! We're all space aliens, my son. We're all in space and to other beings in the cosmos, we're aliens. Let me tell you about space aliens, my friend. Space aliens know we're here but they don't want to visit us because Earthlings are a bunch of bombastic, ignorant, belligerent, paranoid, social retards, so they fly right by our planet."

"Sort of like driving across the country but not stopping in Texas." I smile, but he doesn't find it funny or else chooses to ignore it.

From up on the hood he bends down and gets in my face. "You're not taking it seriously, son. You're not making the Commitment. The Universe doesn't like slackers. Do something half-ass, and the Supreme Being is likely to smite you with a byrnsweord. Hahahaha."

I'm not sure what a byrnsweord is, but my guess is being smited with one would cause pain. I catch myself inching away from his hot breath that smells of old pepperoni pizza. "If you were to get smited by the Lord, it wouldn't be pretty," he hisses. I'm about to say "I'll bet smiting is frowned upon by the Geneva Convention," but think better of it.

Max says, "He's right about making the Commitment."

"Listen to your dog friend," Brother Benny says. "He's trying to help you through your journey. And so far you've had a journey full of twists and turns and bumpy roads."

I nod.

"Commitment to your screen writing. Commitment to relationships," Max continues, "Opportunities come in all shapes, sizes, and forms. Give the man a twenty and we'll be on our way."

"A twenty?" I ask.

"Chaz, didn't you learn anything here?"

"Yeah."

"What?" Max asks, brimming over with impatience.

"I have to make more of an effort to be a writer."

"And... and..." Max says with a heavy sigh.

"And... allow myself to be in a relationship." I say the words like I'm about to walk on broken glass.

"Every lesson in life should be that inexpensive," Max says. I grab a $20 from inside my sneaker and give it to the Holy Man. "So you can hear my dog, too?" I ask.

Brother Benny laughs again and says, "The paths of old souls do cross occasionally."

Max says to me, "There are no accidents," and Brother Benny nods and gets on his bicycle.

I've never been religious, having been raised in a very secular home, but there was something about Brother Benny that made me wonder: Is there a Supreme Being that created everything? That oversees all? That is infinite and omnipotent? Years ago I had the same sense of wonder when I made my own lunch and saw the image of Reverend Billy Graham on a grilled cheese sandwich.

Max and I get into the car and watch Brother Benny pedal along the highway, all the while screech-singing:

"Tall and tan and young and lovely, the girl
from Ipanema goes walking..."

Brother Benny soon pedals around a curve in the road and is out of sight. I fire up Pam Grier and floor it to catch up to the Mystic. It might be good for my soul to talk to him some more, or at least he could be an inspiration for a character in one of my screenplays.

I round the curve in the road but Brother Benny is nowhere to be seen. No trees or rocks for him to hide behind. No buildings or billboards to provide cover. No trace of him at all. As Dorothy Gale said, "My! People come and go so quickly here!" Max sees my shock and breaks into a wry smile.

Oh, well. Brother Benny sure was an interesting character, but it's time to move on. I've been thinking a lot about Clitty and Max is quite aware of that since he has telepathic talents. So I assume we're going to rejoin Clitty soon and give her my answer, but Max says nothing as he hangs his head out the window with his ears flapping and drool flying out the back. I've been thinking of Clitty more than I thought I would. Maybe I should make a commitment.

After driving a half hour we pass a roadside death site. The location where someone had an auto accident and their family and friends mark the place with a cross. Sometimes there are flowers at the site. Or photos. Or a stuffed animal. Have you noticed that it's always a cross that marks the fateful spot? It's never a Jewish Star of David or a Muslim Star and Crescent. Maybe Jews and Muslims are better drivers than Christians. If you're an atheist, there is never a marking. Maybe a lot of atheists lose their lives on the side of the road but we'll never know it.

I once saw a cross with the name 'Bob' scrawled on it. Nothing more is known about the poor unfortunate who lost his life on that particular part of the highway, except his name is a palindrome. Another time I saw a cross with a name on it and beside the cross was a vase of flowers and a beer stein. Perhaps the guy's favorite stein. I wonder if he was drunk when he had the accident?

The saddest roadside memorial I ever saw was four crosses, including photos and baby shoes. An entire family gone in less than a moment.

We pass herds of cows grazing in fields of no worries. On the side of the road is a hand-written sign, red paint on a sheet of plywood, created by a local farmer. In ominous letters it reads: 'No Cow Tipping!' I had never given much thought to cow tipping, but now I wonder: How much do you tip a cow? Twenty percent? What if the cow gives exceptional service, why not thirty percent? It can't be easy to hold a tray of dishes if you have hooves.

How bored can you be to want to knock over a cow? That pastime ranks right up there with watching bowling on TV. Or tossing pairs of sneakers onto an overhead telephone line. I wonder if in Canada they throw pairs of hockey skates onto overhead lines.

Max and I pass a billboard for an approaching roadside diner that specializes in 'Pulled Pork,' which sounds like a euphemism for masturbation. "Hungry?" I ask, and from the back seat a gravelly voice with a New Orleans accent croaks, "Only if you're buying!"

HOLY SHIT! I jump out of both my skin and the driver's seat as I look in the rear-view mirror at Brother Benny with his Jack-O-lantern grin. "Jesus Christ, man! You're gonna give me a heart attack!" I gasp. Max snickers HEHHEHHEH and it sounds like Snoopy's laugh when Woodstock tumbles while ice skating. Next to Brother Benny in the back seat is his bicycle and cross. We travel a few miles with my heart still racing as Brother Benny wails:

> "Candy came from out on the island,
> in the backroom she was everybody's
> darlin', but she never lost her head even
> when she was givin' head, she said take
> a walk on the wild side."

When Benny rasp-sings "And the colored girls sing..." Max throws his head back and yelps the chorus:

"Do-do-do do-da-do-do-do-do-do-da-do..."

The song is interrupted by a couple of knuckle-dragging troglodytes driving a mud-covered old Ford Bronco that I assume used to be white, sitting high atop tires with acute elephantiasis, now speeding right out of some primal ooze mudbug. They are quite elated to be tailgating Pam Grier. An inch away from her rear bumper. Maybe less.

"Get off my ass!" I yell into the rear view mirror.

Brother Benny snorts, "That's closer than tail-gating. That's sodomy! Damn sodomites!" and grabs his wooden cross and hurls it over his shoulder. I glance behind to see the cross bounce on the pick up's hood, spear the windshield with a loud burst and shower of glass, then brakes screech and the yahoos scream and the truck careens off the road and with a loud THUMP lands upside-down in a ditch. Well, happy happy, joy joy, I Ren & Stimpy-ized.

Brother Benny, with a huge grin and great pride says, "Jack Lord works in mysterious ways," as he stands up on the back seat, strikes a surfing pose, then sing-hums the theme from *Hawaii Five-Oh*:

"Da-da-da-da-daaaaah-daaaah-da-da-da-dadaaaaaaah..."

"Very mysterious ways," I say. Benny yells, "Can I have an 'Amen' from the congregation?"

Max and I both yell "Amen" and laugh.

Just ahead is the diner and Max motions me to pull into the parking lot.

Brother Benny makes a beeline for the front door. I don't know how he could 'see' the front door but I try not to question anything. Max always stresses my need for Acceptance.

By the time Max and I enter, Brother Benny has already claimed a table. The waiter arrives with three waters and three menus and a cheery 'Good afternoon, gentlemen."

Brother Benny opens the menu and says, "Sheeee-it! "Thirteen bucks for a sandwich? For that price it should eat me. HaHaHaHa!"

I grab a menu. The first page is blank, so I thumb through the next pages. All are blank. No food items, no prices. Nothing. Brother Benny slaps his leg and roars in laughter. I grab another menu and it too has blank pages. The third menu is also blank.

I should have been tipped off when I saw the chalk board on the way in and it read 'Today's Specials,' but the board was blank.

"How are we gonna order anything," I ask, "when there's nothing to order?"

"You don't," Max says. "You take what's handed to you and make the best of it. It's a metaphor."

The waiter returns with a tray and places a plate of fried haddock and a loaf of bread and a glass of Riesling before Brother Benny. Max is given a glass of port, a plate of braised beef with asparagus tips, a bowl of water, and a rawhide chewie. The waiter eyes me then reaches inside his vest and hands me a black book with the words 'MY JOURNEY' embossed in gold leaf on the front. "Gentlemen enjoy your food," the waiter says and then vanishes in a flash.

"What food?" I ask, but Max shoots me a look, grabs the book and slaps it on the table. "This is a map. Not of roads but a map of your life, and it's more nourishing to your soul then all the burgers and fries in the world."

I'm curious to open the book right there, but I'm afraid. I take off my fedora and reach inside the lining for a joint. I light it, and the swirling clouds of smoke provide a temporary barrier against the harshness of my current universe. Like a vaporized moat fortress around my vulnerable castle.

Brother Benny finishes his meal, then stands atop the table, and sings, "Papa's Got a Brand New Bag" and dances a jig like Walter Houston in *Treasure of the Sierra Madre*. Max chews the piece of rawhide and asks, "Did you ever see *Now, Voyager?*" He doesn't wait for my answer, but continues. "Bette Davis had a line that reminds me of you. She said, "I'm immune to happiness."

I stare at Max and yell, "Fuck you! I'm doing the best I can, considering the circumstances." I open my wallet, toss a couple of twenties onto the table, then grab MY JOURNEY and storm out.

Pain in the ass dog.

Leaning against Pam Grier, I let out a faint, audible whimper, like a Pac Man getting zapped on the screen. Death comes in tiny increments, I once told Max, but he quickly shot back, "Yeah, and so does life." I knew I had to get back on the road, but I also knew there was only so much immortality that the road could provide. I think of Clitty and wonder if now is the time to make the commitment. I kinda wish she were by my side now but perhaps that moment will be revisited one day. It still doesn't feel like the right time.

Max and Brother Benny leave the diner and stroll to the car. Brother Benny says, "If you don't mind, it's time to get back on the road and spread the Word." I grab his bicycle from the back seat and the preacher says, "I'll go back to grab my cross. I'm sure those boys are long gone by now." He mounts his bicycle then turns to me and says, "Chaz, this is gonna be one sweet ride for you. Just learn to float downstream and everything's gonna be all right. Max, 'til next time. Freod. Hahahahaha."

He mounts the bike and as he fades from view I hear his raspy voice attack the Gloria Gaynor tune:

> "Do you think I'd crumble, did you think
> I'd lay down and die? Oh no, not I, I will

survive. Oh, as long as I know how to love,
I know I'll stay alive..."

"An interesting soul," I murmur. Max doesn't say anything, but I feel the tension and blurt out, "Sorry. I didn't mean to blow up."

"Chaz, have a little patience. It's a long road to where you're going and I'm only here to help navigate it. Help you discover answers along the way. It's not always going to be easy." I bend down and hug him.

I whisper, "I think I need Clitty back in my life" remembering the last words she said.

"You think?"

"I... know."

Max knowingly smiles like Clarence the guardian angel. "Not good enough, my boy."

Back on the road we stop at a Holiday Inn Express in Sacramento, the scene of the screenplay pitch fest. Sacramento is not Hollywood, but it is in the same state and the agents in this seminar claim to have helped a few writers land deals and tout themselves as being 'well connected' in the industry. Max is by my side as I pitch *The Frozen Man*, my comedy-drama about a famous writer having an affair but ends up with Locked In Syndrome after totaling his sports car and killing his pregnant mistress. His vengeful wife now makes his existence a living hell. Max thinks it's one of my strongest screenplays. Max is pleased I made a commitment to attend this pitch-fest.

I get "Interesting concept" from a couple of agents who immediately wanted to know "What else have you written?" I want to reply, "A couple of poems, but you'll find them very derivative of Dorothy Parker's early work," but think better of it.

Back in Pam Grier I ask Max if *The Frozen Man* script gives him a hard-on. "Not quite. Semi-flaccid" he replies. I tell him that the experience went better than I thought it would. The agents, or 'dream crushers' as I refer to them, didn't yawn or nod off or even punch me in the head, so I consider that a victory of sorts. I received a lot of "That's not right for us now, but keep trying." I ended up with a pocketful of business cards. Max thought a few of the agents expressed genuine interest. He comforts me by saying, "You've got the talent. So much of getting a script in the right hands is just plain ol' dumb luck. You just never know who'll provide the right hands." I figure my scripts are better than *Showgirls* or *Hudson Hawk*. Even those got sold and made into movies.

I reach inside the glove compartment for MY JOURNEY. I'm shocked to find there is no writing on the pages, but each page is its own movie screen. Like watching rapidly changing videos on a computer screen. The random page I flip to shows redwood trees and beaches and amusement park rides at the Boardwalk, and I immediately know the place. "Ah, Santa Cruz. Max, I think we should go to Santa Cruz."

"That is a good idea."

Faster than you can say "Kowalski's '70 Dodge Challenger," I fire up Pam Grier and head west. I toss MY JOURNEY back into the glove compartment, grin from ear to ear, stretch back in the seat, and yell, "San-taaaaa Cruuuuuuuuuuzzzzzzz!"

Maybe I'm wrong, but I feel you can become immortal by staying on the road. As long as you drive toward the horizon, whatever forces are there to lay you to waste along the way will always be in your rear view mirror and you'll never grow old. Death cannot catch you. It's like what Satchel Paige said about not looking back.

Pam Grier eats up the pavement at 80 miles an hour as I yell "San-taaaaaa Cruuuuuuzzzzzzz" one more time and Max joins in with a long and soulful howl. When I think of Santa Cruz, my mind races with so many memories. I think of Kathy. Long brown hair, big brown doe-eyes, great body, a close resemblance to Valerie Bertinelli in her *One Day at a Time* days. What really got my attention was Kathy's nymphomania. I wonder if she's still insatiable. Probably. I don't think nymphomania is something you grow out of like a pair of shoes.

When I first met Kathy I thought she was the love of my life. On the first date we sat in my car at the park near the Lighthouse, late at night, steaming up the windows, hormones colliding like the elementary particles of the Higgs boson, with the relationship moving past the hand-under-the-bra stage to sprinting around second base faster than Ricky Henderson. She put her head down on my lap and unzipped my pants and put her tongue and mouth on me. God, I was so excited entering this carnal heaven, but quickly lost it and "the calliope crashed to the ground." I didn't have a problem with what she was doing or how she was doing it. The problem was the sound of her doing it.

Kathy had TMJ, and the sound of her jaw clicking while going down on me sounded like a flamenco dancer with castanets dancing on a tile floor. I was so distracted that I went limp and she kept asking, "Is it me? Am I not doing it right?" but I couldn't tell her that her jaw reminded me of the Tin Woodmen's arm before he used the oil can. Besides, to a horny guy, there is no wrong way to do it. Any way you do it is the right way. There's no such thing as receiving bad head. It's just that the steady CLICK-CLICKCLICK distracted me. Maybe I should have put in ear plugs but it was too late. The damage had been done, and Kathy and I only saw each other a couple of more times and the failed attempt at oral sex was never discussed again.

Another memory of Santa Cruz was Delta Montreux. The older woman. Not quite a Mrs. Robinson, but 29 years old to my 18. She had spiked blonde hair that was a different color du jour. Delta was very fit and trim, even though she never worked out. Never biked or hiked. She seemed to fret about everything so perhaps 'worry' was her only form of exercise. She embraced the Chicken Little philosophy and rarely smiled, but came alive in bed, with her eyes igniting in neon rainbows like the sun's rays illuminating a gasoline spill on wet pavement. Once Delta was having sex, the perennial dark cloud above her lifted and she was playful and curious and intense like a kitten strung out on catnip. I wonder if Delta was still in town.

And then there was my father.

We hadn't seen each other for a couple of years although there were the occasional uncomfortable phone conversations. We had a falling out over something stupid. I don't recall what it was but I feel that even though he was wrong, I was wronger. I'm sure it was related to his drinking and fights with Mom. But now it was time for apologies, especially since the last time we spoke on the phone his speech was slurred as he talked about his aches and pains and I realized he was in declining health. I never told him my situation. It was important to visit both Santa Cruz and my father to try and make sense of both of them.

Delta was an artist who specialized in creating plaster of Paris death masks. Maybe it was time to be fitted for one. Max and I were on our way to yesterday.

Chapter 8

"Every exit is an entry somewhere else."
— Tom Stoppard

"Life is a highway, I wanna ride it all night long."
— "Life is a Highway" — Tom Corcoran

I remember Santa Cruz as a heavenly blue mist floating above the Pacific, a seductive temptress never offering excuses, never making apologies, and never compromising, a place where dreams wash up and break on the rocks, where the city elites are surf boys who Corky Carroll called 'tan punks on boards' with surfboards sticking out of the back seat of their VW convertible bugs of psychedelic colors resembling upside down popsicles on wheels, cruising Ocean Street, whistling at young girls in tight shorts and bare midriffs who are visiting with their moms and dads from Nebraska or South Dakota or some other land of naivety, then flirting at taquerias before trying to impress these innocents with riding the big waves at Steamer Lane to a Dick Dale soundtrack wailing in the background, and the townies, always using an older brother to buy liquor unless they're clever enough to create a fake I.D, plying these wide-eyed does with one more beer, oh come on, just one more it ain't gonna hurt ya and besides just think of the stories you'll tell your friends back in Elkhart, Indiana, and holding their warm bodies close when they take the dare and then off to get a small tattoo on their leg of a yellow butterfly or a blue dolphin down on the Boardwalk where all the lights are flashing neon and the rides spin in tempting hedonistic spirals, and then it's a late night stroll to the railroad trestle bridge, yes the same one used in *The Lost Boys*, and these fawns are curious to go there because the shadows dart about like ghosts and the sand is still hot from the summer sun and moist from previous lovers and for a few minutes Time ceases to exist and they revel in their invisibility to the world and thank the beach for having no memory, and yes, there were many days when both big waves and little girls were conquered.

Santa Cruz may look the same, but I've been gone so long I forgot what I look like. Perhaps that's a good thing. It's probably best if it's not easy to recognize yourself. Keeps you on your toes and prevents you from going stale. I wonder if the town will recognize me.

Marini's on the wharf is there for my sweet tooth and Positively 4th Street is still the place to either terminate a hangover or begin a new one. It's usually the kid from out of town who wakes up face down in the sand on the Boardwalk beach as the new sun's orange rays float above the crimson Pacific. He'll close down Positively 4th Street and stagger past the early morning streetlights to the beach, the inside of his head throbbing like a sheet metal factory. Usually on the sand next to his face or splattered on his tee shirt is dried vomit. The poor bastard is in such pain and misery and through half-opened eyes prays that the tide rolls in and mercifully carries him out to the ocean, past the buoys, to be devoured by Great Whites. Of course at 19 the body is resilient and has no recollection of pain, so in a few hours he'll meet friends at Subway and then return for more beers that night at Positively 4th Street or some other hole. The cycle spins around and around like the Boardwalk carousel until the tourists go home by Labor Day and the locals reclaim their town. Students return to the University of Santa Cruz, nestled among groves of redwoods, the cool school where students take calculus and rock climbing, geometry and pottery making, and their mascot is a banana slug, made famous by John Travolta wearing a

UCSC 'Fighting Banana Slug' tee. Santa Cruz then morphs into a different flower that closes its petals and sleeps under the melody of fall.

Santa Cruz is the mecca for bumper stickers. Even more so than Eugene, Oregon, a place I visited years ago with my folks. On one ancient VW bus plastered with stickers was the notice: 'Bumper stickers hold this thing together.' The locals have their Subaru's and VW vans and Volvo station wagons plastered with 'Mystery Spot' or 'Bowlers for Bill Clinton' or 'On the 8th Day God Made Bagpipes' or 'Play the Accordion, Go to Jail. It's the Law.' The rich kids from Silicon Valley drive to Santa Cruz on Highway 17 in their BMW's or Maserati's, and you'd be hard pressed to find a single bumper sticker. Some vehicles don't need decals to make a statement and sometimes the lack of a statement is more powerful than making one.

Driving Highway 17 is an adrenaline rush. It snakes through the Santa Cruz Mountains and if you drive it prior to riding the Giant Dipper and the Tsunami on the Boardwalk, you'll find those rides to be a bit anti-climactic. The amusement park rides may not be as exhilarating as the twists and turns of Highway 17, but they are a hell of a lot safer. The highway always makes the list of 'Deadliest Roads in the U-S,' because Santa Cruz is a party town and most folks leaving for home leaned a little too heavily on the happy horn before getting behind the steering wheel, and those driving to Santa Cruz are in such a hurry to get there they either ignore the speed limit or think the posted 40 mph sign is not an enforceable law but only a polite suggestion.

Every road plays a different song and Highway 17 is no exception. Once you've driven great distances on various roads, you become attuned to the unique sounds of rubber meeting pavement. Highway 17 sings Garcia and the Dead tunes, with an emphasis on the bass. Traveling on Highway 15 outside Ogden, Utah, I heard an angelic choir sounding like a C major triad on a piano. Traveling across Kansas, I-70 sounds very high-pitched and twangy, what you might hear if you pureed Loretta Lynn in a Cuisinart.

I thought it was interesting that I never saw road kills on Utah highways, or in Missouri, or Colorado, but Kansas seemed to have more than any other state. Deer, possum, raccoons dot the interstate landscape in furry mounds of blood. Maybe the wildlife want to commit suicide once they realize they're living in Kansas. Like lemmings off a cliff.

Taking the curves on Highway 17, Dum Phuk urges me to accelerate Pam Grier as I maneuver each dip and turn in the road. He urges me to play rear-steer and I murmur, "Dum Phuk, just go away." How do you eliminate an annoying part of your personality without having a frontal lobotomy like Randle McMurphy?

There's something about driving a '59 Caddy that makes you feel invincible, like you're driving a slick tank. All steel and brawn and an attitude of invincibility. But Max murmurs, "Slow down" and mentions something about messing with the Eternal Plan. At 50 mph I back off the gas, knowing that even if a tank leaves the road and hits a redwood tree or careens off a curve to fly a hundred feet down an embankment, it would ruin my day. And the Eternal Plan.

I grab a smoke from my fedora and fire it up with the cigarette lighter. Max offers a Burma Shave slogan. "Once you arrive, you certainly will find, that Santa Cruz, is only, a strange state of mind. Burma Shave."

"No better antidote, for the blues, than an overnight stay, in Santa Cruz. Burma Shave."

We ride in silence for a few miles, the cool air swooshing through the open Cadillac. It's late September but there's no rain in the forecast. The golden sun plays peek-a-boo through the branches of redwoods, madrones, oaks, maples, and laurels. A mosaic of green shades like a Rousseau painting. An oldies station plays Dylan and Max and I sing along:

"How does it feel? To be without a home.
Like a complete unknown. Like a rolliiin' stone."

Random thoughts collide like bumper cars on the Board-walk. I miss Clitty. More than I could have imagined. Will I find Delta? What'll I say to my father? Does anybody really want to hear my story and why I'm on this journey? Maybe I am a complete unknown like a rolling stone.

Now my thoughts turn to Amber. How awkward will it be to run into her?

The setting sun sizzles into the Pacific Ocean like an egg on a skillet and in ten minutes Max and I are cruising Ocean Street, now dotted with more motels, restaurants, bicycle rental shops, and tee shirt boutiques then I remember from two years ago. Max sings:

"There's two swingin' honeys for every guy
and all you gotta do is just wink your eye."

Santa Cruz is "Surf City," although Huntington Beach tries to lay claim to the honor. To better understand Santa Cruz, it's the only town where Muslim women surf the waves while wearing tie-dye hajibs. And many of the locals think hacky sack should be included as an Olympic sport.

I pull up to the curb at a small bungalow on Seabright Avenue. The front porch light is on. I take a deep breath and think, this should be interesting.

Max interjects, "Don't forget, we are insignificant specks of dust on a meaningless voyage."

"Thanks. Now you've put a big smile on my face."

I open the trunk, remove my cello and bow, then take a tentative walk to the front porch. I sit on a wooden rocker and after a brief tune-up begin playing "Adagio for Strings." About a minute later the door opens and there stands my father, leaning on a cane, with tears running down his cheeks.

I stop playing, lean the cello and bow against the rocker and whisper, "Dad."

His expression is blank and for a moment I'm reminded of Chauncey Gardiner. His voice quivers, "My son used to play that piece. Always made me cry." Both his speech and his face are full of late Winter.

My heart shatters into a trillion sad pieces.

A tall African-American woman wearing a nurse's uniform appears in the doorway behind my father, eyes me up and down, and says, "Yes?" and I let out a deep sigh of despair and realize that everything is not all right.

I tell her who I am and she says her name is Marian and she shakes my hand and invites me in.

"I knew your Dad had a son, but I couldn't figure out how to get in touch with you. Your father had a stroke about six months ago."

I stare at him and he stares back and I feel that for a brief moment or two he knows who I am. At least that's what I want to feel. He doesn't have a scowl. He doesn't seem angry. He has a warm smile, but the twinkle has left his eyes.

"Dad?" I whisper. "I'm Chaz... Chaz?"

He's cordial. "Well, hi Chaz. How are you?"

I glance around the living room at family photos on the wall and on shelves and on the coffee table, but they are not our family photos. The people in the photos are unknown to me. They're the models that are already included in the picture frames you buy.

I ask Marian, "Couldn't he find any pictures of my mother... of me... his family?"

Marian shrugs, "I don't know where he put his personal photos. Maybe up in the attic? He believed his family was the folks in these photos."

I collapse onto the couch, the air knocked out of me, my mind running in a million different directions. A tea kettle whistles, and that jars me back to the here and now, as Marian excuses herself and leaves. I look deeply into my Dad's eyes and he smiles and in a soft voice says, "Chaz, you play very well. I don't know why I cried, but I did." Maybe music opened a door to his memory, a world that was inaccessible by drugs and therapy.

I notice his old violin, the case caked with dust, on a shelf next to a couple of empty whiskey bottles. With Dad playing violin and my Mom playing flute, I remember how proud I was of them, performing in the living room an up-tempo jazz-classical fusion of Satie's "Gymnopedie." Considering their many arguments, the only time they were on the same page and were in sync was when they played music together. That was my fondest memory of being together as a family.

I joke and ask if he's entering a surfing competition being held that weekend and he says, "I would, but I don't recall how to get to the ocean." I want to laugh but he's not joking and my eyes well up. I pat his arm, "I love you, Dad" and he smiles as if a stranger had told him they liked his shirt.

"I just want to tell you I'm sorry. Sorry I was too caught up in my own selfishness. Sorry for being an asshole. Sorry for any embarrassment I caused you and Mom. Thanks for everything." His smile now seems empty and false, like the strangers in the photos on the walls.

Marian returns with two cups and pours the tea and as I continue to stare at my father I notice something strange.

Little by little he is fading away.

I blink and rub my eyes. Maybe I'm overtired. Maybe it's the weed from this morning. No, it's happening. With the passing of every moment his face, arms, legs, and body are vanishing. Like several pixels being removed with each passing moment. He continues smiling as Marian talks about the tea but I'm not listening because I'm mesmerized by my father disappearing and inside I scream, WHAT THE HELL IS GOING ON? but Marian continues to talk but it's only background noise and she's oblivious to what is happening to him, as I can now see through his body and face to the couch behind him like he's cellophane and seconds later all I see of him is the light from his eyes and then in a breath that is gone too.

Marian continues to talk and I catch something she says about my father and then she pauses, "Chaz? Chaz, are you okay?" but a distant calming voice urges me to go outside, so I leap from the couch, dash to the porch and search the darkening cobalt blue sky. I watch a shooting star arc across the void as tears stream down my face. After a couple of minutes I compose myself and return to the living room. Marian asks, "Something wrong? You okay?" and I collapse onto the couch. "Chaz, it didn't seem like you were listening to a word I said."

"Sorry."

"I was just telling you that in the brief time I knew your dad, we got along very well." I stare at her in shock.

"He's in a much better place now," and I nod.

She continues, "Tomorrow I'm going to dispose of his ashes in accordance with his will. I was his caretaker from the time he had the stroke right up until he passed last week. Your father was a good man."

"Yes. Yes, he was. A very good man."

She says his Celebration of Life will take place at J-J's Tavern tomorrow at 9am with the spreading of his ashes near the Lighthouse at 10am. My Father was a frequent customer at J-J's and had his own seat at the bar. It was the Santa Cruz version of *Cheers*. Everybody knew his name.

I thank Marian for her care and tell her we'll meet in the morning to dispose of his ashes. I walk back out to the porch to collect the cello. On the way to the car I see the Cheshire Cat crescent moon hovering low on the horizon.

I cry out to Max, "This has to end in a different way," so I run to the car and grab my laptop. "It has to."

I open up Final Draft and write:

EXT. FRONT PORCH - NIGHT

Chaz and his Dad are seated on the porch, playing "Hu moresque" by Dvorák. They conclude the piece and give each other a high-five.

CHAZ

Good job. We should go on tour.

GEORGE

Good seeing you again Chaz. I miss you.

CHAZ

I'll stop by a lot more. You'll get tired
of seeing me. Love you Dad.

GEORGE

Love you too, son.

They hug.

I'm about to write 'Fade Out' but I can't. The pain is too great. I pray for a sudden cloud of amnesia, like that guy in *Dark City*.

I lean against the car and in slo-mo slide down to the ground. Tears of pain, regret, self-loathing, and guilt. Max rests his head on my leg.

I glance at the crescent moon but this time it didn't resemble the smile of the Cheshire Cat.

I saw my Dad's smile.

Chapter 9

> "We travel not to escape life,
> but for life not to escape us."
> —Anonymous

> "Life has a funny way of sneaking up on you."
> —"Ironic"—Alanis Morrissette

*A*s I drive from the bungalow, Max says, "Chaz, everybody and everything is on a journey. Most of the roads are invisible to us until we're in that dimension. Like your dad. He's still traveling." I find the words comforting, until my wise-ass canine blows the feel-good moment by adding, "Hopefully he won't get stuck on a toll road," then snorts that Snoopy laugh HEH-HEH-HEH-HEH.

That night I went to a bar in Capitola and with a group of strangers, toasted 'journeys,' and after the bar closed down I found myself in a sleeping bag on the beach, peeking in on what the stars were up to. Waiting to see another meteor. Hoping for a sign.

The next morning Max and I drove to J-J's Tavern to meet Marian and a few people I didn't know who I assume were friends of my dad or at least patients of his dental practice, along with a Native American shaman, a priest, and a rabbi. George was always searching for answers to the great Questions of the Universe, so he studied numerous theologies and during various times of his life attempted to become a Jew, a Christian, and a Buddhist, but only succeeded in embracing agnosticism. All of the Holy Men became friends with my Dad and were scheduled to speak at this outdoor service, but as I pull up to the tavern all three are walking in together and it appears to be the beginning of an old joke, 'A shaman, a priest, and a rabbi walk into a bar...' but today there would be no punchline.

I went to the men's room and at the urinal someone had scrawled on the wall: 'It's better to give than receive.' Underneath it someone else wrote: 'Unless you're talking about head.'

The urn holding Dad's remains were placed on the same bar stool always reserved for him. The Holy Men had wonderful accolades to heap on my Dad, even though he never swallowed the religion elixir that each peddled. There was something the Shaman said though that resonated with me. He quoted Black Elk: "At the center of the universe dwells the Great Spirit and that center is really everywhere. It is within each of us."

We raised glasses of beer and wished George well on his journey and then drove to the Lighthouse where his ashes would be spread in a small field among several madrone trees, a place he liked to visit to meditate and write. Marian had the urn in the trunk of her car and gave me the honor since I'm his only kin. Marian also handed me Dad's violin case, as well as a thick, black loose-leaf binder and I thumb through it. Every page is handwritten and includes short stories, poems, a couple of stage plays, a novel, and random thoughts.

"His writings and the violin were the only things he wouldn't part with," Marian said. "Everything else got donated to Goodwill."

I walk to Pam Grier and put the binder and violin in the trunk.

An elderly gentleman, with a gray beard and a tam cocked to the side of his head and dressed in a kilt, played "Amazing Grace" on the bagpipes. My father loathed bagpipes, but I suspect the gentleman was hired by Marian who didn't know George's musical tastes and probably thought it would be appropriate because who doesn't want "Amazing Grace" played at their memorial service? Dad used to say, "Bagpipes sound like a flock of geese being strangled."

I opened the urn and as I flipped it upside down to scatter a gust of wind eddied up and the cremains flew into my face, hair, clothes and speckled many of the nearby guests as well. I couldn't help but laugh and the guests did too. Somebody said, "That's George getting in the last laugh."

As I was leaving, I noticed a couple about fifty feet away from the group but appearing to be interested in the service. I don't know the guy but I recognized the woman. It's Amber.

She's pregnant. Since we had been divorced less than a year, she must have met this guy and got preggers moments after the ink dried on our divorce papers. At least that's what I'd like to believe. It's the romantic in me.

Amber smiles and I hold out my hand but she ignores it and gives me a long hug and whispers "I'm so sorry about your dad."

I thank her for coming, "You were his favorite daughter-in-law." We laugh because she was his only daughter-in-law. She introduces the guy she's with, her fiancé named Rob, and we shake hands.

She saw the obit in the newspaper and wanted to pay her respect. I thank her and ask, "So when's the big day?" She sighs and beams at Rob, "About three weeks," and it's obvious they are very much in love. She then unloads a barrage of questions, "So how are you doing? Where are you working? Still writing? Seeing anybody?" and I responded with a vague, "Everything's great. Just livin' the dream," but Amber knows me well and I'm aware she knows there's more behind the door but it's locked. At least to her. She always knew when I stood at the precipice of a lie and was about to leap, but she didn't press it and try to pry out the answers from my secret place like she would have when we were married.

She smiles and whispers, "I hope you get everything you

want," and I know she's very sincere.

I manage a smile and mumble, "I'm sorry about everything. I'm really, really sorry," and she stares into my eyes and whispers, "No need to apologize. Like you used to say, 'Everyone's to blame and no one's to blame.'"

"But I'm sorry for being an asshole."

"You weren't an asshole."

"Yes I was."

"No you weren't," she says, no longer making eye contact. "Well... there were times when you were assholey."

I nod.

"Chaz, maybe I was assholey too."

Silence.

She's waiting for me to say, "No! You weren't assholey. It was all me!"

I only smile, and I can tell she wants me to own the asshole-iness, but I don't. I smile the smile of someone who just won a chess match. Yeah, it's still easy for us to revert to that jousting mode even though we're divorced.

I walk away knowing I'll never see her again. Nor do I want to.

After the service I drive mindless circles around town, my car and my thoughts all over the map, but realize it would be nice to track down Delta. Her phone number is no longer in service so I drive to her apartment but when I ring the doorbell a guy of about 40 answers and says she moved out about a year ago.

"I think I saw her one day at the Mystery Spot. Maybe she works there," he said, so I jump back into Pam Grier and hustle to the Mystery Spot.

The Mystery Spot has been around for about 70 years and touts itself as a 'gravitational anomaly,' although skeptics call it a scam. Some folks claim perception and laws of physics are twisted because of an alien spacecraft buried in the spot many years ago, causing odd things to happen, like balls to roll uphill, people to lean over without falling, and Democrats to win congressional seats in Alabama. Brainiacs will tell you that the buildings are slanted 20-degrees from the ground, even though our minds perceive the walls to be straight 90-degrees.

You sense you're being taken for a ride, but you don't care because it's still magical and fun. The same description could also be given of Santa Cruz. I always enjoy illusionists performing tricks and never want to know their secrets.

I ask a girl in the ticket booth if Delta works there and I'm in luck because she's just getting off her shift as a guide. I peek in past the fence and get a glimpse of her talking to a group of tourists. Delta looks the same as I remember: Short, spikey orange-red hair, lots of tats and piercings. I walk to the parking lot, jump in Pam Grier, fire up a joint, and wait.

Max is lying in the back seat, chewing on a rawhide strip. "You going to tell her your situation?" he asks.

"Think I should?"

"Honesty is always the best policy... unless you can get away with lying."

Delta comes out of the entrance and I blow the horn and yell "Delta!" She hesitates for a moment then screams "Oh, my fuckin' word!" and sprints to Pam Grier. I spring from the car and Delta bowls me over with a hug.

"Chaz! Holy shit! I haven't seen you for a long time. I thought you disappeared from the planet."

"Not yet. You look great. You haven't changed."

"You haven't changed either."

"No, still pissin' and moanin'."

"Hey, all that pissing and moaning is what makes you, you. Without it I wouldn't recognize you." She laughs.

"I've turned pissing and moaning into an art form."

But she had changed. For the better. She was electric. She

was jumper cable sparks from a battery to bare metal.

"Got a few more tats. Wanna see the latest?" She unzips her pants and yanks down the front to just above her pubic area and points to a tattoo reading 'Mystery Spot' with an arrow pointing down.

"Nice!" I laugh.

She giggles, "It's not a mystery to most people!"

I hand her the joint. She seems much happier than I remember. Almost manic. "Jump in," I tell her and she screams "Wheeeeeee."

Delta eases into the Caddy and says she's met the love of her life. A woman named Jan and I'm glad for her because everyone deserves to be happy. As we drive downtown to Pacific Avenue I think about my dad and mom and Amber and Delta and how things are not what they used to be. Thomas Wolfe nailed it.

Before going to a bar Delta wants to stop at her apartment and freshen up. We're greeted by Jan, her partner. Jan's very Goth with jet black hair and black clothes. She's also very tall and very thin and with her large, black Doc Marten's resembles an exclamation point. Which is the perfect complementary character standing next to Delta.

I ask Jan to come along with us, but she has a client coming over in a few minutes but would love to take a rain check. Jan tells me she works full time as a cab driver, but she and Delta also have a side business: They sell plaster of Paris molds of male and female genitalia.

"Come here." Delta grabs my arm and I follow her to a back room where the walls and shelves are decorated with hundreds of plaster sets of breasts, along with vaginas and penises with testicles, all looking very realistic, complete with pubic hair that is placed into the plaster before it hardens, and others painted with glow in the dark psychedelic colors or decorated with polka dots or stars. One set of male genitals is painted to look like a basketball player: The penis head is the 'head' of the player, the shaft has a numbered jersey and shorts, and the testicles are painted basketballs so it gives the illusion the 'player' is dribbling two balls.

Another plaster of Paris penis is painted to look like President Nixon. Tricky Dick.

Delta comes out of their bedroom and asks, "What do you think, Chaz? Wanna get a life mask?"

"Delta, you've graduated. You used to make death masks."

"Death is sooooooo yesterday!"

She embraces Jan and says, "We'll cast your dick for you and let you pick out the colors. We can paint stars or stripes or op-art on it."

"Monet water lilies," Jan interjects.

"Whatever. It's all very tastefully done."

Jan nods.

"Yeah, with Christmas coming up, that would sure make a nice stocking stuffer."

Delta smiles at my sarcasm then says, "I'm ready, let's go" and we leave.

We drive on Pacific Avenue and the change is striking. Downtown was once a festive, noisy, colorful aggregation of creativity exploding from the sidewalks with street musicians and performance artists, panhandlers, and oddballs, but the plague of gentrification crept in and strangled the city, and the colorful and quirky people have been eased out, or sometimes forced out by the BMW driving yuppies who made a financial killing in Silicon Valley, bought up real estate in Santa Cruz, and then influenced members of the City Council to change ordinances and make the city more "respectful." Downtown no longer had the fun, edgy, street fair vibe it used to. It was now like driving your car around the inside of a Brooks Brothers store. I didn't recognize downtown Santa Cruz and perhaps the feeling was mutual. You can rest assured the suits of the world usually find a way to fuck things up.

I remember one street performer who called himself 'Puppet Man' but was perhaps the worst puppeteer of all time. He had a small, make-shift stage and his show always centered around the exploits of James Bond. There was a marionette named James Bond and other marionettes were either Bond girls or villains and the guy would play the James Bond theme on a boom box while 'performing' his skit. He used his own nasally voice for each character and never even attempted to give each marionette a different voice. Invariably the marionette strings would get tangled after a few minutes of the characters 'running' or 'fighting' each other on the stage and that would be the end of the performance. It was sad but laughable and folks would stare wide-eyed at this train wreck but always left tips in his upside down cowboy hat because they felt sorry for him. In a perverse way he sure was entertaining. To this day, whenever I hear the James Bond theme I don't think of Sean Connery or Pierce Brosnan. But as we drive down Pacific Avenue that night, Puppet Man is nowhere in sight and the world is a much emptier place because of it.

Max follows as we enter a sushi restaurant on the wharf, a place Delta sings the praises of and knows the chef. But Delta knows just about everyone in Santa Cruz, either intellectually, spiritually, or carnally. Some of those friends can even boast of hitting the trifecta.

Delta calls herself a quasi-vegetarian because she only eats animals that have died of natural causes, so when she inquiries about the eel sushi I ask the chef if the eel died of old age. He laughs and asks Delta, "Where'd you find this guy?" and she deadpans, "Under a rock." Delta orders "the usual" which is cucumber sushi. I tell the chef, "Make that the usual for the un-usual."

The conversation and the laughter and the sake flows freely. She talks about her art: "It's not uncommon for guys, after having their genitals cast in plaster of Paris, to ask if I can add an extra inch or two of plaster. One guy asked, 'Can you make my nuts bigger?'"

Her relationship with Jan: "We'll grow old together." On being a lesbian: "I realize you and I finally have something in common. We both love women." We even talk about the proper etiquette of passing gas, and she says, "Here's what you should do when walking a trail and you have to fart: First check to see if anyone is behind you, and then only fart if it's someone you don't like or someone who's deaf or missing a nose. Nothing worse than drifting through someone else's fart cloud."

As I we walk to Pam Grier, Max tells me that Delta has a dog by her side but she can't see or hear it talk yet, but she will in 24 days.

My jaw dropped. It was the same feeling I had when I got the news that Marcel Marceau had died. I was speechless. Which is exactly what he would have wanted.

"No! You kidding me?"

"Motorcycle accident," Max says.

"No way!"

"I don't make this up. Of course, why should you believe me? I'm only a fucking talking dog."

I drive Delta home and we walk to her front door. I hug her for a very long time and didn't want to let go.

On the drive back I don't feel very well. Sort of sick to my stomach and my head is clogged. I hadn't felt this nauseous since the first time I heard "Wing Beneath My Wings." As I trudge on the warm sand while carrying my sleeping bag to the Boardwalk beach, my *Charlie's Angels* ring-tone sounds and the text NOT NOW is displayed on the screen. "Jesus, what the hell..." I say to no one in particular.

That night I popped a Marinol and smoked a Blue Frost on the beach at the Boardwalk and flashbacked to a time when I had reached a personal ebb and feared the tide would never turn. I closed my eyes and spiraled into a daydream, or maybe a nightmare.

It was Christmas eve. I was 18, before I met Amber, and very much alone. I didn't want to be with my folks and I didn't have any friends to hang with. It was raining and I took my fake ID to a strip club in Bakersfield. The place was empty, except for one other drunk at the end of the bar with his head in his hands, the bartender who checked his watch with bored frequency, and five strippers. One stripper after another paraded onto the stage, inserting quarters into an old Wurlitzer jukebox, and with half-hearted gyrations removed their clothes. I soon realized that management probably couldn't get the really pretty girls to work Christmas eve, it was definitely not the A-Team, but I was drunk and it was naked female flesh and for all I cared it could have been Bea Arthur and *The Golden Girls* and I would have watched.

Each dancer looked bored, wishing they were somewhere else on Christmas eve, as they performed their lackadaisical bumps and grinds and reluctantly went through the motions of sliding up and down a pole. It was getting close to a midnight closing when the bartender yelled, "Last call."

For some reason or other, maybe she got into the holiday spirit or just felt sorry for the few pathetic patrons, but the last stripper put several quarters into the jukebox and grabbed a candy cane hanging from a nearby Charley Brown Christmas tree. Here I was, drunk and alone on Christmas eve, watching a stripper gyrate to "Little Drummer Boy":

BRRUMMM...BRRUMMM...

BRRUMMM-BUMMM-BUMMM

The dancer then sat on the edge of the stage, spread open her legs and inserted a candy cane into her vah-jay-jay, threw her head back and yelled, "Here's your present, boys! Merry Fuckin'

Christmas everybody!"

The drunk at the end of the bar raised an empty shot glass and mumble-slurred "God bless us everyone!" which made me ponder what the future held for Tiny Tim if he became an alcoholic. I pushed away my unfinished beer and began to sob in self-pity.

And that, boys and girls, is what the spirit of Christmas is all about.

I left the club, turned my collar to the wind and rain, and trudged back to my one room studio. One very merry couple who were very giggly in love passed me with a very jolly, "Merry Christmas!" and I murmured, "Fuck you, but Happy New Year!" and they laughed in hysterics. I realized then that I had to stop living off my parent's handouts and start a career before I drowned. It was my Ebenezer Scrooge moment after he had been visited by the ghost of Christmas future. The very next day I applied to several radio stations.

Chapter 10

"Every day is a journey, and the journey itself is home."
— Matsuo Basho

"I want something else, I'm not listening
when you say good-bye."
— "Semi Charmed Life" — Third Eye Blind

The sun is a melting candle of dripped oranges and reds sprinkled on the white cloud bank above the Santa Cruz Mountains as Max and I cruise south on Highway 1. I'm sneezing and my nose is stuffed up. My head is a mucous factory. Max calls it being "Awash in a sea of snot," and I ask him if that's a line from a Keats poem. He replies, "Yes, Ode to a Runny Nose." I once thought of writing a parody of a Noel Coward play involving a character with a very bad head cold. In a scene, a young English girl greets a stranger at the door who asks to see her dad, and she replies, "Father is in the drawing room expectorating."

I reach into the glove compartment for MY JOURNEY. "Now where to?" I ask Max. I think about what may lie ahead without ever wanting to go back. You can't move forward if you're always looking in your rear view mirror.

"You're writing it," Max says, "It's your journey." I open the book at random and watch the page become animated like a movie on a screen and it plays out a panoramic view of Monterey, with pelicans perched on the pier and boats bobbing in the harbor and then a slow pan of Cannery Row. Monterey, a favorite of Clint Eastwood, where *Play Misty for Me* and *Sudden Impact* were shot. I decide to flip through the book to see what the final page holds but there is no final page, and every time I think I've reached the last page, more pages suddenly pop up in this bizarre book that has no beginning and no end.

I turn pages toward the front of MY JOURNEY, and stop at a page where I'm in the high school principal's office. I think I hold the Harbor High School record for most detentions in a single year. I'm still waiting to receive the trophy. At least be invited back to put my handprints in wet cement.

I flip pages toward the front of MY JOURNEY and see ancient images in sepia tones of a Japanese woman in a kimono standing on a footbridge in a garden, a young girl with a large family surrounded by palm trees, an old tintype of a solemn black man dressed in a Union uniform. I don't know these people. At least I'm not aware of knowing these people, but I have an uncanny feeling they know me.

Max says, "You probably never saw *The Steel Helmet*, did you?" Max doesn't wait for the answer he already knows. "It's a movie I wrote and directed about the Korean War and instead of having 'The End' after the final credits roll, I included 'There is no end to this story.' Capeesh?"

After a stop at a Safeway to buy honey and brandy, we're on our way. A local jazz station plays "All Blues" and I sip my concoction and steal glimpses of the Pacific Ocean and the heaven above and I'm engulfed by the lyrics:

"The sea, the sky, and you and I,
I know we're all blues, all shades, all hues."

I think of Clitty and see her precious smile when she said my music was "cello-licious" and wonder when we'll reconnect. I feel different about her than anyone else. All my life I always looked for relationships below the waist, but now I wanted the whole package. Max calls her a "tumbleweed" with random thoughts being blown about in no particular pattern and in no particular direction, and I realize the same description can be said of me. Right now I'm missing that tumbleweed. Missing enough to make a commitment?

We pass a recently harvested strawberry field in Watsonville and see a small roadside stand advertising fresh picked fruit so I ease Pam Grier off the highway and onto the dirt parking lot. A pretty woman in her mid-20's is behind the counter talking in Spanish to a young boy who is busy packing artichokes. She wears a colorful summer dress and her shiny black hair moves in the breeze like raven wings in slow motion. I approach and say "Buenos dias" but she replies with something which I don't understand then smiles after realizing that I speak little Spanish. Her perfect smile is sunflowers on a late August afternoon and her voice nectar. I'm sure a hummingbird would flutter at her mouth to slide its bill in and out of her sweet lips. I would give anything to be that hummingbird. I take a container of strawberries and make small talk about the weather and she realizes I'm stuffed up and suggests I also get broccoli and bell peppers to help my immune system.

"On vacation?" she asks.

"Just exploring,"

"I like your car. My uncle had one like that in Tijuana when I was a little girl. But his was red and it wasn't a convertible, but it had those big fins like it could fly to Jupiter." She giggles and her laughter is a capriccio born of heaven.

I've had lots of folks drool over Pam Grier since it's so long and solid and powerful. When guys look at the Caddy they have car envy. It's definitely car porn.

The boy, who I assume is her son, interrupts with something in Spanish and she firmly responds in Spanish and I gather from his angry reaction that he wanted to stop working and go play with his friends, but he scowls and continues with the artichokes.

I introduce myself and she tells me her name is Valentina. In the explosion of that moment I want to tell Valentina to close up the produce stand and run off with me and I don't care if you're married and yes, you can bring along your son but please I want to get to know you because right now I would walk barefoot across a bed of scorpions just to caress your cheek and you're the center of my universe and no, you can't go home first and pack a suitcase because I want you now and I would do anything for you so hurry grab some strawberries get in the car and let's fly to Jupiter.

But I don't.

Max smiles because he knows what I'm thinking and he says, "How quickly you forgot about your little tumbleweed."

"I haven't forgotten. Just trying to stay in practice, that's all."

I would so like to ask Valentina if she wants to ride in my car but I fear that I would never bring her back to the produce stand and to her son and to her life of which I will never be a part of, so I smile and say, "Thanks, Valentina" and she says "Nice meeting you, Chaz" as I trudge toward Pam Grier and put space between me and a very delicious dream.

Max consoles me with "Maybe next time around" as I fire up the car and wave goodbye to paradise. At least the entire time I ignored the shouts of Dum Phuk in my subconscious to "Grab her! Tie her up. Throw her in the trunk. She'll eventually fall in love with you. It's a Stockholm Syndrome thing." I figure I must be getting more mature to no longer pay attention to the rants of my inner lunatic. Dum Phuk, get out of my brain and never come back. Good riddance!

Back on Highway 1, I think about my lack of friends and relationships. I've always been somewhat of a loner, not the ominous time-bomb personality of a Travis Bickle, but someone who easily makes friends but doesn't have the interest to keep them.

I've always believed that when it comes to company, I have my own, and sometimes that's better than nothing. Well, okay, I'm learning that it's rarely better. I miss Clitty and I'm getting close to asking Max to make her reappear.

All the way to Monterey I sneeze and blow my nose into tissues and continue sipping the mixture of honey and whiskey, not sure if the concoction is getting rid of my cold or just making the germs drunk. I flash back to Paula Walker, the love of my life in the first grade. Paula was so cute but the only thing I remember about her was her runny nose. It seemed as though she always had sinus drip. The mad crush may have lasted three weeks, which is forever when you're six years old. I wonder if Paula ever cleared up her perpetual head cold.

My mind now pinballs to Sandra and I thank Eros and Cupid and Venus for not bringing us together. Sandra was very much like her mother, both extreme gregarious blondes, very animated, wore lots of pink, and over-the-top bubbly. Sandra could kill you with her perkiness. But underneath that facade of effervescence lurked a bitch who always harped about some guy not being wealthy enough or handsome enough or intelligent enough. Her poor father was emasculated and anyone who ended up with Sandra would surely have to check his balls at the door. Under her mom's tutelage, Sandra was a C.I.T: Castrator in Training. At the age of sixteen I thought I wanted to be with her but in retrospect all I wanted was to spend a few weeks getting to know her breasts.

Like her mom, Sandra had huge breasts, larger than your average honeydew melons, the largest boobs in high school and she used those assets to lure guys into her web and then devour them. That December I took Sandra to the Snow Ball and she kvetched about the type of flower on the corsage, the limo I rented was not long enough, and the restaurant not fancy enough. She wished I played guitar rather than cello. She preferred quarterbacks over

JV basketball team bench warmers. She didn't think I was making a wise financial decision to aspire to be a disc jockey rather than a dentist. She didn't like the crowd I hung out with, especially after one of my wise-ass friends wrote in the yearbook under my photo: 'Voted most likely to be found shot in a motel room.' Sandra was a grinder, but oh what tits, and when you're a horny guy you can stumble through a gauntlet of bitchiness just for the opportunity to feel someone up.

I never got into the rah-rah bullshit of high school. I think the principal and teachers knew that and it angered them, even though I aced all the tests and was chosen to be the class valedictorian. More about that clown show later.

I tried out for the J-V basketball team and since I was one of twelve who tried out, I got on the team. But I always rode the pine and never got into a game unless we were losing by a gazillion points with ten seconds to go in the second half. I had the vertical leap of your average box turtle. I thought of quitting but I stayed on the team to support a couple of friends who played, and I always thought it strange how we'd play a team from a religious school, like St. Francis Academy, and we'd kick their asses all over the court. Even though prior to the game that team formed a circle on the sideline, bowed their heads, and prayed to God for a victory. God must have had money riding on our team.

I never had to bust my hump for grades. I seldom studied but aced all the exams. It just came easy, like breathing. I always retained everything I ever read, having a photographic memory. But high school was boring and the teachers were boring and I thought it to be an unfortunate place to be trapped for four years, like a prison sentence, but with a slightly better rating than Ju-Vee Hall. Sandra Big Tits loved high school though, especially being a cheerleader and being the center of the universe. I noticed when she started cheer-leading as a sophomore, there seemed to be more and more fathers attending their son's games. Kind of like that movie where Lester stares at Angela dancing on the gymnasium floor.

In spite of Sandra being a harpy, the Snow Ball turned out to be a minor victory as I did get my hand under her bra but that was as far as things would go, although that was enough fuel to ignite my masturbatory fire that night. I figured another date would move things further along on the road to bliss, so I spent fifty bucks for a pair of tickets to a program of holiday music by Tchaikovsky and that Saturday night I took the ball buster to the *Nutcracker*. After the show we made out in the car, steamed up the windows, and went all the way. It was exciting. At least for me. Over the next two weeks we would have sex on several more occasions, but she always seemed detached, distant, and I felt like a lone polar bear riding an ice floe.

While making love Sandra never whimpered, groaned, or screamed. She probably made more noise in a library. One time I lost it when in the heat of the moment I caught her checking her watch and that resulted in a big fight. The next attempt at sex was a disaster as I was unable to get hard, and eventually having sex with her was almost as much fun as pruning an apple tree on Arbor Day. The ill-fated relationship lasted about five weeks.

As we near Monterey, I realize I'm doing a lot of reminiscing, but if you have no future what else can you dwell on? I usually try to not dwell on the pain of yesterday but maybe there are lessons to be mined. Max tells me to be more like a dog and stay in the moment. The Here and Now.

"Concentrate on your breathing. Practice mindfulness. Take a deep breath and slowly let it out. Think only of the air entering your lungs and then flowing out."

This from a dog who pants and drools after licking his crotch. He's suddenly getting all Buddhist on me. I take his advice and inhale a deep breath of Blue Dream and feel better already.

I look for a diner for breakfast, remembering that old adage my mother used to say, "Feed a cold and starve a fever." Or was it "Starve a cold and feed a fever?" Either way something's got to eat so I pull into a strip mall where a small cantina advertises 'Authentic Mexican Food' which is too bad because I really wanted 'Fake Mexican Food.'

Max follows me in where I grab an empty booth and leaf through the menu. I tell the waiter about my cold and he recommends sopa de tortilla. "I fix it up good for you, Señor. Your cold be gone like that," he says, snapping his fingers. In a few minutes he returns with a bowl of soup, and even though it was very tasty I struggled to eat it since I was sweating from the added Chile peppers and jalapeños, my hair and shirt were soaked as I performed self-immolation by releasing an inner Hell. I glanced at the front counter and the waiter and cook were smiling and nodding and talking in Spanish as they watched me catch fire. They probably were waiting for the spontaneous combustion of a gringo. But I could feel my sinuses clear as the cold germs were quickly being burned alive.

As I paid my bill the waiter asked, "You okay, Señor?" and I gasped "Never... felt... better," but in all honesty I was thinking of ripping the fire extinguisher off the wall and spraying the contents down my throat.

"What did you put in that soup?"

"Red Savina habanero," he grins. "So hot you would want to take a bite from the Sun to cool down. Here, amigo" he hands me a paper cup loaded with ice cubes.

"Thanks," I hiss and filled my mouth with cubes. I wave and manage a smile to the waiter and cook as I practically slide out the door on a tidal wave of perspiration. Mucho fuego caliente!

There's a chill in the air but in my overheated condition the convertible top comes down. Pam Grier's tires humming on Highway 1 whisper that everything is possible and the promise of a new day awaits and I hear Vivaldi's "Spring" from the *Four*

Seasons. Years ago my parents drove the Northeast on Route 1 and the uneven pavement and occasional potholes provided an ominous future, the futile pessimism and dark melancholia of a Shostakovitch String Quartet. When I mention this to Max he shrugs, as much as his little dog shoulders allow him to shrug, and says, "Knock off the weed. Highways all sound the same." I tell him, "These roads are the perfect place to smoke. It's why they're called 'high'-ways."

I am feeling better and the head cold has all but disappeared. My throat though may have permanent third-degree burns from the Red Savina habanero. That stuff is potent. Maybe it could even cure cancer.

Max and I drive along Cannery Row, past boutiques and cafes, still alive with tourists even though Labor Day has passed. We find a parking space near San Carlos Beach Park and a brief walk takes us to the pier to watch sea lions and pelicans and gulls, and the low tide reveals many starfish and sea anemones cling-ing to shiny rocks in the surf. A group of scuba divers ease their way from the beach into the surf and disappear below the waves. About thirty yards from shore a sea otter lies on its back in a bed of kelp, floating on the currents, warmed by the ocean breeze, oblivious to the anger and sadness and indifference of the uni-verse and appearing to be in control of its own world.

"That's the life. Contented. No cares, no worries," I tell Max. "I'd like to be reincarnated as a sea otter."

Max points to a fin slicing through the ocean surface about fifty yards away from the otter and then submerging to the depths below.

"Okay, on second thought, maybe reincarnated as a shark."

"Then get hunted so your fins are made in to soup."

"Damn, it's a no-win situation."

Max leans in close. "It's your ego. Remove your ego from the equation and the ride is a helluva lot smoother. You think you're in control, you want to be in control, but you're not. No one is in control. Nothing is in control. Existence is pain and chaos and fear and there's nothing you can do about it. So just close your little otter eyes and surrender to the energy of the wave. Let it go."

"I'm just trying to find the Answer to it all."

"You have a better chance of finding D. B. Cooper," Max says.

I burst out laughing because lately Max is sounding like some New Age bullshit artist and I tell him so and he laughs too, but I know he's laughing at me and not with me and he blurts out, "Oh, you poor little insignificant speck of cosmic dust. Everything is just a minor annoyance. That's all! You've got a lot to learn!"

"So much to learn, so little time!"

"You know what, Chaz, let's script it."

"Script what?"

"Some random thought from your strange little brain. Maybe one of your latest dreams. I could use a good laugh and you could use practice writing."

I run to Pam Grier, grab the laptop from under the front seat, and dash back to the beach to write the dream I had the previous night:

EXT. FOREST - NIGHT

A flock of crows, with human heads, the gama yuns of Russian mythology, swoop down next to a wooden table under a full moon. A piano soundtrack of Satie's "Gnossienne" plays. The heads on the gama yuns are people familiar to Chaz: his parents, Amber, relatives, friends and teachers. The creatures flutter in from the heavens grasping jigsaw puzzle pieces in their b e a k s and carefully place each piece in its correct place on the table. The puzzle, a head-to-toe portrait of Chaz, takes shape, except for one piece missing on the side of his head. FADE UP stabbing violins like those used by Bernard Herrmann. The crows are wide-eyed in panic as they dart through the trees in search of the lone puzzle piece. A wind picks up and blows the puzzle pieces off the table and scatters them onto the ground and then they become airborne and soar above the trees and vanish into the night sky.

"What do you think, Max?"

"Interesting. I could see Tim Burton shooting it. Quite an insight into your psyche."

"But do you like it?"

"I like it."

"So it gives you a hard-on?"

Max laughs and says, "Yes, my boy. A huge, huge hard-on!"

Chapter 11

"We travel, some of us forever, to seek other places,
other lives, other souls."
— Anais Nin

"I take a deep breath and I get real high
And I scream from the top of my lungs
What's going on?"
— "What's Up?"—4 Non Blondes

After driving south on Highway 1 we find a beach near Big Sur. While sitting in the sand my head starts to ache, and the pain intensifies as I squint my eyes and exhale an anguished "Fuck, that hurts." And then a wave of nausea. I take a Marinol as my brain feels like it's being squeezed by the strong hand of some invisible ogre. My hands are shaking as I reach inside my fedora for a joint of Vortex, fire it up and take a deep breath. After a few minutes the headache loosens its death grip and I fall back onto the mother warm sand, my breathing slows and the searing pain and nausea ebbs. But I know it will return again like an angry tide and keep returning with more frequency until...

"A bad one, huh?" Max asks, and I nod like I had just stepped on broken glass. I take another drag.

"Felt like death."

"You'll know it when it really happens."

"Well Max, I'm still a stranger to death. I guess I haven't quite got the knack of it yet."

A flock of seagulls hover above, surfing a sea breeze. They seem harmless enough. This isn't Bodega Bay. A few yards away one of the gulls lands on a bronzed piece of driftwood near a patchwork quilt of yellow and pink ice plants and a couple of green leafy chalk live-forevers that are nestled between a mound of gray pocked rocks. I recently learned that ice plants are native to South Africa and are an invasive species to California. The ice plant always seemed so Californian like it should be wearing sunglasses and have its own agent. The bird tilts its head and eyes me, hoping that I'm eating something that I drop onto the sand so it can pounce on the morsel and fly off. Maybe it knows I'm consuming a hallucinogenic and wants a drag.

I blow a big cloud toward the gull and he shakes his head and ruffles his feathers and I smile and blow more vapor to the bird and he hops off the log and edges a few feet closer onto the rocks. Max is enjoying this scene as I hold up the remainder of the joint and ask the gull, "You wanna hit?" so I snuff out the burn on an ice plant and check with my index finger to make sure the fire is out then flick the small roach toward the gull and he jumps on it, stabbing it with his beak, and quickly flies away about twenty yards to the beach, landing in the wet sand where the waves tease the shore. The bird swallows the marijuana and it lets out a screech and I tell Max, "Jerry Garcia has returned as a seagull."

The bird then flies away with about forty or fifty other birds. "Flock of Seagulls," Max says and I sing:

> "I just ran. I ran all night and day.
> I couldn't get away."

as we watch the seagulls fly away parallel to the shore and I carefully search the flock for that one erratic gull who's flying in circles or making loops or nosediving into the ocean or flying upside down or just plain "Truckin." Where's Jerry? All the gulls look the same and there is no one gull eating more than its share of fish or lying on its back laughing at images it imagines in cloud formations or reading passages from Ferlinghetti.

"Do you know his poem *Dog*?" Max asks.

I shrug.

Max says, "Ferlinghetti says the dog is 'looking like a living question mark into the great gramophone of puzzling existence.'"

"I can relate to that."

I lay my head down onto the warm sand and it engulfs me like a lover as I sink into its soul and become a part of it and close my eyes with the sun on my face and slip away for perhaps a minute or a millennium because time is a blur. But in a wink I sense a nearby presence and my eyes flicker open to see a woman sitting several feet away on a driftwood log. She's staring at me but also looking past me, with a bemused smile and her long brown hair lightly tossed by the breeze. The woman wears a long cream-colored dress and carries a pink parasol that seems to have been crafted in another era from spun cotton candy. The lady is speaking to someone so I turn around to see if someone is behind me, but there's no one else on the beach but her and me.

She says, "Joe, when I say the line, 'My darling will come back. I know in my heart he will,' do you want me to turn to the ocean and look off in the distance or just fall to my knees?" Who is she talking to? Her gaze continues right through me as she nods her head and after a few moments says, "My darling will come back. I know in my heart he will," then falls to her knees and sobs for about thirty seconds, and then rises with a smile and asks, "How was that? That a take?"

Her voice sounds like Kathrine Hepburn, with the upper crust lilt of an exclusive finishing school in Connecticut when she pronounces words like 'haaht' and 'dahling' and she smells of lavender soap. Max is also curious about what is happening.

I ask, "Max, what's going on here?"

"She's on another plane of existence."

"You mean like a parallel universe?"

"Yes. Ask her what movie she's making."

"Excuse me, miss..." but the lady is startled and furrows her brow before turning away and asking, "Joe, did you just speak to me?" then with an embarrassed laugh says, "I swear I just heard someone say, 'Excuse me, miss.'"

Max urges me, "Tell her who you are. Find out if she's in the future or the past."

"Ah miss, I know you can't see me but I know you can hear me and I can see you..."

The lady looks wild-eyed as she turns and furtively looks around and says, "I think I'd better sit down. Maybe it's the sun..." and she collapses onto the driftwood.

Chaz continues, "I'm sorry, I don't mean to frighten you but we seem to be in parallel universes. In two different times and things are getting crossed up. I don't know how long this time-space convergence is going to last. What's your name?"

She doesn't respond.

"Please. What's your name?"

The lady takes a deep breath and murmurs "Pauline" as her eyes dart about.

"Are you shooting a movie?"

With trepidation she says, "Yes. I can't see you. Where are you? Who are you?"

"My name is Chaz. Where I am it's September 28th, 1999. What time are you in?"

"It's..." she stands up and looks past Chaz and says, "Yes, a glass of water, thanks," and someone hands her a glass and she drinks. Chaz sees that her image is fading.

"What time is it? Tell me about the movie."

The lady closes her eyes and whispers, "It's July 18, 1915."

Max says, "A silent. With a voice like Kate Hepburn that no one will ever hear."

"Why does she say a line if it's a silent?"

"Because the audiences back then could read lips."

I still don't know if she entered my future or I entered her past. Either way this time-travel bedazzle has occurred without the help of Doc Brown installing a flux capacitor.

She continues, "We're shooting *The Threads of Fate* and my director is over there. Mr. De Grasse and..."

I stare at her image but it is vaporizing, with the beach and the waves coming into view beyond her. I shout, "Pauline? Pauline!"

I hear a very distant whisper "Chaz..." a voice from another time, and then an even more faint "Chaz..." and then she disappears like the receding tide on the sand.

I'm blown away and tell Max, "Was that the coolest thing or what? How'd that happen?"

Max says, "Damned if I know."

"I thought you know everything. This ever happen to you before?"

"No, but I've heard of it happening. Somehow the four-dimensional space-time continuum gets messed up, journeys crisscross, worm holes appear within wormholes, time gets tweaked and turned inside out, the laws of physics get shredded, and..."

"A friend of mine once said the same thing would happen if you nuked a mirror in a microwave."

"Then we'll need a DeLorean and not a Caddy."

"Isn't there some big creator who oversees everything that ever happened and everything that will happen? A Supreme Being who could have caused this to happen."

Max laughs. "A 'God'? Is that what you're asking?"

I nod and Max continues, "There was a God who created everything billions of years ago, did a pretty good job until the sixth day when he created Man and then he was judged to be insane so they locked him away. I'm told the next universe will be created by a committee, that way they can spread the blame around."

"So you do know just about everything."

"I do know what God spelled backwards is."

I light up a joint and take a deep drag. "It's all too much for me to comprehend. But wasn't it Socrates who said, 'It takes great wisdom to admit you know nothing.'"

"Your problem, Chaz, is that you're thinking in reality. You have to start thinking in abstract and then everything will make perfect sense. Like Einstein said, 'Time is a stubbornly persistent illusion.'"

I fall back onto the sand and realize I'm lying next to a chalk live-forever plant and smile at the irony. I don't understand any of it but perhaps I'm not supposed to because things will play out the way they are supposed to play out and there's nothing I can say or do that will alter that fact. For twenty years I've had to deal with the rhythm of life, but now I have to get used to the unseen rhythm of death. Maybe grasping the meaning of it all would be like trying to put a bra on an eel: It would be difficult, but more importantly, what would be the point?

I only know I'm afraid. Afraid of the next moment. The unknown. The inevitable, and no amount of New Age babble from a talking dog trying to draw life's lessons from film noir is going to make me feel any more comfortable about the future.

The beach seems like the right place to spend the night so I walk back to the car and grab my sleeping bag and a bottle of tequila, a small jar of salt, a couple of lime wedges, and several Reese's Peanut Butter Cups.

I blend a handful of dry and a can of dog food for Max and then open a can of Coors and pour a little into his dog bowl. I tell him, "I know you can't hold your liquor, but let's celebrate."

"Celebrate what?"

"Oh... just being a part of it all. Just to rejoice in the Moment. I'm here. You're here."

He takes a few licks of the beer then makes a face like he has a thorn in his paw, but continues drinking. I lick salt off the back of my hand, take a deep chug of tequila, and bite into the lime. "Here's to the Goddess of Blue Agave!" I shout, and Max continues downing the Coors.

Max looks me in the eye and asks, "You ever see my movie *Shock Corridor*?"

"It's on my bucket list."

"The main character is a newspaper man trying to win a Pulitzer Prize so he goes undercover in a loony bin after he convinces everybody that he's crazy."

"Good premise. I'm getting a hard-on."

"Every one of my movies was gritty realism."

"And every Russ Meyer movie was titty realism."

Max ignores me and continues, "So the psychiatrist says to him, 'What's wrong with you is characterized by childish behavior, hallucinations, and emotional deterioration.'"

"And your point?"

"I'm describing you, Chaz. You're over-medicating yourself."

"This observation from a dog getting drunk on Coors."

"I'm serious."

"Helps ease the pain."

"Escaping like your dad did inside a bottle."

"Yeah, I'm so fucked up I believe I hear a talking dog."

"Believe what you want. Your life will be vastly improved by self-reflection, not self-medication."

"Don't get preachy."

"Would explain your kleptomania and pyromania."

"Hey, I haven't done that shit for years. I was in therapy for a long time."

"Too much booze makes you do stupid things," Max says, then teeter-stumbles to a nearby ice plant, lifts a hind leg to pee, loses his balance and topples over. I smile and applaud. Max, a bit humiliated, gets back on all fours and manages a smile. "All

I'm saying," he says, "Grab life by the throat and spit in its face. Don't run away from it."

I'm about to pour the rest of the Coors into his dog bowl but think better of it. The bar is shut off to that canine lush.

"You're talking about Clitty," I say.

"Things went bad in high school so you quit. Things went bad with your father, so you quit. Things went bad with Amber, so you quit. I'm seeing a pattern of retreat."

"Yes, Max. Yes, Max. Yes, Max" I say, nodding my head up and down.

"And don't neck-fuck me!" he says. "You know I don't like to be neck-fucked!"

I close my eyes and exhale deep, the ocean breeze and pounding surf now providing the soundtrack as I think about choices I've made and decisions I didn't think through. I flash-back to the time in high school when I stole a tennis racket even though I never played the game. I didn't want the racket. I had no use for the racket. But I had a need to take the racket. My psychologist diagnosed me as a kleptomaniac, until he caught me trying to steal his watch. Then I became "a common thief."

My mind jumps to thoughts of my mom. She was so happy with her new husband and new life. They sent me an all-expense paid round trip airline ticket to stay with them for a month in Spain and I was to fly from SFO on a Thursday morning, but that Sunday night I got a call from a police official in Barcelona informing me of the car accident. I had just spoken to my mom the day before, and that Saturday would be the last time I heard her voice.

I tear up and pound my fist into the sand, then break down in uncontrollable sobs. But after a few moments I feel an energy next to me. A warm, powerful Presence, all loving and knowing, I feel a oneness with a gentle, trusting and compassionate force, and I wipe the tears from my eyes and smile. No words needed to be said, no apologies needed to be made, but I felt my mom and I were communicating, and she let me know that everything is good and there is no need for worry and no need to be afraid. It was almost the Bardol Thodol of the *Tibetan Book of the Dead*. The 'liberation' of experiencing the death plane.

I speak to the Presence. "I'm so sorry for all the pain I caused you and Dad. So very sorry."

I sigh and watch the orange sun being consumed by the ocean and ponder what this moment means, and the next moment and the one to follow. Moments that are irretrievable. Scraps of time rising like ashes into the air never to be experienced again.

Chapter 12

"Not all those who wander are lost."
— J.R.R. Tolkien

"Anywhere you go, I'll follow you down
I'll follow you down, but not that far."
—"Follow You Down" —Gin Blossums

I awake from a very vivid dream to the sound of ocean waves, the breeze, distant gulls, my heart, the breath of the universe. In the dream, Clitty appeared as a large kite of vibrant colors, a thousand feet tall and hovering a mile above, smiling down at me, her dress and hat rippling in the warm air currents, the kite string wrapped around her finger with the other end of the string held in the mouth of a dolphin breaking the sea green waves far away on the azure horizon. Clitty beckons to me, luring me to join her, asking me to play in the clouds to shape each white vapor into images of new animals that have never existed, pleading with me to float above the earth together until the sun disappears then we'll grab the stars to rearrange them in iambic pentameter in the night sky as sonnets to our love.

Max interrupts with, "Where to now?"

I'm not going to tell him about the dream. "I need a stimulant. Let's find a Starbucks."

"Blueberry muffin time!" he salivates.

I roll up the sleeping bag, collect the dog bowl and the tequila bottle and walk back to the car. Back on Highway 1 we head north and find a Starbucks in Salinas. I'm not so sure you ever find a Starbucks. They seem to have an unsettling way of finding you, like you're a young coed alone on an island with Freddy

Krueger.

I pull into the parking lot and enter the store and order a grande with sugar and a blueberry muffin. I'm not a big fan of Starbucks, or as Max refers to it 'Starsucks,' but it's coffee. At least I think it is. It's hot and brown and has a distinct and peculiar taste. Of course I can think of something else matching that description.

We take a slow drive on the main drag of downtown Salinas, past a small park where several older Mexican hombres in pure white cowboy hats stare and smile at Pam Grier. One gives the '59 Caddy convertible a thumbs up. This is Steinbeck country and I imagine seeing the Joad family resting at a picnic table. The downtown has a few pickup trucks and classic cars. An older Honda Civic, with primer on the body, blue wheels, and missing a muffler, roars past us as the sub-woofer breathes deafening fire with a bass of death rhythmical BOOM-BOOM, BOOM-BOOM, BOOM-BOOM that pierces your chest and rattles nearby windows and sets off a seismograph in San Francisco. It would make the Joads want to hightail it back to the relative quiet and calm of the Dust Bowl depression of Oklahoma.

Max and I sit in Pam Grier and finish the coffee and blueberry muffin and then fire up the Caddy to cruise down town and in a short while Salinas is in the rear view mirror.

Minutes later we fall under the hypnotic spell of winding roads nestled in the beige rolling hills between Salinas and Watsonville, the madrones dotting the sun-kissed slopes, explosions of dark green on hills of golden honey.

I pull off the paved road and enter a long dirt road of many memories surrounded by fields of tall amber-brown grass, where I turn off the engine and listen to a family of very talkative lark sparrows in a madrone. A warm breeze tickles the nearby grass and every so often I hear a distant semi shifting gears as it gathers speed to climb the entrance ramp leading onto Highway 1.

I light up a joint and think about my radio career, brief as it was, which began not too far from here. I recall how my folks thought my infatuation with the medium was only temporary. An impulsive childhood phase I would soon kick to the curb before coming to my senses to pursue something more practical. They believed that not wanting to attend college was only temporary insanity until I had an attitude adjustment, and after a few months of 'finding myself' I'd enter college and follow in my father's footsteps to attend med school and then on to the exciting world of dentistry.

To hell with that.

Disc jockeys get groupies, dentists don't. Yeah, dentists make more money, but I don't need a lot of money. Just enough for beer, smoke and pizza. When I told them college was not in my plans, the announcement caused a mountain of disappointment and anger on the home front.

"You ungrateful... BLAHBLAHBLAH We work hard for you... BLAHBLAHBLAH How could you let us down...BLAHBLAHBLAH." Mom offered to teach me the real estate business, which I thought was boring and told her so.

Even though I was almost 17, I looked older, so my fake I-D helped land a job at the station, the youngest jock they ever hired. I worked the overnight shift and it felt totally cool. It was an old-ies format and the play list were songs my parents played when I was growing up. I had been exposed to music from the 60's, 70's, and 80's because my parents loved that stuff and always had either a radio or a CD playing.

It was KKOX, and its slogan was 'Your Ox in the Central Valley,' and the logo on bumper stickers and on the side of the station van showed a mean-looking pepper red ox, its nose snorting, holding a boom box to its ear. One day I approached the sales manager and suggested we change the station call letters to KOX and have an icon of a dick holding a boom box to its head. He stared at me for what seemed a year before he shook his head and snarled, "Goodbye."

After working as a DJ for a year, my parents got used to their son on the air. I believe or want to believe, that Mom actually became proud of me. Well, at least not as ashamed. Dad though continued to pester me about college and that resulted in lots of fights. "Don't you want to be successful?" he'd ask. He couldn't comprehend that happiness is more important than success and if you're happy you are successful. Pursuing your passion is more important than the dollar. I'm sure my unyielding tenacity was the subject of many conversations over martinis with their country club friends. "Where did we fail? Where did we go wrong? How can we convince him that we're right?"

Just let it go, just let it go, JUST LET IT FUCKING GO!

It took a while, but their embarrassment subsided and my folks were finally able to be out in public without wearing paper bags over their heads. Mom told me she was driving clients around looking at houses one day and I came on the radio and the clients said they were fans of my show and it made her feel very proud. Dad came up with the occasional, "How's that radio thing going for you?" like it was some phase I would grow out of like wearing my hair in a Mohawk. Then he'd make a face like he swallowed his own bile.

I think about a local rock station in Salinas and wonder if my friend was still working the morning shift. He used to call his show 'Terry-O in Stereo' on 92.7 FM. When I met him a few years ago he was an institution in town, having worked at the station for almost 40 years. He'd go into any diner, any bar, and know everyone and never have to pick up a tab for a meal or a drink. The big fish in a little pond.

I was the new kid, the overnight DJ, and I often talked radio with Terry-O, not only to learn the biz but also to hear his stories. And he had tons of stories. Terry-O always looked like he just climbed out of bed, his hair disheveled, his clothes wrinkled, torn sneakers. He once told me, "Radio is like masturbation, you don't have to look your best to get the job done."

His show could be corny. He'd read jokes from old copies of *Reader's Digest*. I recall once after he played a real tearful ballad, he said, "Why, that song is sadder than a whooping crane with a whooping cough." I never understood his appeal but lots of people liked his act.

Terry-O told me that he was never going to retire. The only way he'd leave the studio is if he's carried out on a stretcher. He used to bring in a loaded handgun in his duffel bag, next to his bottle of grape Nehi soda, bag of Wise potato chips, and tuna fish sandwiches his wife made the night before. He'd wave his gun and point it to the studio door and laugh, "If the suits try to take away my mic, there'll be hell to pay!" and he'd cock the gun and then growl, "BOOM-BOOM-BOOM!"

It'd be nice to hear Terry-O's gravel voice again and some more radio stories, so I figure I'll stop in, but when I fine tune the FM dial to 92.7, it's an avalanche of disappointment. Tejano music pours from the speaker like candy from a ripped-open pinata and the DJ, who sounds like he's overdosing on cheerfulness, says something in Spanish. Oh well...

Guess I'll never know if Terry-O in Stereo exited the studio on a stretcher or with guns a blazin'.

When Terry-O came in early before his morning shift he'd hang with me in the studio and share some stories about radio back in the day, a time when many stations were family owned, the DJ's played vinyl records, commercials and PSA's were on carts, and phone calls were edited on reel-to-reel tape machines. Terry-O told me about a DJ named Juicy Brucey that he worked with in the early '70's. JB, as Juicy Brucey was called, worked the overnight shift, the perfect time to avoid seeing the boss and having long phone conversations with horny groupies who can't sleep or are up all night cramming for finals. Terry-O found out that whenever JB would play all seventeen minutes and five seconds of "In-a-Gadda-Da-Vida," that meant his girlfriend was in the studio and they were going at it. One night at about 2 a.m., "In-a-Gadda-Da-Vida" came on the air, but about three minutes into the tune the stylus suddenly skimmed across the record with an ugly SCREEEEEEECH and then... nothing. A whole lot of white noise. The silence of the Avant Garde recording "4'33."

JB had placed the record on one turntable and he and his girl decided to strip down and mount the other turntable, with his naked ass on the turntable and his girlfriend straddling him while their heaving flesh rotated at 33 rpm. This revolving sex ride seemed to work at first until one of them nudged the turntable speed lever and cranked it up from 33 rpm to 78 rpm and they went spinning out of control and were thrown off the turntable and onto the floor where they were both knocked unconscious.

For the first time ever, the program director just happened to be listening to the overnight show, and he called the studio 'hot line' but JB didn't answer so the PD decided, since he was close by, to stop at the station to see if everything was all right, fearing that there might be some medical emergency. The PD ran from his car into the station then dashed down the hall and heard a woman's breathless voice pant, "Don't hold my ears, I know what I'm doing." The boss then looked through the glass into the studio and saw the naked couple on the floor, the woman's head bobbing up and down like an oil rig in an Oklahoma field.

And that was the end of Juicy Brucey.

Terry-O also told me about an afternoon DJ in a small town station who had the unenviable task of having to read obituaries on the air. The sales manager sold time to a local funeral parlor who sponsored the death notices so the DJ had to grab the local newspaper and in his most somber voice read the obits from the paper, which were always printed in alphabetical order. The DJ did this every afternoon at 5:10 with no problems, but one day he finished reading the obits, then paused and asked, "Isn't it interesting how folks around here always die in alphabetical order?" The boss didn't hear him but the owner of the funeral parlor did and jumped on the phone to the boss and threatened to cancel his advertising contract, and that was the DJ's last broadcast on that station.

To paraphrase Alexander Pope: To 'air' is human, to forgive divine. It's rare that the suits in radio forgive, especially if it costs them revenue.

I started working as an intern at a radio station before graduating from high school, and I figured this was going to be a better education than anything I would ever get in college. I figured there must be more to life than trigonometry, Sartre, and beer pong. When I tell that to Max he says, "Sartre was full of shit. There are plenty of exits. Just no entrances."

Yeah, my parents were disappointed and pissed off when I told them I didn't want to enter my senior year and only wanted to travel and see the world. My grandfather Maxie thought it was a good move. "Your best education is outside of a classroom," he said. "In the real world. That's where you'll succeed. Of course it helps to find a rich woman."

I figured I could be a writer without a degree, like Capote or Faulkner or Orwell. I enjoy the use of words and I know them all and maybe someday I'll even figure out how to put them in the right order like writers who are recognized and published and admired. "I just want to create art," I tell Max.

"If that's what you want, don't be afraid to offend," Max advises. "Any art should exhilarate, raise your blood pressure, get you pissed off, start conversations, mess with your emotions..."

"And make you think."

"Yes, Chaz. Art should make you think."

I reflect on this conversation for a moment. "Max, I got it

figured it out. Amber was too left brain. Analytical. Logical. But me..."

Max interrupts, "No brain."

I ignore the little mutt. "...I'm right brain. More intuitive. Creative. Like Clitty. See? That's why Clitty and I click."

Max has a smile like thrown confetti.

It seems like I've been waiting forever for Clitty. It would have taken less time to wait for Godot.

Yes, the moment had finally arrived. No longer would I run away from Commitment. It was time to embrace it. It was time to embrace Clitty.

Maybe all I need to create is the right inspiration. Not the muse at the bottom of a bottle but the muse of a beautiful woman.

Chapter 13

"Travel brings power and love back into your life."
— St. Augustine

"We gotta get out while we're young, 'cause tramps
like us, baby we were born to run."
— "Born to Run" — Bruce Springsteen

"Max, I'm ready."

"I knew it."

"Glad you could read my mind."

"It's light reading." He Snoopy-chortles HEH-HEH-HEH.

In slo-mo the breezes sweep in through the hills from various directions and merge together like warm water caressing summer flesh while scattering glistening vapor particles into kaleidoscope colors, and the shimmering molecules swirl to crystallize into a form, as an angelic crescendo swells the heavens and breathes life into the shape with rivulets of heat that slowly morph into a woman. A very, very beautiful woman.

Clitty blinks several times then murmurs, "Chaz, do you want to make love?"

I whisper, "Thought you'd never ask" and we embrace for a very long and very wet kiss. We slump down onto the front seat and wriggle free of clothes and inhibitions and we melt together as one. Sweaty bodies rubbing against the car's vinyl seat sounds like Jacques Cousteau removing a wet suit.

Making love to her is heaven.

Clitty and I lay there in the afterglow for eons. I offer her a joint of Violet Delight, singing with a terrible Sinatra impersonation:

"Come fly with me, come fly, let's fly away."

There is the occasional giggle about nothing and every-thing, and we'd finish each other's sentences with non-sequit-orial nonsense.

Clitty: "So what would you like to be..."

Me: "...when I emerge from inside a cantaloupe."

Me: "If you could be any sea creature..."

Clitty: "...I'd have dual exhausts and run on STP."

Clitty: "If I don't go to the bathroom soon..."

Me: "...my canvas will explode with colors."

With her honey-drenched smile she whispers, "Oohhhh, that was nice. Really, really nice."

I giggle in her ear and whisper, "Fuckalicious!" and her laughter is a popped bottle of champagne.

With my index finger I trace the small purple infinity tat on her right shoulder.

"It's cool if something doesn't have a beginning or end," she explains.

Then I slide my finger over flesh, taking the scenic route over her breasts, then down to her left forearm, where I finger a blue and yellow butterfly tattoo.

"My birthday present to myself when I hit eighteen."

She uses her finger to slide to my right calf above the ankle and stops at a series of musical notes.

"Got that one when I was sixteen," I tell her.

"What's the tune?"

"A Brahms cello sonata." I caress her back and see several small portrait tattoos. "What about these?"

"Oh. The Presidents..." she says, her voice trailing off.

There were three tats, each about the size of a quarter, side by side on her upper back above her right shoulder blade. "It was just a phase," she adds with some embarrassment.

The tattoos are of Millard Fillmore, Franklin Pierce, and

James Buchanan. "I got sucked into the presidential tattoo fad that was so popular a few years ago. Blame it on my youth," she laments.

"I know. Everybody was doing it back in the day."

We stare into each other's eyes for an eternity and I whisper that she is the northern lights that envelop me in a spectrum of shimmering sheets across the night sky.

Max sticks a paw in his mouth and pretends to gag. I shoot him an angry look.

"Never did it in a '59 Caddy before," she giggles. "Once on top of an Army tank."

Naturally I was curious about that story.

"I was seeing this guy who was in the Arizona National Guard and he snuck me on base at night and we decided to christen a tank. I tried to talk him into firing off the gun at the same time we came, but he wouldn't do it."

"Like hooking up to the '1812 Overture.'"

She leans in close and we kiss again. "Are you hungry? I am starving. I could eat a horse."

I was hungry too, although I sensed a headache about to make an appearance and that would have brought on nausea and that would have killed my appetite. I couldn't tell her that having sex brought on my headache and nausea, but it may have.

"Let's find a place," I said, grabbing a Marinol from the bottle in the glove compartment. We quickly dressed and drove back down the dirt road to Highway 1.

"Where we goin'?" she asks.

"No where."

"When are we gonna get there?"

"Never." I laugh.

"Come on, are we headin' south?"

"Yeah, why?"

"I still want to get to L-A."

I felt somewhat deflated. I made the Commitment. Wasn't she supposed to also?

"Maybe you can be my agent," she continued. The lazy-ass I got now never calls. Never texts. When I call him it's always, 'Yeah sweetie, I'm working on something. Don't worry. Big things are gonna happen.' The asshole is just strokin' me."

"Well, if he never gets you anything you can't give him ten percent of nothing."

"I swear you could do better. Get a website. Business cards. You're a disc jockey. You know how to talk."

Max interjects, "Now might be a good time to tell her about yourself, my boy."

I dismiss his suggestion with a slight shake of my head. Don't need to bring this party to a crashing halt with talk about death. My ring tone plays and the screen reads: NOT NOW.

"It would be easy for you," she continues. "I'm highly marketable. Once directors saw my talents, your ten percent would be the easiest money you ever made. So much of the job is just schmoozing. I'm sure you know how to schmooze. What do you say?"

"Well..."

"I know I may have a few faults. Some stuff I could work on. But I"m sure you'll agree that even my imperfections are perfect. What do you say... is it a good idea?"

I suddenly slam on the brakes with a deafening SCREEEEECH as Clitty braces herself against the dash and Max flips over in the backseat. I pull the car to the gravel shoulder, throw open the door, lean out of the seat and vomit. I didn't take a Marinol in time.

"Geez," she gasps, "I guess that's your way of saying it's not a good idea."

Still leaning outside the door I close my eyes and wipe my mouth. "No. No, I'm just not feeling too well. I haven't been this nauseous since I read Tori Spelling's autobiography."

"Come on, Chaz," Max says. "Now is the time."

"I'll be okay," I tell Clitty, easing back onto the seat and closing the door.

"Chaz..." Max is impatient.

"I got just the remedies," Clitty says, reaching into the back seat for her suitcase. She opens it to reveal more pharmaceuticals than you'd find at a Walgreen's. She offers several small plastic containers, "Vicodin, codeine, LSD, morphine?" like a flight attendant offering bags of peanuts or pretzels.

"All of it. Mixed in a bowl with Ben and Jerry's New York Super Fudge."

"Seriously, what do you want?"

"Just to finish this part of my journey."

"You're getting your color back. Feeling better?"

"Clitty?"

"What?" and she waits for what seems like eons.

"I'm dying," I tell her in a very soft voice. And time stops.

Clitty falls back against the seat and murmurs a feint "Oh" and stares at me. Does she believe me?

She blurts out a denial, "Chaz, we're all dying, just at different speeds."

After several moments her look of grave concern gives way to a smile and then she hugs me, kisses me on the lips and bursts out with "Congrats! It's not that you're dying. You're graduating. Graduating from the School of Life. So let's celebrate!"

She sounds like the old lady in *Harold and Maude*, as she turns on the ignition, cranks up a tune on her CD, leaps on top of the engine hood like a cat pouncing on a mouse, and dances. A 1930's ragtime version of "Get Happy" blares from the speaker and Clitty sings:

> "Pack up your troubles and just get happy,
> You better chase all your cares away."

She has taken crazy to a whole new level, but for one brief wonderful moment I forget my pain.

> "Shout Hallelujah, come on get happy.
> Get ready for the judgment day."

I break into a smile and forget my sickness.

> "The sun is shinin', c'mon get happy.
> The Lord is waiting to take your hand."

I watch her dance as I keep rhythm with my hands thumping the steering wheel.

> "Shout Hallelujah, c'mon get happy.
> We're goin' to the Promised Land."

In one lightning flash, Clitty helped me see the absurdity of it all. The short time we feel, either pain and suffering or joy and laughter. How unimportant any of it is, with the significance of the insignificance being the only thing that truly matters.

Max enjoys her performance. "Chaz, it's all meaningless, so you'd better just laugh at it. Have fun with it, because there's really nothing else to do."

"Let's find a restaurant," I tell her and she jumps down from the hood and slides into the passenger seat and turns off the music. I fire up Pam Grier and soon we're back on Highway 1 and it seems as though I'm not touching the gas pedal but we're accelerating faster as if gravity evaporated and the Earth is now tilted and we're going downhill like on a giant ski jump, launching off into space. The image makes me laugh out loud. Clitty doesn't know what I'm laughing about, or at least I don't think she does, but she laughs too. Maybe it's a relief that it isn't my moment to change highways and that I still have more time on this trip.

I grab her hand. "Maybe that's the secret. But how do you make dying a fun experience?"

"You add balloons?" she asks.

The conversation turns to relationships, which is common when a couple is developing their own relationship. Clitty tells me about the first boy she kissed.

"I can still remember his name. Gerald Tinsley. We were in the second grade. He lived down the street and invited me up in his tree house. We kissed. He pushed his tongue so far down my throat he almost tickled my tonsils. Then he dropped his pants and asked me to kiss his wiener. I screamed and jumped out of the tree house and broke my ankle. Usually guys break my heart. Gerald Tinsley broke my ankle."

I told her about my first experience. I was in the fifth grade with Jacqueline. I thought she was so exotic because she was bilingual, having been born in France but her parents moved to the States when she was six. My parents weren't home one day when Jacqueline and I decided to use our hot tub, but I thought the experience could be so much more erotic if it were a bubble bath, so I poured an entire bottle of liquid dish detergent into the swirling hot water. We slid into the foamy wet heat and kissed, but after about five minutes I saw my mom's car pull into the driveway. Jacqueline jumped out and ran across the lawn, soap suds flying off her naked body as she ran down the sidewalk. The suds spilled out onto the deck and began covering the lawn. My mom later confessed that even though she tried to play the role of the stern parent, when she saw the sudsy mess it took much effort to hold back her laughter.

In Pacific Grove we find a Safeway. Clitty jumps into a shopping cart and I race her up and down the aisles like Jake and Elwood driving their '74 Dodge Monaco through a mall, taking corners on two wheels. She growls, "VROOM-VROOM-VROOM" at one point almost colliding with an elderly lady on an electric cart who put her cane down long enough to flip us off. We stop in the produce section, where Clitty grabs a banana and slowly and seductively peals it then bites off an end and slowly rolls it around the inside of her mouth with a seductive giggle.

I whisper, "You tease," as I grab the hose used to water and freshen the produce and spray the front of her blouse. I then reach in to the carriage, pick her up and toss her onto the bin filled with strawberries, and the red stains her clothes as she squirms. I leap on top of her and unbutton her soaked blouse. I'm unzipping my pants just as a produce clerk, a young girl with huge green glasses and braces on her teeth, scampers up to us and hisses, "What are you two doing?" The question seemed strange, since it was obvious what we were doing.

"I'm calling the manager!" she fumes, and I wonder: Is she calling the manager because it's against store policy to make love in the produce section, or is she calling the manager because she doesn't know the answer to her own question "What are you two doing?" and she's hoping the manager can explain it to her?

Clitty spits a strawberry through the air and it lands between the top buttons of the clerk's Safeway shirt and rolls down between her breasts. The clerk's eyes widen and she whimpers like a scolded puppy and storms off. Clitty jumps out of the strawberry bin as I zip my fly and we grab a couple of apples and a bag of grapes and dash out of the store. Much laughter as we jump into the car and race through the parking lot and fly back on to Highway 101 with tires smoking, like Bonnie and Clyde being pursued by Frank Hamer. Clitty says, "I'm thinkin' we'll never be allowed in Safeway again."

"Next time let's do it in the salad bar. Re-create the scene in 9 1/2 Weeks."

It isn't long before we're a few miles outside of King City. We pass a minor league ballpark, with a sign out front reading: 'Ken Griffey Jr. Bobble-head Night.' A few miles later we pass a planetarium with the sign: 'Stephen Hawking Bobble-head Night'. Minutes later a sign in front of a church promoting: 'John the Baptist Bobble-head Night.'

Clitty leans tight against me with her hand slowly rubbing the inside of my thigh.

"My mom gave me some advice when I was twelve. She told me how to hold on to a man so he'd never stray."

"What's that?"

"She said, 'Keep his stomach full and his balls empty.'"

"I think I once saw that line in *Reader's Digest.*"

"My family was always talking sex," she says. "When I was a little girl my grandmother had a framed crochet doily with writing on it hanging from the wall in her home. At six years old I didn't know what the writing meant, but as I got older and had a lot of relationships with assholes, I finally understood. The sentence read: 'The bigger the dick, the bigger the dick.'"

"I was about fourteen when my dad tried to give me the birds and bees speech."

"Fourteen? A little old, isn't it?"

"Something he'd been putting off for a few years. He was very uptight about sex. I remember smelling the whiskey on his breath. He needed a few pops before attempting the talk. His mom was sexually repressed so it was in his DNA. He was wound as tight as the inside of a golf ball." I smile as I remember the scene. "Wanna see it?" I ask.

"Yeah." I pull off the highway and into the parking lot of a bar called 'Hurry Inn.' At the lot entrance a white sign on wheels reads 'Karaoke Night! Fun! Cash! Prizes!' so I figure with such a generous use of exclamation points it must be worth a visit, so I maneuver the Caddy several spaces away from at least eight Harleys, a Chevy pickup truck, an older Ford Bronco, a Toyota hybrid, and a dented-up Miata.

I reach into the glove compartment and remove MY JOUR-
NEY and thumb the pages toward the beginning and find the
scene with my Dad. The page comes alive like a movie I scripted and I hold it for Clitty to watch:

INT. GARAGE - NIGHT
George stands in front of a blackboard. Chaz enters.
CHAZ
Mom said you wanted to see me?
*George grabs chalk and draws a side-view of a penis
and scrotum on the blackboard.*
GEORGE
Do you recognize this?
CHAZ
A satellite view of Lake Michigan?
GEORGE
That, young man, is your penis and scrotum.
CHAZ
If it is, then I'm horribly deformed.
GEORGE
Your mother thinks it's time we had a little
talk. A talk about your penis.
CHAZ
Dad...
GEORGE
I know how it is. Your ol' Dad's got one too,
you know. And believe me, sometimes the little general
can lead you into dangerous territory, so...
CHAZ
I learned all about this in sixth grade biology
class.
GEORGE
You learned about erections?

                    CHAZ

We learned about erections.

                  GEORGE

Ejaculation?

                    CHAZ

We learned about ejaculation.

                  GEORGE

What about... cunnilingus?

                    CHAZ

We had an oral test.

George removes a hot dog from his jacket pocket.

                  GEORGE

Well, what about this?

                    CHAZ

I know all about hot dogs.

George takes a condom package from a pocket.

                  GEORGE

I'm sure they didn't show you this in biology
class.

He unrolls the condom down the length of the hot dog.

                  GEORGE

Now pay close attention. There's a valuable lesson to be learned here.

*The hot dog breaks, with half of it falling to the floor. Chaz
winces and squeezes his legs together.*

                    CHAZ

The lesson is... if not handled carefully, a penis
can break in two?

                  GEORGE

All right son. We'll talk again. Just... just be care
ful. Okay?

Clitty smiles and says, "Oh, your poor Dad!"

"Yeah, he was sweating. No, we never talked about it again. But for my fifteenth birthday party he snuck me a porn video and said, "Don't tell your mother I gave you this." It was pretty cheesy. The guys all had those porn moustaches. The girls all had big boobs and acted like inflatable dolls. But the soundtrack was cool, with the wah-wah guitars."

"It's too bad you never hear a cello in a porn soundtrack," Clitty wondered.

I place MY JOURNEY back in the glove compartment and look at the front door of the Hurry Inn. "Feeling brave? You said you were hungry enough to eat a horse. Trigger is probably on the menu."

"I'm sure the menu is in French and the chef is a grad of a Parisian culinary school."

"Don't judge a book..."

"*Oui garcon, le cheval avec fromage.*"

Max follows and as we get closer we see a small sign on the front door. It reads: 'Close the door. Don't let the rats out.' Inside a woman's voice sings:

"I love rock and roll put another
dime in the jukebox baby"

Once inside we look around for a place to sit. It's all dark wood and it appears to be stuck in 1960, and at any moment I expect to see Patrick Swayze as the bouncer. There are two pool tables, with one woman in leathers, strumming a cue stick like a guitar, with the occasional Townsend windmill, sitting on the edge of a table. Next to her is a baby wrapped in a blanket and sucking on a pacifier. A couple of biker guys shoot pool at the other table, every so often looking up at the woman on the small, makeshift stage, doing her best Joan Jett impersonation. One of them yells encouragement, "Go Maggie! Damn woman, that's good!"

"I saw him dancin' there by the record machine,
I knew he must a been about seventeen…"

At the bar a couple of guys in leathers. They're both wiry, probably this side of 40, with long, gray-brown beards. I mumbled to Clitty, "I always wondered whatever happened to Z Z Top." The two guys are watching a reality TV show on a small TV screen above the bar. On the show a nearly naked man eats a tarantula.

"'And I could tell it wouldn't be long
til he was with me, yeah me…"

Two other biker couples are dining in a booth. Their heads bob to the beat.

"I love rock n' roll, so put another dime
in the jukebox, baby…"

On one end of the bar near the cash register is a three gallon jar filled with pickled eggs and pig's feet. Clitty sees the jar and makes a face. "Think I'd rather eat scorpions," she says.

"Just ask. They're probably kept in another jar."

On stage, Maggie the biker chick tries her very best, throaty Joan Jett growls, OOWWWWWWWWW!" but it doesn't quite come out right and I feel that she may soon be spitting up blood.

A much older woman, maybe in her 60's, wearing a white dress and a broad-brimmed sun hat, her long gray hair falling past her shoulders, is alone in a booth and engrossed in a book. The book has a white, leather cover, and embossed in gold on the front are the words Holy Bible. The woman takes an occasional sip from a straw impaled into a red, fruity drink garnished with a small, yellow decorative parasol. She seems totally out of place but not uncomfortable in her surroundings.

At the end of the bar are two older guys, also in their 60's, one who's bald but has long tuffs of hair sprouting from his ears like gray bonsai shrubs. The other has long hair, boot-polish black, in a pony tail under a Chicago Cubs cap, with Max Schreck ears. Before them lots of glasses of whiskey, behind them lots of rough roads. They look like two old dogs from a George Booth cartoon and you can almost imagine flies swirling around their heads. They're playing cribbage and mumbling indecipherable gibberish, except when one loudly proclaims, "I am the eggman!" and the other guy acts all pissed off and screams, "No, I am the eggman!"

"Hey, I said I'm the eggman."

"Fuck you! I am the eggman, he is the walrus," gesturing to the bartender.

The bartender, in his 20's, is engrossed in Tetris Plus on a Game Boy and by his dour expression has heard this dialogue many times before, and without looking up from his game, murmurs, "Knock it off! You're scarin' away my customers. You old farts should be institutionalized."

"We were," one of them says loudly and proudly and high-fives the other.

"Ten years at Agnews," says the other, like he's displaying a badge of honor and they high-five again.

"So what was I sayin'... oh yeah, you're the walrus, I'm the eggman. Coo coo ca-joob."

Together they yell, "COO COO CA-OOOOOOOOOOOB!" and then erupt in laughter.

I watch the duo and from their grins I see they've lost most of their teeth. I tell Clitty, "They must be rich from the tooth fairy."

"He was with me, yeah me singin'
I love rock n' roll. So put another dime

in the jukebox, baby..."

Clitty and I ease into a booth and she teases, "Buy me a beer and I'll pretend to love you."

We lock eyes and smile. "Well, I can live with pretend until the real thing comes along."

The bartender approaches and says, "My apologies. They go through that every night. Sometimes it gets out of hand and I have to throw 'em out." He tosses a couple of menus on the table.

"What do you win for karaoke?" I ask.

"Twenty-five bucks and a bottle of Jack Daniel's," the bartender says. "So what'll you guys have?"

"Coors" I say and Clitty says "Make it two."

"I-D'S? Sorry, I gotta ask."

I pull out my wallet and show him my California license. He looks at it, then at me, and nods. Clitty says, "I don't have a driver's license."

"Well..." he says.

"I can pee in a cup for you."

"That won't be necessary..."

"Oh," says Clitty, "I got this." She digs down into her backpack for a Kodachrome photo of a woman holding a baby, and scrawled in ink on the white border reads: 'Clitoris at 10 months old, 1974, Taos, NM'.

He shrugs and says, "Okay. We only have a breakfast menu. It's what we serve all day. Gimme a yell when you're ready."

"We're ready. I'll get a veggie omelet and she'll have a plate of veggies." Max paws my leg.

"You have blueberry muffins?"

The guy hesitates and says, "Don't think so. We may have a doughnut somewhere in the back though," which certainly doesn't sound very appetizing and gives the impression that the doughnut was once discovered in an archaeological dig. Max mumbles, "Okay, that'll do." I tell the bartender "Thanks" and he returns to the bar.

Clitty grabs my license and studies it up close. "Cool! Good job."

"Cost me 250 bucks. The guy is an artist. I think he did time at Leavenworth for forgery."

The biker babe karaoke star finishes to a loud round of applause and whistles. She's beaming. She curtsies before jumping off the stage then hustles back to the pool table where she swigs back the rest of the Bud.

One of the biker pool players yells to the bartender, "Ryan, Maggie was the best tonight."

"Maggie was the only one tonight," Ryan says. "Nobody else signed up."

"She was fuckin' great! What does she win?"

A biker guy at the bar chimes in, "Hey, what about me?"

Ryan looks at the woman who sang "I Love Rock and Roll" and shrugs his shoulders. "Sorry," he mumbles. The biker guy makes a slow slide off the barstool, or falls off the barstool is more like it, then staggers like a newborn colt to the stage.

Max eyes the jar on the bar.

"Want a pig's knuckle?" I ask him.

"No, I'll stick with the prehistoric doughnut."

"How about a pickled egg?"

"God, that swill smells bad."

"This from a creature that greets other dogs by smelling their butts."

Max glares up at me. "We'll go for a walk and he'll find an old turd," I tell Clitty. "He's not very discriminating."

"Especially with who I hang around with," Max snarls.

"This dog can stop and sniff a turd for ten minutes. I'm always yelling at him 'Come on, let's go! What else do you need to know? It's dog shit.'"

Max is proud. "I can tell you what breed, when he pooped, what he ate, when he had his rabies shot, and if he still has his nuts."

I pat the top of his head, "Yeah, he's one of a kind."

"At least I don't eat it," Max continues. "I saw Divine do that and it made me sick to my stomach."

Ryan brings our beers to the table as the biker taps the mic and croaks, "Hey, can you hear me?"

His biker friend at the bar yells, "Yeah, unfortunately."

The biker on stage clears his throat, looks at the lyrics on the screen, and in a gravely voice bellows:

"I was tired of my lady, we'd been
together too long. Like a worn-out
recording of a favorite song..."

His buddy screams and makes coyote noises HA-ROOOOO-HA-ROOOOO and loudly interrupts:

"If you like pina colada,
gettin' caught in the rain"

as the karaoke biker yells into the mic, "Shut up, asshole!" and without missing a beat continues singing:

"So while she lay there sleeping,
I read the paper in bed. In the personals
column there was a letter I read..."

The elderly woman in white approaches the bar. She leans on a cane and walks with difficulty. She has the expression of someone who's been waiting in line at the DMV for a very long time. She whispers to Ryan.

"A good lookin' dog," Clitty says scratching Max. "Too bad he's neutered. You could have had little Max's running around."

"I wonder if he has phantom balls. You know like amputees."

"You ought to see him at dog parks. He tries to hump them all. Great Danes, chihuahuas, you name it. Shooting blanks, but not very discriminating."

Max shoots me a look. "You were more appealing as a stranger, and less dangerous." It sounds like a line Gloria Grahame may have said in a film noir.

The cook, a burly guy with a goatee and wearing a stained Hawaiian shirt, brings our meal. "You guys want Tabasco? Ketchup?" We shake our heads and he says, "Enjoy."

"That didn't take long," I say.

Clitty responds, "They made it last year and just re-heated it." On a separate plate is a plain doughnut I place onto the floor.

All of the bikers are now screech-singing:

"If you like making love at midnight,
in the dunes of the Cape. I'm the love that
you've looked for, write to me, and escape."

The biker leaves the stage to loud whistles and applause as his biker friend yells to Ryan, "Does he get the money and Jack? He kicked ass."

Ryan says, "Well, we got one more." The elderly lady approaches the stage, her walk is slow and labored like a car trying to move on four flat tires. The bikers look at each other as if to ask, "What is this all about?"

The woman avoids eye contact and takes the mic from the stand and picks out a song. After seeing her reading the Bible, I expect her to sing a hymn. All eyes are on her and no one makes a sound. She presses a button on the karaoke machine and through the speakers blares the opening chords to "The Low Spark of High Heeled Boys." I turn to Clitty and whisper, "Well, this should be good."

> "If you see something that looks
> like a star and it's shooting up out
> of the ground..."

Her voice is soft and quivering and vulnerable like a baby rabbit.

The two old guys at the bar stop playing cribbage and state at her with curious smiles.

"Food is pretty good," I tell Clitty.

"I've had worse things in my mouth," she responds.

> "... the thing that you're hearing
> is only the sound of the low spark
> of high-heeled boys..."

I recall from my DJ days that the song is more than eleven minutes long so I know this performance is going to take some time. Max has already wolfed down the doughnut so I give him a slice of toast and my hash browns. As discreet as I can be, I slip a vape pen from my shirt pocket, take a few hits, then pass it to Clitty. She sucks in hard like trying to pass a golf ball through a garden hose and I tell her, "Just a little. It'll lay you to waste."

> "... but it wasn't the bullet that laid
> him to rest, it was the low spark of high-
> heeled boys..."

The woman steadies herself with the cane as she closes her eyes and gently sways to the music. Her voice is stronger now, more confident. I overhear one of the bikers at the bar tell his friend, "You can kiss that fuckin' money and Jack goodbye." His head is lowered in defeat.

His friend replies, "Yup. Ya never gonna beat an old lady with a gimpy leg."

Ryan ignores the karaoke performance and is immersed in Tetris Plus.

> "...and the sound that I'm hearing
> is only the sound. The low spark
> of high-heeled boys."

The woman continues to sway with her eyes closed as the music fades. Then applause. The biker at the bar who had sang earlier gets off the barstool and approaches the woman, grabs her hand and murmurs, "That was great, lady. Just great." She acknowledges the clapping with a slight grin and a quick wave of her hand as she shuffles back to the booth. Ryan walks toward her and places the Jack Daniel's bottle on her table and hands her a twenty and a five-dollar bill. She says something to him that I can't hear, but Ryan picks up the bottle and brings it to Maggie, the woman who sang "I Love Rock and Roll." He says something to her and Maggie looks at the woman in white and puts her thumb and finger in her mouth and lets out a shrill whistle to get the woman's attention, and then Maggie gives the lady a thumbs-up and yells "Thanks! I appreciate it!" The elderly woman nods.

Clitty and I get the bill and pay up and leave. In Pam Grier we enjoy another hit or two from the vape pen. It's early evening and a huge burnt-orange moon hovers low in the sky like a round glowing lantern. I lean against the car and draw Clitty close and we stare into each other's eyes forever. I'm reminded of the sensuous scene in *Picnic* when Kim Novak and William Holden held their gaze forever as they embraced on an outdoor dance floor with Chinese lanterns shimmering in the background. I don't know how much time passed, but when I came back down to Earth we were on the highway.

"Where we goin'?" she asks.

"No where."

"When we gonna get there?"

"Never," I laugh.

We were in motion, and I know that I had to keep driving. The road never disappoints. It will always take me somewhere.

Chapter 14

"may came home with a smooth round stone
as small as a world and as large as alone."
— e.e. cummings

"It's the end of the world as we know it
and I feel fine."
— "It's the End of the World"—R.E.M.

Clitty is curled up on the front seat, my right thigh a pillow for her head. The dashboard lights illuminate her face. Her eyes are closed and she's smiling, lost in a dream.

In the distance is the mournful wail of a train. The car's canvas top is up as the night air chills and Fall appears to be very anxious to push Summer aside. It doesn't feel like the tires are touching pavement as we soar past fields, houses, strip malls, and alongside a railroad track. For a couple of miles we run parallel to a freight train rumbling along. We're both doing about 42 mph, many of the boxcars containing mysteries are tagged with graffiti of colorful letters and gang symbols. Several flat cars are loaded with lumber from Oregon. I press the accelerator to catch up to the engine, a dirty yellow powerhouse with 'Union Pacific' in red letters and a faded Stars & Stripes on her side. Between looking at the road, I sneak glances at the engineer, wearing a blue cap, his eyes locked in on what lies ahead. He appears to be about 50 and is lost in the rhythm of the steel wheels kissing track. Where he's going? How long has he been driving the rails? Does he wish the train would become airborne to take him somewhere that's not a predetermined destination? Is anyone waiting for him at home? Does he even want to go home?

The road gradually veers to the left and the train and I are going to have to part company. I take one last glimpse of the conductor, and he must sense it because for a brief moment we make eye contact. He expresses no emotion, and looks back to the track as woods quickly separate the road from the rails and through the trees I watch the train disappear into the night as it races to overtake the pale orange moon.

I'm not tired, although I probably should be. Max is spread out in the back seat. He wants to know, "Are we driving all night?"

"Not sure."

"*They Drive By Night.*"

"I remember that one. Film noir with Bogie?"

"He was a truck driver and his girl was Ann Sheridan. I think Clitty is your Ann Sheridan."

"That's a compliment. I'm definitely not Bogart."

"Bogart wasn't Bogart. His on-screen persona was different than the real man. You are who you are. For better or worse."

"Maybe we can find an all-night diner and get coffee."

"And a blueberry muffin," Max salivates. "Or two." I wonder if Pavlov enticed his dogs with blueberry muffins.

Clitty stirs awake, rubs her eyes and looks up at me. "Are you really dying?" she softly asks.

It catches me off guard, but after thinking about it for a moment I yell, "Hell no! I'm living!" I must have thought a loud response would scare away the Angel of Death. I always seem to have much cockiness during the day but at night I always feel alone, vulnerable, and scared. But now as blackness descends, with Clitty by my side, I feel strong and invincible.

"I had the strangest dream," Clitty says. "I was alone in a field and it was raining, but each raindrop was a fortune cookie and inside was a message, so I was tearing open raindrop after raindrop to read these messages."

"What did the messages say?"

"Just words like 'Emotions.' 'Joy.' 'Trust.' 'Anticipation.' You know, that kinda stuff. I wonder what it means."

"It means you're happy. It also means you had a nice hit from the vaper."

She smiles and closes her eyes and I brush strands of hair away from her face.

The miles pass in silence until Clitty asks, "Chaz, how come you set fire to things?"

Another question that is totally unexpected. I blurt out, "I was just trying to keep warm."

"Wise ass."

"Well... I felt neglected at home and it was a way to get attention. Ever since I was young, fire turned me on. I know, it's kinda weird, but... well, to me the flame represents life. If something is glowing, it's alive. Darkness is death. Thoreau called fire 'the most tolerable third party.' I always liked that quote."

"Does quoting Thoreau legitimize your pyromania?"

"I told you... I don't do it anymore. The psychologist 'shrinked' it out of me."

"Okay," she murmurs and closes her eyes again.

About forty-five minutes later I pull the Caddy into the parking lot of an all-night diner. I put on my tux jacket so we don't get refused service. There's only a couple of cars in the parking lot. Clitty and I enter and see a long Formica counter with round polished silver stools, circa 1950. There's one customer at the counter, a man wearing a suit with a half-knotted tie, with a coffee in hand and the sports section of a *USA Today* spread out in front of him. Working behind the counter is a thin guy wearing a white shirt. Clitty and I take a seat and the clerk brings us a couple of menus. Max curls up at my feet.

"No thanks," I tell the waiter, "Just coffee." He pours two cups as the man seated across from us mumbles "Damn Broncos" to no one in particular. "God damn Broncos!" he hisses through a smile like a steel-jawed trap. The man looks like the character actor Paul Douglas, who I saw in the movie *Panic in the Streets*.

Clitty looks around and says, "I feel like I've been here before." I survey the scene and gasp. "It's *Nighthawks*. You know that painting?"

"We're in it?" she gasps.

"We are! This is eerie. I feel like we should hear a Theremin playing in the background. EEEEEOOEEEOOOOOO-WWW-WWWOOOO."

"If I'm gonna be in a painting," she says, "I'd rather be Christina stretched out in a field of grass. I can twist my right arm back like that," and she demonstrates the pose.

"At least we're not in *The Garden of Earthly Delights* and my ass is being impaled by some rat creature."

The man with the newspaper looks up and says, "Pardon my French." I ponder that expression for a moment: In France, when someone utters a profanity, do they say, "Pardon my English?"

The waiter asks, "Where ya headin'?"

I start to reply but he cuts me off with, "Everybody who stops here is goin' somewhere."

"Eventually L-A" Clitty replies.

"I got a cousin down there. A mechanic. Once changed a flat tire for Harrison Ford. Got a signed photo of him next to the movie star and Harrison is holdin' up the nail that my cousin yanked out of the tire."

Clitty and I nod as the clerk takes a rag and cleans up several round coffee stains from the Formica counter top.

"Yeah, everybody's got a story," he mumbles.

The Broncos fan jumps in, "Anybody wanna hear my story?" but before we can respond he says, "I just drove up from L-A."

"On vacation?" Clitty asks.

The Bronco fan shakes his head. "Business. Trade show. I'm an inventor. I come up with a lot of clever shit. Geez, there I go again... pardon my French."

Clitty says, "Don't worry. I've heard those fuckin' words before," and the man breaks into a grin. "Ha! That's a good one, lady."

When you're a writer, it pays to observe people and make conversations. Helps feed your writer's soul. Gives you material. There are always speech patterns, physical qualities, or manner-isms that you can use in a screenplay. And hopefully the per-son whose characteristic you stole doesn't see himself on the big screen one day and sues your ass. But I think I'd be protected by the 'Any similarity to any person living or dead is merely coinci-dental' disclaimer.

Max, always eager to display his knowledge of cinema, says, "That came about by the movie *Rasputin and the Empress*. MGM got their ass sued. Look it up." I nod and turn back to the Bronco fan.

I ask, "What do you invent?" and that seemed to be the cue he was looking for. "Mind if I...?" he says like a spider spinning a web, as he grabs his coffee and briefcase and crawls onto the stool next to Clitty.

He offers his outstretched hand, and moves in a little too close. "Ben," he says and Clitty and I shake his hand as he at-tempts to crack bones with his firm handshake. He has a large grin with a barbed wire smile. I notice that he's wearing dentures and from the staining it's evident he likes to drink a lot of coffee. Clitty and I are overwhelmed by his body odor. It's obvious he's never had the suit dry cleaned. Clitty and I introduce ourselves, but she calls herself 'Pam' to avoid a long conversation about the origins of her real name.

"Ben Mazotti. But everybody calls me Pawny."

"Interesting name," Clitty prods. "Pawny. How did you get it?"

He grins again. "You really wanna know?"

We nod. He lowers his voice and, without making much eye contact, murmurs, "I've got three" and he points toward his crotch.

Clitty furrows her brow. "Three... what?" she says, taking a sip of coffee.

"I was born with three balls... uh, testicles, so when I was younger everyone said I was like a pawnshop, you know... you've seen pawnshops with three balls hangin' over the sign? So everybody started callin' me Pawny."

Clitty does a spit-take as coffee shoots out her nose. I hand her a napkin. "You okay?"

"Yeah," she rasps, "Meeting a guy with three balls just caught me off-guard."

Pawny smiles, a smile like broken glass.

"One more ball and you could walk to first base," I say. His forced grin makes me believe he's heard that line a thousand times before.

"So... Pawny..." I pause, "What do you invent?"

"Right now I'm peddlin' something I call the 'Swiss Army Seat.' It is gonna be a smash hit. Wanna see it? I've got a prototype. Patent pending." and before Clitty and I can respond he opens his briefcase and removes a small model of a toilet seat.

"Tiny toilet seat," I say. "Where'd you get it? You break into Peter Dinklage's house?"

He totally ignores me but Clitty rolls her eyes. Pawny shows us the side of the seat, which has layers like a Swiss Army knife, containing various components that accomplish various tasks. He pulls out a section that resembles a music stand so one can sit on the toilet seat and have a place for a book or magazine.

"Cool!" Clitty responds.

Pawny continues, "And over here you can pull out this accessory, which is a cell phone holder."

"Cool!" says Clitty.

"Did you know," Pawny says, getting very serious, "The average person in their average lifetime destroys three thousand, six-hundred and ninety-eight trees? Trees made into toilet paper. Just because you wipe your ass doesn't mean you have to contribute to global warming." He takes a quart of water with a hose attachment from his briefcase and hooks the other end of the hose to a spigot sticking under the toilet seat.

"Cool!"

He taps a tiny button on the front of the seat and a spray shoots out of the spigot and lands on the floor. "Voila! You're own bidet!" The clerk sighs and makes a move for the mop.

Clitty is about to say "Cool" again but I give her a look and she freezes in mid "Coo..."

Pawny is on a roll now as his voice rises and he gets more animated as beads of sweat form on his brow. "And now the piece de resistance." He pulls out a section that looks like a rubberized bladder. "If suddenly your home is flooded, God forbid, all you have to do is sit on the toilet seat, pull this plug and this part inflates and becomes an emergency raft."

I didn't mean to crush his enthusiasm, but I had to ask, "So... how often does it come up that you're taking a crap when your house gets flooded?"

He gets very serious. "Many folks get killed every year because of tsunamis, because they crash into a house without a moment's notice, and if these poor unfortunates were alive today they would probably wish they had owned one of these." Pawny awaits a response, as he looks from me to Clitty and back to me again. "Could save your life one day."

"Well... cool!" I blurt out, and Clitty gives me a smirk. "Have you sold a lot of these?"

While placing the Swiss Army Seat back into his briefcase, he says, "Not yet, but it's early. I'll let you in on a little secret," he says, edging closer and lowering his voice.

"The public is really stupid. The average American is below average. Genius is usually not recognized right away. Sometimes it takes a while for John Q. Public to catch up."

He slams the briefcase shut and with a smile says, "But they will. Oh, they will, all right." He grabs a very used handkerchief from his pocket and pats his forehead dry.

"Cool!" Clitty and I say in harmony.

"By next Spring, these will be selling out on eBay and Amazon and I'll be livin' on Easy Street" he grins.

The clerk comes over with a coffee pot and tops off our mugs.

"Now you two look like you're intelligent, know a good deal when you see it," Pawny says, and I can tell he's about to go fishing.

"I'm lookin' for some venture capitalists, somebody who makes a small investment and in a short time is up to their necks in moola."

I look down at Max by my feet and he's looking up at me with an expression that says: Walk away. Walk away as quickly as possible. No, don't just walk away. RUN!

"Investors for the Swiss Shitter?" Clitty asks.

Pawny forces a smile. "The actual name is 'Swiss Army Seat' hon', but no... I've already got that covered. It's another invention of mine that is gonna take the world by storm. I call it 'Sole Food.'" His sincerity seems over-rehearsed.

"Soul, like your spirit or psyche?" I ask.

"No. S-O-L-E. Like the bottom of your shoe. Did you folks know that there are more than twenty-three million joggers in the United States? And millions of more folks who walk. Now sometimes when you're out walkin' or joggin', you get hungry but there's nowhere around to get a bite to eat. Well, I've taken care of that with the ever-so-handy 'Sole Food.' It's an attachment that works with any shoe or sneaker. You fill it with soup or a sandwich and it heats up because of the constant motion of your feet. So after jogging for an hour, you sit down, remove this attachment from your sneaker, open it up and voila... you got yourself a hot roast beef sandwich. Or hot apple pie, just like mom used to make."

Pawny seems to pause waiting for a "Cool" from one of us, but it doesn't come. Perhaps the universe only allows you to say so many "Cool's" and we may have used up our quota.

"Only nineteen-ninety-five," he says catching his breath. "You kids should get in on the ground floor of this multi-million dollar enterprise before it's too late. They're gonna sell like hotcakes."

I hear Max say, "Holy fuck! Run away! Run away!"

"Well..." I say, and Pawny quickly tears open his wallet. I catch a glimpse of his numerous credit cards, displaying more plastic than in Carol Doda breasts, as he digs out a business card and hands it to Clitty.

"Give it some thought," he says. "Let it sink in. Just remember: Opportunity doesn't knock twice."

Pawny removes a five from the wallet and tosses it on the counter. "Nice meeting you folks. Call me if you got any questions," he says. Then turning to the clerk, "Larry, thanks. See you next month," and he grabs his briefcase and is quickly out the door. I'm hoping the clerk opens a few windows to air out the joint.

Clitty says, "We can now inhale."

The clerk laughs to himself as he mops the floor. "I hear that spiel once a month," he grins. "I could recite it in my sleep."

As I leave money on the counter for the coffees, Clitty and I laugh too. As we leave the diner the laughter builds and by the time we're at Pam Grier, we're almost crying in hysterics. I open the front door and Max jumps in, taking a place in the back seat, then Clitty just about falls onto the front seat and I collapse on top of her, now weak with laughter.

"Cool!" Clitty says, and we laugh some more. Good. She hasn't used up her quota because it's cool to hear her say "Cool."

"The Swiss Shitter" I laugh and we're doubled over in convulsions.

"You know," she says, "There are just some people who should be laughed at."

For some reason though I kinda felt sorry for Pawny. He seemed so alone. Probably the only Christmas card he ever receives is from his insurance agent.

"You'd think that a guy with three balls would have a deeper voice," she says, and we laugh even louder.

"That may be your chance to be filthy rich."

"After talking to him I just feel filthy."

"Don't you wanna be a big success?" I ask.

She pauses. "The way I figure it, my pursuit of wealth has not worked out so I'm trying a different approach. I'm gonna pursue poverty."

"Oh, yeah?"

"Yup. I figure trying to be poor is much easier than trying to be rich, and so far I'm doing very well at it so I consider myself to be a success."

"Well, I've got nothing," I say, "But you're welcome to it."

"Where would I put nothing?"

"Nowhere."

"At least it would fit in my suitcase."

"All my life I've had the label of being an underachiever," I tell her. "Well, I worked hard to be an underachiever. It didn't come naturally."

"Yeah. Have no expectations and you'll never be disappointed."

"Yes. Aim low."

I remove a Blue Dream from the inside brim of my fedora and light it up. I stare up at the moon, its illumination peeking through the blackness like a round hole had been cut out of the sky and was letting in the breath and light of a distant world.

We sit in silence for a long time, alone in our thoughts, until Clitty whispers, "Tell me about your death." I close my eyes and smile.

"Oh, didn't I tell you that it's all in my head?"

"So you're imagining it? Ha! I thought so!"

"No. I'm serious. It really is in my head. A little spot that can't be operated on. And that spot is getting larger and larger as I get smaller and smaller until one day the spot will be huge and I will disappear."

The gravity of the situation cascades on Clitty like an avalanche. "I'm so sorry."

"When I was a kid there was a neighbor across the street who had a sick dog. He loved that dog, but he knew the dog was old and sick and suffering and wouldn't recover, so one day he took out his hunting rifle, told the dog he was sorry, and shot it in the head. He thought he was doing the right thing, and maybe that's what the dog wanted too. Do you understand what I'm saying? There'll come a day when I hope you use your gun."

Max rolls his eyes, "Oh Jesus, Mr. Melodramatic. Now he wants to go out like *Ol' Yeller*."

I ignore him and stare at Clitty. "I have nothing to say," she Johnny Belinda-ized.

We held a gaze for a long time, until she turned away and sobbed.

Chapter 15

The next morning we awake in a nearby Super 8. Clitty insisted on showering after the conversation with Pawny. We shower together, the water washing off memories of the previous night and circling the drain. We load up on bananas, apples, Danishes and coffee from the continental breakfast and get back into the Caddy, pull down the convertible top and dine *alfresco*. Max wolfs down several blueberry muffins with a side of Iams.

Clitty tells me about her Uncle Gus who appeared to be cut from the same cloth as Pawny. "Ever hear of the 'Pet Tumbleweed'?" she asks.

"No."

"Uncle Gus was driving through Texas late one summer and he had to dodge a lot of tumbleweeds flyin' across the highway, but it gave him an idea. He thought he'd cash-in on the Pet Rock idea so he took all of his and Aunt Lila's savings from the bank... about ten thousand... to try and market the Pet Tumbleweed. Aunt Lila thought it was a dumbass idea. His brother Johnny thought it was a dumbass idea. His kids thought it was a dumbass idea. His friends thought it was a dumbass idea. But he said he had a vision, like St. Bernadette at Lourdes. Besides, the guy who invented the Pet Rock made a fortune. So he figured he'd hire a truck and crew and drive along Texas roads and pick these things up and give 'em cute little names, put 'em in fancy packages and sell 'em. Complete with their own certificates of authenticity. He even made a TV commercial of a man walking alongside a tumbleweed that's rollin' along and the guy is talkin' to it like it's some pet dog or something. The video played a few times late at night on local TV stations."

"So what happened? Did he get rich?" I Bill Gates-ed.

"Fuck, no. Nobody wanted a Pet Tumbleweed. He rented a warehouse and filled it with tumbleweeds, and they may still be there now for all I know. And he and Lila were out ten grand. Everybody was right. It was a dumbass idea."

"You can't always get what you want."

Max jumps in:

"But if you try some time, you just might find,
you get what you need."

"Well, sometimes you just gotta ignore everybody and listen to your gut feeling." I heard my ring tone and glanced down at my cell phone. On the screen was the same cryptic message NOT NOW and I put the phone away and repeated to Clitty, "Yeah, you just have to ignore everybody."

Clitty licks the Danish frosting from her fingertips. "What about you? Any get-rich-quick schemes?"

"Screen writing, but that's more get-rich-slow, if you get rich at all. You could spend a lifetime paying your dues."

"Why do you do it?"

I shrug. "I'm a masochist, I guess."

"Can I read one?"

"Sure. Then you'll be a masochist, too."

She says "Fuckalicious" and playfully punches my arm.

"Yeah, you can read 'em. If you get really bored with your

life. They're in a tote in the..." and no sooner had I said those words then I'm swept over by a tsunami of nausea. I fling open the door and vomit. I close my eyes and moan. I wipe my mouth with my sleeve and gasp and vomit again.

"We've gotta get you to a doctor," Clitty said.

"I'm past that." I reach inside the glove compartment, grab a bottle and pop a Marinol and then remove a joint of Northern Lights and quickly fire it up. I take a deep drag, "Sorry. That came out of nowhere. Damn! I haven't felt this nauseous since the Pauly Shore Film Festival."

"Anything I can do for you?"

"Yeah. Reach in your handbag, take out your gun, and shoot me in the head."

Max says, "Chaz, if you want it done right, do it yourself. Remember the line from *Out of the Past*? The Jane Greer character shoots a guy four times but only connects once, so the Steve Brodie character says, "A dame with a rod is like a guy with a knitting needle." Besides, shooting yourself is a cliché. So mundane."

"Too Hemingway."

"Yeah, but that was a big deal because Ernest was already a famous writer. You're not, so if you blow your brains out, it won't even be picked up by Fox News."

"Maybe you should go out like *Thelma and Louise*," Clitty says. "Something that'll make the news, something dramatic, something that'll get you fifteen minutes of fame."

"Especially if you invite reporters and a camera crew," Max says. "They'll find out you wrote screenplays and studios will want to read them. The *60 Minutes* crew will ask, 'Who was that troubled genius ignored by Hollywood?'"

"You have to go out with a bang, not a whimper," Clitty urges.

Max and Clitty are right. Getting published posthumously is

better than not at all.

I manage a smile to Max and then stroke the top of his head. We sit in silence for about twenty minutes. The nausea is gone but I'm too relaxed to drive because my legs are like jelly. A feeling like I had been de-boned. I get out and stagger to the passenger side and motion Clitty to get behind the wheel. "Where to?" she asks.

"Anywhere that's not here."

Clitty asks for a hit and she fills her lungs and says, "Okay, we're off to see the wizard to get you a new brain," as she eases Pam Grier into 'Drive' and we accelerate down the road.

I tell Clitty that when Max and I were driving around the country earlier in the year we passed through Kansas and saw billboards advertising the Wizard of Oz Museum in the town of Wamego so we stopped in. I didn't want a flying monkey grabbing Max and disappearing into the sky. I remember some old guy ahead of me in line waiting to pay the entrance fee and he asked the clerk if he could get a discount because he is a senior, and the clerk said in a very condescending tone, "Sir, no one is ever old in the land of Oz," which I thought was a pretty bad cop-out so I paid his way and the old man was very appreciative. The clerk seemed to have a real attitude problem and should have given him a break. Maybe a house will fall on top of her.

I start thinking about places Max and I visited. South Dakota is not only the land of Mt. Rushmore but also the land of billboards, a countless amount of billboards blocking the beautiful rolling Black Hills, advertising a T/A Truck Stop, Wall Drug, and signs for 'Reptile Gardens,' with the billboards always reading 'Experience the thrill,' so Max and I created our own Reptile Gardens billboards. We came up with:

'Reptile Gardens — Experience the thrill of being swallowed whole by an anaconda!'

A photo of a beaming Mom and Dad looking lovingly at

little Johnny with the caption: 'At Reptile Gardens, they'll never forget when they lose their meddling fingers to a snapping turtle!'

'Reptile Gardens, where doctors are standing by.'

'Reptile Gardens — Play Frog Roulette! Six harmless frogs in the pond and one poisonous dart frog. Reach in, grab a harmless frog and win a prize!'

When I was young my parents drove across the country, and at the New Jersey state line was a sign reading 'Welcome to the Garden State.' A few thousand feet down the road someone had posted another sign: 'New Jersey, Smell the Difference.'

Near Pasa Robles Clitty says, "Let's see where this takes us," and we quickly ease onto a side road off Highway 101. We pass a strip mall with a liquor store, an H & R Block, and a boarded up magic shop, which prompted Clitty to observe, "The magic shop disappeared. Nice trick."

Next to the abandoned magic shop is a dry cleaning shop named 'J-C Cleaners.' "They must specialize in robes and swaddling clothes," I tell her.

We pass an adult store that appears to no longer be in business. Weeds overrun the parking lot, windows are boarded up, and paint is peeling. Out front a large dilapidated sign advertises: 'Mother's Day special: 20% off all toys.'

I tell Clitty, "Yeah, nothing says Happy Mother's Day quite like giving Mom a dildo."

"I think I once saw that in a Norman Rockwell illustration."

"Hey, it's one of the freedoms in the Bill of Rights to give Mom a ten inch black love python."

Clitty salutes and says, "God bless America."

Now we pass forests and fields, with the occasional house or trailer on a patch of land. There are no other cars on this stretch of road. I think it's seen less traffic than the dental supply aisle at a Wal-Mart in Mississippi.

Clitty drives the Caddy like it's an extension of her very essence, taking each curve and playing each bend with a delightful ease, a euphoric ride into the unknown but always in command, carrying me aloft to dizzying riffs like a Lennie Tristano improv. Her driving turns me on. I lean over and plunge my face into her lap, although in my weakened condition I sort of fall into her lap.

She plays "Tubthumping" on the CD and sings:

> "I get knocked down but I get up again
> You're never gonna keep me down."

She turns down the volume and asks, "You wanna play rear-steer?"

I expect to hear Dum Phuk yell "Yes! Yes!" in my ear but he must be gone for good. I tell Clitty "No, thanks. I appreciate you driving."

"If neither one of us drives, we'd be goin' nowhere fast," she replies. "It's like what the Dalai Lama used to say, 'Somebody's gotta fuck the yak.'"

"Did the Dalai Lama really say that?"

She doesn't respond and turns up the volume:

> "He sings the songs that remind him of the good times
> He sings the songs that remind him of the best times."

as my one speaker shakes like it's inflicted with St. Vitus's Dance.

I close my eyes and inhale the sweet moment of now. It could be the weed, or it could be echoes from the past, but my thoughts turn to Grandpa Don, my mom's dad. When I was very young my family visited Don and Helen's farm near Ames, Iowa. Or what was left of it. When my mom was a little girl on the farm, it was prosperous. Don and Helen had several hundred acres, along with a herd of about a hundred Holsteins, pigs, sheep, and chickens. Life was good. But things changed after Mom left for college and her older brother joined the Marines. Don and Helen tried to run the farm on their own but had little success, and things took a really bad turn for the worse when Don fell and suffered a skull fracture while repairing the barn roof. Helen said the accident changed him. He was a different man. Their life together would never be the same.

I remember Don being a man of few words, like it hurt him to speak. Perhaps it did.

I was six when I saw my mom's childhood home. The old red John Deere tractor was rusting in a thorny clutch of briars and weeds with a steady stream of arrivals and departures of hornets near the radiator. Brown, moldy, rotting bales of hay were stacked inside the barn while the fields became overgrown with weeds and brush. Even the weather vane on the barn roof rusted stuck and no longer twirled. The livestock had been sold and the farm was dead, except for a couple of Plymouth Rock chickens.

I only met Grandpa Don a couple of times and I don't recall seeing him prior to his accident. I remember looking at him after his fall and saying to myself, 'If I ever get that old I hope I never act that old.' He was short but very overweight, resembling Orson Welles in the later years of the actor's life when he was selling wine, and Grandpa always wore very worn denim bib overalls over a flannel shirt. Photos I saw of him in younger days when he worked the farm were of a robust, wiry man, but he gained weight after his fall.

My mom thought he was chronically depressed and suffered PTSD from his service in the Korean War. She said the accident left her father a recluse and often described his behavior as being "a little odd." Grandpa Don would sometimes mumble to no one in particular like he was having a conversation with imaginary folks. Grandma said, "If it wasn't for the voices in his head, he wouldn't talk to anyone." It was around this time I realized that mental illness didn't just run in my family, it galloped like it was nearing the finish line.

Both of the times we visited, Don was in the chicken coop talking to the chickens, while a tune by the Ray Conniff Singers played on an old, dusty, cob-webby cassette player hanging from a wooden peg in a beam. He insisted the hens produced healthier eggs while laying them to the sounds of the Ray Conniff Singers. It always took a lot of yelling by my grandmother to pry him out of the coop to come back into the house and have dinner and socialize with guests.

Don would stay for hours in the coop, talking to the chickens Henrietta and Mimi. During one visit, as my parents were in the kitchen having tea with my grandmother, I decided to wander out to the hen house to see what Grandpa was up to. I knocked on the dusty coop door, not too firmly for fear that it would fall off the hinges and crash to the ground, and I asked, "Grandpa?"

He bellowed, "Come on in, Chazy."

Inside, the Ray Conniff Singers' "Windmills of Your Mind" played in the background as Don sat on a milking stool with one of the chickens facing him atop a bale of hay. "Chazy," he said, "Watch this!" He clapped his hands in front of the chicken's beak, then held up his index finger in front of the bird's eyes, and slowly moved it back and forth, with the fowl's head moving back and forth to follow the finger. "I can hypnotize it! Pretty good, huh? Yupyupyup!"

> "Like a clock whose hands are sweeping
> past the minutes of its face. And the world
> is like an apple whirling silently in space."

The bird did look dazed and vacant as it stared off into space, like the Robinson Stone character in *Stalag 17*. Don smiled and watched the bird for a couple of minutes, then snapped his fingers and the chicken shook its head and staggered off the bale of hay.

I wasn't sure what to say but I blurted out, "That's great. You... you hypnotize it so it'll lay more eggs?"

My grandfather looked confused. "Weeeellllllllllllll," he slowly drew out the word, "Never thought about that. Nope. Hmmmm. Not a bad idea though. Yupyupyupyup."

"Like a tunnel that you follow to a tunnel of its own.
Down a hollow to a cavern where the sun has never shone."

Grandpa shook his head, like the chicken, to clear his thoughts. He reached under Mimi and pulled out an egg, then held it up in front of my eyes, as he sputtered, "Yupyupyup. Know what this is?"

"An egg?" I hesitated, fearing that it might be a trick question.

"It's the universe," he said, breaking into a Jack-O-Lantern grin. "It's you and me and the state of Iowa and the pyramids in Egypt and the Bay of Fundy and Marilyn Monroe and Saturn and my manure spreader and the Chicago Cubs and Che Guevara and everyone's ego and thoughts and dreams and religions. All inside here. Yupyupyup."

"Oh" was my weak and unsure response. I had no idea what he was talking about or where he was going with this conversation.

"And the world is like an apple whirling silently in space."

He moved the egg back and forth in front of my face and I wondered, "Is he trying to hypnotize me?"

"Chazy, it wouldn't take much to break this egg. But it would be folly to do so. Yupyupyup. Ruin everything in the universe. Disrupt the Great Eternal Plan." His voice grew louder and more agitated. "Mountains would go crashing into the sea. The Earth would get swallowed by the Sun. Mother Nature would take her last gasp of air and every single sperm in the Almighty's ejaculate wouldn't be worth a plugged nickel because it would be impossible to create a new tomorrow. You hear me? IMPOSSIBLE! YUPYUPYUP." His voice was now thundering.

He caught his breath and continued. "That's why it's our responsibility to take care of this egg. Nurture it. Respect it. Never assume it's gonna be here for another minute. Another hour. Another day. You understand, boy?"

I nodded, although I was baffled and somewhat frightened, and at the age of six, what I knew about a metaphor could fit into a flea's navel.

"Like a circle in a spiral, like a
wheel within a wheel. Never ending
or beginning on an ever-spinning reel."

"Grandson," he said, now holding the egg on the bridge of my nose so my eyes crossed, "This is very fragile. Treat it right and it'll give us Time. Yupyupyup."

Grandpa's eyes twinkled and I replied, "Yupyupyup."

"Yup," he said.

"Yup," I echoed, as he placed the egg in my hands. As I gently cupped it, he put his strong, massive hands around mine and said, "Chazy, thank you. Now seize the day." His strong, massive hands were just a bit too strong and massive, like Lenny cupping a rabbit, because we heard a sharp CRACK and watched in shock as yolk oozed between our fingers and drooled in glops onto the chicken coop floor. I felt my heart race. With great apprehension I looked up into his eyes. His eyes had gone dull and were no longer twinkling. I murmured, "Yup" but he didn't respond with "Yupyupyup." Damn, I had destroyed the Universe. At least his.

It seemed like forever before he finally spoke, "Oh well, there'll be other eggs." He exhaled a deep breath. I made a bee line out of the hen house and that would be the last time I saw Grandpa Don.

"Like the circles that you find
In the windmills of your mind."

Years later my mom told me that the relationship between Don and Helen reached the tipping point because of the attention he gave Henrietta and Mimi, or as Helen described it "Over friendliness bordering on unspeakable," and on more than one occasion she read him the riot act. "It's either me or the chickens," she'd snap, but he never offered his choice. The final straw was the day a FedEx van arrived and delivered a package addressed to Don. Helen was curious and opened the box and inside was a plastic bag of Frederick's of Hollywood panties, the crotchless style. Her immediate assumption was that Don was going to dress up the chickens in provocative outfits. She hit the roof. Later that same day Don had a massive stroke and died. Word was Helen had discovered his body in the chicken coop, but no other details were ever forthcoming, and whatever caused Grampa to die from a massive, sudden heart attack in the coop was never divulged. That piece of information went with Grandma to her grave. I'd like to think that Don bought the panties for Helen, with the intention of spicing up their marriage. It's the romantic in me.

It's not known whatever became of Henrietta and Mimi, but my guess is they aspired to bust out of the chicken coop, leave cosplay behind, take to the air, and soar like eagles.

I was still feeling the elation of Northern Lights when I returned from my flashback and I asked Clitty, "What is the point of it all?"

"There is no point," she replied. "There's no reason for any of it and it's all very unimportant. Once you accept the nothingness of it all, everything is cool."

"Thanks, Nietzsche. I can always depend on you to leave me laughing."

"Cool!"

"Cool and Fuckalicious!" I laugh.

Chapter 16

"Life is either a daring adventure or nothing."
— Helen Keller

"Life is but a dream for the dead."
—"You Know What They Do" — My Chemical Romance

I remember the date like it happened yesterday. August 24th, 1995, four years ago, when I told my parents I was not returning to school in the fall to complete my senior year. I was done. School had no appeal. The teachers were uninspiring. My fellow students were jerks. The school psychologist thought I should be locked up. In a room with nothing flammable. The news was not a warm and fuzzy warmly received by Mom and Dad. It all hit the fan.

August 24th was an ugly day I try to block out of my memory. I wish I could delete that file. Who in their right mind would want to float down the River Styx and return to that inferno? It was just one more fire I set, but unlike any other. Max tells me to write it all down and that will help me process the anger and pain. I take the laptop from under the front seat and write in Final Draft:

EXT. BACKYARD - DAY
George and Sara are seated at a table on the deck as their son Chaz leans against the railing.

GEORGE
What do you mean, "You're quitting high school?"

CHAZ

It's pretty clear. How else can you interrupt that?

GEORGE

Don't be a wise-ass.

SARA

Chaz, have you given this a lot of thought?

CHAZ

Yeah. At least the last ten years.

GEORGE

What a disappointment. After everything your mother
and I—

CHAZ

Yeah, Dad, I shouldn't have been born. It's all your fault
for having me.

*George jumps from the chair and approaches Chaz, getting
right in his grill.*

GEORGE

Listen here, you little ungrateful bastard. If it wasn't for
the sacrifices your mother and—

SARA *(angrily)*

George!

*Sara goes to Chaz as George returns to the table and pours
himself another drink. Sara puts her hands on Chaz's shoulders.*

SARA

Honey, your father and I don't want you to
make the wrong decision. If you want to be successful
you need an education. Maybe you just need sometime
away from school.

GEORGE *(sarcastically)*

So he can find himself?

*Sara begins to sob and Chaz puts his arm around her
shoulders.*

I can't finish this scene. It's too painful. I want to escape the future and not the past, but this scene is an exception. I fold up the laptop and slump down in the passenger seat. Clitty bobs her head to some tune on the radio. The tune playing in my head is 'There's no more time left to criticize. I've seen what I could not recognize. Everything in my life was leading me on. But I can be strong.' Max leans into the front seat and licks my left ear. "What's that for?" I ask.

"Just thought you needed a display of kindness," he said. "I'm a dog. That's what we do. That and the loyalty thing."

"Thanks," I murmur, wiping the dog drool from my ear lobe.

"Besides, I like the taste of ear wax."

I turn to Clitty and grab her arm. She turns down the volume on the CD and I ask, "Where are we goin'?"

"Nowhere."

"When are we gonna get there?"

"Never!"

She cranks the music back up and continues rocking. I'm in need of a major chill so I take a Cookies & Cream from inside my fedora, light it, and take a long drag. I offer a hit to Clit but she doesn't give a shit. I figure we'll drive for a couple of hours then crash in a motel. Sliding into a deep relaxation, my thoughts turn to Grandmother Grace, my Dad's mom. I remember years ago during a Thanksgiving dinner when she announced in a clear, bold voice, "I've found Jesus!" No one said anything for what seemed like hours, until I blurted out, "I didn't know he was missing." My Grandfather Maxie laughed but everybody else got pissed off. I suppose I was disrespectful, and I can certainly understand why she would turn to religion after dealing with Maxie for all those years. Maxie was Jewish, although he never practiced, and even though Grace was baptized Methodist, I don't think they ever gave their religious differences a second thought.

Grandma Grace was tight with her church, always going to

Sunday service and pot luck suppers and teaching Bible class. Every fall she'd make replicas of the Nativity Scene using various vegetables to represent Joseph and Mary, the Three Magi, and Baby Jesus, along with cows, sheep, and chickens. She would buy small balsa wood cradles, along with tiny eyes and pipe cleaners at a local arts and crafts store to make the characters a little more realistic. Joseph was a cucumber and Mary would be a small gourd, both with pipe cleaner arms and legs. Joseph and Mary would have eyes much larger than the Baby Jesus, who usually had two tiny eyes glued to a large green olive as it lay on a tuft of hay in the cradle. Two beady, unblinking eyes looking in different directions. Jesus looked like Marty Feldman.

Grace made the animals from apples and pears. She would stick corn kernels on top of the fruit to represent the animal's ears and then she'd glue on eyes. She'd sell these Nativity scenes at local craft fairs and church bazaars and they were a big hit.

At first, Grandma made the Nativity scene in October so by the time Christmas rolled around, the characters took on a different look, like they had been left in the care of Tim Burton. The apple and pear animals shriveled up to where they resembled livestock with anorexia. Joseph and Mary shriveled up and turned gray and quite often developed holes from some worm parasite. When Christmas came, the green olive Baby Jesus had turned brown with wrinkles and now resembled Moms Mabley. The crèche appeared to be assembled by George A. Romero. After a couple of years of seeing the rapid deterioration of the characters, she wisely started the creative process in late November.

Grandma Grace's vision was deteriorating and sometimes she'd place the wrong eyes on the characters. In one Nativity, the cow wore the tiny eyes intended for Baby Jesus and Baby Jesus had two huge yellow corn kernels for eyes. One year Grace bought the wrong eyes from the arts and crafts store. Very large eyes that you'd find on a stuffed teddy bear, so for that particular

Nativity scene every character appeared to be frightened beyond belief.

That night in a motel bed we shared a Blue Dream. Clitty asked about the time I spent on the road away from my parents.

I told her the story:

I was reluctant to tell my parents that I planned to return to school after a few months but I first needed some time to find myself. They didn't think I was missing, but I was. They seemed to be fighting all the time so they had their own problems to worry about. They needed some time to find themselves. So instead of entering my senior year, I set off on The Great Adventure.

I inherited the '59 Caddy from Grandpa Maxie as soon as I turned 16 and got my driver's license and had been driving it for more than a year with no tickets and no accidents. Mom and Dad gave me permission to take to the road as long as I returned in three months. They figured I would get the wanderlust out of my system. My folks said they were concerned for my safety, so they laid down the rule: I could only drive around California. I laughed to myself, but I assured them that I would not venture into the other 49 states because it would be too dangerous. I felt like I was running away from home, but with my parents blessing. Wise old Grandpa Maxie used to say, "You're never too old to run away from home."

Dad filled the gas tank, which only got me a couple of hundred miles away, Mom packed the cooler with soy milk, frozen veggies, and cheese, and I made sure I had plenty of meds in one tote as well as cash hidden in various compartments. I was surprised they said yes to my road trip, but they talked it over with my school psychologist who said it would be a good thing to get my mind off of my mind. I told my folks, with tears in my eyes, "Even at my age I have a 'bucket list.' None of us know how much time we have left." I sold it real good and that must have clinched it because that afternoon they were helping me plan out my trip. They had a map of California spread out on the kitchen table and my mom would say, "Oh, you have to see Yosemite" or "Don't forget to go to Alcatraz," and Dad would say, "You should hang around Hollywood, maybe you'll run into some stars, like the girl who played Julie McCoy on the *Love Boat*. You can give her one of your scripts."

My parents also gave me a platinum credit card with a gazillion funds to use, with my mother's warning, "Spend responsibly. Don't do anything rash," which I always thought was a strange expression, kind of like "Don't come down with a skin condition." I assured her I wouldn't. My Grandma Helen gave me a couple of thousand dollars in cash and said, "Now don't tell your parents. This will be our little secret." I knew she had a lot of money after the sale of the farm and her husband's life insurance policy, but it was still a nice gesture and I thanked her tons.

My parents made me promise three things: I would check in every day with a phone call to see if I was okay and so they could track my progress. They made me promise I'd be home for Thanksgiving so I could start my senior year in December and only miss three months, which I could make up blindfolded while standing on my head. I wanted to come back before Christmas and they wanted me back before Halloween so we compromised on Thanksgiving. They knew that with my IQ I'd breeze through and graduate with my class in June.

They also insisted I practice cello every day. I swore on the soul of St. Cecilia that I would. I love to practice. I don't think of it as drudgery, but a form of escape. Kind of like weed, but without the side effect of making you hungry.

There were a lot of tears when I drove the Caddy down the long driveway of our home. It felt strange to leave, although the previous year I had already been away from home for a couple of months in Ju-Vee Hall, but this time it seemed like I'd be gone forever. It was something I needed to do, like Will leaving to see Skylar.

In case I needed to defend myself, Dad gave me a small canister of mace and suggested I find a pit bull to take along for the ride. Mom gave me the cordless Black & Decker meat carver we use for Thanksgiving for protection. I figured if I was ever assaulted by a flock of angry turkeys, I'd be able to defend myself.

I left the house and had just stopped at the end of the driveway when I heard my cell ring tone blare the theme to *Charlie's Angels*. I answered. It was Mom. "Where are you now?" she asked.

"At the end of our driveway."

"Oh," she sighed, like someone had pulled a dark curtain over her light. "It already seems like you've been gone so long."

"Mom, don't worry. I'll be fine. Call you tonight."

"Sure you don't want to get a good night's sleep and start first thing tomorrow morning?"

"Bye, Mom."

I took a stick of Blue Dream from my glove compartment, lit it and inhaled the madness. I looked both ways on the road, wondering whether to go left or right. It really didn't matter which direction I took, I just wanted to get miles away from me. I looked one more time in the rear view mirror down the driveway toward the house. At that moment I thought, "When I return, things are not going to be the same."

And they weren't.

Chapter 17

"Wandering re-establishes the original harmony
which once existed between man and the universe."
— Anatole France

"Give me one reason to stay here
And I'll turn right back around."
"Give Me One Reason" —Tracy Chapman

My first stop was the local animal shelter. I didn't know
if I wanted a pit or a German Shepherd or a Chocolate Lab. It
just seemed like it would be cool to have a traveling companion.
Something to talk to, even if it didn't talk back. I thought if I
drove around the country with a dog it would be like *Travels With
Charlie* on acid. Maybe I could teach the dog to roll over, play
dead, and smoke a joint.

Without a doubt, I hit the dog lottery when I chose
Max.

It was after I paid the shelter, put the collar around his neck,
hooked up the leash and got him in the back seat that I realized
this was not an ordinary dog. I jumped in the front seat and we sat
there looking at each other for the longest time. I said to myself,
"I'll think I'll call you Max. After my grandfather. What do ya
think? Wanna be called Max?"

The dog turned its head and looked off in the distance for a
few seconds before looking back at me with a head tilt. There was
a brain at work there! Damn, as I looked into this dog's eyes I felt
like it was trying to talk to me. I thought about that for a moment
then put the joint into the ashtray. Maybe I better hold off on any
more drags before reality is completely shredded. The dog pawed
me on the shoulder and whined. I could almost hear the word

"Chaz," and at that point I snuffed out the stick.

"Okay, this is really gonna be a long, strange trip." I continued staring at my new companion. I put the Caddy in 'D' and tore off down the road, all the while looking at the canine in the back seat.

"A strange trip, indeed!" I Timothy Leary-ized

First stop was the local dog park. How social would this dog be with other dogs? Yeah, the shelter swore that it was social, but what does that mean? It's friendly with dogs larger than him, but will eat smaller dogs?

I hadn't been to a dog park since I dated a girl in my sophomore year who had a Chihuahua named Pinky. Pinky had a little pink harness and pink leash and was an irritating little shit who I expected also shit pink turds. I acted like I cared for the dog because I wanted to have sex with its owner. But I never did, even after spending a small fortune on rawhide chewies. People are just so ungrateful.

Some folks have problems with dogs humping at dog park. They always try to separate the dogs. They should just let dogs be dogs. Years ago their parents should have been separated while humping.

I entered the dog park and let Max loose. Faster than the Madeleine LeBeau character who stood at attention when the band played "La Marseillaise," a male poodle approached my dog and sniffed its butt. My dog sniffed the poodle's butt. The poodle's owner approached me and for a second I thought he was going to sniff my butt but he did not. He mentioned what a good looking dog I had. I lied and returned the compliment even though I really don't care for poodles.

Later at the dog park some guy said, "Don't let your dog play with poodles. He'll go gay."

"Not that there's anything wrong with that," I Jerry Sienfeld-ized back to him.

I soon realized Max did have a mean streak. I yelled at him for some reason or other while I was driving, so he lifted his leg and peed on the rear left speaker as I was listening to the radio, because it suddenly went BUHZXXCCZZ and I thought it was blowing up.

I recognized Max's hostility for what it was: An attempt to be Alpha dog. I didn't care. If he wanted to be in charge and make decisions, that was fine. I was never one to embrace responsibility, and in fact I get a little anxious if it's in the same room with me.

We drove all day and I must admit there was a twinge of pain and guilt when I saw the road sign: 'Welcome to Nevada.' I promised to stay in California, but I had exploring to do before going home for Thanksgiving. I figured I'd pay cash for everything outside of California rather than leave my parents a trail of receipts from other states.

The next sign read 'Speed limit 80' so I gave the Caddy the gas and it flew above the highway. I knew it had a lot more speed left in that grand engine and if I pushed the pedal to the floor it would create sonic booms. I likened the black missile's speed to a cool vivacissimo.

My Grandpa Maxie, a life-long Democrat, used to say that the red states had higher speed limits so liberals could drive quickly through them to minimize the discomfort. I didn't care if I was crossing red or blue states or green states with yellow polka dots, it just felt great to be on the road, the convertible top down, and the radio cranked up to a rock and roll tune. I never felt so free in my life.

I took one of the Reno exits and cruised down Virginia Street in The Biggest Little City in the World. Some guy on the sidewalk whistled and yelled, "Nice black beauty you got there, buddy." I nodded and then it hit me: I should name this Caddy. There was a sudden flash in my brain and I thought of the movie star Pam Grier, of *Foxy Brown* and *Sheba Baby* fame. She's like an old lady now, but in those blaxploitation films of the '70's she sure was hot and she sure went topless a lot.

I drove up and down Virginia Street, with the occasional side street, and observed that Reno is just a puppy dog. So eager to please, yet independent. A little out of control. A little impetuous. Undisciplined. But something you could eventually care for and love in spite of its shortcomings.

A few times I nearly ran the curb or hit parked cars while staring at the fine-looking women parading the street. Lots of legs. Lots of cleavage. I was getting so hot and I remembered what a guy in Ju-Vee Hall used to say, "I was so horny I'd fuck a porcupine if you held it for me." I wasn't quite at that point but the ladies were sensuous fireworks of neon colors lighting up the Nevada sky. I had lots of money. More money than courage, so I thought I'd give it a try. I pulled the Caddy to the curb near a tall brunette with latte-colored skin stuffed into a sparkling blue dress. She was talking on a cell phone.

I took a deep breath and asked, "Excuse me... you... ah... would you like some company?" She didn't hear me and her back was turned to the street but I heard her yell into the phone and she was upset with somebody named Jason. She said, "Jason, don't be a prick. Well, you're acting like a prick. I know you. You can be very pricky." I noticed what a deep voice she had. I tried to get her attention again and she screamed something into the cell and then turned to me, in a very feminine voice, "Hold on a second, sugar," and then continued to blast Jason. As she took a few steps toward a streetlight I saw what large biceps she had and a little voice inside said that it was time to leave. So I put the Caddy in drive and slowly pulled away from the curb, as the lady yelled, "Hey, sugar! Where ya goin'? Get back here!" and then back to the phone she screamed "Fuck you Jason, now you did it, you little prick," but I was gone as quickly as you could sing "Lola, la la la la la Lola."

I thought I heard Max give out a snort-laugh, but it was probably the weed playing tricks on me. I spent a few more hours in Reno. Tried to play a slot machine in some casino but got tossed out when I showed my driver's license but they could tell it was a forgery. Tried to talk with a girl working at a Subway. Her name tag read 'Heather' and we seemed to connect while she was making my Italian with "extra cheese and hold the onions," but she mentioned that she was meeting her boyfriend after work so that affair had the lifespan of your average gnat, but at least I had some extra cheese and she held my onions, although I thought of other things I'd rather have her hold.

That night I slept in the back seat of Pam Grier at a rest stop off I-80 just a few miles outside of town. I could see the lights of Reno illuminating the western part of the sky while the Eastern sky dazzled with natural lights, like I was inside a dark box but there were thousands of pin holes letting in distant energy. Later in a dream, or more like a nightmare, I was back home. My parents were not there, but I wasn't alone because there was this being that would not leave the house, some creature that had invaded my space, but nothing I did could force it to leave. I felt it was going to kill me. I jumped awake, with my brow covered in sweat.

That morning a combination of a chill in the air and the rising sun woke me. Max had already jumped out of the front seat and was marking territory. I grabbed a can of dog food and put it in a bowl on the ground. Then I walked to a nearby tree to mark my own territory. I figured we'd stop at the next coffee shop and grab a muffin. I didn't know where the next coffee shop was. I didn't know where I was going, but was hopeful that any place would be better than where I've been.

I lit up the remaining roach from last night's joint and my mind was soon colorful confetti. Max finished his meal and I was wondering if his previous owner had taught him any tricks. "What if I adopted some brilliant dog that could do all kinds of tricks?" I Lassie-ized.

I knelt next to Max. "Can you shake?" and he offered his right paw. Good boy!

"Can you roll over?" and the dog sank to the ground and rolled over on his back. "Can you drive me around the country?" and the dog jumped into the front seat behind the steering wheel and stared at me with a tilt of his head.

Okay, this dog was now freaking me out. "Would you help me write a screenplay?" I Syd Field-ized. He could probably do a better job, at least not get bogged down in the Second Act. I can think of great beginnings and great endings but it's that great middle that seems to be so fucking elusive.

We're back on I-80 heading toward the sun. I thought of my writing. I wrote more than a dozen screenplays. At least they're in the screenplay format. A Hollywood producer or reader may think they're garbage. Someday I'll grow the balls needed to attend a pitch session with producers and agents. I'd like to write screenplays for a living, although my parents think I'm daydreaming and not being realistic. Dad wants me to be a dentist and Mom thinks I should be a high school English lit teacher. I love to read and have devoured all the classics, from Dostoevsky to Faulkner. They once suggested I go to a Waldorf school, but I have no interest in learning how to make salads. I told them a billion times how much I hate school. It doesn't challenge me. I get so bored in classes. I don't know what I'm going to do, but I know whatever it is, I'll be good at it. I've always had an interest in being on radio and I could do it without sweating out a college degree. I could work as a DJ until I sell a screenplay.

I have a need to write and I think with time I'll be pretty good. Good enough to get published. Maybe I need more life experiences. The experts say, "Write about what you know," but what do you write if you don't know anything? Yeah, maybe getting in radio will lend itself to some real-life experiences.

A guy I knew in high school had an uncle who was in radio in Minneapolis. My friend said his uncle had done some jail time for larceny, but he had a smooth voice and could talk a nun out of her habit, so he was hired by the radio station manager. The suits don't care about your past. Can you sell a product in a commercial? So even with my Ju-Vee Hall record, I could still bullshit my way into a DJ job. In the employment application I'm not going to mention I was in Ju-Vee Hall. I don't think they check that stuff anyway.

Once I graduate in June I'll be about a month short of my 17th birthday and then I can leave my parents uncivil war, I Gettysburg-ized to Max. Be on my own. I'm tired of their arguing. He drinks too much so their fights get nasty. They're loud. Even when they're not talking to each other, the silence is loud with tension and it gives me a headache.

Dad yells at Mom for always working at the real estate office, putting in lots of hours at night and on the weekends. Mom yells at Dad for drinking too much in his quest to write a novel. I know she feels neglected. He sits in a recliner for hours writing in longhand, with a glass of whiskey on a stand next him. I've never seen anything he's written. She's never seen anything he's written. Maybe what he's written is good, maybe not. He says he's not going to show it to anyone until it's finished.

I think they should lighten up on each other. At least she knows where he is every night. In the recliner, rather than in some bar putting moves on a waitress. And he should stop writing for one night a week and take her out for dinner or to a movie. He should be glad she has a job she loves and makes good money. I hope they stay together, but I don't think it's in the stars. A divorce would really suck.

I have a feeling they're staying together for my sake, but

they shouldn't worry. I can take care of myself. I'm proving it now by being on the road. I know they went to counseling for a few months but it stopped and I don't know if they'll try it again.

I look in the rear view mirror at Max, his head out the window, ears flapping every which way. He's living a simple life, but my life is problematic. It wears me down. I've got a suitcase full of suck. It would be cool to be a dog. Not a neutered dog like Max, but a dog that has his equipment and does what he wants. Having the freedom of no one telling you what to do. Living in the moment. A life where you didn't have to answer to anybody. Just then my cell phone rings. It's my mom.

"Hi Mom. Yeah, sorry I didn't call last night. I tried but I couldn't get cell service. I was near Yosemite. You know how it is with all those mountains. Everything's great. I'm happy. My dog's happy. I named him Max, after Grandpa. Yeah, he drools just like Grandpa. So... how's Dad? Well, tell him I miss him too. Okay, gotta go. Yep, love you too. Bye."

I look back at Max and he eyes me like he wants to say something. The Dog. The noblest of creatures. I don't believe in a God, but if there is one, He must be a Dog. Full of unconditional love. If it's true that God made man in his own image, then God must be an asshole too, because there are a lot of assholey people out there, but you'd never find an assholey dog. I think God has a big laboratory where He was mixing different solutions together and adding different ingredients to come up with human beings. My guess is Mankind is an experiment that went horribly wrong. Like something from a William Castle movie. If God submitted the universe as a project to one of my teachers, He would have received a B-minus.

I look back at Max and ask, "What do you think, Max? Are you God?" He doesn't answer but sticks his head out the window and the passing wind fills his mouth as his flapping cheek makes a rhythmic THWACK-THWACK-THWACK noise and drool flies from his mouth.

The Caddy skims across the road like a stone skipping on a pond as we cross Nevada. My CD player is cranked and "Nice Guys Finish Last" blasts from the speakers. Green Day doesn't quite sound the same with the constant THWACK-THWACK-THWACK accompanying the lyrics.

I've had this idea for a screenplay pin-balling around my brain for the past week. It's about a young, hot, high school teacher who's into S & M games and the student who has a crush on her. I'll take some notes on it later and see where it goes. Maybe that'll be my ticket to immortality.

I could use some of the students I know but not use their real names. A few teachers, too. I know this one guy from calculus class, his name is Geoffrey, but everybody calls him Jeffrey and that pisses him off, so he's always correcting you by saying, "No! It's Joff-ree. Joff-ree! Got it?" and the kids continue to say "Jeff-ree" just to watch him get riled up. His face gets red and his fists tighten and you expect his head to explode like *Scanners*. He doesn't have many friends, but I think he's okay. I know him from being a band geek. I think the music teacher is desperate to fill the horn section, because he uses Geoffrey, even though he plays the trumpet like he's constipated.

Geoffrey's the kind of guy who just can't tell you "I've got to go to the bathroom" or "I've gotta go take a dump." No, he'll say something like, "I've got a turd knocking on my anus door," and he's so serious when he says it. He cracks me up even though he doesn't even try. One day we were talking about getting laid and he said, "If I get myself drunk I can usually take advantage of myself," and I nearly pissed myself laughing.

Geoffrey was the first person I told when I was asked to be the class valedictorian. He said, "Maybe you can set fire to the school the day before so you don't have to deliver it."

When Geoffrey was growing up, his parents always vacationed at Disneyland. They loved the place and collected cartoon cells from Disney movies that decorated the walls of their house. Once I visited his house and had to take a leak and noticed the walls of the bathroom were plastered with cels of *The Little Mermaid*. When we were sophomores, we had a formal Winter Ball and Geoffrey asked Heather to go and she said yes. Now Geoffrey wasn't a bad looking dude, he just acted a little strange, that's all. Maybe a little ADHD. Throw in a little Asperger's. The next day in class I asked him about his date with Heather. "Did you get any?" He just blushed and grinned and whispered, "Sex with her was even better than 'Mr. Toad's Wild Ride.'"

Everything is sex in high school. Everyone's hormones are exploding like the night sky on a Fourth of July. There were so many classes that I walked out of with a book in front of my crotch to hide my hard-on. Sitting next to girls with great breasts. Watching the ass jiggle of my English teacher with her back to the class as she wrote on the blackboard. I masturbated so much I figured that over the course of a man's lifetime he must spend more time playing with his dick than with any friend.

I remember one night last year a bunch of us had a party down on the beach. We had a fire going in a metal barrel and somebody had a boom box blaring and everybody had chipped in for beer, either slipping a few bottles from their parent's refrigerators or begging an older brother to buy a six pack. A couple of friends of mine who supply me with good weed came by to sell some smoke. A girl named Linda was there. Now I was somewhat surprised to see her, because in school she pretty much kept to herself and didn't hang out with anybody, but somebody must have invited her to this beach party because there she was. Linda was okay to talk to, but she really wasn't very pretty. At least not to me. She didn't pique my interest or anything else. She was not a wharf I wanted to tie my boat to. A friend of mine even went so far as to say Linda had the sex appeal of a slag heap.

She could have used a makeover. Maybe if she put on make-up and had a hair style that was of this century she would be okay. Linda had potential. Like Laney Boggs with her big glasses and dumb ponytail. I asked a friend what he thought about Linda, and he said, "Better than sticking your dick in a beehive." I always thought that was a ringing endorsement.

Linda was a dumpy-frumpy girl. If she had been in a Dickens novel, she would have been selling matches on a London street corner. But during that party, no matter where I turned, I found Linda next to me and wanting to touch my skin. She was all over me like a swarm of mosquitoes.

I knew she was coming on to me but I didn't want to be rude, even though I ended up being so. Linda put her hand on my arm, looked into my eyes, and murmured, "This summer I finally discovered sex."

I blurted out, "Oh, you're starting to masturbate?"

As soon as I said it I felt bad, but the damage had been done. She quickly removed her hand and hissed, "You make me want to puke," sounding like the Jean-Paul Belmondo character talking to Jean Seberg. She then stormed off.

"I'm sorry. So sorry." I Brenda Lee-ized, "It was just a joke."

But I would never talk to Linda again and every time I passed her in the halls between classes we never made eye contact. Just a few months ago I saw her at a restaurant playing tongue-tag with the quarterback of the football team, a real good looking guy. She must have had a Jenny Jones makeover because she was a Bo Derek 10. I'm sure to her I'm just a distant, ugly memory.

I think when I get old, in my 40's and 50's, high school will hold a lot of distant, ugly memories for me. One of them was Lexi Cornwall. Some guys called her Cornhole. Her friends called her Cornie. We dated for a few months. We were only freshmen so neither of us drove. These were chaperoned dates so either her parents or my parents dropped us off at the movies or a restaurant and then picked us up later. It really sucked. She was real pretty with long brown hair and sparkling blue eyes and we used to kiss a lot. After a month or so she finally let me put my hand under her bra even though she didn't have much to hold on to. I could have been grabbing my own breast, it felt about the same. But that was all she'd allow. Nothing more. She wanted to save herself for when she got married. I respected that. I respected it but I still had needs, so soon I hooked up with one of her friends, a girl I knew who was not waiting to get married. I thought we were being pretty discrete, but somebody must have seen us and tipped off Lexi who got all pissed, so just after I got my grandfather's car, I think it was Lexi who took a key to it, carving DICKWEED into the front hood. Although with my track record there could have been a few other kids who were eager to trash it up.

My so-called genius got me in trouble, because I was asked by the principal to deliver the valedictorian address. Mr. Harrington wasn't happy with the idea but the school went strictly on a student's GPA and mine was 4.0, even though I missed a few months at Ju-Vee Hall in '94 and then a couple of months driving around the country in '95. Yeah, I may have had the highest GPA in school history, but I was in a class of underachievers, students who should have gone to class and not fallen asleep. Open a book instead of a bottle of beer, like John 'Bluto' Blutarsky. Okay, so my GPA was perfect, but I really didn't have much competition. I had some friends, but most of the kids were boring and very forgettable. Empty shadows that dashed across the pages of my memory.

Mr. Harrington was at the podium onstage and he introduced me through clenched teeth, "Ladies and gentlemen, Chaz Chase will now give the valedictorian address." There was polite applause and a few kids whistled as I made my way to the podium, dragging my cello along. I removed my sports jacket and then my tie and then my shoes as a few people snickered in the audience and Mr. Harrington stormed back to the podium and asked, "Mr. Chase, what are you doing?"

"Didn't you say the 'valedictorian undress'?" and many of the kids laughed. The parents didn't and my folks politely smiled, although it appeared to be more like the expression you have when you're trying to pass a kidney stone. I took a seat near the podium and fingered the cello. Then I talked. I didn't have anything prepared but I ad-libbed how life sucks but enjoy it while you can and make the best of it because as you get older it'll only get suckier once you get into a meaningless marriage and have ungrateful kids. As I rambled on I played "I'm Only Happy When it Rains" and some kids knew the tune and would sing-shout the lyrics "Pour your misery down on me!" as the parents and faculty looked wide-eyed in confusion, dismay and fear, knowing there was something going on but they didn't know what it was although it was something menacing that turned their world upside down and destroyed the norm and they didn't like it and IT MUST STOP NOW.

I continued with this nihilistic spew until I finished the tune, grabbed a lighter from my pocket and yelled, 'Now get out there and set the world on fire!" then lit up the cello. It quickly went up in flames because earlier in the day I had brush stroked a little turpentine at the base of the cello. It wasn't the expensive cello my parents had given me, but for the stage theatrics I had purchased a cheap cello at a used musical instruments store. Quite a few of the kids applauded, a few parents screamed, some shouted and booed, and Mr. Harrington ran to the stage with a fire extinguisher and doused the flames. I looked up to see my parents. My mom had her hands up to her face, all I could see were her eyes, which were wide with disbelief and resembled Sponge-Bob SquarePants. My dad's face was magenta and he had steam coming from his ears, like Elmer Fudd being out-witted by Bugs Bunny. He was visibly shaken and pissed off and ready to sell me off to some child trafficking ring. I watched as they snuck out the back door. I still have the image of Mr. Harrington, holding the fire extinguisher and staring at me with such hatred, hissing, "Mr. Chase, get out of my school and never come back." That was fine with me. It was like being kicked out of Hell by Satan.

After the ceremony I went to a senior class party but it was void of fun because there were so many parents chaperoning us like the prison guards in *Shawshank Redemption*. Later when I got home my folks were waiting up for me, which I expected, and although my Mom didn't say much but seemed to take my side or at least play the impartial referee, my dad was super pissed off. Let me screenplay it for you:

INT. LIVING ROOM - NIGHT
Chaz sits in a chair with Sara sitting nearby. George paces like he's trying to wear out the carpet.

GEORGE
Dammit Chaz, what the hell were you
trying to prove?
CHAZ
Just something different. That's all.
GEORGE
Something different, alright. A goddamn
embarrassment is what it was. The newspaper
was there, your little stunt will probably be
on the eleven o'clock news tonight...
SARA
George...
GEORGE
Jesus Christ don't take his side again. I knew
somehow this would end up being my fault—
He pours himself a whisky.

CHAZ

Mom, can I stay with you tonight? He's just—

GEORGE *(interrupts)*

You little ungrateful shit. All your mother
and I have done for you and this is how you show your
gratitude, with a public display of humiliation...

*George approaches Chaz, his fist clenched. Sara jumps
between George and Chaz.*

SARA

George! Calm down! It's not the end of
the world.

CHAZ

Mom, it's no use. You know how he is.

SARA

It was unique, like our son. You wouldn't
expect him to deliver some cookie-cutter speech that
you've heard a billion times.

GEORGE

Yeah, what the hell do you care? You don't live
in this town anymore.

CHAZ

You're overreacting.

*George rips a couple of epees from the wall and tosses
one to me.*

GEORGE

En garde, you little shit!

*George and Chaz duel for several minutes, knocking
over a table lamp and an aquarium.*

Okay, so the dueling part of the scene I made up. I think
writers have to embellish the truth to make stories bigger than
life. Hemingway may have taken two minutes to land a trout in a
lake in Idaho, but he embellished the story and came up with *The*

Old Man and the Sea.

I'm sure Mr. Vadim, my high school counselor, would have found sexual imagery in the dueling scene. He was so Freudian. I can hear his voice now saying the epees were penis substitutes and my Dad and I were fighting for the attention of my Mom. Geez, that is really twisted, but that's how his mind rolled.

The rest of the scene played out like I wrote it, and throughout the scene all I could think of was the aggressive, angry music of "Mars, Bringer of War." It was the perfect soundtrack for me and my Dad's hostilities.

But in retrospect maybe I did get carried away and was a little over the top. I didn't want to embarrass my folks. I just wanted to make a point and make the valedictorian address something memorable that would be the topic of conversation during our fifty year class reunion.

My first best friend was Jimmy Arroyo. He wasn't very bright and was sure goofy looking, but he made me laugh. It took him five years, but he finally graduated from high school, and in his yearbook he was voted by the senior class as the student 'Most Likely to be Arrested for Beastiality.' It was an 'honor' he seemed to be proud of.

When we were both six years old he lived down the street from me. We spent a lot of time looking at his dad's collection of porn magazines, but we also used to play Gas Olympics. We'd try to out-fart or out-belch each other in a competition and give ourselves scores. I'd let out a loud fart and say, "Nine point-three!" and Jimmy would try to top it. It was just dumb shit.

Six-year-olds do a lot of dumb shit. Sometimes it's a combination of dumb and dangerous shit that causes them to get maimed or die. Years later you get to thinking about your childhood friend Bobby, who thought it would be cool to put a firecracker down the front of his pants, and how awkward it must be now for him to tell potential dates the reason why he can never have kids.

It's usually a guy thing, although I'm sure there are some girls who also get Darwined out of the gene pool. *America's Funniest Home Videos* has tons of examples of guys trying to jump over a car on a skateboard or leap off a bridge holding a plastic bag as a parachute. I admit to doing dumb shit, but never putting my health at risk. Okay, so Rear-Steer is an exception. Yeah, 20 year olds and 60 year olds also do dumb shit, so I guess six-year-olds don't have a monopoly on dumb shitiness. Sometimes as you get older the dumb shitiness has more serious consequences and you could quickly go from dumb shit to deep shit.

I didn't have a lot of friends growing up and I have fewer now. I figure friends are like leaves on a tree in Autumn. Some are gone right away, others linger for a while, but eventually they all fall to the ground and are swept away by the wind.

Somewhere on I-80 I feel like I'm in a dream as the miles peel away. Probably the effects of smoking Northern Lights. I'd like to close my eyes and fall asleep. I must have nodded off because the angry blast of a car horn and tires screeching jolts me awake as Pam Grier scrapes the right bumper against a guard rail sending sparks everywhere. Under my breath I yell "Fuck!" and then I hear a very calm voice say, "Now is not the time for you to die."

I check the radio but it's turned off. I look in the rear view mirror to see if someone has jumped into the back seat. I know I heard a voice, and it wasn't mine. The voice sounded like an older man, somewhat gravelly, but with perfect diction. Like John Huston in *The Wind and the Lion*. I put the rest of the joint in the ashtray and checked the radio again. Still off. As I look again in the rear view mirror I hear the words, "It's never wise to mess with the Divine Plan" come from Max. I crush the brake pedal with my right foot. "Holy Shit!" I yank the steering wheel to the right off the highway where we skid to a stop in a cloud of dust and surrealism.

"Holy shit again!"

I spin around in the seat and stare at Max. I'm hyperventilating and I hear my heart thumping in my chest as I ask, "Did you just talk?" like Kirsty Alley in *Look Who's Talking Now*.

Max doesn't make eye contact but stares off to a distant horizon. "Christ, I gotta lay off the meds. I swear you said something. I swear I heard words..."

"Just drive, dipshit," Max says.

I'm stunned. I giggle and turn around in the seat, shift Pam Grier into drive, and ease our way back onto the highway, all the while looking in the rear view mirror at my talking dog.
Hot damn! My dog just talked and told me to drive!

And drive I did.

Chapter 18

"The end of all our exploring will be to arrive where
we started and know the place for the first time."
— T. S. Eliot

"They just drove off and left it all behind 'em
But where were they going without ever
Knowing the way?"
— "The Way" — Fastball

Being on the road is so cool. It's a freedom I never knew before. It's going from inside the bird cage to soaring through the clouds. It's more rewarding if you share the experience with a dog. Especially a talking dog.

For mile after mile I stare at Max, with the occasional glance at the road. "Say something!" I demand a few times. He doesn't, but throws his head back and lets the passing air flap his ears, with the occasional drool flying out the back.

"Are you gonna talk again?" Still no reaction from Max.

"God dammit, I've got a talking dog who won't talk. I know I heard you talk. And it wasn't because of the cannabis. At least I don't think it was."

A few more miles pass and I yell, "Come on, speak! Speak, you little ball-less wonder!" Still nothing. Maybe it was my imagination. Maybe my drug diet had finally fried my brain.

"I swear, you're like that dog in the science fiction movie with the guy from *Miami Vice*. What was the name of..."

"*A Boy and His Dog* starring Don Johnson, The dog's name was Blood." Max says, looking at my eyes in the rear view mirror.

I laugh in hysterics, "YESYESYES! You can talk!" I scream.

Max rolls his eyes and mumbles, "Pull over somewhere, I'm

feeling poop-ish."

I'm grinning from ear to ear and yell "YEEESSSSSSSS!" as I take the Lovelock exit. I stop near a vacant field and Max jumps out and walks to a nearby tree, all the while I'm staring at him. Holy shit, a talking dog!

Lovelock is a cool name, but there isn't much there. I drove to the Cowpoke Cafe to grab a coffee and while I'm waiting I thumb through the menu. I'm surprised they had a veggie burger, so I order one with curly fries topped with fry sauce and then meander toward the outskirts of town until I come across a field of brown weeds, discarded beer bottles and a couple of old tires. Max leaps out of the back seat to find a place to leak so I get out of Pam Grier and set up the food on the front hood and sip my coffee. The day is heating up fast and the sun is a slow fireball climbing to the top of the sky. I remove my tee shirt and the embrace of the warm breeze feels good like the embrace of a lover.

My dad suggested I keep a diary to write down everything that happens. I've tried to do that, typing in my laptop where I am and what I'm doing and what I'm thinking. But for the most part I've just been enjoying the experience and not keeping a written track of it. I guess he figures I'll have stuff to show my own kids someday. I had an English teacher this year who said I should keep a journal of my daily activities and it'll help me with creative writing. Mr. Marsden thought my essays showed "A real creative flair." He's the only teacher I can think of who was encouraging.

One of the promises I made to my folks was to play the cello every day, so I decide to play a tune in this dumpy field next to some rusted Chevy memory. I take the cooler from the trunk to use as a seat and tune up the cello and then launch into "Eleanor Rigby." Here I was without a shirt, playing cello like Charlotte Moorman. It felt totally rad.

About half-way through the tune I stop when I ponder the

lyrics, 'All the lonely people, where do they all come from?' and I lose interest in playing. I pack away the cello and the cooler into the trunk and drive off. My mind feels stormy and I don't know why.

After gassing up at the local Stop & Go, Max and I are back on the highway, where I start feeling better. My personal dark cloud seems to have passed, once I think about Max and how I must be the only person in the world with a talking dog. The day accelerates and I feel like I'm cramming hours into seconds as I shoot across the dry, arid land. Speed limit is 80 so I can push the Caddy to 85 without a state trooper pulling me over. I love how the big states have big speed limits on their highways. I've never been there but I'm sure the speed limit in Rhode Island is 40, because if you drove faster than that you'd run out of space to stop and you'd go flying into the Atlantic Ocean.

I know I've only been on the road for a couple of days, but there are a few things I've learned that I want to share. When I left home, I opened the plastic bag of ice cubes and dumped them into the cooler. But now I've found that if you leave the frozen bag intact and set it inside the cooler, food will stay fresh longer and you don't have all the water sloshing around inside the cooler. Another tip is to be careful when opening a first aid kit. I brought one along on the trip in case something happened. It did. Opening the kit was a challenge because the manufacturer had made it child-proof. I accidentally cut myself opening the first aid kit.

I also write in my journal that sometimes while driving you should find a restroom, even though you think you're about to fart, it could be a turd masquerading as a fart, and before you know it things could get nasty. Just a word of advice. Yes, I speak from experience.

On the distant horizon are rolling dark clouds, with splashes of light toppling over each other, like the waves of Hokusai. I pull into a clearing off the road to prop Pam Grier's top back up and as soon as I get out of the car I sense someone nearby. At first I see an older Jeep, parked on a dirt road about a hundred feet away from the highway. Then I hear the POP-POP-POP of a 9mm handgun. I don't want to become porous, so I scramble for cover behind Pam Grier and crouch down to the ground, like a low camera shot by Ozu. I quickly look around to see who's shooting. A voice cries out, "I'm not shooting at you. Sorry to scare you."

I get to my feet to see a large man with a gray-flecked beard appearing from behind a long abandoned Greyhound bus. He appears to be a Hassidic Jew, wearing black pants, white shirt, and a black tie, slightly over-dressed for the desert heat. He's also wearing a camouflage yarmulke.

"If I wanted to shoot you, I would have." He eyes me, approaching, "But you're not very shootable."

"Thanks," I mutter.

"Give me a reason to shoot you, and I will," he says, not very menacing as he offers his hand.

We shake. "You just gave me a little scare, that's all."

"I'm Jacob," he says, stuffing the Glock into a shoulder holster inside his jacket. "Don't worry. I've got a concealed carry permit. I'm not some Fascist gun nut."

"Chaz. Target practice?"

He nods. "I actually hate these things. We'd all be better off with no guns. But the way the world is today..." His voice trails off. "What I prefer to shoot is a Canon."

"You shoot cannons?"

He smiles. "The camera. I'm a wildlife photographer."

"Oh."

"My gear is in the Jeep. I roam all over the Nevada desert. You could call me a wandering Jew."

"You take any photos today?"

"Got a red-tailed hawk. A kit fox," he pauses. "And a Hadru-rus arizonensis." He practically whispers, staring me in the eye. Whatever it was, he made it sound terrifying.

"What's that?"

"Latin, for giant hairy scorpion." He laughs.

"I didn't know..."

"Scorpions are very common around here. Just a heads up if you decide to camp overnight in the desert."

"Thanks."

"They only come out at night. About a year ago I was a few miles from here taking photos under a full moon, and I was shooting one of these critters just a few feet away. I was so concentrating on this one scorpion, when another little bastard crawled up from behind and bit me on the tookus. My own fault. Such a mashugana!" He chuckles.

"Did you have some antidote or something?"

"No, hurt like hell. Like a bee sting. Not enough venom to kill you, unless of course you're allergic, which I'm not."

"Damn!" is all I can reply.

"It's like that old joke" he says. "A beautiful woman gets bit on her titty by a poisonous snake, everybody wants to suck out the venom. An old man like me gets bit on the ass ... he's gonna die!"

"I saw that in a Woody Allen movie."

He smiles and stares off into the distance for a moment. "That scorpion? I'll bite it back someday. What goes around comes around. Like Ouroboros."

"Oro...?" I ask.

"Ouroboros is the ancient snake that eats its own tail," he laughs. "What's to be accomplished by that, right? You eat your-self until you disappear. Don't try that yourself. Get your parents' permission first." And he laughs at his own joke.

"I won't."

"I could eat myself," Jacob says, "I'm kosher." We laugh together. He asks, "What's your story? You run away from home?"

I shake my head. "I'm just tryin' to figure out who I am. Where I'm going. You know, that kinda stuff."

"And your parents don't understand you, that's why you ran away," he Professor Marvel-ized.

"How'd you know?"

Jacob laughs again. "Can I offer some advice from someone who never takes advice?"

"Yeah."

"Do it all. Try everything you can. Get it out of your system. That bucket list you want to do, check them all off. Don't leave anything on your plate. Climb your ladder. Shoot your wad. With all the stories you collect you'll be a raconteur. The more stories you have the more parties you're invited to, the more women you meet, the more chances you'll get laid. Just leave the world better than how you found it."

"Thanks. I'll try my best."

He offers his right hand. "Goodbye Chaz. Yishar koach."

I shrug with ignorance. "'You should have strength' is what it means," Jacob explains.

I shake his hand. "You too," and he withdraws his pistol and walks back to the abandoned bus. As I fill the water bowl for Max, I hear POP-POP-POP-POP fill the air and think that I don't want to be like the snake that eats itself.

A few miles along the highway I think about Jacob. He sure seemed like a wise man. I hope to be that wise when I'm his age. All I know is that I don't have any answers and I'm usually in the dark about stuff. But I guess it's okay to know nothing. Don't worry about the questions. If you have an imagination you can create your own answers.

From the back seat Max howls, and it almost sounds like a

laugh. I crank up the CD and listen to old school Aerosmith. I know I'll have to return home sometime, but I can't think about that now. There are items waiting to be checked off my list.

Chapter 19

"The road is life."
— Jack Kerouac

"We know where we're going,
but we don't know where we've been."
— "Road to Nowhere" —Talking Heads

The miles blur like the scene in *Clockwork Orange* accompanied by the "William Tell Overture" and I imagine taking my hands off the steering wheel as Pam Grier drives herself, taking me to who knows where. Through Utah with its cool looking rock formations and then into Wyoming with its cool two-headed car. At a gas stop in Rawlins are the two front ends of an older car welded together so they're facing in opposite directions. Two steering wheels and two front bumpers. If you tried to drive that car you wouldn't know which way to go. I claim it as a metaphor for my life.

After being away for a couple of weeks, I thought I should return to Cali again, but before heading west I look around Rawlins for about an hour. It seems like a sad place, a town fighting back tears. Hours later we're back in Utah and driving south on I-15 to Moab, even though I dislike the interstates. Max and I spend time wandering the main street and visiting the dog park where I practiced my cello while Max worked on his doggie socialization skills. I played for about twenty minutes until this one ADHD Dalmatian ran to where I was sat on a stump and tried to pee on my cello. Damn, everybody's a critic. Later I took Max for a walk along the Colorado River, which always seems to be in a rush to get somewhere.

Back on the highway I pass a sign for Pumpernickel Valley and wonder: Does the valley look like the bread or is it where Pumpernickel bread was invented? Further along the road a sign advertises the Dinosaur Festival in the town of Big Water. And all this time I thought there was nothing to do in Big Water.

Somewhere in Utah my phone rings. It's Mom. Dad had a stroke and is in the hospital. She says it was minor but the doctors are going to run tests on him for a week or two. "So if you want to come home..." her voice melts into a pool of sadness.

"Of course. I'll be there tonight."

She was sad but didn't cry. My freedom on the road would soon be coming to an end, not with a bang but with a whimper. My three months quickly shrank to three weeks.

It took me about twelve hours to get from Ogden, Utah to San Jose and I arrived at the hospital at about 8:40pm and found my dad's room. My mother greeted me with a hug and asked, "Where were you when I called?"

"Oh, southern California. Near Needles."

Dad was hooked up to lots of high tech machines and he seemed okay, except his speech was a bit slurred like he had been drinking. He just sounded normal.

"How long you gonna be here?" I asked. He shrugged..

Mom said, "Dr. Lansky says probably by Sunday he can go home, but he's going to have lots of physical therapy. He'll have to sharpen his cognitive skills, his speech..." I'm reminded of that Harrison Ford character who survives a shooting.

"It sucks, Chaz," my dad said, looking at the fluids in the intravenous bottle. "Not what I want. If you add a little scotch in there, I wouldn't mind staying here."

He managed a smile, even though one side of his mouth didn't cooperate and just sort of drooped like a basset hound's ear.

"So... where have you been? You take lots of pictures?" he Richard Avedon-ized.

"Oh yeah. Lots. So... how'd it happen?"

It seemed to pain my folks to make eye contact. "Well..." he said.

Mom jumped in. "Your father and I were having a discussion."

"Is that what you call it?" he mumbled.

"Okay. An argument. Well, suddenly he fell to the floor and..."

"Jesus Christ, what's wrong with you two?" I yelled. "Can't you guys just lay off each other for five minutes?"

"Chaz..." my mom pleaded.

My father turns to her, "She's always got to stick the knife in and twist it. I can't even—"

Mom interrupted. "I've tried to get your father to a counselor, but..."

"We're too far down the rabbit hole for that."

"... he says he's okay. I'm the crazy one..."

"If the straight jacket fits..."

"... If I could get a counselor to meet us in a bar, he'd probably go..."

"SHUT UP!" I screamed. "Just shut up. You have no idea how nice it was to be away from you two, and your bullshit arguments..."

A nurse raced into the room and said, "You're going to have to keep it down. There are other patients trying to sleep."

"Sorry," Mom said. She couldn't even look at him when she said, "George... I'll be back tomorrow."

"I ain't goin' nowhere," is all he said.

"We're leaving anyway," I told the nurse. "Sorry about the yelling."

I wanted to go to my dad's bedside and hug him, or at least pat his shoulder or hold his hand. Tell him that everything was going to be okay. I couldn't. I was too angry with both of my parents. I just needed separation. I looked at my father for a few moments and murmured, "Okay Dad. Hope you feel better soon" and then turned and left. I didn't hear him say goodbye. All the way through the hospital corridors, down the elevator and out to the parking garage, Mom and I walked in silence. But as I got into the Caddy she said, "Chaz, I'm sorry. Very, very sorry, but your father and I are filing for divorce." Now the tears flowed.

"Mom..." I said, giving her a hug.

I wasn't surprised by the announcement, and in fact the news was a relief. Maybe once apart they would be civil to each other.

On the drive home, I thought of my parents divorcing and realized it would be for the best. I also thought of getting back to school and acing every test and flying through my senior year so I could graduate in June and move out. Maybe I could find a job in radio. Or mix tunes in a club. Or maybe some studio will buy one of my screenplays. Or maybe I can just set up my cello at a BART station and play for tips. Or maybe I could just get in Pam Grier and keep driving forever until I pass the horizon and drive into the sun.

That senior year flew by. I got an intern job at a local radio station helping the morning disc jockey with show prep. He had me find lots of show biz gossip shit on the computer that he used on his show. I didn't make a cent, but every so often he gave me free certificates to local restaurants.

I kept up with my cello lessons and had a recital in January. That's when I hooked up with Marie, the violinist. Pale skin, straight dark brown hair, almost Goth, but with bright blue eyes. She was so beautiful I would have drunk her bath water. When I watched her finger the violin neck, I fantasized it was me, and half-way through the concert I was hard. I know she couldn't see my pants hidden by the cello, but she gazed up during the performance of the Brahms "String Quartet Number Three," and she smiled and winked. We saw a lot of each other for the next two months, and I do mean a lot of each other. And she did finger me as well as she fingered the violin.

My dad and mom separated as they awaited for the divorce to be finalized. He stayed in the house and she moved away. He recovered from the stroke and eventually went back to work and for the most part laid off the booze. Doctors told him he had to, but Mom said on occasion he'd cheat and sneak a sip of scotch. She knew because she marked the label on the scotch bottle and she saw the amount diminishing. She didn't mention it to him. Maybe she thought "If he wants to end his life that way, oh well..." but I hope that's not true. I'd like to think she let him sneak a drink because it made him happy and she wanted him to be happy. It's the romantic in me.

Dad still spent many hours in his study working on his novel. Mom spent a lot of time going to various real estate seminars and conventions. They didn't see each other very often, but when they did, it was civil. Before Mom moved out, they slept in separate bedrooms, but that was nothing new. They hadn't slept together for a couple of years.

When the divorce came through, they agreed to put the house on the market in April because, as she said, "It had too many unpleasant memories." I told her I didn't agree. The house had a lot of good memories, too. She smiled, nodded, and said, "Oh, sure. You're right," but I knew she would have been hard pressed to remember many.

I graduated with a perfect GPA and had several colleges knocking on my door willing to pay for my ride anywhere, but none offered scholarships in either Slacking or Aimless Wandering, which are the two subjects I wanted to major in. I was through with school. At least for now. I could always go back, and that really pissed off my parents. First they launched the guilt missile about "how much we sacrificed for you" and "you don't respect us and you're just being ungrateful" and blahblahblah. Then it was the anger missile, with "we're taking that car away and your allowance" and "we're not allowing you to end up bagging groceries at Safeway for the rest of your life" and blahblahblah. I noticed that if I was stoned while being brow-beaten, they sounded like the muted trumpet WAH-WAH-WAH of Charlie Brown's parents. Finally they caved in. "You're a young adult. You can make your own decisions. Maybe you just need to sow some wild oats for a few months, and then you'll have the right mind set to get a college degree. You know we love you and we'll support anything you decide to do."

They were right. I knew at some point I'd go to college, but for right now I wanted to be 'in' life and not just read about it in some old dusty college book.

That summer I landed an on-air job at an oldies station and worked there for six months. It was then I met Amber. I was on the station softball team and got hit on the head from a line drive and ended up in the hospital where Amber was a nurse. I remember her joking around with me, saying, "Geez, couldn't you catch it? Do you wear a glove like Michael Jackson for no apparent reason?" I was attracted to her wit and intelligence. She was 22, four years older than me, but we hit it off and started seeing each other.

Things between Amber and me moved at the speed of light. In a month she asked me to move into her apartment. In three months we were engaged, and several months before I turned 19 we were married.

I take a deep drag from the Blue Dream and turn to Clitty, "That's my story and I'm stickin' to it." She's sound asleep. I whisper, "If you ever have trouble sleeping, just ask me to tell you my life story." I kiss her on the forehead, then roll over and go to sleep.

Chapter 20

"Everybody goes home in October."
— Jack Kerouac

"I'm looking to the sky to save me,
Looking for a sign of life.
Looking for something help me burn out bright."
— "Learn to Fly" — Foo Fighters

Back on the road the next morning, Clitty asked about the moment I found out about the tumor. My rude awakening happened in June of this year. I told her:

When I first saw the image, I recalled a photo of a distant world in an astronomy book I had as a kid. I admired the beauty and grace of the Cat's Eye Nebula even though I was unable to make sense of it. It was taken from the Hubble telescope and showed the lone bright spot of a distant, dying sun amid cosmic particles and gases and it was extreme in its mysterious, otherworldly perfection. My MRI image also showed a lone bright spot, and when my neurosurgeon pointed it out, I knew it was not perfection. I also knew it represented, as Camus said, the end of my "invincible summer." I brought the image home and framed it to help me feel more empowered and less of a victim, and perhaps convince myself that the tumor was on the wall and not in my head. When I was told I had four to six months to live with a Stage IV glioblastoma multiforme, I immediately thought, "How strange that I'm going to be killed by an unpronounceable word." I was 20 and was told I wouldn't live to be 21. The docs said I would not live to see the new year, the new millennium. It's so unfair. Fucking Fate!

I first sensed something was wrong last winter when I started getting frequent headaches, blurred vision, and nausea. My family doctor referred me to a Dr. Salinger and he gave me a series of tests along with the MRI and a year's supply of Marinol. Although he implied I probably wouldn't use the entire bottle.

My first reaction was to tell my parents, but in the same moment I realized that my mom was gone and my dad disowned me. At least that's the word he used. I thought it strange because he never owned me to begin with.

I had to face this by myself. There was no one to share my oncoming personal apocalypse. I was divorced from Amber and there was no one from high school or radio who I could call, just to either piss and moan or to cry on someone's shoulder. I hadn't kept in touch with any of my old friends and over the years I had set up an impenetrable wall of Alone. All I had was Max. I remember the drive home from the hospital and the conversation with my dog.

"I'm gonna get a third opinion."

"Chaz, the two neurosurgeons you spoke to are the best on the west coast."

"Then I'll go to the east coast. Get a ninth, a tenth opinion. I'll find somebody who says it's not a tumor."

"Go to your auto mechanic. Have him read the MRI. Maybe he'll give you a different opinion."

"I didn't see any certificates on Dr. Palmieri's office wall. How do I even know he's a doctor?"

I pull Pam Grier over to the shoulder of the road and cry. It's apparent I'm going to bypass all five stages of death and go directly to the stage 'hysterical sobbing.' Max nuzzles my arm and lays his head on my right leg.

"Remember that quote from the movie *The Lady From Shanghai*?"

"Which one?"

"One of the actors said, 'Killing you is killing myself. But, you know, I'm pretty tired of both of us.'"

"It's all the boyhood fears I had lurking under my bed now living inside my brain."

"Don't think of it as a monster. That only feeds it. Drive it around the country. See places you've never seen. Meet people you've never met."

I stare at Max in disbelief. "Yeah, I'll take my tumor out for an ice cream cone. We'll go see a movie. Take it to the ball game and hope I don't get hit on the head with a foul ball. Wouldn't want to harm it. Maybe even give it a cute name. Boomer the Tumor. I'll kill it with kindness."

"Compose a song to it."

I can't believe I'm going to die. Fuck!" I hiss. "God damn God! Proves He doesn't exist if He can allow so much shit to happen."

"Maybe God is just apathetic. He's got his own problems. He probably says, 'You little pissants on Earth. Stop asking me to save the life of your pet cat, or prevent famine, or have your favorite football team win the Super Bowl. I got better things to worry about. You're on your own.'"

"Yeah. Makes sense to me." I close my eyes. "No, none of it makes sense to me."

"Welcome to reality, Chaz. One day our bodies will give out and things break down and we're all just a few minutes away from smelling really bad."

"You always know how to cheer me up. Death is supposed to be what happens to old people. Fuck! I'm only twenty!"

Max chuckles and tilts his head back, the wind flapping his ears. "Happens to everyone and everything. Don't panic. Everything is temporary. Except temporary. Temporary is permanent. Okay Chaz now howl with me. You'll feel better." Max breaks into a soulful, "HHHHAAAARRRRROOOOO!"

"Sorry, I don't feel like it," and pounded my fist against the steering wheel.

I tell Clitty, "And that's how it happened," but she doesn't respond.

I fantasize about shaking my head violently and shooting that pea-sized tumor out of my ear and into space, where it ricochets off planets and asteroids, like a silver ball in a cosmic pinball machine, and then is swallowed up by a Black Hole. Clitty says, "As Pope John Paul used to say, 'Sometimes ya get jerked around when ya rather get jerked off.'"

"When Pope John Paul retires, will he be replaced by Pope George Ringo?"

She shouts, "Amen! The Pope is a wise man."

We travel in silence. I think about the time bomb inside my head and my eyes get watery. How many more ticks before it explodes? A deep sigh, then I ask Max, "You have any words of wisdom, my little furry friend?"

Max says, "Someday the sun will be in the box and the box will be closed."

"Sounds like a fortune cookie message written by T.S. Eliot," I said.

He then laughs, that contagious, Snoopy laugh of his, HEH-HEH-HEH-HEH, and he throws back his head with his ears flapping in the breeze. The image makes me smile, and before too long I'm laughing too and I threw back my head, but my ears aren't flapping, and I yell, "FUCK IT ALL!"

I repeat it, yelling "FUCKITALLFUCKITALL!" over and over again and Max joins in howling, "FUCKITALLFUCK-ITALLFUCKITALL!" and we continue the madness for miles like we're the Charlie Brown characters stoned from Peppermint Patty's mom baking special Alice B. Toklas brownies as Clitty joins in and raps the steering wheel like a drum and we're screaming "FUCKITALLFUCKITALLFUCKITALL!" in a sing-song rhythm of defiance as my little insane asylum on wheels rolls merrily along to oblivion.

After a few miles the crazy sing-along stops and we're alone with our thoughts as Pam Grier continues her quest to transport us somewhere.

"Happy New Year, Clitty. And happy new millennium," I tell Clitty.

"It's not December thirty-first."

"I'm not going to live to see 2000. The next century. Just the thought of that amazes me."

Clitty says, "You're not going to miss much. I already saw the trailer, and it's going to be very similar to the 20th Century. Clothing and hair styles will change. Higher tech shit. People will be more assholey. A lot more violence. In fact the world doesn't make it to the 22nd Century."

"So what you're saying is that I'm checking out at the right time."

She turns away. The escape of laughter was fun, but a temporary denial, and now reality seems to have returned with a punch.

"Will God make an appearance on Earth?" I blurt out. I don't know why I said that, because I've never been religious and have always thought of myself as an atheist. At least during the day. Alone at night, to hedge my bets, I think I'm an agnostic.

"There's no God," Clitty said, "And if there were, He wouldn't let young people die. I know the dude wouldn't hang out on Earth, that's for damn sure!"

"It's a loser planet."

"The only special ed planet in the galaxy."

Max chimes in, "The *Bible* says that God made the world in 7 days. It was a rush job. He should have taken his time and done it right. Was He on some kind of a deadline? Maybe just doing drugs. Like Groucho in *Skidoo*."

"When I was a young boy, I had all the answers. Now that I'm dying, I only have questions."

"The only answer is to be nice," Clitty says. "Nice to people, animals, trees. Even bugs." As soon as she said that, a fly lands on the dashboard and she grabs my paperback copy of *Ulysses* from the glove compartment and smacks the fly into a squishy black mush.

"Except for flies," she huffs. "Be nice to every other bug. Except flies."

"I finally understand the meaning behind that book. It's meant to squish flies."

I see something we pass that catches my eye and I tell her to turn around.

"What is it?"

"A nursing home. I've got an idea. Let's go back and do something nice," I say.

As we pull into the parking lot of the Cypress Senior Center, I tell Clitty "Let's entertain."

"Nice gesture, Chaz."

"I'll try not to vomit on my cello."

I take the cello from the trunk and Clitty and I walk into the front office lobby and approach a woman behind the desk. She's about 50 with gray-tinged black hair in a bun and the name tag 'Carly' above her heart on her light blue scrubs.

"Hi, my name is Chaz and this my wife Cli... ah, Doris, and we're musicians and we'd like to entertain your residents."

"Well..." Carly is taken by surprise. "We usually require some advance notice so our recreational director can schedule it and..."

"My grandparents were in a nursing home and I know how important music is for their well-being."

"How long did you plan on..."

"Half hour."

"... being here because we're getting close to serving lunch so...

"Only a half hour. Please?"

Carly sighs, "Well, okay, but I can't allow you in there without any pants on."

"I lost my pants in an earthquake," I moan, and Clitty kicks my leg. "It was a five-point-eight quake near Salinas. My house was okay, but my clothes closet collapsed and I lost my entire wardrobe."

Carly sure looks skeptical. "That's a good one," as she walks back to a room behind the desk and returns with teal scrubs. "Here. Put this on and follow me."

I slip on the scrub pants and we follow Carly to a large sunny rec room where an unwatched TV drones in the background. The residents are either reading, playing cards, sleeping, or staring off trying to piece together memories like chards of broken glass.

Clitty grabs my arm, "What do you expect me to sing?"

"You said you know show tunes."

She exhales apprehension, shakes her head, and mumbles, "Well... yeah, but Jesus, that was a long time ago."

"Fake it. I'll follow along."

Carly said, "You can set up right here. What's the name of your group?" she asks, lowering the volume of the TV.

The question catches me off guard, but Clitty bails us out. She had caught a glimpse of a book one of the residents was reading. "We call ourselves the Mockingbirds," Clitty says. I open the case and tune the cello.

As Carly announces, "Excuse me everyone, I have a surprise for you today." I catch sight of the Harper Lee novel one of the residents is reading. "Here to entertain you... for just thirty minutes," she says eying me and Clitty, "Let's give a warm welcome to... the Mockingbirds."

Carly and several seniors applaud and then Carly takes a

seat and glances at her watch.

Clitty whispers, "Ah... let's try 'What I Did for Love' from *Chorus Line*. Okay?"

I nod. "I know the tune. Slow tempo. Follow my lead," and I begin to finger the strings and bow. I play an intro and nod to Clitty when to jump in. She does and when it's over we both breathe a sigh of relief and burst into giggles, surprised at how well it sounded as Carly and several residents applaud with much enthusiasm. Clitty now has her confidence and says, "If I Were a Bell" from *Guys and Dolls* and we launch into it.

As Clitty sings I watch the faces of the seniors. Some move their heads or tap their feet in rhythm with the music. Most are smiling. I envy their white hair, their wrinkles, and their long life of memories. How wonderful and natural it would be to grow old.

Clitty and I play several more show tunes, then for the final song we perform "Oh, What a Beautiful Mornin'."

After the applause, Clitty and I walk around the room to shake hands and thank the residents. Carly thanks us several times as we walk to the front office and she asks us to come back real soon. I return the scrubs and as Clitty and I return to Pam Grier, we both keep repeating, "Nice. Nice. That was really nice."

I'm feeling stronger so I decide to drive, but we're a few miles away from the senior center when I feel my head being ripped off my neck. The intensity of the explosion of pain was unlike anything I had ever experienced before. For a moment I blacked out and swerved the car into the oncoming traffic lane. Clitty grabbed the wheel and screamed as Max is bounced around the back seat as I skidded Pam Grier to a stop on the gravel shoulder. I put my head down towards my lap and moan. Clitty holds me as the pain in my head is excruciating and I can't open my eyes. I can't describe how pukeulous I feel.

Clitty keeps me close until I break from her embrace to

throw open the door and vomit onto the ground.

"Want one of your pills?"

I shake my head. "I took one about an hour ago. They're not working anymore. My fun sticks are not workin' anymore. Nothin's workin' anymore. The doctor said this would happen as I got closer..." It's too painful to verbalize the thought.

Clitty lays her head on my shoulder, holds my hands, and cries. Max's cold nose muzzles the back of my neck. Max said, "You're not taking the journey alone. I'm here with you."

I force a smile.

My 'Charlie's Angels' ring tone sounds and the message on the screen reads NOT NOW.

A few minutes later the black cloud has passed and I'm feeling better, but I realize I shouldn't drive anymore, so I hand the keys to Clitty. She wipes tears from her cheeks.

As the miles past I stare ahead at the passing white painted markers in the middle of the road and want so much to escape from myself. I think: *Believe that your death is not the last sentence in your story, it's only a chapter in an eternal book. The road may take different forms and we may take different forms but the journey is always continuous. A road without end.*

Max hears my thoughts and murmurs "Burma Shave" and I smile. It's good to be on the road. Clitty is driving very fast so nothing can catch me. I've always felt that home represents birth and death but the road represents movement. You have a pulse. You're alive. Maybe I wasn't running away from something, maybe I was running toward something. Soon I'll close my eyes and drift into a soft endless dream. Like Max has always told me, this existence is only one highway you travel. When you leave it, there are other paths to take with more adventures, so passing on from this path is a wonderful thing. Something to look forward to. Discovering what lies ahead is all we have. Things are always better on the horizon.

I rest my hand on Clitty's leg and ask, "Hey! Where are we goin'?"

A deep sigh then she whispers, "Nowhere."

"When are we gonna get there?"

"Never," and she wipes tears from her eyes.

"I think I'm around for a little while longer. It just doesn't feel like it's time."

I grab MY JOURNEY from the glove compartment and search for the final page to see how and when it ends. But there is no final page. When I think I've turned to the last page, more pages suddenly spring up.

"You should go to L-A and meet with your agent. You've got a career to pursue."

"No," she says with the force of a kick.

"What do you mean 'no'?"

"I'm gonna hang with you. I ain't leavin'. You're stuck with me."

"Until the end," I sigh.

She doesn't respond and looks off to the distance.

"So, where to?" I ask.

She takes a deep breath. "Someplace with no worries."

Chapter 21

"Arriving from always, you will go everywhere."
— Arthur Rimbaud

"I'm the kind of guy who laughs at a funeral.
Can't understand what I mean? You soon will."
— "One Week" — Barenaked Ladies

We drive all night and part of the morning before finding ourselves in Barstow, although I doubt anyone finds themselves in Barstow. Clitty tells me she once visited Barstow.

"Why? Did you lose a bet?"

"No, I was young. My parents stopped here on the way to Joshua National Park."

We pass a historic sign for Route 66. "See?" I said. "This is where we can get our kicks."

Max picks up the tune from the back seat:

"It winds from Chicago to L.A.
More than two thousand miles all the way.
Get your kicks on Route sixty-six."

It's obvious that Route 66, like me, has seen better days.

We grab a couple of burritos from a lunch wagon near a park and I pop the Caddy's trunk and scoop out Max's food and fill his water bowl and he slurps it down. The trip was somewhat uneventful. I only had to stop once to vomit. I'm noticing a correlation between the amount of times I gas up Pam Grier and the times I get nauseous, and I'm averaging about two pukes per gallon.

Clitty is at a picnic table reading one of my screenplays. I leaf through my Dad's binder of writings and soon I'm immersed. His writing style is good. Kind of a bare-bones Ernest Hemingway with a shout-out to Raymond Chandler. I wish there was some way to get his writings published, a way to honor him. I only wish he had shown Mom his creative side. I think she would have been impressed. Maybe it would have been the glue that held them together. At least that's what I would like to believe. It's the romantic in me.

I want to swallow a Marinol but need a beer or water to wash it down. A hungry and curious crow waits at one end of the table waiting for a morsel of food.

"You don't need this," I say, holding up the pill. "You're lucky. Crows don't get brain tumors."

"This is good," Clitty says. "I like your writing style."

"You're only saying that because I'm dying."

"Fuck you. You've got real talent. I could totally see this as a movie."

"My Dad was a writer. He wrote some pretty good stuff. Must be in the D-N-A."

Across the street is a Circle K and I ask Clitty if she wants anything. "If Johnny Depp is in there, send him over."

I manage to cross the street, almost getting run over by some yahoo in a mud-caked Dodge Ram pickup. Shit! I should've used the crosswalk. My own damn fault. A sudden thought: Has Dum Phuk re-entered my mind? I almost became roadkill and I didn't want to go out like that. But maybe we're all roadkill. Perhaps we all end up getting run over by something, even if it doesn't have four wheels. The simple act of crossing the road left me drained like I had just run a marathon.

Inside the convenience store I hit the rest room and stand in front of the urinal where a miniature plastic football end zone with a tiny football strung between goal posts sits at the bottom of the piss bowl. And like every other guy who has ever stood there, I try to hit the football with my stream of piss. When guys stand at urinals, we need something to aim for. We'll shoot at plastic footballs, a fly if it lands on the porcelain, a piece of dirt. It's like a video game. It's primal. We have to shoot something, like our prehistoric ancestors used to shoot woolly mammoths with spears. Freud referred to it as 'piss dominance' or 'piss aggression.'

I felt weak, like I should lie down, but I force myself to go back into the store to grab a six pack of Coors and a blueberry muffin for Max. I put the items on the counter but there's no clerk to ring me up. I tap a desk bell and a minute later the clerk appears from a back room and shuffles behind the counter, lumbering along like a sick manatee. She's a middle-aged woman, wearing a red 'Let me tell you about my grandkids' tee shirt.

She barked, "Let's see some I-D, sonny," with a facial expression like she just regurgitated her own bile. Gee lady, I lost interest in the beer. I'd rather have you tell me about your grandkids. I'm sure it would be so much more intoxicating.

When she opened her mouth to speak, I saw she had only a few teeth, and her sallow skin pulled tight across her face made her look like the creature in *Aztec Mummy*. I would guess she only had tooth numbers 23, 24, and 25 on the bottom, and only numbers 4, 5, and 9 on top. I pull out my fake driver's license and she eyeballs it quickly and then rings me up. I feel sad that she never told me about her grandkids. It'll go down as one of the great disappointments in my life.

I also bought a lottery ticket, something I never do. I figure if it hits, it'll be good money to take care of Clitty. I remember my Grandpa Don saying that buying a lottery ticket is like marriage: You have great hope but then you end up paying for disappointment. If I can believe that my dog talks, then anything is possible. Even winning the lottery.

Behind the counter a white sign in black Gothic scrawl caught my attention. It read:

> 'Since the fire at St. Mary's last May, Father Procopio is now hearing confessions in the back room. Please be quiet and respectful of others. God bless you.'

I ambled back to the picnic table and popped a Marinol with a Coors chaser.

"This is really good," Clitty gushed.

"Which one are you reading?"

"*Rocky, My Fairy Godmother*. Very unique."

"You want something unique? You know what they got in the back room of that Circle K?"

"Hookers?"

"No, something else that'll make you scream, 'God, I'm coming!' A confessional booth."

"You're kidding. Why?"

"Seems the church burned down and that's the only place they can have it."

I smile at Clitty and she returns my smile and says "Fuckalicious!" and faster than you can say Father Merrin, I toss the beer, food and Dad's binder into Pam Grier and Clitty throws the script onto the back seat and we cross the street with Max at our heels.

As we arrive, an elderly lady resembling Beulah Bondi, with a black shawl draped over her shoulders and her head bowed, murmurs prayers as she fingers a rosary and then enters the confessional.

Clitty whispers, "Maybe you get a free beef jerky with every sin you confess."

"What are you even here for? You've never sinned."

"Yeah, that's me. The Singing Nun. Fuck, if I have to atone for all my sins I'll be in that booth for months."

After about ten minutes the elderly lady exits the booth, folding her rosary into her purse.

"Can we go in together?" Clitty whispers, but it's loud enough for a man behind us to say, "Sorry, Father only takes you one at a time."

"You go first," she says to me. As I enter the confessional, Clitty says, "See if he'll bless the lottery ticket."

I've never been in a confessional before, but when you're dying, you tend to do things for the first time knowing they'll be the last time. Besides, it might even be good for my soul. If I have one.

I slide into the dark booth and close the door. A few moments pass but it seems like hours, and then the Priest speaks through a darkened screen. A very monotone, soothing voice, almost hypnotic, and I guess his age to be about 40. He introduces himself and asks if I have anything to confess. I blurt out my name and where I'm from and then my mind races for something else to say.

"Uh... Father... this is my first time, and I'm not sure..."

"It's okay, son," Father Procopio says. "Tell Our Heavenly Father when was the last time you confessed."

"Well, I was twelve. At the police station. They caught me setting fire to my neighbor's tool shed."

"No, I meant confess your sins to a priest. You may say you are sorry for that sin and all the sins of your family."

"I'm sorry for that sin and all the sins of my family."

"I give you the Sacrament of Penance to help you resist future temptations. In the name of the Father, the Son..."

I interrupted him. "I've got another one Father that I've never told anyone."

"Yes, my son?"

"When I was twelve... no, maybe I was thirteen, I was in Target with a girlfriend and we got laughing so hard over something that I kinda lost control and I shot out a turd that rolled down my pant leg and scooted across the floor, and then it was stepped on by a blind man walking his dog."

There was a long pause. A really long pause. I said, "I always felt bad about that."

I hear the Priest clear his throat and whisper, "I absolve you of that sin. Please say the Act of Contrition and..."

"I don't know the Act of Contrition."

"Very well, son. God has forgiven your sins. God bless you and please, go in peace."

"Thank you Father." I wanted to say, "Tanks, Fadda," like Huntz Hall but I think better of it. I leave the booth and as Clitty enters I say, "I think I screwed up. I'm going to hell."

"Is there room for two in that hand basket?"

"I'll be out in the car." As I exit the Circle K, I realize I forgot to get the lottery ticket blessed.

I take a bite of the burrito and take a swig of Coors as Clitty emerges from the Circle K and runs across the street with Max following.

"How'd it go?" I ask.

"I confessed that young priests make my nipples hard."

She laughs, but she won't tell me what she said to Father Procopio.

Later Max told me, "Clitty didn't confess anything. She asked the Priest to pray you have a peaceful journey. And some other stuff, too." I've never been a Believer, but when you're in a situation like mine, I figure I can use all the help I can get.

I was now exhausted. I had only walked across the street, but I felt like the Red Buttons character in the movie about dance marathons. A quick stop to gas up Pam Grier and our little unholy triumvirate is soon covering asphalt. Clitty continues raving about my screenplay, and repeats lines of dialogue and laughs. I'm flattered and tell her so.

As Clitty drives toward Joshua Tree National Park, I think about my last will and testament, something I hadn't given much thought to since August when Max and I were on our way to Monument Valley. Maybe I didn't finish it then because I was still in denial of my outcome. Or because I really didn't have anyone to leave my stuff to. Now I did.

As soon as we checked into a motel in 29 Palms, I crashed onto the bed for about three hours. When I awoke, Clitty was re-heating the rest of the burrito that I couldn't finish. I picked at it and forced down a couple of bites before my stomach told me to stop. I took a Cookies and Cream stick from my fedora on the nightstand and sat up in bed to finish writing the will on my laptop. I was ready to enter her last name onto the document but I didn't know it. After all we've been through it seems like something I should have known.

"Clitty, what's your..."

"You ever hear of chaparral?" she interrupts.

"No."

She reads from a website on her laptop. "It's a plant that grows in the desert and it supposedly fights cancer."

"Maybe we can call room service and have them send up a few plants."

"I'm serious. It says here that Native Americans have been using it for centuries because it has nor-di-hi-hydro-... shit, I can't pronounce it, but it's an ingredient with an anti-tumor agent."

I force a smile and lie back on the bed and stare at the ceiling.

"You've given up, haven't you?"

"It's too late. I'm the opposite of "Symphony Number 8." *That* remained unfinished."

She was angry. "Why are you giving up? God damn it Chaz, don't give up!"

"I know what the doctors told me. It's coming down fast.

I'm always tired. No appetite. More nauseous. My eyesight is blurred. My headache is constant. My head is slowly breaking apart."

"Maybe chaparral can help."

"I just don't wanna get my hopes up, that's all. Shit, if I thought it was going to work, I'd run out into the desert tonight and wolf down a few plants."

"You don't know unless you try."

"What are you getting all pissed off for?" I asked. "You're in my will. I ain't got much but it's all yours."

"Fuck you, Chaz!" she yells and storms out of the room.

I was about to say, "I refuse to argue if you're going to interject logic into the conversation," but the slamming door stops me in mid-sentence. Only a week ago I could have jumped out of bed and chased her down, but now I just want to lie here and close my eyes.

I fell asleep. Maybe it was a combination of the Mexican food and the joint, but I had the craziest dream: I was very warm and alone and floating in liquid although I had no feeling of having a body. Only my thoughts. No feeling of Time, but only the Time before I was aware, or at least I was aware that I was aware. No one was around but I felt the presence of someone or something. I wasn't afraid. There was no danger. Just a nice sensation that I didn't want to end.

I awoke from the dream and wondered, what the hell was that all about? The same question I had years ago after watching *Ishtar*.

When Clitty returned a couple of hours later, I tell her she's experiencing the 'denial' stages of grief but I had already trudged through the first four and was now on Acceptance. She cried as I held her in my arms.

"Acceptance," Max says. "Like the Sterling Hayden character in *The Killing*."

"Didn't see it."

"And at this point you probably never will," Max says, making me smile. "At the end of that movie, Johnny could have run from the cops, but he says, 'What's the difference?' and he accepts his fate."

"I'll put it on my bucket list."

"You're going to need a bigger bucket," Max says, channeling his inner Martin Brody, and then he snorts out a Snoopy-laugh HEH-HEH-HEH.

Clitty sighs, "We have to talk." The four words that strike dread in every man. Usually when a woman says that, the guy thinks, 'Uh-oh, here it comes. Now what did I do wrong?' She stares into my eyes for what seemed like eons.

"Chaz... I'm pregnant."

It hit me like a left hook from Rocky Balboa. "You're kidding."

She shakes her head. "My periods have always been all over the place, but this time I'm late. Really late. I just came back from the clinic down the street, peed on a stick, and..."

I'm still reeling but I break into smile, a smile like I had never had before. Then a giggle. "I guess... congratulations. To us?" and I give her a long kiss and our tears flow.

I sit on the edge of the bed, not knowing what to say or do. All I can mumble is, "Oh, man... this is amazing. You really are..."

"Preggers."

"Oh... wow..."

Clitty says, "If it's a boy I'll name him Cool. If it's a girl... Fuckalicious."

"Too common. Everybody names their kids that." We laugh and she rubs my shoulders.

Clitty rises from the bed and straddles my legs, then cups my head and nestles it against her belly. It's warm like a flowering meadow in Spring. I have no thoughts of yesterday or tomorrow but I'm in the moment of right now. For the moment nothing else exists in the world, and I know I could not feel any more elated and I know I am at peace.

"I love you, Clitty."

"I love you too, Chaz."

I hold the moment close, not thinking of anything else.

"So what do we do now?" Clitty wonders.

I struggle to get up and shuffle to the bureau. I select a tune on the CD player. "I think we should celebrate with a dance."

"At Last" blares from the tiny speakers as I offer my hand to Clitty, she gets to her feet, and we embrace. Our movement is more of a gentle sway than a dance. A slow motion meshing of bodies, a need to become One. I knew she was using every bit of her strength to support me and keep me on my feet.

As the song fades, we kiss and stare into each other's eyes and I know that nothing else exists in the universe but us and we're twin stars linked forever.

She repeats. "Now what happens?"

"First thing in the morning, we head north to Vegas. Get married. And someday you'll have great stories to tell either Cool or Fuckalicious."

Clitty forces a smile.

That night we hardly slept. I had renewed energy and we talked like it was our last day together. We said everything that entered our minds and we laughed and cried.

I told her about the visit to my subconscious by Dum Phuk who suggested my final scene and I describe it to her. I know it's going to be the last time I hear from Dum Phuk, but his idea is good. In the last few years I've tried to silence that inner voice, but this time I'm taking Dum Phuk's suggestion and running with it. He said I had to go out with a bang. Much better than the Virginia Woolf suicide I was going to copy by putting rocks into my overcoat pockets and throwing myself into the Salton Sea. Max listens as I describe my Grand Exit to Clitty. I ask him if he's excited by it.

"Huge hard-on," he Snoopy-cackled HEH-HEH-HEH. "Huge!"

Perhaps the only thing that lasts forever is Forever, but I really don't know. That night, lying close to each other, I can't think about yesterday or tomorrow, but only the beautiful and mystical impermanence of Now. All my life I lived for what's coming up next, but now the most important thing in the world was to be in the moment.

Chapter 22

"Has anyone supposed it lucky to be born?
I hasten to inform him or her it is just as lucky to die."
— Walt Whitman

"It's something unpredictable, but in the end it's right
I hope you had the time of your life."
— "Good Riddance" — Green Day

The next morning I awoke before Clitty and watched her sleep. The slow rhythmic rise and fall of her chest reminded of the "Canon in D," the elegance of Pachelbel. Her hair and face collect the sunlight. Her lips are full like a warm shower in May. We're caressed by a new day and I've never felt happier in my life.

After much effort I finally rise from the bed and she helps me take a shower. I almost fell asleep under the falling water. Clitty repeatedly asked, "You okay?"

Clitty checked the lottery results. No winning ticket. In a Hollywood ending, we would win the lottery AND I'd receive a new treatment that would save my life. Welcome to reality!

Las Vegas was about three hours north. Clitty drove and when we arrived she said I slept the entire trip. That disappointed me, because I want to take it all in, the small towns, junk yards, slow-moving freight trains, fields of cattle, distant mountains, billboards, and folks walking their dogs. All of it. And the road. Especially the road. I wanted to experience it all and not miss a single molecule or a single second.

Max says, "You didn't miss much. Everything was a bore. The only entertainment. Was hearing you snore. Burma Shave."

My brain has checked out, because I had no rejoinder to

Max. I've always been able to return with a clever comeback, but not this time. Max paws my shoulder.

"Don't worry. You'll think of one."

"I narrowed it down to three places for us to get married," Clitty said. While driving she steals glances at her notes. "There's 'Graceland Wedding Chapel' and..."

"No," I interrupt. "Not Elvis. I'm nauseous enough as it is."

"Okay. There's the 'Chapel of Love.' She sings:

"Goin' to the chapel, and we're gonna get married."

I knew it was an oldie but I couldn't think of the artist. Max says, "Dixie Cups," and I sigh, "Oh, yeah. Guess the files in my brain are being deleted." For the first time in my life, the inner jukebox seems to be unplugged.

"I can't believe I'm getting married again in Vegas," Clitty says.

"Second time will be a charm. Don't worry, I won't divorce you. This marriage will last forever. Or... at least a couple of days. Whichever comes first."

"Stop it," Clitty snaps. She didn't want to think about the future. At least what there is of it.

I tried to joke about the situation. "For a wedding gift I hope you don't give me a calendar."

"Chaz..." Her voice trails off in anguish. "Please." My imminent demise was no laughing matter. I know I'm in the final stage of Acceptance when I can joke about my own demise.

"Sorry." I kiss her cheek.

"The third place is called 'Endless Love.' They have a bunch of theme rooms."

We find Endless Love off East Desert Inn Road. It's in a large, single story building with lots of flickering white lights surrounding a large heart of red lights.

We walked in, well, Clitty walked and I shuffled like I'm 90, with Max following, and we approached the front desk where a clerk is playing solitaire on a computer screen. The clerk is of a questionable gender and I think of a carnival barker chirping, "Guess the sex and win a stuffed animal."

The clerk greets us, "Good evening. I'm Leslie" which didn't clear up the sexual identity confusion.

Max knew what I was thinking. "Leslie Howard, from *Of Human Bondage* or Leslie Caron from *An American in Paris*."

"Leslie Nielsen," I mumble. "*Naked Gun*."

Leslie shakes our hands. "Feel free to look through our booklet for the multitude of themes we have to ensure your wedding ceremony is unforgettable."

"I don't think I can stand up," I whisper to Clitty. I felt like my legs had been de-boned.

"Is there a ceremony where we can lie down?" she asks Leslie.

"Whatever you want," Leslie says, "We'll accommodate you."

Clitty goes through the theme notebook and then stops on a page. "What's... The Cave?"

Leslie snaps his fingers. "Oowww, good choice! If you prefer not to stand, The Cave is your answer. Follow me."

Leslie leads us down a long hall to a door with 'The Cave' scrawled on the front. Inside is a tacky version of stalagmites and stalagmites made of paper-mache with small plastic bats dangling from the ceiling.

Leslie eyes us from head to toe. "Wait here" and scampers from the room. He returns a few minutes later carrying two black bat costumes with dark gray gossamer wings.

"Change into these. I'll be back in five minutes."

He runs out the door again and Clitty and I look at each other, shrug, and burst into giggles.

"Chaz, this is truly Fuckalicious," as we slip on the costumes.

"I'm Batman," I Michael Keaton-ized to Clitty.

Leslie returns, now wearing a long white robe with purple beads around his neck like an Indian mystic. He says we must complete the scene by being suspended upside down. There are two clamps dangling from the ceiling which he electronically lowers by pushing a button near the door. He secures the clamps around our ankles and then asks, "You ready?" and the clamps begin a slow rise toward the ceiling, lifting us aloft, and faster than Adam West could yell "To the Batcave!" we were hanging upside down. I had a sudden fear that this was all a ploy for Leslie to get unwilling victims into an S & M scene.

The ceremony was mercifully brief, because the blood running to my head made me feel worse. When Leslie asked Clitty her last name, she replied, "Bang." As strange as it may seem, I never knew her last name. I tried to ask her the other day but got sidetracked. 'Clitty Bang.' It sure has a nice ring to it.

After pronouncing us husband and wife, Leslie says, "You may now kiss the bride." We struggle to hold on to each other while inverted but manage a quick kiss. Leslie takes several photos for our album. He then pressed the button at the door and we eased back down onto the floor where he unhitches our ankle bracelets.

"I have a yummy surprise for you," he squeals. "Don't go away."

'What are we gonna do, fly off into the night?" Clitty asks. "You okay?"

I nod. She says, "Like Mother Teresa used to say, 'Things could be worse. We could be sucking on a leper's toe.'"

Leslie returns with a platter holding a cake in the shape of a large mosquito. He presents us with the photos inserted into a small album, along with a marriage certificate, and we are now officially, according to the great state of Nevada, husband and wife:

Chaz Chase and Clitty Bang.

Within twenty minutes we're heading south on I-15, now Mr. and Mrs.

Maybe hanging upside down invigorated me, because I don't feel so tired and Clitty and I talk the entire five hour drive to Salton Sea. As she drove, I typed on my laptop and together we screen played the final scene. My Great Exit. She stopped at a gas station and then later at a Safeway to buy something.

Clitty returned from the store carrying a small pink box with a string that looked like it contained pastries. I assume it must be our breakfast for tomorrow morning.

After writing the script, Clitty and I talked about carnivals and freak shows. Maybe it was Leslie or Las Vegas that triggered those thoughts, or some heavy weed usage, but Clitty said she had a distant cousin who appeared in some freak show that traveled around Mississippi and Alabama in the 1950's. He was double-jointed and called himself 'The Human Pretzel.' He could bend his body into the oddest contortions and according to lore was actually able to put his own head up his ass.

"Don't know if that actually happened. But that was the family story that got passed along over the years. Pretty cool if it's true, huh?"

"The guy could give himself his own colonoscopy," I said.

I gave Clitty my debit card and told her about my secret hiding places in Pam Grier for money and weed. I signed off the title to Pam Grier. She says she'll take my screenplays to Hollywood and find a publisher for my Dad's manuscript.

"Chaz, I'll get your screenplays sold. I promise."

I know she will.

An hour later we arrive about three miles from Bombay Beach on the east shore of Salton Sea. How we got here I haven't a clue. If I had to find my way here again I wouldn't be able to. It was a total happenstance that got me here. Perhaps it's total happenstance that takes us anywhere. There have been many times in my life when I wish I had never been born, but now when I think about sunsets over the Pacific splashing colors of pink, orange, and red or hear Yo-Yo Ma play Bach's "Cello Suite #1" or stare into Clitty's eyes and see her radiant smile, I know it's all worth the price of admission and I'm so grateful for my life, as brief and tumultuous as it's been.

The sharp fireworks in my brain are unbearable and bring tears to my eyes. I know the time has come. The pain is extreme and my entire body feels like it's being torn apart and eaten by some wild beast. Every living thing passes through a door and now it's my turn.

I was fighting fatigue all day and I just wanted to close my eyes and float away like the red balloon the kid chased around the streets of Paris. I take a Cookies and Cream stick from inside the brim of my fedora, and place it between my lips. Clitty lights it, and with a few draws I become the soul of a soft warm flower in a meadow.

For about the tenth time Clitty asks, "You sure?" Once again I nod. It's time to jump off the carousel. Or at least grab the brass ring and stop it. She tries to remain strong but can not hold back the tears. "You guys can do this," I tell her, placing my hand on her stomach. "One of us has to be strong. Don't let me down, Mrs. Chase," I force a smile. I hope Clitty isn't losing her nerve because I need her to help me escape this world.

"I never will, Mr. Chase."

"I'm probably the only screenwriter to ever write his own personal final scene."

"I believe you are, Chaz," Max agrees.

"I got something for you at the store this morning." She runs to the trunk and returns carrying a small cake with a single lit candle in a swirl of chocolate.

"Everybody gets a birthday cake," she says. She reveals a small cake with my name and today's date written in vanilla icing.

"But only you would think of a death day cake."

Clitty brings the cake close to me and whispers, "Make a wish!" I wish her and our child long, happy and healthy journeys. With some effort I blow out the candle and she offers a bit of the icing dabbed on the tip of her finger. As nauseous as I feel, I lick it off.

My sense of taste is gone, and the other four senses will soon follow. I tell this to Max and he jokes, "Your sense of decency left years ago." The only sense that's still very much alive is my sense of pain, and I'm very eager to shut that down as well.

For the first time in my life, my inner jukebox is silent. No tunes enter my mind and I can't recall any. I still have a few files remaining though. Movie files. Max tests me by asking, "Is this the end of Rico?"

I rasp, "Edward G. Robinson. *Little Caesar*."

Max smiles. "Good one, my boy."

I can barely walk, but Clitty manages to drag me out of Pam Grier and steadies me as I stagger to the end of the pier. She returns to the Caddy to grab the cello case and the gas can and sets them next to me. With her blood red lipstick she writes 'KIS-MET' on the case. Clitty sits beside me, her feet dangling in the water with my head resting on her lap. I want it all to end.

With half-opened eyes I gaze out at the Salton. I am so through with this journey, except for one more wish.

"One last sunset," I whisper. "Please, just one more." We remain at the edge of the pier, she stroking my face, and with half-opened eyes I watch the last orange streaks flare across the water and disappear behind the horizon.

As I stare at the darkening waters of the Salton Sea, I recall

Oscar Wilde's final words in his fight with the wallpaper in his room. The Salton and I are in a race to see who'll die first, and the smart money is on me.

I was so pleased that my wife and I scripted the final scene together. If you can't share in a suicide, then life isn't worth living. The last scene would be something similar to a Viking funeral. It was a suggestion from Dum Phuk and it will give me an opportunity "to not go gentle into that good night."

Max says, "Let's shoot it!" and faster than a beam of light, the shadowy crew races around to set up Klieg's, arrange microphones in place and assemble a camera tripod on the pier.

Max tells the crew, "There'll be only one take, so let's make it good." He looks at me and asks, "This is almost like the last scene in my movie *China Gate*. At this point I won't even ask—"

I interrupt, "I'm going to shock you, my little dog. I did see it. The Lucky Legs character does herself in at the end along with a few thousand Chinese."

"Chaz, my boy, you never fail to amaze me."

I smile and pat the top of his head.

He inhales deeply, "Chaz... you ready?" I nod. He nuzzles under my chin and licks my face.

"I love you Max," my voice barely audible. "Thanks. You've been a great guide."

"This is your screenplay, Chaz. Congratulations. It's the best you've ever written."

I scratch behind his ears, "Now make sure—"

He interrupts, "I'll watch out for her. Don't worry. Have a good journey. See you on the other side," he Ghostbuster-ized.

"This is getting as sappy as the last scene in *Love Story* where Jenny is dying in the hospital. Have you seen it?"

"I'll put it on my bucket list," Max says, and that makes me smile.

Max disappears behind the camera next to the cinematographer. I hear my ring tone. Clitty has my cell phone and she takes it from her pocket and looks at the screen. She holds it close for me to see. The text message reads: NOW and blinks with an intense urgency NOW NOW NOW NOW.

I manage to whisper to Clitty, "Where are we goin'?"

"Nowhere."

"When we gonna get there?"

She stares at me for several moments, her finger to my lips, and smiles, "Soon."

Max yells, "Roll audio. Roll camera. Okay, slate it." A shadow figure runs in front of the camera with a clapper board and snaps the boards together. Max says, "Last scene. Last take."

Max holds my gaze for a few moments then says, "And... action!"

EXT. SALTON SEA — NIGHT

On the pier, Clitty places the cello case into the water and with great difficulty manages to drag Chaz onto the case. She kisses him.

CLITTY

Chaz, are you sure? You're certain...

CHAZ *(struggling to breathe)*

Help me, honey. Please. Help me do this.

Clitty hands Chaz the gas can and he clutches it to his chest.

CLOSE UP — Clitty and Chaz

He removes his fedora.

CHAZ

Here. In case you ever find yourself in a film noir.

Clitty places it on her head.

WIDE SHOT — pier

With considerable effort, she pushes the cello carrying
Chaz away from the pier and it drifts away some 30 feet.

CLOSE UP — Chaz

He looks toward the night sky.

CHAZ (V.O.)

With every beat of my heart more and more stars appear in the sky like welcoming mile markers on my dark highway home.

MEDIUM SHOT — *The cello case. It's*
some 80 feet away from the pier.

MEDIUM SHOT — Clitty

She reaches into her handbag and pulls out her hand
gun. With deliberation she raises the barrel, then lets it fall by her
side as she wipes tears from her eyes.

CLOSE-UP — Chaz

CHAZ (V.O.)

Come on, Clitty. Please. You can do it.

If you truly love me...

CHAZ POV — *Clitty*

She raises the gun again and draws a bead on the gas
can.

BACK TO CHAZ

CHAZ (V.O.)

Come on Clitty, do it. Now. Please!

CLOSE UP — Clitty

CLITTY

I love you, Chaz.

She squeezes the trigger for a single shot.

LONG SHOT — *Salton Sea with the*
explosion lighting up the sky.

CHAZ (V.O.)

The night sky is ripped apart. It's The Big Bang in a rapidly swirling reverse with a dazzling shattered calando of countless pixels.In that trillionth of a milli-second, everything became clear. Everything made sense. Everything was good. And there was no more pain. The orange and red waves consumed the inferno with my essence everywhere in the molten sea and atmosphere.

                    MAX *(deep breath)*
          That... is a wrap.
                    CHAZ (V.O.)
          The shadowy movie crew figures recede
    into the darkness like phantom fog rolling
    over a hill in the night air. The camera, micro-
    phones, and lights fade away. This is where the
    final credits roll but Clitty and I never wrote a
    'FADE OUT.' My wife got a blanket from the
    car and all that night she sobbed while curled up
    in a fetal position at the end of the pier with Max
    snuggling next to her. As a new day is born,
    Clitty and Max walk to the Caddy. She sits in the
    driver's seat and for a long time stares out at the
    at the Salton Sea, then turns on the engine, hugs
    Max, and they drive west to Los Angeles, slowly
    being consumed by the rising sun to their backs
    as they melt onto their own never-ending
    highway. There are now only ashes playing on
    the water, but the fire still burns. The flame never
    dies out. It burns forever as it lights the path of
    my journey.

And now I know:
Death is the ultimate road trip.

APPENDIX of EPHEMERA from JOURNEY THROUGH A LAND OF MINOR ANNOYANCES

Page 9 "Planet Claire" is a song by the B-52's released in 1979

Page 9 Margaret Hamilton cackled as the Wicked Witch of the West in *The Wizard of Oz*

Page 10 Pat Welsh was an actress who provided the raspy voice of E.T.

Page 10 Bengt Ekerot was the actor who portrayed Death in the 1957 film *The Seventh Seal*

Page 12 Dennis Weaver was chased by a semi truck in the 1971 movie *Duel*

Page 14 Man's Best Friend was a sci-fi, horror film from 1993

Page 15 David Lean directed *Lawrence of Arabia,* the story of T.E. Lawrence

Page 16 "What a dump!" is a line uttered by Bette Davis in the 1949 film *Beyond the Forest*

Page 17 Fizzy Lifting Drink was the soda in Willy Wonka and the Chocolate Factory from 1971

Page 19 Annie Wilkes was the deranged character in the 1990 movie *Misery*

Page 20 Jack Torrance is the name of the character played by Jack Nicholson in *The Shining*

Page 21 Norma Desmond was the faded Hollywood star in the 1950 film *Sunset Boulevard*

Page 25 Levi Stubbs gave the 'voice' to Audrey II, the man-eating plant in the 1986 movie *Little Shop of Horrors*

Page 26 Maria Ouspenskaya was the actress who played the old gypsy woman in a couple of *Wolf Man* movies in the early 1940's

Page 26 *Un Chien Andalou* is a surreal short film from 1929 by Luis Bunuel and Salvador Dali

Page 31 Ginger Baker was the drummer for the 1960's rock group Cream

Page 32 Willis O'Brien was a motion picture special effects wizard who won an Oscar in 1950 for his work on *Mighty Joe Young*

Page 34 Russ Meyer was a screenwriter and director who

specialized in sexploitation movies featuring large-breasted women

Page 35 Slim Pickens was the actor straddling the H-bomb in Stanley Kubrick's *Dr. Strangelove*

Page 38 Preston Sturges was a screenwriter and director who mastered the screwball comedy format

Page 39 Dr. Szell is a sadistic character in the 1976 thriller *Marathon Man*

Page 41 Pan Galactic Gargle Blaster was a potent drink introduced in the novel *The Hitchhiker's Guide to the Galaxy* by Douglas Adams

Page 44 Dr. Jack Griffin was portrayed by actor Claude Rains in the 1933 movie *The Invisible Man*

Page 47 Rod McKuen was a poet, singer, and songwriter

Page 50 Gizmonic Institute is the fictional research laboratory that employed Joel on *Mystery Science Theater 3000*

Page 51 Gregor Samsa is the character in the 1915 Kafka novel *Metamorphosis* who turns into a giant insect

Page 56 Commander Shears is the character played by William Holden in the 1957 film *The Bridge on the River Kwai*

Page 58 Busby Berkeley was a film director and choreographer known for his elaborate musical productions

Page 59 Esther Williams was an actress and swimmer who appeared in several movies in the 1940's and 1950's known as 'aqua musicals'

Page 59 Robert Mitchum was an American actor who performed in several classic film noirs

Page 64 Paul Henreid and Bette Davis shared a smoke in the 1942 film *Now Voyager*

Page 66 Dean Moriarty was a character in the 1957 Jack Kerouac novel *On the Road* who urged the Sal Paradise character to drive to Mexico

Page 66 Alfonso Bedoya was the Mexican actor in the 1948 film *The Treasure of the Sierra Madre*

Page 69 *Howl* is a book of poems published in 1956 by Allen Ginsberg

Page 69 Roy Hobbs is the fictional baseball player in the 1952 novel *The Natural* by Bernard Malamud

Page 72 George Bailey was the character played by James

Stewart in the 1946 movie *It's a Wonderful Life*

Page 73 movie shot at Devil's Tower' is a reference to the musical notes played in the 1977 film *Close Encounters of the Third Kind*

Page 73 the movie directed by Michelangelo Antonioni was the 1970 drama *Zabriskie Point*

Page 75 Eugene Felsnic is the nerdy character in both *Grease* and *Grease 2*

Page 77 Alfred Beach was an American inventor who designed New York City's earliest subway

Page 77 Myers and Carvey refer to Mike Myers and Dana Carvey, stars of the the 1992 comedy *Wayne's World*

Page 84 "Kashmir" is a rock song released in 1975 by Led Zeppelin

Page 91 Billy Pilgrim is the time traveling character in Kurt Vonnegut's 1969 novel *Slaughterhouse Five*

Page 93 Humbert Humbert is the fictional character from the 1955 novel *Lolita* by Vladimir Nabokov

Page 94 'scene with Flick' refers to the 1983 film *A Christmas Story*

Page 97 Tony Curtis and Sidney Poitier played the escaped prisoners shackled together in the 1958 movie *The Defiant Ones*

Page 102 the Steve McQueen movie is *Bullitt* from 1968

Page 103 the song lyrics are from "Smells Like Teen Spirit" released by Nirvana in 1991

Page 110 Peter Max is an artist known for his brightly colored psychedelic paintings

Page 110 William Least Heat-Moon is the author of the 1982 book *Blue Highways*

Page 113 Rondo Hatton was a horror film actor in the 1940's who suffered from acromegaly, which disfigured his head and face

Page 116 "The Girl from Ipanema" Antonio Carlos Jobin

Page 117 Dorothy Gale is the fictional young girl character in *The Wizard of Oz*

Page 118 Lou Reed

Page 122 Clarence the guardian angel is the name of the character in the movie *It's a Wonderful Life*

Page 123 Kowalski's '70 Dodge Challenger is a reference to the car in the 1971 road film *Vanishing Point*

Page 128 John Travolta wore a UC Santa Cruz shirt in the 1994 film *Pulp Fiction*

Page 129 Randle McMurphy is the protagonist in the 1962 novel *One Flew Over the Cuckoo's Nest* by Ken Kesey

Page 131 Chauncey Gardiner was the fictional name of the Peter Sellers character in the 1979 movie *Being There*

Page 140 Thomas Wolfe was an early 20th century author who wrote *You Can't Go Home Again,* published in 1940

Page 149 Travis Bickle was the unhinged character in the 1976 movie *Taxi Driver*

Page 152 the character Lester is infatuated with a teenage girl in the 1999 film *American Beauty*

Page 155 D.B. Cooper was the man who hijacked a Boeing 727 and jumped somewhere over the Pacific Northwest while holding $200,000 in ransom money. He was never found.

Page 157 Bodega Bay is the location in Northern California where scenes from the 1963 film *The Birds* were shot

Page 161 Doc Brown is a character in the movie *Back to the Future* from 1985

Page 161 the DeLorean was the automobile used as a time transport in *Back to the Future*

Page 167 the Joads were the fictional family in the novel *The Grapes of Wrath* by John Steinbeck, published in 1939

Page 171 "4'33" is the avant garde piece by John Cage, composed in 1952

Page 180 Jake and Elwood drove through a shopping mall in the 1980 comedy *The Blues Brothers*

Page 185 "I Love Rock and Roll" Joan Jett

Page 186 "...Townsend windmill..." refers to the style of guitar playing by Pete Townsend of The Who

Page 187 Max Schreck was a German actor known for his role as the vampire in the 1922 horror film *Nosferatu*

Page 187 Tetris Plus was a video game that was released in 1996

Page 190 Divine was a character in the 1972 film *Pink Flamingos;* "Escape" is by Rupert Holmes

Page 198 Nighthawks is a 1942 oil painting by Edward Hopper

Page 198 Christina is a reference to the 1948 painting Christina's World by Andrew Wyeth

Page 198 The Garden of Earthly Delights was a triptych oil painting by Hieronymus Bosch created around 1500

Page 205 *Johnny Belinda* was a 1948 film about a young deaf-mute woman

Page 207 "You Can't Always Get What You Want" Rolling Stones [not Donald Trump]

Page 221 George A. Romero was a filmmaker best known for horror movies involving zombies

Page 223 Saint Cecilia is the patron saint of musicians

Page 224 Will leaving to see Skylar is a reference to the two c haracters in the 1997 drama *Good Will Hunting*

Page 226 Timothy Leary was a psychologist and writer known for being a proponent of LSD

Page 226 Madeleine LeBeau was an actress who appeared in *Casablanca*

Page 230 Syd Field has written numerous books on the art of screenwriting

Page 232 William Castle was a filmmaker who made many classic horror 'B' movies

Page 235 Laney Boggs was the name of the character in the 1999 teen comedy *She's All That*

Page 235 Jean-Paul Belmondo and Jean Seberg starred in *Breathless,* a 1960 crime drama written and directed by Jean-Luc Godard

Page 236 John 'Bluto' Blutarsky was the character played by John Belushi in the 1978 comedy *Animal House*

Page 237 "I'm Only Happy When It Rains" is a 1995 song by the rock group Garbage

Page 244 Charlotte Moorman was an avant garde cellist who occasionally performed topless

Page 245 Hokusai was a 19th century Japanese artist best known for his masterpiece The Great Wave Off Kanagawa

Page 251 the Harrison Ford character was in the 1991 drama *Regarding Henry*

Page 251 Richard Avedon was a famous fashion and portrait photographer

Page 269 Father Merrin was the fictional character in the 1973 horror classic *The Exorcist*

Page 271 Huntz Hall was an actor in the 1930's and 40's who

had a very distinct New York accent

Page 271 the Red Buttons character was in *They Shoot Horses, Don't They?* a 1969 movie about dance marathons during the Great Depression

Page 272 *Symphony Number 8* by Franz Schubert was a composition he started writing in 1822 but never finished

Page 274 Martin Brody was the character in the 1975 film *Jaws*

Page 282 "...the red balloon..." is a reference to the 1956 French film of the same name

Page 284 "See you on the other side" is a line from the 1984 movie *Ghostbusters*

As a morning disc jockey for more than 30 years, **Al Kline** wrote comedy every morning at a handful of radio stations all around the country. He's also written several stage plays, as well as a couple of dozen screenplays, several of which have been made into award winning short films. Al was also a commercial copywriter for a chain of radio stations and wrote a weekly humorous syndicated newspaper column for several years. *Journey Through a Land of Minor Annoyances* is his first book, and he hopes you have as much fun reading it as he had writing it. He recently completed a second book, a Young Adult fiction, and has begun work on a third. Al lives on the coast of Maine with his black lab Max, a very intelligent dog, although Max doesn't talk.